Fearless

Devon Hartford

COPYRIGHT NOTICE

Want to get an email when the sequel is released?

Sign up here:

http://eepurl.com/B7crf

DEDICATION

To Barzel Segal, the original New Adult Bad Boy. A dear friend, and fellow adventurer. They broke the mold after they made you, my man.

Chapter 1

I was disastrously late for my first college class ever. My master plan to live at the beach while remaining close to the San Diego University campus had blown up in my face. I had left out one variable: suck-ass traffic.

Nobody had given me the memo that the Pacific Coast Highway was the route that half of San Diego County took to work in the morning.

At least I had a scenic view of the beach while I waited behind a line of cars at a red light in my raggedy VW. I watched a bunch of surfers skimming across the top of the ultramarine Pacific Ocean.

I did my best to relax, clicking my nails on the steering wheel, keeping time to Born This Way by Lady Gaga. I didn't care what people said, Gaga wrote great music. Girl Power!

The cars in front of me had moved. Finally. Horns blared behind me.

"All right!" I shouted at them. Not watching what I was doing, I reached for the stick shift and knocked my Venti Americano out of the cup holder. The lid flew off and coffee poured all over my bare legs. "Shit!" Fortunately I loved half-and-half, so the coffee didn't scald me. But the cup had been nearly full. Creamy coffee coated my legs and the footwell. At least none of it got on my new print dress.

"Move it!" someone yelled behind me.

Seriously? I had the BP oil spill turning my car into the Gulf of Mexico and I was supposed to worry about traffic? I threw napkins at the mess, but I didn't have enough to make a dent.

I frantically grabbed the stick shift and put the car back into first. My foot slipped off the clutch as I put on the gas. I lurched forward and the car stalled. Crap. Coffee sloshed against the floorboards and waved into the back seat. Craptastic.

"Go, you dumb broad!"

I glanced in my rearview at a red-faced guy in a gaudy gold Mercedes convertible. He stood up in his car and leaned over his windshield impatiently.

Flustered, I twisted my keys in the ignition and nothing happened. What was wrong with my car now? I hoped nothing serious because I didn't have spare cash for a replacement thingamajig or whatever. I took a deep breath. Duh. I'd forgotten to push the clutch.

Red Face shook his fist at me. "You made me miss the light, stupid bitch!"

Bitch...

I leaned my head out my window and prepared to give this guy a dose of feminine fury. My face was nearly sliced off as a motorcycle lane-split between my car and the sedan next to me.

"Hey!" I turned to shout at the motorcycle. "You almost killed me!"

The psycho guy on the roaring black bike didn't hear me. He rolled to a stop at the red light a few cars ahead of my VW, planted his boots on the ground, and revved his engine. I noticed his thin white T-shirt flutter in the breeze, revealing sculpted bronze back muscles that led to what was clearly an amazing ass hidden under his jeans. The way he straddled the racing bike made me blush. Was he wearing any underwear?

I wish I was that motorcycle. Shut your dirty mind, girl! Thoughts like that will get you into all kinds of trouble!

Maybe I liked trouble.

His narrow waist led to broad shoulders that were equally amazing and stretched the cotton material of his shirt impressively. Yum.

Hold up, girl! He almost beheaded you with his handlebars! No special passes for insane bikers. Even if they are hot from the rear.

"Psycho!" I shouted. He didn't hear me.

"You made me miss the light, idiot!" I whipped my head around. Red Face had gotten out of his Mercedes and stood right behind my door, his fists planted on his hips. He wore a toupee and gaudy gold chain. His swollen gut, wrapped in a silk button-down shirt, hung over his expensive slacks.

I might have liked trouble, but not this kind.

"Don't call me an idiot!" I shouted. "And quit yelling at me! I'm swimming in Lake Americano here!" My pulse raced. I knew guys like this. Asshats to a man.

He eyed my coffee mess and smirked. "It's stupid broads like you who cause all the accidents."

"Excuse me?" *Broads?* Was I trapped in a 1940s gangster film? A thatch of curly hair puffed out of his open shirt collar. More like a 1970s mafia movie.

"Dumb bitch! Get off the road! Leave the driving to the men!"

Bitch...

How many times had I been called that in the last two years? I learned I didn't have to take it from *them*, so I certainly wasn't going to take it from this prick. I cranked up my window furiously. Half way up, Red Face grabbed the glass and pushed against it. "Hey! I'm talking to you! Get off the road, slut! You're blocking traffic!"

Slut...

I knew that one, too. But I was no slut. Uh-uh. I flashed my teeth at him. If I were a werewolf, now would've been the moment when I bit his fingers off. No such luck. I tried to turn the window crank, but Red Face pushed down so hard on the glass, I couldn't budge it. "Hey, asshole, get off my car or I'm going to pepper spray your face!"

"Don't back talk me, whore!"

Whore...

I glared at his insane eyes. I knew the look. He was trying to intimidate me. My face was suddenly hot, and I felt tears welling. I willed them to dry up. I'd promised myself no one would ever intimidate me again, and I certainly wasn't going to cry for *this* sloppy bastard.

But old feelings leaked into my awareness anyway. Red Face had managed to bring me right back to that night two years ago. The night that had started all the dirty looks, the labels, the name calling, and the ejection from high school society.

For a second, I almost fell apart. But I had plenty of practice holding myself together under stress. I took a deep breath and shoved my old pain behind the emotional walls I'd worked so hard to build.

When I regained my composure, I spoke to Red Face in a calm, commanding voice. "Remove your fingers from my window and get back into your car. Now."

He ignored my request. "Move it, skank!"

This guy was plain crazy. He probably didn't know what day of the week it was, let alone his own name. He needed a handler with a leash. Where was Animal Control when you needed them?

What to do? I didn't have pepper spray. Even if I did, it would be buried in my purse underneath the hoarder's paradise I kept inside it. I considered biting his fingers once again. Until I noticed he had hairy knuckles. Ew. That made *him* the hairy werewolf in this scenario.

I considered gouging his eyes with my nails, but the way he was standing, I couldn't get an angle. I looked around for help. No one was jumping out of their cars. I was on my own on this.

Shit, when wasn't I?

Red Face kicked my car door with his pointed loafer. "Hey! I'm talking to you, pinhead!"

I noticed motion out the corner of my eye. Psycho Motorbike had put his kickstand down and swung his leg over his motorcycle. Helmet still on, he swaggered toward my car.

Psycho Motorbike stopped short of Red Face, who hadn't noticed him. Psycho Motorbike's front side was as impressive as his back. His broad chest flexed under a V-neck t-shirt. The tanned edges of his sculpted pectorals danced in the open collar. Muscled arms covered in tattoos hung at his sides. Leather gloves covered his fists.

I couldn't see much of his face with the helmet on, but his sapphire blue eyes pierced my heart. "You gotta problem?"

Was he talking to me or Red Face?

Red Face swiveled to confront blue-eyed Psycho Motorbike. "Who the fuck are you?"

"This guy bothering you?" Psycho Motorbike stared into my eyes, clearly talking to me. *Sigh.*

"I'm talking to you, you fucking prick!" Red Face shouted at Psycho Motorbike.

Psycho Motorbike never took his eyes off me. I gazed into his two blue oceanic jewels and nodded slowly.

"The lady wants you to leave," Psycho Motorbike said to Red Face.

"What? I don't take shit from you, punk. Get the fuck outta

here," Red Face growled.

Psycho Motorbike took a step toward him. "Back off, buddy."

"Fuck you, prick!" Red Face lunged toward Psycho Motorbike.

In one fluid motion, Psycho Motorbike side-stepped and punched Red Face in the gut. The fat man went down in a crumpled heap. Nope. this wasn't a gangster movie or mob drama. This was an old west showdown! *Woo hoo, Psycho Blue Eyes!* I almost clapped. Almost.

Psycho Motorbike leaned over, grabbed Red Face by the back of the shirt and pulled him to his feet. The muscles in his tanned arms bunched and stretched beneath his intricate tattoos. Wow. Red Face coughed and sputtered as blue-eyed Psycho Motorbike led him somewhat politely to the curb and dropped him there like a sack of rice.

"You need an ambulance?" Psycho Motorbike asked Red Face while towering over him.

Still coughing, Red Face's eyes bulged from their sockets. Surprise, embarrassment, and anger warred on his fat face. He looked up at Psycho Motorbike and shook his head no, then hung it between his shoulders in defeat.

I rolled my window down as Psycho Motorbike walked over and leaned onto my car. I noticed the material of his shirt was an expensive knit, and slightly transparent. *Quiver.* One of his well-toned forearms rested on my windowsill.

I inhaled the faint scent of his cologne, which hit the manly sweet spot somewhere between dusty cowboy and crowned prince. Strength and style. *That's not the only spot it hits. Down, girl!*

There was no way he could see anything beneath or through my knee-length dress, but I squeezed my thighs together, just in case. *Just in case I jumped him. Rawr!*

Now that he was my knight in see-through armor, maybe I should stop thinking of him as Psycho Motorbike and call him Motorknight.

"You okay?" A dimple twitched beneath his cheek. I detected a cocky smile. I couldn't see his lips beneath the helmet's face mask, but I could imagine them. *Swoon.* He looked at me expectantly.

"Uh…" *Pick up your panties and grow some ovaries, girl! Loosen that corset or you're going to faint right here!* "Thanks, yeah, I'm okay."

His face twisted. "Why do you smell like coffee?"

"Um...new body spray?" I said hopefully.

He noticed my legs and the coffee spill. He chuckled. "Looks like you had an accident."

Boy, he was really looking at my legs. I wanted to squirm. "Yeah. Accident." I sounded like an idiot.

"What's your name?" His eyes melted my good sense, like Superman's laser beam eyes, except blue.

"Sam—"

Cars started honking again. The light had cycled back to green.

"—antha."

"My work is done here. Sam. Antha." More dimples. Wow. Was this guy for real?

He slapped the roof of my car, swaggered back to his bike and rocketed down the highway. I wanted to shout "My name's Samantha Smith! My cell phone number is—" but I had a small fragment of self-respect remaining.

I started my car and tried to follow, but he was long gone. All I had left of that horrible-magical moment was a car floor soaking in coffee and my outfit equally in need of a wash and detailing.

Psycho Blue Eyes had made me forget all about Red Face. But Red Face had brought back everything else.

Bitch.

All because of something *I* did...

Slut.

A mistake *I* could never undo...

Whore.

Something *I* would regret for the rest of my life...

Horribly late, I pulled into the north parking lot at SDU. Coffee sloshed around the soles of my flat sandals every time I braked or accelerated. I would have to deal with it later.

The parking lot was the size of a small town, and packed with cars. I grabbed the first available space. I had to shoehorn my VW between the two jackholes who had parked Daddy's BMW and Mommy's Lexus over the white line on either side of the space.

My car door bumped into the Lexus when I opened it, leaving me no more than a mail slot to squeeze through. I was by no means fat, but I barely made it out of my car.

I jogged across the lot toward the business school. My feet stuck to my sticky sandals, peeling off with very step. Lame. My book bag felt like it was loaded with bricks. Sweat would be running down my face by the time I made it to the lecture hall. Stupid traffic.

At the end of the lot, a black motorcycle parked with the others caught my eye. Was that the bike blue-eyed Psycho Motorknight had ridden? I wasn't sure. I doubted a guy like him went to college. He was probably heading to an early-morning drug buy or gang fight, by the looks of him.

My cell phone jangled. A text from my first and only friend in San Diego, Madison Lockhart.

Where r u? Class has started!

I texted her back. *Late. Running. No pun. >:|*

Her reply: *Look 4 me at the back. I'll save u a seat.*

I shoved my phone in my pocket and maintained a fast walk. Although I knew where everything was, I didn't remember things being so far apart.

When I finally reached the business school and crept into the back of the immense lecture hall, nobody paid any attention to me. The professor didn't even notice. Yes, I half-expected the entire class to stand as one to point and name-call at the new girl, but no one did.

The nice thing about giant schools like SDU was that I could disappear into the crowd. Nobody cared about Samantha Smith.

I was finally anonymous.

I hoped it would stay that way.

I slid into the seat next to Madison. She and I had met last week during the orientation tour. She was total BFF material. When I'd told her I was from D.C., she'd offered up her SUV to haul the new furniture I needed to buy, and helped me set up and decorate my apartment. "Hey, Mads," I whispered.

"What took you so long?" she hissed.

"I got stuck in traffic."

Madison wrinkled her nose. "Why do you smell like coffee?"

"Long story," I groaned. I considered skulking to the nearest bathroom to rinse my feet in the sink, but my coffee odor would have to wait.

"Don't worry," she whispered, "I'll email you my notes later. You haven't missed much."

That was for sure. Fundamentals of Accounting. One of the lower division classes for my major. Gag. I was on the fast track. I couldn't wait to graduate and get my CPA. My mom and dad would be so proud. Yay. Sort of. Who *really* wanted to be an accountant?

I pulled out my laptop and turned it on. I had a moment to look around at the other students in the room. They all seemed to be earnestly following the professor's every word. Was I the only one who didn't really want to be taking accounting? I mean, I know college is an amazing opportunity that not everyone gets. But why did my major have to be something sensible and boring like Accounting?

Because you're good with numbers, my mother had encouraged. Rah, Mom. *Because accounting is a safe, dependable career*, my dad had said. Go, Dad. Maybe they were right. I screwed up everything else I tried. I had the scars to prove it. Maybe something safe and dependable was exactly what I needed.

Might as well make the most of it.

Samantha Smith, CPA.

Groan. My name was as boring as my major.

Chapter 2

After class, Madison and I packed up our laptops and skirted outside. A throng of people poured out of the surrounding lecture halls and onto the wide walkways between the various buildings. Laughter and first day of school excitement ricocheted everywhere.

"Where's your coffee, Sam?" Madison asked. She already knew about my caffeine addiction, and harbored one of her own. "I thought you told me you felt naked unless you had one at all times."

"Ha, ha. I'm wearing it," I pouted. "I spilled it all over myself on the drive over."

Madison grimaced sheepishly. "Oh, good. I didn't want to say anything. The smell was a bit strong. I was worried you were trying out a new body spray." She wrinkled her nose.

"Funny, I said the same thing earlier."

"To who?"

"Nobody."

"I see your eyes twinkling," she singsonged. "What?"

"I'll tell you later," I grinned. "Right now, I need to wash off my Parfum de Starbucks. Is there a restroom around here?"

"Yeah, around the corner."

When I rinsed my feet in the restroom sink, and then my sandals, only about eight girls gave me the stink eye.

Madison noticed after the third one. "What are you looking at?" she snapped at the gawker. "Aren't you late for class?"

The gawker rebutted with an upturned nose and a huff before stalking outside.

I used a wad of paper towels to dry off. I felt like a homeless woman taking a sponge bath in a public restroom.

"Ignore them," Madison consoled. "Wait till it happens to them."

"Thanks, Mads. I don't know what I'd do without you."

She smiled. "All clean?"

"Yeah. I think I got up on the ass side of bed this morning." We walked outside.

"We need to turn your frown upside down, girl. You need more caffeine." Madison was such an enabler. "I've got an hour to kill before Spanish. When's your next class?"

"Eleven."

"Cool. Let's stop at the Student Center and grab you another brew."

My sandals squished wetly as we walked. I hoped no one noticed the trail of wet foot prints I left behind. Ugh. They were like a road map pointing to the idiot.

Unlike me, Madison, was the picture of stylin' beach coolness in her flip-flops, board shorts, and surf t-shirt. You could see that she wore a neon bikini swimsuit top instead of a bra. She was tan from head to toe. Her hair was golden blond from the sun. You couldn't get that color from a bottle. She was a genuine California Girl.

I was her polar opposite with my dark print dress, drab hair, and pale skin. I examined my fingernails. They were short, chipped, and flecked with remnants of black nail polish.

Emo. Goth. Witch. Sorceress. Suicide Watch...

That's what they had called me back home in Washington D.C., after my life fell apart. My solution to the rejection was to check out completely. I hid behind black clothes and buckets of black makeup. But I wasn't an Emo, or Goth, or anything else. I just wanted to be left alone. It was the only way I could keep my secrets to myself.

After two years of solitary misery, I was ready to move on. I wanted to reinvent myself here in San Diego, and rise from the ashes of my life like a fiery phoenix.

I was determined to shed my bleak wardrobe and frosty skin and finally get a tan. I believed the sun's rays would burn my old memories and my pain completely away. With any luck, it would only be a few short weeks until I was tan like Madison. And sooner or later, my dishwater blond hair would lighten naturally, like hers.

Then, any signs of my gothish past would be wiped away forever. Hopefully the bad memories would disappear just as easily.

Bitch. Slut. Whore...

The enormous Student Center contained a food court, a movie theater, various meeting rooms, the campus bookstore, and tons of outdoor seating. It was packed with people.

We got in the long line at the campus coffee shop, Toasted Roast. It was so long, it ran out the door and into the courtyard.

"Check out those hot guys over there," Madison motioned with her chin. A bunch of tan, athletic guys sat on top of a table. Was everybody in San Diego tan except me? The guys rough-housed each other and laughed. "I'm pretty sure they're on the rugby team."

"Whatever," I scoffed.

"Come on, Sam. Don't rule them out. You haven't met them."

"Have you?"

"No, but it doesn't mean they're jerks. Some of them are pretty cute."

"Yeah, well, fine for you. You have the whole 'hot surfer chick' thing going. I don't have time for dating anyway."

"Don't sell yourself short, Sam. You're totally hot. I'm sure guys fell all over you in D.C."

"Yeah, whatever." The story of me and guys always ended in disaster.

Madison's eyes lit up. "Hello, GQ biker dude!" A new jock had joined the stud farm at the table. "I saw him first!" Madison squealed. "I call dibs!"

GQ Biker had dark, naturally curly hair and was taller than the rest of his pals, but equally tan, and very muscular. He wore a white t-shirt and motorcycle boots. Tattoos criss-crossed his arms. His face was turned away, but I could tell his jawline was masculine and rugged.

Madison was breathless and close to fainting. "That guy is seriously hot."

"You can't even see his face."

Then he turned. It was Psycho Motorknight, jeweled blue eyes and all. He was stunningly hot.

Madison fanned her face. "O. M. G. I'm sprung." Madison was in love, no doubt about it.

"Geez, I hope your panties are drip-dry."

Madison smacked my arm. "Shut up! I'm busy swooning."

"He's all yours, Mads. Go get him." I was happy she was into him. Not that either of us knew the first thing about the guy. Other than he was gorgeous.

"Bitch alert." Madison frowned.

What was it about sorority girls that was so identifiable? Was it their impossibly long legs, perfectly fake breasts and cookie-cutter beauty? I'm pretty sure the three that had just walked up to the table of hot guys were manufactured in the same factory as Barbie dolls because they had the same plastic looks and perfect proportions.

Two of the sorority girls wrapped themselves around Psycho Motorknight. He sat down on the table top and grabbed the third robot doll by the hip and pulled her onto his lap. Her hair was blond and wavy. She draped her arms around his neck. They were nose to nose. She tongue kissed him. He indulged her.

Psycho Motorknight was enjoying himself like a lion on the savannah. I imagined him rolling around on his back in the tall grass while lionesses fed him and stroked his ego. Men. Maleness transcended all species. Ugh. I couldn't watch anymore. I turned away. "Gross! Somebody get me a barf bag."

"Slut," Madison said, faux-wounded but still curious. "What's he doing now?"

I couldn't help but look. Psycho Motorknight had set Blondie down. He stood and motioned like he was playing charades. "I think he's telling a story."

Psycho Motorknight suddenly dropped into a crouch and swung a fist through the air. I had seen him do that this morning. Was he telling his groupies about saving me? I hoped not. When he finished, his buddies clapped him on the back. I was expecting him to start signing autographs when he looked right at me. His blue eyes blinked recognition. Oh shit.

I heard him say faintly, "That's her!"

All of them stared at me. Oh no. The sorority squad scowled and narrowed their eyes, targeting me with their daggery sneers. This was how the negative notoriety started. The scrutinizing glares. Crap.

I turned around, looking for cover. Luckily, the line for coffee had made it into the building. I hid behind the doorframe of Toasted Roast. "Shit, shit, shit," I hissed.

"What's wrong, Sam?"

"Hide, Mads! Don't let them see you." She had no idea what was going on. Did I want her to? She seemed so smitten with Psycho

Motorknight, did I want to tell her that he'd punched a guy out while defending me this morning? How would that make her feel? What if it turned out she was totally jealous? I didn't want to find out. I'd only known her a week and didn't want to test our friendship this soon.

I yanked her through the door by the arm.

"Hey!" She stumbled, nearly falling, and eyed me like I was crazy.

"Girls like that can smell fear!" I hissed. "I don't want them to get any ideas."

"What? I'm not scared of them! Now I'm totally confused."

"When bitches like that smell competition, their claws come out. I was just watching out for you."

"Are you sure you're not over-reacting?"

"Can I take your order, please?" the barista asked. Saved by the bell.

Madison and I ordered our coffee. When we had them properly creamed and sugared, we walked outside. The lion and his pride of catty bimbos were gone, thank god.

"What's your next class?" Madison asked, swirling her cup.

"Life Drawing."

"I thought you were an accounting major?"

"I am, but I'm taking drawing as one of my electives. I need to balance the bitter taste of business with something fun. I sort of want to minor in art."

Madison sipped her coffee. "Have you bought any of your books yet?"

I face palmed. "Crap! I'm supposed to bring drawing supplies to the first class! I don't have any."

We walked into the school bookstore. It was more insanely crowded than the courtyard outside.

"O. M. F-bomb!" Madison's eyes goggled. "It's worse than I imagined! I've got class in fifteen minutes. Can you get your supplies later, when the rush dies down?"

"No, I have to buy them for the first class."

Madison's shoulders slumped. "Sorry girlfriend, but I'm going to have to throw you under the bus on this one. Spanish lab has like twelve people and if I walk in late, I'll have my calabaza handed to me on a plato."

"I totally get it. Thanks anyway."

"We'll get lunch later, okay?" Madison gave me a sympathetic look.

"Yeah, okay." When she left the bookstore, I returned my attention to the mob in front of me. How was I going to get all my books and supplies without getting stabbed or shot by some hyper-ambitious over-achieving honor student? I reminded myself it was no worse than the subways in D.C. during rush hour. I could do this.

There were so many people stuffed into the textbook wing, it looked like Black Friday at Walmart. Scratch that. Books later. Art supplies now.

Thankfully, the art department was empty. I quickly found what I needed. A gigantic clipboard, a huge pad of drawing paper, vine charcoal, and a kneaded eraser. I wrestled everything to the register and paid. They didn't have a bag big enough for the giant clipboard. No surprise there.

I checked the time on my phone. Crap. I had nine minutes to get across campus to the visual arts building with my XXXL clipboard and drawing pad for titans.

I butt-bumped the release bar on the door of the bookstore and backed out into the courtyard of the Student Center. I spun around, and blundered right into blue-eyed Psycho Motorknight.

Those muscles of his were as solid as a marble statue. I think I bruised myself on his abs.

"I'm so sorry!" I backed up, frazzled. His eyes were much bluer than I remembered. Wait, was he wearing mascara? Nope, naturally dark lashes, thicker than mine. Bastard. His dark hair and olive complexion further contrasted against his sapphire eyes. They glowed.

His smile was far better than I had imagined. His cheeks dimpled and his succulent lips revealed dazzling white teeth. Without his helmet squishing his face, I could appreciate his high cheekbones and rugged jawline.

I'm pretty sure I saw one of those wall-mounted Automatic External Defibrillators for heart attack victims inside the bookstore. Good thing, because I needed a hit right about now.

He drilled me with his Superman laser eyes again. My chest was melting, as were other biological destinations south of my rib cage, including my toes. *Swoon. Double Swoon.*

"Sam. Antha."

He remembered! Sort of. Where was that AED? Cardiac arrest was imminent.

Red light! Warning flag! I needed to get a hold of myself. Madison was into this guy, not me. Now was the appropriate time for me to run away. Before trouble got the best of me.

I took one step and my ginormous drawing pad slipped out of my arm and took flight. The immense pages fluttered as the pad fell to the ground.

"Let me help you with that." His low voice was a resonant baritone. Deep, full and manly. I felt it in my chest. And other areas. He dropped to one knee. He looked like he was about to propose.

Gulp. "That's ok, I've got it, thanks." I bent to retrieve the traitorous pad. I kept my head down, hiding my glowing red cheeks. I'm sure I looked hideous. Broiled lobster, anyone? I rolled my eyes at myself.

The pages of the drawing pad flapped in the slight breeze, making it difficult to flatten them back into the pad without tearing them.

Blue Eyes held out his hand. It was quite large and very tan. Was I supposed to shake it? I peered at it like it was on fire. Maybe it was.

I avoided his eyes. I knew that if I looked into them at this range, I'd be frozen in place. This guy was like a male Medusa. Only he was a *Man*-dusa, and instead of being ugly, he was so good looking, he turned innocent virgins to stone with a single gaze.

With eyes like his, I was pretty sure he could de-virginize unsuspecting young women with a single gaze as well.

"Uh, what's your name?" I mumbled. Crap! Why did I ask him that? He must have hypnotized me. Otherwise, I'd already be cowering in the nearest bush.

"Adonis."

I scoffed. "What, like the Greek god of beauty and desire?"

"Yep."

Eye roll.

"It fits, don't you think?" He winked at me.

Gag. "No." *Yes.* "Ego much?"

He cocked that perfectly crooked, dimpled grin. "Don't blame me. My parents picked it out. Guess they knew what they were doing."

This guy's ego was so monstrous, he was definitely a Man-dusa. The kind that's ugly on the inside.

His hand still waited to be shook. Crap. I didn't want to be a rude bitch. I shook it. It was very large, and engulfed mine. But it was also gentle and kind.

I swear, I had no intention of looking into his blue, blue eyes again. I froze. Stupid Man-dusa.

Wait, what? Why was he lifting my hand to his lips? And kissing the back of it? Oh no. Electric tingles slid up my forearm. I realized he was caressing my palm with his large fingers. My eyelids fluttered. I felt betrayed by my own body. Stupid hormones. "I'm late for class, I have to go."

I jerked my hand free from his. I would be lying if I said I didn't want to stay right there, staring into those eyes, until the next century. But I bolstered my feminine independence, picked up my traitorous drawing pad, and trotted off to class.

With Madison already making wedding plans, the last thing I needed was for Psycho Blue Eyes to be gazing into *my* eyes like that.

Those eyes spelled trouble.

Chapter 3

As I hurried to class, I passed the three Fembot Barbies who had been hanging on Adonis in the Student Center earlier.

I gave them a wide berth on the cement pathway. I couldn't help overhearing their conversation. Clearly, all three believed they should be upstaging Christina Aguilera or the Queen of England, based on their volume.

The brunette cackled. "Did you see the way she skulked off when Adonis pointed at her?"

"Like a frightened rat," the blond with the stick-straight hairdo said.

"She should really do something about that dishwater hair of hers. She looks like a chambermaid," the brunette continued.

Chambermaid? Who stuck me in a time machine and sent me into a Charles Dickens novel? I was used to deflecting bitchery like this. I could handle it. I held my head high. I passed them as quickly as I could.

I heard giggled whispers. "Oh my gawd, that's her."

Enough of this. I had sworn to myself I wouldn't let my peers beat me down anymore, like they had in high school. I stopped in my tracks and spun around. "You three *ladies* have a problem? Say it to my face."

They recoiled and stumbled over each other.

The blondest and tannest among them, and the obvious leader, walked toward me with her limp hand extended. I envied her long, slender legs.

Her salon-fresh wavy hair rippled impressively. She wore a Delta Pi Delta t-shirt. Her shirt, knotted above her waist, revealed her flat stomach and stretched over her double-D Deltas. Her short shorts left almost nothing about her Pi to the imagination. I knew there was a reason why Delta Pi Delta made me think of Breast Vagina Breast. This girl looked like the cover of a trashy men's magazine.

"Sorry about them," she said. "They have no manners. My name is Tiffany Kingston-Whitehouse. Pleasure."

Was that a name or a title? I'm pretty sure her tailored nails dripped venom, even if I couldn't see any. Yet. Sure, I hadn't heard her gossiping about me, just her henchwoman cronies. But that didn't mean she hadn't been snarking about me before I'd caught up to them. I shook her hand reluctantly.

"You must be new here. East coast?"

"How did you—"

She smiled, but I didn't believe it was sincere for a second. "Your outfit. I saw some Manhattan socialite wearing your dress at some country club thing I found online."

I'm pretty sure that wasn't an insult. But a hint of iciness in her tone kept me on my guard.

"San Diego is a bit more…*casual* than the east coast." She eyed me from head to toe.

I detected the faintest sneer when she said the word "casual." That was definitely an insult gift-wrapped in niceties. Oh, she was good, this one. I frowned at her. "So I've noticed."

The brunette snapped her gum. "You must feel pretty special to have the hottest guy on campus come to your rescue." Her white day-glow teeth beamed at me, nearly as bright as the sun.

Great. There went any hopes I'd had for anonymity. Adonis must have told them everything. How long would it take for my story to get around campus? I prayed that SDU wasn't as gossipy as my high school had been.

And I hoped Madison wasn't too into this Adonis guy. Guys surrounded by gossip, who went for women like Tiffany and her ilk, were a mess. I had seen it firsthand in high school. I would have to break the news to Madison lightly. She deserved better.

"You should totally pledge our sorority," Tiffany said.

Was this a keep your enemies closer thing? She couldn't possibly think I'd fall for that. I had visions of hazings, scandal, and my face plastered all over the campus newspaper.

"If Adonis likes you, you're in like Tim," The brunette said.

Liked me? Geez, I hoped that was just an expression. I wanted nothing to do with him *or* these three. "You mean Flynn?" I scoffed. When she wasn't getting it, I had to explain. "The saying is 'in like

Flynn,' dear. Flynn."

For a moment, Brunette was confused. Then she gave me the "I may be an ignorant ditz but my teeth cost more than your car" smile of superiority.

I hated that smile. I'd had enough of the Three Stoogettes. My mouth raced ahead of my brain. "Does Adonis have to screw, cough, I mean approve all your members?"

The brunette's high-watt smile was hit by a rolling blackout. "No."

I smirked. *Great comeback,* I thought.

Brunette's face screwed up. "You don't have to be such a bitch about it. Let's go, you guys."

And...I felt like a total bitch. There was no reason for me to say that. I didn't need to be like them. But the brunette *had* called me a chambermaid.

Tiffany scowled over her shoulder and shot me some daggers. "Stay away from Adonis." The three of them pranced off in identical strides.

I didn't know what Tiffany was worried about. She had the looks all guys went for. She was perfect for Adonis.

In general, I think my biggest problem in high school could be traced back to all the times I'd said what I shouldn't have, right at the perfect moment. Had I been protecting myself from bitches like Tiffany & Company, or sabotaging my social life?

In either case, my troubles were my fault. I was a walking curse. Only not a cool curse, like Curse of the Mummy. More like a social disease everybody knew to avoid. I was a walking STDon't.

And so it began. I was so good at being an outcast, I had cast myself out of the inner circle without ever having been inside it. That was okay. I was used to it.

But it didn't mean I wasn't sick to death of it.

Two hours into my first day of college and it was shaping up to be a gruesome misfire.

Could I get a do-over?

When I got to the Visual Arts building, the path split. I hesitated, unsure which one led to the studio wing.

A guy with a drawing pad similar to mine tucked under his arm stopped next to me. "Looking for Life Drawing? It's this way."

He wore an elaborate burgundy coat with black cuffs and intricate embroidery. It had this steam-punk cosplay thing going that I believed was standard bedroom attire for vampires everywhere. His silver-tipped black leather shoes matched his coat. "Come on, girl. We're going to be late and get a shitty spot if we don't stop dragging our fat asses."

"Isn't it a bit warm for such a long coat?" I was over-heating in my thin print dress and sandals in this end-of-summer San Diego weather.

"It's never too warm to be fashionable, darling." He had such a sincere and yet smarmy look on his face, I couldn't help but grin.

"Are you wearing a monocle?"

"Why, yes. Do you find it fetching?"

Fetching? Who is this guy?

He turned so I could get a better look at his monocle. It popped off his cheek and swung from the black thread attached to his jacket button. He fumbled for it and squeezed it back into place, holding it there with a one-eyed frown.

"Aren't you worried your face will stay like that if you wear the monocle all the time?"

"Well, mothers everywhere do warn of such evils. But we all know good fashion is dangerous."

"So you're okay with looking like some sort of two-faced monster for the rest of your life?"

"You mean like Two Face? From Batman?"

"Who's Two-Face?"

"One of Batman's arch enemies. One side of his face was burned by acid, and looks terrible. The other half is normal."

"Are you sure it wasn't from wearing his monocle too long?" I quipped.

"No, silly. It was because of the acid." He smiled pleasantly. "The damage to his face drove him crazy and he became a villain."

I smiled. "Okay, so you don't mind living like an arch enemy for the rest of your life? Committing crimes while being shunned by society?" I joked. How had I gotten sucked into such a bizarre conversation?

"When you put it that way, how can I resist? I'd be rather pleased with the idea of Batman chasing me all over Gotham City for eternity, while he manhandled me every step of the way. I think you and I are going to be friends. What's your name?"

I smiled. "I'm Samantha Smith. People call me Sam."

"Pleasure to meet you, Sam."

"I'd shake your hand but I have gigantic drawing equipment in both of mine. I asked the guy in the bookstore if they had anything larger, but this was the biggest they had," I said sarcastically. I held up my gargantuan 18 x 24 pad and clipboard.

"You know, you can actually clip the drawing pad into the clipboard."

Duh. I suddenly felt stupid. Why hadn't I figured that out? Maybe I was better off in accounting.

"Don't fret, Sam. You don't have to figure everything out on the first day. You have the rest of the year to make a fool of yourself." He chuckled and did an elaborate courtly bow while twirling his free hand with Renaissance flair. "Romeo Fabiano, at your service."

I smirked. "That can't be your real name."

"It certainly is. But if you prefer, you can simply call me Fabulous. All my friends do."

"They don't call you Fabio?"

"Well, if it wasn't for my lack of luxurious locks," he had a short, meticulously groomed faux-hawk, so he flipped imaginary hair, "my mammoth pectorals, and about ten inches—not in the pants, naughty girl, I meant height—then yes, Fabio would be appropriate. But Fabio is so 1992. Twenty years is a tad too vintage for my taste. I'm all the rage! I'm *Fabulous!*"

I shook my head and grinned.

"Come now, dearest Samantha. We have to get to the studio, or the door will be locked."

I followed after him. "Locked, why?"

"They always lock the door during Life Drawing."

"Oh." I wasn't sure why that was. To punish the late students? Hopefully I wouldn't have to find out. I sped up until we were both walking as fast as possible without running through a eucalyptus grove. "Can I just call you Romeo? Fabulous seems a bit much."

"As long as you don't fall in love with me, fairest Samantha. It would only lead to heartbreak. My heart is already sworn to a certain Julian."

"Ok, now you're making that up. You aren't in love with someone named Julian."

Romeo looked suddenly hurt. His shoulders slumped, like I'd murdered his mother.

"Oh, I'm sorry. I didn't—"

He cracked a grin. "Gotcha!"

I slapped his shoulder. "I bet your name isn't even Romeo. It's probably Ralph. Ralph Farquhar."

He scowled. "Please, Sam, I thought we were friends. How can you wound me like that?"

"Well come on, is your name really Romeo Fabiano?"

"Yes, I swear. But no, I'm not in love with anyone named Julian, or Juliet. Promise."

I laughed. "I'm still not calling you Fabulous. Romeo will have to do."

"Perfect. Here we are." Romeo held the door open for me. "Life Drawing. And we're in luck. They still haven't locked the door."

With that, we walked into the room.

The drawing studio was nothing like the impersonal lecture hall I'd had for Fundamentals of Accounting this morning, which had no windows and was lit by cold banks of overhead fluorescent lights.

In the studio, a wall of windows allowed ample natural light. It was bright and inviting. Prints of famous paintings hung from the remaining walls. Van Gogh, Monet, Rembrandt, Picasso, and a bunch I didn't recognize.

Easels filled the room, surrounding a black dais. On the dais were a selection of solid-colored pillows, several sheets of colorful textured fabric, a barstool and a waist-high grecian column.

This was an oasis compared to the vacant wasteland of my accounting class.

About twenty students buzzed around the room. Some were still setting up. Others were already busy sketching. An old guy with glasses on the tip of his nose worked intently at his easel like he'd been there for awhile.

Although I'd doodled in my school notebooks for as long as I could remember, I'd never done life drawing. I guess life drawing meant working while standing? Because it was more lively that way?

"There's two open spots in front," Romeo pointed. "We'll get a great view."

"Of what, the colored pillows?"

He led me over to the empty easels and set his clipboard on one of them. I did likewise. "Hey, Kamiko," he said to an Asian girl sketching next to him. "This is my new friend Sam. Sam, Kamiko."

Kamiko held out her charcoal-dusted hand. "Nice to meet you, Sam."

"You too." She seemed sweet. I hoped it wasn't an act. Now I had charcoal all over my fingers. I guess life drawing was messy too?

"Kamiko is amazing," Romeo said. "You should see her sketchbook. She's like this wunderkind drawing prodigy."

Kamiko blushed. "Shut *up*, Romeo!" She punched him in the arm.

"Ow!" Romeo rubbed his arm vigorously. "When are you going to learn to hit like a girl? I bruise easily. Besides, I thought I asked you to leave your false modesty at the door."

Kamiko grinned to herself while she continued sketching.

"Seriously, did you bring your sketchbook? I want to show it to Sam."

"It's in my bag."

Romeo dug it out of her lime green knapsack. A little cartoon figurine hung from one of the zippers by a keychain.

"That keychain on your backpack looks familiar," I said.

"It's Finn the Human, from Adventure Time," Kamiko replied.

"I've seen that show. It's on Cartoon Network, right?"

Kamiko exploded with glee. "Ohmygod! You know Adventure Time?"

"I've seen it once or twice." *I think.* Bonding over cartoons. Whatever worked. Better than the Fembots from Delta Pi Delta.

"Girl crush," Romeo said. "It's her favorite show. You shouldn't have lit her fuse. Now she's never going to shut up."

Kamiko raised her fist threateningly at Romeo.

He covered his arm protectively. "Ow!"

Kamiko smiled. "I didn't even hit you yet, baby."

"Here, Sam, look at her sketchbook before she murders me," Romeo said.

I flipped through it. It was filled with the most amazing japanese-style manga and anime drawings, many in color. Way better than I could do. Who was I kidding taking an art class? Maybe accounting really was the path for me. I was sure everyone in this room could draw better than I could. "Wow, Kamiko, you're really good," I said despondently.

"Thanks," she said nervously.

"Don't worry, Sam," Romeo said. "Kamiko came out of the womb with a sketchbook and pencil in hand. She can draw in her sleep. She's a freak. I think the government is going to hire her for some special drawing wizard thing to fight terrorism."

Kamiko rolled her eyes.

"You must be an art major." I handed the sketchbook back to Kamiko.

"Actually, I'm pre-med," she said. "My parents would kill me if they knew I was taking art classes. All I want to do is draw manga, but if I tell them that, they'll disown me. So I'm going to be a doctor. But I'm minoring in Art."

I sighed sympathetically. "You've got sensible parents too? Mine think I should be an accountant. After looking at your drawings, maybe I should."

"Don't talk like that," Kamiko said warmly. "I'm sure you're great."

I liked her. "Thanks." But I didn't think she had any idea how much better she was than me. If she was going to be a doctor, and she was this good at drawing, who was I kidding? Oh well, I signed up for this. Time to get to it.

I looked around, unsure what to do. Where was the professor?

The door opened and Psycho Motorknight Adonis walked into the room. He closed the door behind him, locking it. The entire class looked at him expectantly. The other females, and Romeo, were obviously drooling.

Blue Eyes walked to the dais with the colored pillows in the center of the room and stepped onto it. All eyes followed him. Was Adonis the *professor*? No, please no.

How did I end up with *him* as my professor? Madison would be jealous for sure. She'd probably want to transfer into this class as soon as I told her.

Adonis stood only a few feet away from me. He glanced at me and smirked his dimples at me. Oh god. I rolled my eyes. This was too much. I would have to drop this class immediately. I didn't need one of my professors hitting on me. The last thing I needed was further scandal.

Maybe accounting was the way to go. My Fundamentals professor looked like Dwight D. Eisenhower. Accounting was safe, boring and scandal-free.

Wait, what? Why was Blue Eyes taking his shirt off?

Gulp.

Chapter 4

"All right, class, we'll start with short poses. Beginning with one minute quick sketches." It was the old guy with the glasses on his nose. Was *he* the professor? "Remember, you want to focus on the gesture of the pose. Don't worry about details." He was. *Phew.*

"Didn't I tell you we'd have a good view?" Romeo gaped at Adonis. His eyes blazed with desire. "Look at those abs!"

Adonis stood on the dais with his shirt off in an elegant pose. Holy shitburgers! He looked like a Greek statue. Or a Greek god. His parents *had* named him appropriately. His jeans rode low on his narrow hips, revealing the sculpted V that arrowed down to his... YIKES!

How was I supposed to concentrate? I realized I'd been holding my breath for quite some time when Adonis changed poses. His abs rippled when he twisted his torso. His motion was fluid, like an experienced dancer performing a practiced routine.

Did he have an eight pack? More like an eighteen pack. His body was unbelievable. His thick pectoral muscles and defined shoulders popped when he settled into his next pose.

I took note of his elaborate tattoos. Aggressive tribal blades on his arms, wings on his shoulders, and the word "Fearless" in elegant script across his chest. From what I knew of this guy so far, it was an accurate description. He didn't look afraid of anything.

My god. Shivers ran up the backs of my legs and spun through my stomach before raising a flock of goose bumps along my arms. I couldn't do this. This had to be the wrong class. I considered running for the door, but Adonis had locked it. I imagined myself yanking on the doorknob with both hands and a foot, unable to escape. "I gotta get out of here," I whispered, panicked.

"Why, when we have such a magnificent view?" Romeo replied.

That was an understatement.

"Start drawing, girl," Romeo encouraged.

He was right. I needed to woman up and get a hold of myself. It was only a drawing class. It's not like Adonis was going to jump off that dais and wrap his manly arms around me and...goodness. Where was my mind going? I wasn't *this* boy crazy, was I?

But seriously, how was I supposed to draw perfection? I glanced around the room. Everyone was busily sketching away. Were they all master artists? How could they possibly capture all of the deliciously perfect muscles on Adonis' body? Not to mention his intricate tattoos? They were works of art in themselves.

"I'm drowning here," I hissed at Romeo.

"Make a few lines. These are quick sketches. Not masterpieces."

The first drawing on Romeo's pad was nothing more than scribbles, but it reminded me of Adonis' first pose. Kamiko's was of course elegant and masterful. Much better than Romeo's. But he didn't seem to care. The girl to my right had a drawing about as good as Romeo's. Maybe I *could* do this.

I looked at Adonis again. Deep breath. My hand shook so much I didn't think I could draw a straight line, let alone him. But I had to try. As I started scratching my charcoal on the paper, he changed poses again. I tugged on Romeo's arm and whispered. "How am I supposed to draw him if he keeps moving?"

"Long lines," the professor said. He stood to my right and drew a simple stick figure on my pad, but his confident lines evoked the essence of Adonis' current pose.

"How'd you do that?" I was amazed.

"Practice. Start with stick figures, try to match the pose. You'll get it." He looked at me over his glasses. Silver hair and a matching trim goatee framed his face. He wore a tweed jacket over a maroon turtle neck, and tan slacks. His outfit, that warm smile, and those glasses made him look like an avant-garde Santa Claus. I could work with that.

Some time later, I'd filled several pages of my drawing pad with over a dozen stick figure drawings. They weren't very good, but I could tell what each pose was.

"The model will now take a break," the professor said.

The students stepped away from their easels and circulated throughout the room. Two girls across from me walked up to Adonis and chatted with him. His back was turned to me. The girls whipped their hands through their hair like preening flamingoes while their eyes slid all over Adonis. I hated them.

"Professor Childress is great," Romeo said.

Romeo's words pulled me out of my hate fantasy that involved a rusty butcher knife, the two Flamingoes monopolizing Adonis, and a steaming cauldron. Now, why would I care who was talking to Adonis or not? I didn't want to think about it. I turned to Romeo. "Yeah, once the professor showed me that stick figure trick, I could actually sort of draw."

"Did you wipe the drool off your drawing pad?"

"What?"

"I saw the way you were staring at the model," Romeo said coyly.

"I wasn't staring!"

Romeo grinned. "Then how'd you do all those drawings? I know *I* was staring at him the whole time," he tittered.

I huffed, fresh out of retorts. I walked around the room, surveying the work of the other students. Some were pretty good, others not so much. Kamiko, on the other hand, was much better than everybody.

There's always a genius in every bunch. It didn't have to be me. I was okay being in the middle of the crowd, even if I trailed near the rear of the middle. At least I wasn't completely terrible. For a second there, when I'd started drawing, it felt like being here was a pipe dream joke and I would have to be smoking crack to think I wasn't wasting my time on art.

Maybe I *could* do this.

"Okay, everybody," Professor Childress said, "next we'll do some five minute poses." Everyone returned to their easels. "These poses will be full nude."

What, WHAT?!

Adonis stepped onto the dais and removed his boots and socks, then unzipped his pants and pushed them down. I barely restrained a face palm. No underwear! I had been right.

Adonis was completely naked. He struck a standing pose with his back to me. I'm sorry, but I had to look at his ass. Only for a second. I couldn't help myself. Oh gawd.

I was going to faint. I definitely needed that AED from the Student Center bookstore. Heart attack was imminent. This was not going to work. My body broiled from head to toe. I'm pretty sure steam was coming out of my ears, and my face was as red as a stop sign.

What was I doing here again? Was this a real class? Had I missed the part in the course description that said HOT NUDE GUYS? Why wasn't there a mile-long line of young women outside waiting to get into Life Drawing?

"Do you need oxygen," Romeo whispered. "I know I do." He was equally flustered. For Kamiko it was business as usual. From the look on her face, she could've been drawing a basket of fruit or a vase of flowers. She must have done this before, or else she was a lesbian, or maybe asexual. How could she concentrate?

I wanted to fan my face. I wanted to run out of the room again. Both would call more attention to myself. I surreptitiously glanced around. Was I the only person not drawing?

Even the preening flamingo girls were drawing where they stood on the other side of the room, albeit with lusty looks on their faces. Maybe they *had* known the secret about life drawing class. Adonis' back was to me. Which meant his fully-nude front was facing those flamingoes. Which meant they were staring at his—

"Long poses are intended to give you more time to focus on the anatomy and structure of the model," the professor said to the class. "Lay in the same gesture you did for the one-minute poses, then add three-dimensional form on top."

Concentrate, girl. This is school, and you're in class. You're here to learn. Who was I kidding? This was an educational environment? Was I being graded for staring at a naked, beautiful man? If so, I was going to ace this class. If I could only stop staring long enough to draw.

"Start again with the gesture."

I jumped.

Out of nowhere, Professor Childress was drawing on my pad again. I'm pretty sure my heart stopped for real this time.

The professor drew another stick figure on my pad, matching Adonis' pose. "Then add structure." He drew cylinders and cubes on top of the stick figure. Watching him work was magical. "Now you try." He smiled and walked away.

Deep breath. Relax. Okay, one more deep breath. I started drawing and focused all my attention on copying the professor's drawing on my pad. I didn't look at Adonis. Well, maybe once or twice, to make sure I got the butt right.

A few minutes later, Adonis changed his pose.

Help!

Adonis faced me directly, in all his glorious splendor. I think I heard angels sing. I looked everywhere except at Adonis. The ceiling looked pretty good. I took a moment to appreciate Romeo's shoes. They really accented his outfit.

Romeo giggled. "Are we having a problem?"

"No. I. Uh."

"It's okay. It doesn't bite."

"What doesn't bite?"

Romeo snickered.

Oh, duh. Now would've been a good time for Kamiko to punch him again.

Speaking of Kamiko, what else could I look at that wasn't the naked man five feet away from me? She held her charcoal at arms length, toward Adonis, and squinted at it. I'd seen artists do that before, but I didn't know why. Maybe I could try that.

I held my charcoal out toward Adonis. *Oh, I get it. The charcoal is there to block the model's—*

"You haven't drawn anything. Is something wrong?" Professor Childress asked.

Caught red handed. Or should I say red-faced? "It's just that I, well, I've never done any drawings like this before."

The professor nodded encouragingly. "It's nothing more than shape and form. Tubes—"

Did he say tubes?

"—and boxes."

Crap. He said boxes. Tubes in boxes. I mean tubes AND boxes. Did someone turn up the heat in here? I swear it's like a hundred degrees and totally humid.

"Give it a try. You'll do fine. I promise."

I managed to finish my drawing using Kamiko's charcoal-eye-shield trick to black out the, um, tube. I had to hold my charcoal close to my face to block out all of Adonis' uh, you know. My drawing was sort of empty in the center, since I couldn't see his, ahh, yeah, that. But I drew his head, er, I mean face, and arms and legs. It looked okay.

Thankfully, the next two poses were sitting, and Adonis angled himself in such a way that I didn't have to use the charcoal-eye-shield trick to hide his tube from view.

"The model will now take a break before we start the contour drawings."

"Wow, Sam, those are good," Kamiko said.

"Really?"

"Yeah," she smiled. I wasn't sure if I believed her. She was *so* talented.

"Seriously," Romeo chimed in, "not bad for a first time."

"Thanks guys." I smiled uncertainly.

"Because it's pretty obvious you're a life drawing VIRGIN," Romeo gasped scandalously.

I swatted his arm. "Am not!"

"Well, not anymore. Now that your charcoal cherry's been popped!"

I swatted him again.

"Ow, ow, ow! I think you dislocated my shoulder!" He was fine.

"Baby!" I giggled.

"So what if I am?" Romeo tilted his head back proudly and shook his imaginary locks. "I'm a sensitive artist."

Professor Childress walked over and examined my drawings and smiled. "Nicely done. I knew you could do it." He walked to the next student.

I was so busy basking in all the praise, I almost missed Adonis putting his pants on for the break. What a relief. Now he was only shirtless, and I could steal glances at his amazing body without embarrassment.

There's something indescribably sexy about a man wearing nothing but pants, like he'd just jumped out of your bed and thrown them on. Where was my butterfly net? My stomach was filled with them.

I decided it would be wise to stop thinking about Adonis and bedrooms because he was busy with the two flamingoes again. One of them was tall and had a perfect hourglass figure and beautiful hair. Adonis was putting her phone number into his phone. She did the same while the other girl thrust her mammoth breasticles out at him. Bitches. I wish those two girls would flamin*go the fuck away.*

What was I thinking? This guy wasn't for me. Madison wanted

him way more than I did anyway.

"For the next drawing," Professor Childress said, "I want everybody to do a blind contour drawing. Fold back your pad to a fresh, blank page. Then lift the blank page and draw beneath it, with the paper covering your hand, so you can't see what you're doing. The purpose of this exercise is to focus on seeing. Don't worry about your drawing."

Adonis walked onto the dais, put his cell phone into his pocket, and slid his jeans off. Oh, my. Again? Could someone get me a bucket to collect the drool pooling at my feet?

"This will be a ten minute pose," the Professor said. He punched some buttons on a small kitchen timer and set it down on the dais where Adonis could see it.

Adonis sat on the colored pillows and faced my general direction. He propped himself up on one tattooed, muscled arm and draped the other over his hip like a lounging gladiator reclining on a roman couch. All he needed were laurel leaves and a handful of grapes to complete the ensemble. He bent his top leg, shielding his manly business from my view.

Okay, this I could work with.

"Start moving your pencil freely," the Professor continued. "Pick any point on the outline of the model and follow it along the contour of his body." I could do that. "Imagine that where your eye touches, so does your pencil. Imagine that your fingertip is literally sliding across the surface of the model."

You've got to be kidding me! How am I supposed to get any drawing done thinking like that?

"Don't think about what you are drawing on your pad. Think only about what you see in front of you."

Hot guy. Amazing body. Perfect muscles. Aggressive tattoos. Pant, pant.

I wasn't going to get anything done at this rate, so I started at his toes, just to be safe. Toes and ankles weren't nearly as sexy. Some minutes later, I had made my way up to Adonis' shoulder. I wondered what my drawing would look like.

"Don't be tempted to look at your work," the Professor said. "Concentrate on looking only at the model. Take note of every curve, every muscle, every bulge."

The only bulging I could think about were my nipples pressing against the cups of my bra. I'm sure glad I wore my print dress this morning. Perfect camouflage.

Deep breath. Sigh. My eyes worked around the shape of Adonis' head and hair. I stole a glance at his eyes across the length of his impressive body. He caught me peeking and winked back. Could I draw his eyes? Was that part of his outline?

I flashed on the image of him exchanging phone numbers with one of the flamingoes. And the fawning Delta Pi Deltas. And him kissing Tiffany Kingston-Whitehouse-Snootfest. I felt bad for Madison. She had no idea what she was getting into falling for Adonis. He was a total player.

Luckily, I didn't have to waste my time on him. That made it easy to focus on my work.

Several minutes later, the timer started beeping. "Time's up, everybody," the Professor said.

"Lift up your paper," Romeo said. "How'd you do?"

I almost forgot I'd been drawing anything, I'd been so focused on looking. I lifted the blank page, expecting the worst. I was surprised to see a quivering line around my paper that somewhat resembled Adonis' pose. Romeo had produced similar results.

"Nice work, Sam." He patted me on the shoulder. "You're pretty good at this."

Even Kamiko's contour, while better than everyone else's, wasn't perfect like her other work. Maybe I wasn't so bad after all.

The last drawing of the class was another long pose. This time we were supposed to look at our work. Adonis sat on the stool with his side to me, in the classic Thinker pose, chin resting on his knuckles. This was the least distracting pose so far. I focused entirely on my drawing. And how bad it was.

The more I drew, the worse it got. Romeo wasn't struggling at all. He looked repeatedly from his pad to Adonis, laying down lines with assurance.

Kamiko was halfway through a masterpiece, complete with shading.

I was making a mess. I was sweating again, this time from stress. My drawing sucked ass. Pretty sure my armpits were dripping. Good thing my print dress disguised what were likely frisbee-sized sweat stains. I felt like my wardrobe decision was the only good thing that had happened today.

I set my charcoal down before the pose finished. I was spent, and not in a good way. Every line I drew had made my drawing worse. It was a charcoally black mess. Romeo worked enthusiastically on his, too busy to help.

I'd hoped Professor Childress would come by and encourage me, but he was working with the other students. Finally, the timer beeped. Adonis began dressing, not that I cared. I felt like a failure.

The other students folded their pads closed. I did too. I didn't want anyone to see my horrible drawing.

I glanced at Kamiko's pad. She was adding final touches without having to look at the model. Her drawing was amazing. It looked like Adonis, right down to his facial features. How did she do that? She'd even pulled out a blue colored pencil at some point to do his eyes. She got that right too.

The face on my drawing was a black smear. I know, because I had rubbed it out with my fingers earlier.

I wasn't an artist. Who was I kidding? I belonged in accounting, with smelly coffee feet, taking notes on a laptop like everyone else. I wasn't meant to do something special or romantic like art.

Emo. Goth. Witch. Sorceress.

Shit, I was none of those things. Those things had a spark of originality. I was completely common. I couldn't make anything magical. I was plain old Sam Smith. Boring CPA.

Adonis walked out of the room. Hourglass Flamingo had her arm around his waist and her breasty minion in tow.

Blue Eyes took the last of the magic with him when he'd left the room. Well, except for Kamiko's drawings, which were pretty damn magical. Unlike mine.

College sucked ass. What was I thinking when I decided to move across the country, leaving everything behind? Did I think I could change my life so easily? My parents had been right all along. I was nothing special. Why bother trying? I should go home and be miserable in familiar surroundings. At least I knew how to do that.

Professor Childress folded his arms across his chest. "How was your final drawing?"

I sighed heavily. "Not so good."

"Can I see it?"

I was reluctant to unveil my failure. "It's not very good."

"I'll be the judge of that. Let me see it."

Great. Now he was going to judge me. *Have at it.* I lifted back the pages until I revealed my final drawing.

The professor stroked his goatee thoughtfully. "Mmm-hmm. Mmm." He cocked his head. "Mmm."

What the hell did that mean? "It's horrible, I know."

"Horrible? Is that what you think?"

"You don't have to say anything." I hoped he didn't hand me a bunch of b.s. fake praise. I hated the "everyone's a winner" syndrome. Not everyone could take first place. Or second, or third. Or twentieth.

"Have you done much drawing in the past?"

"A little. Sometimes I draw in my sketchbook." I fidgeted. *Get this over with already!*

"Your line work is very strong. See your s-curve on the extended leg over here? It's confident and true."

"Yeah, but the rest of the drawing's terrible!"

"It's fine to take note of your failures. In the beginning stages we have many. Don't forget to celebrate your successes as well. That one line shows me you have talent. You have only to develop it."

"But everyone else's drawings are so much better than mine. Kamiko's—"

"You're referring to the young asian girl?"

"Yeah."

"She showed me her sketchbook before class. What about her?"

"Kamiko's drawing's are *so* good. I can't compete with her."

"You're not competing with her. You're competing only with yourself. Kamiko has had years of vigilant practice. Your goal is not to best her. You goal is to improve. Remember the beautiful s-curve you drew on the extended leg?"

"Yeah?"

"Next time, strive for two beautiful lines. That's it. Let the rest of them be messy and terrible. It's through the process of making countless mistakes that we approach, but never achieve, perfection. We get better one step, or in this case one line, at a time."

"Really?" Was it that simple? Maybe it was. "Thanks Professor Childress!"

"See you next class. What was your name?"

"Samantha Smith. People call me Sam."

"Pleased to meet you, Sam. I expect good things from you. I've been doing this a long time. You have what it takes, I know."

"Really?"

"Yes."

Wow! I didn't suck!

Chapter 5

Romeo, Kamiko, and I went to the Student Center for lunch. I was ready for a distraction. I texted Madison where we were going, but she didn't reply.

Romeo introduced me to fish tacos. I had no idea you could put fish in a taco. I loved the white sauce! So good.

I munched on tortilla chips while Kamiko talked about Adventure Time. I learned more about that cartoon than I ever thought I would. She was so enthusiastic about it, I couldn't bear to stop her.

Romeo dipped a chip in his salsa. "So, Sam. I was worried about you during Life Drawing. I was ready to call 911. You were dangerously close to paralysis."

"Yeah, I think I have PTSD," I said.

"That guy was Muy Caliente!" Kamiko laughed.

I was surprised. "You noticed? I thought you were too busy drawing to care."

"I'm not blind! That guy was super hot! And he was totally checking *you* out."

"No he wasn't," I scoffed.

Romeo wiped his hands on his napkin. "You are totally in denial, Sam! His eyes were glued on you."

Great. Not what I wanted to hear. "Then why did he leave with that girl? She had her arm around him."

"Well, he sure acted like he wanted to get to know *you*."

I winced. "He kind of already does."

Romeo almost jumped out of his seat. His monocle swayed from the button on his coat. I noticed he hadn't worn it once since we met. "What!" he shouted. "Have you been holding out on us? I want to know everything!" He propped his elbows on the table and rested his chin in his cupped hands. "Details."

"Fine. I'll tell you." It's not like this could get any more awkward. "This morning, on my way to campus, our model totally saved my ass."

Romeo did a double take. "Stop! Rewind! The art model *saved* you?"

"Yeah. I was waiting at a red light and spilled my coffee. This fat guy in a gold Mercedes got out of his car and started yelling at me. Our art model—whose name is Adonis—was there, and he punched the fat guy out."

"You know his name?!" Romeo's jaw dropped. "That is *so* not fair! I wish I could be a damsel in distress."

"Poor baby." Kamiko patted his arm reassuringly. "So let me get this straight, Sam. Some random hot guy saves your ass this morning, and two hours later he's totally checking you out in drawing class? How lucky are you?"

Considering that Madison, my only other friend in San Diego besides these two, was crushing on him, I would say not lucky at all. How would she feel if she knew Adonis had his eyes all over me while I had my eyes all over him? I felt like a total jerk.

"Do you have Sir Lancelot's phone number?" Romeo pleaded. "When do you think you'll see him again?"

"Uh, probably never."

"Or right now," Kamiko murmured, staring at her plate.

"Samantha?"

I whipped my head around. Adonis stood behind me, holding a plate with a sandwich and chips on it.

"Uh, hey, Adonis."

Romeo stood up, eyes sparkling, and pulled out an empty chair. "Care to join us?"

"Looks like you guys are almost finished."

"Oh no, we're just getting started. Join us!" Romeo picked up a fistful of chips and shoved them in his mouth. He jawed them nervously. Crumbs rained on his lap.

Adonis sat down and set his plate on the table.

I made a mental note to kill Romeo later. In the meantime, I'd have to satisfy myself with stomping on his foot under the table. Too bad I was wearing sandals and not stilettos.

Romeo's eyes popped and he stifled a grunt. I smiled back at him innocently. He coughed several times on his chips. Served him right.

"You okay, buddy?" Adonis asked.

"I'm, *cough*, fine. *Cough*," Romeo gagged.

When Romeo's choking spree subsided, everyone at the table stared at Adonis like idiots. I guess introductions were up to me. "So, um, Adonis, these are my friends, Romeo and Kamiko. Everybody, Adonis."

Adonis saluted everyone with his sandwich pickle. I was pretty sure Romeo was remembering him naked.

"So, how'd everyone's drawings turn out?" Adonis asked.

Romeo nodded mutely.

"Excellent!' Kamiko tittered nervously.

"They usually do," Adonis replied. "Considering the subject matter. How could anyone possibly do a bad drawing of me?" His dimples winked at me sarcastically.

I rolled my eyes and laughed in his face. "Don't be bashful, Adonis. Tell us what you really think."

Adonis' luscious lips spread over his brilliant teeth, revealing that perfect smile again. Stupid dimples. He was un-hatable. But I could still give him a hard time.

"Are you going to be able to fit your head in your motorcycle helmet later?" I sneered. "I think it's twice the size it was this morning."

Romeo's jaw dropped. He stomped *my* foot under the table.

"Adonis!" A young woman I'd never seen before pranced up to the table on dancer's legs. She had bouncy auburn hair. Her dress was what I'd describe as nouveau hippie. It seemed like an affectation. Somehow I imagined her paying top dollar for what was supposed to look thrift-store vintage.

I suspected the two man-magnets bouncing on her chest were artificially enhanced. She immediately started massaging Adonis' shoulders with both hands.

Oh my god, how many women were wrapped around this guy's fingers?

A slow smiled spread across Adonis' face. "Hey, Skylar. How you doing, babe?"

"Better, now that I tracked you down. You've been M.I.A. since our last date."

"Date?"

"Don't you remember? Onyx? The club downtown? We danced

till they closed? My place afterward? The kitchen table after breakfast?"

Adonis squinched his eyes thoughtfully.

Oh, Lord. Did he even remember having sex with this woman? Guys like him were all about the fuck and run. What a nightmare.

"Oh yeah." Adonis grinned thoughtfully. "I remember now. That wasn't a date. We were just hanging out."

Jesus, what did a date involve for this guy? A sex swing with an audience?

Skylar was undeterred. "When can I see you again? It's been weeks." She draped her arms over his shoulders and rubbed his chest. Had she no shame?

"I'm pretty busy."

"Come on, Adonis," she begged. "I totally need to see you tonight."

"You don't *need* to see me. You might think you do, but you don't. There's plenty of other guys out there."

"Yeah, but none like you, Adonis."

"That's true."

Oh, God. Barf. Did he really talk like this? Or was I trapped inside a bad porno movie? I shot to my feet. "Okay! We have to go now. We'll leave you two in peace. Come on, you guys."

Romeo hadn't heard me. I smacked his arm and he jumped. "Oh! Right! Let's go, Kamiko."

Adonis was too busy with Skylar to notice our departure.

None of us had class until the next hour, so we emptied our trays into the trash, and the three of us walked to the Central Fountain. Lush green lawns surrounded it. Shade trees dotted the grass. We collapsed beneath one of the trees.

My phone jingled. It was Madison. "What up, Mads?"

"Where you at?"

"I'm over at the central fountain with some new friends. You wanna join us?"

"Yeah, I'll be there in five." She arrived a few minutes later holding a soda. I introduced her to Romeo and Kamiko, and explained we met in Life Drawing class.

Madison sat down and pulled a bag of mini peanut butter cups out of her backpack. "I brought treats! Anyone want any?"

We all fought to jam our hands into the bag at the same time. A chorus of "Thanks, Madison!" followed.

I was so glad I'd met her. She was so thoughtful and generous.

Madison sipped her soda. "So, how was life drawing, you guys?"

I had hoped she wouldn't ask anything that would lead to the topic of Adonis. So much for that. Well, I didn't have to say anything. No matter how hot Adonis was, I wasn't going to let him come between me and Madison.

Romeo swooned. "I declare, I'm absolutely in love with the model."

Madison frowned. "Model? I don't get it."

"The Life Drawing model," Kamiko said. "The one who posed for us today."

There was no getting out of it.

"Wait, so you guys drew a model, like a live person?"

Romeo popped a peanut butter cup into his mouth. "Yup. And he was quite dashing. Winsome, if you will."

"Romeo means he was hot," Kamiko translated.

"And naked," Romeo grinned.

Madison sputtered on her soda. "Holy shiznet! For real? Naked? Like, birthday suit naked?"

Madison looked at me. "Yeah," I answered dismissively. "He wasn't that hot," I lied.

"Liar!" Romeo shouted. "He was *so* hot and you *loved* it!"

Shit. Romeo was not helping.

"Really." Madison arched an eyebrow. "Do tell. Was he circumcised?" She giggled and swatted my arm.

"I didn't look that close!"

"I did." Romeo grinned. "And yes, he is cut."

"Eww, Romeo." Kamiko grimaced. "T. M. I."

I *really* needed to steer the conversation away from Adonis, for Madison's sake. If I couldn't manage it myself, a sudden earthquake or swarm of killer bees would suffice. "Can we change the subject?" I pleaded.

"I think not," Madison said. "You spent class time drawing a hot naked guy. You have to give me details. What did he look like?"

"Kamiko," Romeo said, "show her your drawing. It totally looks like him."

No, no, no. There was no way I could stop this. Where were those bees? Crap.

"I don't want to drag my drawings out, Romeo," Kamiko moaned. "They're terrible."

Thank god for Kamiko's false modesty.

"Come on you guys, now I'm totally curious," Madison said. She set her soda on the grass.

"He was tall, like a warrior," Romeo mused. "He had dark hair, sculpted muscles, tattoos, and the bluest eyes you've ever seen."

"Hey, that sounds like the guy I saw this morning when we were at the Student Center," Madison said.

Oh no.

"Did Sam tell you he *saved* her on the way to campus? Like a damsel in distress?"

Fucktastic. I shot Romeo a "shut the fuck up" look. He didn't notice. Where were those damn bees?!

"Who? The model?" Madison asked.

"Yeah. His name is Adonis," Romeo said innocently. "Sam's totally into him."

I sighed. I couldn't blame Romeo. He didn't know that Madison had a thing for Adonis.

Madison's brows snapped up and her eyes flashed at me expectantly.

I decided the best thing to do was be honest. "I admit it. I was totally staring at him. But how could I not? I was supposed to, for class." Did I have to tell her I thought Adonis was hot? Could I leave that part out?

Madison folded her arms across her chest and leveled a shrewd look at me. I think she was reading my mind.

If she was going to hate me, at least I still had Romeo and Kamiko. I wasn't entirely sure I wanted a blabbermouth like Romeo around at this point. But I wasn't in a position to be choosy about my friends. I never had.

Madison tilted her head back, waiting for the rest. May as well give it to her.

"Okay, don't hate me, Mads. I admit it. Adonis is totally hot. But I will stay away from him, if that's what you want."

She didn't look like she was buying it.

"I have to warn you though, he's probably slept with half the women on campus, and I think he's working his way through the rest of them. The way they throw themselves at him, I'm surprised he doesn't tell them to take a number. He probably hosts orgies every weekend."

"Do you think he'd invite me?" Romeo asked sheepishly.

Kamiko smacked him. "Shut up, Romeo!"

I gave Madison a pleading look. "Do you hate me?"

For a second, I was sure that she did.

But then Madison's lips relaxed into a smile. "Did you think I was that into him?" She shook her head. "I know better, Sam. Yeah, he's hot. But I saw those girls melting all over him. Did you think I was going to be jealous if you liked him too?"

"Yeah. Sort of." I examined my fingernails and the peeling black nail polish. "But I totally don't like him."

"Methinks the lady doth protest too much," Romeo said theatrically.

"Whatever," I scoffed. "He's a total man-whore."

Madison leaned over and gave me a big hug. "Oh, Sam. You were worried over nothing, There's tons of hot guys on campus. I'm not going to obsess over one. Now eat a peanut butter cup. Sugar and fat cures all ills."

I hugged her back. "Thanks, Mads. I thought you were gonna kill me for sure." I grabbed a handful from the bag.

"Nope. But if you eat the last peanut butter cup, I will!"

Romeo grabbed for the chocolates in my hand. "Gimme those, glutton!"

I dodged expertly. No one was getting my peanut butter cups!

We still had a few minutes before everyone had class.

"So, Kamiko," I asked, "how come you're not an art major? Your drawings are amazing."

She pulled her knees to her chest and sighed. "My parents are paying for college. They want me to be a doctor."

"Isn't it weird how money can be a trap sometimes?" Madison asked.

"I never thought of it that way," she sighed. "But my older brothers and sisters are doctors or software engineers. I don't have any choice."

"Don't you feel like your talent's going to waste?" I asked.

"Sort of. But I owe my parents. They worked really hard so I could go to a good college. I can't disrespect them by throwing it all away."

"I get it." It didn't make me feel any better. "But if I was as good as you, I don't think I'd be studying accounting." Kamiko was so good at drawing, I worried she really was throwing away her *true* talent. "Romeo, what's your major?"

"I'm doubling in Art and Theater. Between the two of them, I'm sure I'll be out of work on a regular basis. But heck, I've always wanted to be a barista, and I hear Starbucks has a great health plan."

I felt the weight of our futures pressing down on all of us. I looked at my newfound friends and saw the stress and fear tightening around our throats. Except for Madison. She seemed impervious.

What happened to college being the launch pad to our bright and wonderful futures? We were all paying dearly to ensure our future success and prosperity. We should've been jumping for joy. Not drowning in a blue funk of worry.

Madison stood up. "Come on, you guys! That's years away. We should be enjoying this amazing weather. Besides, we're late for class!"

That afternoon, we all had separate classes. I was sitting in Sociology when Romeo texted me halfway through class.

Me & Kamiko r going to the campus art museum after class. Wanna come?

Yup, I texted back. *Where is it?*

Meet you at the fountain in 30.

K.

I didn't realize there was a campus art museum. That sounded fun. Even if I was destined to be an accountant, I could enjoy myself for now.

The Eleanor M. Westbrook art museum was huge. One of the signs going into the galleries said that Eleanor had married a prominent Hollywood movie producer in the 1940s. They had retired to San Diego with their fortune. Eleanor had outlived her husband, and upon her death, donated a ton of money to the university.

Romeo guided us around the museum. He was familiar with many of the artists, and told us about them as we went from room to room. I'd never heard of most of them, but the paintings were beautiful.

Kamiko had her sketchbook out the entire time, and made dozens of tiny pencil drawings of the different paintings, or drew the various sculptures. She was *so* good.

"I can't get over how many talented artists there are that I've never even heard of," I marveled. "So much beautiful work."

We stood in front of a huge painting of cliffs and the ocean after a thunderstorm. Sun rays shone between cracks in the clouds. It kind of reminded me of the view I'd seen when I was driving to school, except cloudy and darker. It was so realistic, I almost thought I felt the chill air and smelled the ocean.

Who had painted it? I read the placard.

Spiridon Manos (1952—   )
"Shrouded Paradise"
Oil on Canvas
1973
130" x 55"

"Whoever this Spiridon guy is," I said, "he's a freaking genius. He was twenty-one when he painted this."

Romeo read the description below the placard. "I've never heard of him. But you're right." Romeo half-laughed. "He's really, really good."

Romeo was clearly impressed. Kamiko was too, based on the intensity in her eyes while she sketched the painting. "The composition is amazing," she said.

"Composition?" I said. "It's like a photograph!"

"Yeah, but look at the shapes of the clouds, how the light seeps through the cracks between them. Clouds don't stay like that all day. He had to pick the perfect moment and capture it before it was gone. He probably made a small oil sketch on location and finished this large canvas in the studio."

"How do you know all this stuff?"

"I read about art whenever I'm not studying medicine."

"When do you read? You're always watching Cartoon

Network," Romeo joked.

Kamiko ignored him.

My depression returned. Between my crappy drawings this morning, Kamiko's genius sketchbook, and this guy Spiridon's über-genius painting, I sucked hairy ball bags. "I'm fooling myself, Romeo. I'll never be this good."

"Aw, cheer up, Sam. Van Gogh didn't start painting until he was in his late twenties."

"Really?" That was hard to believe. But I felt a hopeful chill rush up the back of my arms anyway.

Romeo's eyes goggled at something behind me.

"Yup, and Kandinsky didn't enroll in art school until he was thirty," Adonis said.

I whipped around. I caught Adonis sliding the tips of his index fingers up the backs of my arms, hence my chills. Cocky bastard. "What're you doing here?"

"Looking at paintings."

"What do you know about Kandinsky?" I asked haughtily. I didn't even know who Kandinsky was, but I wasn't telling him that.

"I know that Kandinsky gave up a career teaching law and economics to enroll in art school, where he excelled. I also know that he wrote extensively about the spiritual aspect of art. He even theorized that there was a direct connection between color and sound, that specific colors corresponded to specific musical notes."

How the shizzle did everybody know so much about art except me? I fought to hide my awe. This guy didn't need me stroking his ego. Instead, I stared into his eyes. I'm sure a tube of expensive blue paint was named after them.

Why was this guy getting so far under my skin? I didn't like it. He may have known art, but he was still a player.

"So," I blurted. "What happened to Skylar?" I sounded about thirteen years old when I said it, but I swear I didn't mean to.

Adonis nodded and grinned. "She's not into art."

"What about that girl from life drawing class?" I sniveled. "She seemed like she was into art."

"If you mean she was into me," he grinned his cocky grin, "then yeah, she's into art."

My eyes flashed. "You're no work of art."

"Oh no she didn't," Romeo murmured. He backed away until he stood behind Kamiko. "I think they're going to fight."

Adonis chuckled, cool as could be. "Do you need a whetstone to sharpen those claws?"

"I don't know," I sneered, "are you done talking about your harem?"

"You brought it up."

I had. Why was I turning Superbitch all of a sudden? I blamed Adonis. I was doing fine until he showed up and molested the backs of my arms. Perv. "Are you stalking me?"

"I was already here. I saw you guys walk in twenty minutes ago."

"Fight, fight!" Romeo whispered.

I glared at him. "I heard that!"

He ducked behind Kamiko.

Adonis smiled at me. "So, you like the museum?"

That caught me off guard. He wasn't allowed to change the subject and act like a sane person. "Uh, yeah, it's great."

"We're lucky to have such an amazing art museum on campus. There's some paintings in here you're not going to see anywhere else in the world. You like landscapes?" He motioned toward the cloudy beach scene I had been admiring.

"Yeah, it's great." I blinked and looked at it again. It really was amazing. "I feel like I could throw my leg over the picture frame and step right into it."

"It's a view from near where I saw you this morning on the PCH," he mused thoughtfully.

"No wonder it looks familiar! How'd you know that?"

"I grew up around here." He shrugged.

I'm sure he added the shrug on purpose, because it drew attention to his impressive shoulders. My belly warmed as I remembered the rest of what lay beneath his V-neck t-shirt in detail. I'd had plenty of time to scrutinize exactly how his shoulders attached to his breathtaking chest and muscled back during Life Drawing.

Was the room shrinking around me? Woo. Heat.

"The weather rarely looks like this." He no longer sounded flirtatious, but rather as if he was remembering. He motioned toward the painting. We both turned back to face it simultaneously.

My shoulder brushed against his elbow. "Usually the wind blows the storm clouds out to sea in the afternoon, if we have any. You can't beat San Diego weather."

My shoulder tingled where it had kissed, I mean rubbed, Adonis' elbow. Standing in front of the painting, I felt like we were a couple out for a nature hike and we had stopped to enjoy the view.

I almost fell for it. Not.

He probably took all his girls out for "get back to nature" hikes. This guy knew what he was doing. He wasn't going to enchant me with his pathetic charms.

Time to go. I turned around. Romeo and Kamiko resembled a couple watching a romance flick at a movie theater. Romeo bit his lower lip and clutched Kamiko desperately. Kamiko swooned, her sketchbook dangling forgotten at her side. All they needed to complete the tableau was a bucket of popcorn and the flickering lights.

"Enjoying the show?" I sneered. "Let's go, you guys." I strode toward the exit without checking to see if Adonis followed.

Chapter 6

I didn't have anymore classes that day, so I said my goodbyes to Romeo and Kamiko outside the museum. I stopped at the Student Bookstore and was able to buy my textbooks, which weighed a ton. I headed for the parking lot.

Thankfully, the jackhole cars bookending my VW this morning were gone.

When I opened my car door, the smell of coffee curdled cream punched me in the face. It had baked in the oven of my VW all day. Shit. I'd forgotten about that.

I wished I had a crane to turn my VW on its side. Then I'd shake the coffee out. Otherwise, the coffee was going to slosh against my feet on the drive home. I needed a plan B.

The likely solution was about 200 napkins, or some good rags, to mop up the mess. Unfortunately, I didn't have either.

If I had notebook paper, I would've used that. But all I had was my laptop. Groan.

Options. I could find the closest dining hall and ask to borrow a case of napkins. Or the nearest restroom, where I could wind out an entire roll of paper towels. I'm sure someone would call campus security on me and accuse me of grand theft blotto.

Maybe I could sop it up with dirt? The parking lot was surrounded by hedges. But then I'd be stuck with coffee flavored mud. Why did that make me think of Rocky Road ice cream? Gross.

A motorcycle drove up and stopped behind my car. "Hey, Samantha."

I knew those arms. "Adonis."

He flipped up his visor. "Need some help?"

Yes. I mean no, not from you. "Sort of. Remember I spilled my coffee all over my car this morning?"

"Yup."

"I'm debating whether or not I want to drive home without

cleaning it up. I don't have enough napkins."

"How big was your coffee?"

"I don't know, gallon sized?" I couldn't help but laugh at my predicament.

He took off his helmet and brushed his hair back. Dimple alert. Why were dimples so damn sexy? He got off his bike and inspected my car. "That's not too bad." He climbed inside and sat in the driver's seat.

"Hey! What are you doing?"

"We need to air this thing out."

We? Why did I like the fact he said we?

He leaned over and opened the passenger door. Then he grabbed the sopping napkins I'd thrown at the spill this morning and chucked them out of the car. "I'll pick those up later. Right now, we need something to absorb everything. We can get some paper towels from the dorms over there."

Hey, that was my idea! Sort of. "I thought the dorms were private."

"So?" He walked his motorcycle into the open space next to mine.

"What kind of motorcycle is that?"

"It's a Ducati."

"I thought all real men rode Harleys," I said defiantly.

He scoffed. "If I want to sit on a couch, I've got one at home. Most Harleys don't make it past one-ten. One-twenty on a good day. I've taken my Ducati up to one-seventy-five."

"Is that fast?"

He threw his head back and laughed. "Is that fast? You wanna find out?"

I was suddenly nervous. "Now?"

"No. Later," he smiled. "When it's dark. No traffic. Fewer cops."

I'd never been on a motorcycle before. Let alone gone more than maybe eighty-five in my parents' Honda. 175 mph? Jesus. "Um, I don't know. It sounds dangerous."

"It is." His grin shone confidently.

In-SANE! I smelled death wish. So why did the idea turn me on? Maybe I was the insane one.

"Anytime you wanna go, you let me know." He smiled confidently, like he went 175 mph every day.

"I'll think on it. Right now I need, like, a million paper towels for the epic coffee tragedy in my car. Who's going to give us that many?"

"We'll find some. Come on."

We walked to the dorm building adjacent to the parking lot. When we approached the main doors, he stopped.

"What are we waiting for?"

"You need a key card to get into the building."

"Then how are we going to get inside?"

The doors opened and two guys with skateboards walked out. Adonis grabbed the door before it shut. "This way."

"Isn't this breaking and entering?"

"I didn't break anything, did I?"

"So we're entering?"

"Yup."

We walked inside together. He surveyed the entry hall. It split off in two directions. We turned left. A barefoot girl wearing an SDU t-shirt, holding a bowl of Cheerios and milk in one hand and her textbooks in the other, struggled to open a door to one of the suite of rooms. She fumbled to get out her key card. She was about to set down her books when Adonis intervened.

"Let me help you with that." He took hold of her books.

"Thanks." She smiled. When she got a good look at him, she raked her eyes up and down his body. "Thank you very much." She blushed.

"My pleasure." Adonis cocked an eyebrow.

She dug out her keycard and waved it in front of the lock. The mechanism clicked.

"I'll get that." Adonis opened the door for her and held it. "Never can be too careful, what with all the psychos around." He flashed his award-winning grin.

"No, you can't," she smiled bashfully.

Put your underwear back on, Cheerios! You're getting milk on the floor!

Cheerios walked through the door and Adonis followed. He handed her books back to her then looked at me and cocked his head. "Come on."

I grabbed the door before it closed.

He walked right into the suite's bathroom. A girl in a bathrobe had just stepped out of the shower. She jumped when she saw Adonis. "Who are you?!"

"Don't worry about us," he said confidently.

"You guys can't be in here!"

"Just need to borrow some paper towels. Ours ran out. Had a little mess. Be gone in a sec."

Shower Girl's eyes pivoted from side to side like a caged rat.

Adonis spun the dispenser's handle, causing his forearm muscles to dance hypnotically. The spell broke when I saw he had wound out at least twenty feet of paper towels. He smiled at me. "You think this'll be enough?"

"Uh, yeah."

He wadded them up, and tore off a small chunk, which he ran under the faucet.

"What are you doing?" Shower girl asked.

"Gonna clean up a mess. Wet towels work better." He balled up the wet towels. I could tell he was trying to keep as much water in them as possible. They dripped all over the floor. He thanked Shower Girl on our way out. She was horribly confused the entire time.

I was halfway to crazy myself.

"Better move before someone calls campus security," he joked. He didn't seem to be taking this very seriously.

"That's not funny. Someone might."

"For what? Entering and Borrowing?"

"Are you going to return the paper towels when you're through with them?"

"I could. It would be messy, but if you think it's the right thing to do." He winked at me.

I smacked his arm. "You're crazy."

"To a degree."

At my car, Adonis blotted up the remaining coffee with some of the dry towels, then went over everything with the damp towels. I watched. His back muscles did amazing things while he wiped.

"Let me help you with that," I suggested.

"Relax. There's not much to do. I'll be done in a minute." He dried up with the remaining towels. Why was a sexy men cleaning twice as sexy? I had no answer, but new it as fact.

He picked up the soaked napkins he'd thrown on the asphalt earlier and added them to the dirty wad he held in his hand. "Well, it's not perfect. But it'll do until you have a chance to hit up a car wash."

"Thanks, Adonis. That was really sweet of you. You're quite the Boy Scout."

"Just trying to earn my carwash merit badge. I need to throw all this away." He held up the sopping wad. He started back toward the dorms.

"I'll come with you."

"You sure? We might get arrested for Clean and Run."

"Okay, that's stupid."

"Assault with a cleaning weapon?"

I shook my head.

"Mess-slaughter?"

I giggled. "Nope."

"No? Well, what have you got, Shakespeare?"

"First Degree Maider?"

He groaned.

I smiled. "You're dripping."

We looked behind us. We had dripped all the way from the car.

"Well, it's almost as good as a trail of bread crumbs. We can follow it back to the wicked witch's VW. It's not gingerbread, but it smells like coffee."

I gave him another smack for that. I was no wicked witch.

We found a trashcan and he stuffed everything inside.

Why was I thinking in terms of "we" all of a sudden? And why was I letting a guy who I'd just met, then stared at naked a few hours ago, clean my car?

Because I was certifiable. That's why.

Or maybe because my first impression of Adonis had been wrong. Maybe he wasn't really a self-centered bad boy. He'd saved my ass this morning when he punched that fat guy. Now he was cleaning my car for me? That was hardly selfish. I'd been ready to write him off, but maybe he deserved a second chance. Otherwise, I'd feel like a judgmental bitch.

We arrived at my car.

"Thanks again, Adonis." I shifted from foot to foot nervously. I needed to go, but I didn't want to.

He was staring at me with his amazing eyes.

I stomped my foot and stifled a giggle. "What?!" I didn't want to sound like a giddy teenager, but I did.

"Just looking."

"At what?"

"A work of art."

"Shut up! That's *so* stupid." I reached around and twirled my finger through my pony tail.

Then I realized I was being played. He'd probably said the same thing to Skylar and a hundred other women this week alone. It was a variation on the some crap I'd heard a thousand times in the past from similar men.

Guys like Adonis were a dime a dozen. No, make that a penny a dozen. Scratch that. You couldn't pay me to take anymore of this sort of verbal fertilizer. I'd had my fill a long time ago. "Thanks again for all your help, Adonis. But I've got a buttload of homework, and I need to run some errands on my way home. So I've really got to go."

In the corner of my eye, I noticed a police car turn into the parking lot. It drove toward us.

"When can I see you again?" Adonis was determined, I'd give him that.

"I'm not really—" The police car pulled to a stop right beside us, blocking my car and Adonis' motorcycle. Two officers got out of the car. Was this campus security?

"Good afternoon," the office with a mustache said. "Can I talk to you two for a second?"

Adonis didn't respond. I saw his jaw muscles dance.

"Sure," I said, eyeing the other officer, who was female. "Is something wrong?"

"We received a complaint about a tattooed man and young woman trespassing in one of the dormitories," the female officer said. "Do you two know anything about that?"

Caught. This was ridiculous. We took some paper towels. So what? I glanced at Adonis. He didn't appear ready to talk.

"Are you both students here?" Mustache Cop asked.

"Yeah." Well, I was. I'd *assumed* Adonis was too. But maybe he wasn't. He hadn't been carrying any books or a laptop, or even a regular old notebook. Maybe he wasn't a student. And in that case, what was he doing on a college campus? And how old was he, anyway? Was he even in college? I took a deep breath. I was getting ahead of myself. He obviously was the art model this morning. So even if he wasn't a student, he was supposed to be here.

"Can I see your I.D. and your Student I.D.?" mustache cop asked.

Adonis pulled out his wallet while I dug through my purse. It was going to take awhile to find anything in my bag. I swear it was bigger on the inside than it was on the outside. I found an old tube of black lipstick I thought I'd thrown out.

Emo. Goth. Witch.

I would've tossed it into the bushes but I didn't want to get fined for littering. Adonis handed two I.D.s to Mustache cop. I recognized one was a student I.D. So Adonis *was* a student. Or had been at some point.

Mustache cop sat down in the police car and started typing into the car's computer. I kept digging for my I.D.s. I glanced at Adonis.

His hands rested casually on his narrow hips, and was drumming his fingers on his jeans. He stared at the ground, ignoring me.

The female cop narrowed her eyes at Adonis and put the heel of her hand on the butt of her gun. Was I missing something?

Mustache cop fingered the radio on his shoulder and mumbled something into it.

After what seemed like forever, I found my wallet and both my I.D.s. I offered them to the female cop. "Here you go," I said with as much lightness and merriment as I could muster.

She looked at them. Looked at me. Looked at the I.D.s again. Flipped them over. Looked at me, then glanced at her partner, who nodded at her.

A second later, another cop car pulled into the parking lot, lights flashing, but no sirens. Mustache got out of the cop car and walked around Adonis until he was behind him. "Sir, please step up to the vehicle and put your hands on the hood."

What was happening?

The other cruiser stopped behind the first one and two more officers got out.

"Sir?" Mustache asked again.

Adonis' face screwed up tight while he ground his jaw. His full lips compressed into a thin white line and his eyes swiveled menacingly. He looked ready to spring.

What was he going to do?

The female cop stepped toward Adonis. "Sir, up against the vehicle and place your hands on the hood."

Finally, Adonis moved. He walked up to the cop car and leaned his hands on the hood. Mustache stood behind him and pushed Adonis' legs apart by bumping them with his knees. He patted Adonis down thoroughly. "Place your hands behind your back, sir. You're under arrest."

I panicked. "Wait! What're you doing?"

"Please step back, ma'am," the female cop commanded, her palm held up like a stop sign.

Adonis did as ordered. Mustache pulled out a pair of handcuffs and slapped them on.

"Is this because of the paper towels?"

"Paper towels?" The female cop was confused.

Mustache opened the back door of the cruiser. "Please step into the vehicle, sir." Adonis complied.

"We took some paper towels. From one of the dorms."

Now the female cop eyed *me* suspiciously.

I was making this worse. I took a deep breath and blinked back sudden tears. "I spilled my coffee all over my car this morning. I didn't have anything to clean it with. We were just trying to clean up the mess. We went into one of the dorms to find some paper towels. We, uh, borrowed a bunch from one of the suites. If that girl hadn't—" I stopped myself before I said too much.

The female cop frowned. "What girl?"

Shit. Damage control. "The one who's bathroom we took the paper towels from. To clean up my car. I guess she was mad we were taking so many paper towels. But it was a big cup of coffee." I hoped that made it sound more innocent.

She nodded, satisfied. But Adonis was still in the back seat. I tried to catch his eye. He didn't notice. Like he'd forgotten I was there. "So, um, why are you taking him in again?"

"There's a warrant out for his arrest, ma'am."

Shell shock. "What?! A warrant? For paper towels?"

"For assault, ma'am."

"He didn't hit anybody!" My mouth Oed then clamped shut.

This morning. Red Faced fat guy and the Mercedes. But it couldn't be. That guy swung first, hadn't he? I wasn't entirely sure anymore. But Adonis was protecting me. Isn't that like self defense? Shit, this was my fault.

Mustache Cop was already in the car, and the female officer was climbing into the driver's seat. Before she closed the door I blurted, "Wait! Where are you taking him?"

"Downtown. To book him."

"No! You can't!"

"Please, ma'am," she said. "You should go home. You don't want to waste your time on a guy like this."

What a bitch! I can't believe she said that! Adonis cleaned my car!

Adonis brooded in the back seat, leaning forward because of the handcuffs. His head hung between his shoulders. As the police cruiser drove off, he drilled me with his jeweled eyes for a brief second before his thick lashes slid closed. He looked…pained.

A wave of nausea bloomed in my stomach, overshadowing my sadness. It was obvious that Adonis was trouble with a capital T.

The cops showing up had scared the shit out of me. Maybe I was better off with Adonis gone. There was a good chance that after his arrest, I'd never see him again.

Why did that suddenly make me feel so damn sad?

I'd known the guy for less than twelve hours. That wasn't enough time to get to know anyone.

The only thing I knew for sure was that I missed him already.

I stopped at the grocery store on the way home. When I caught my reflection in the rearview mirror, I noticed my mascara had run. When had I been crying? I hadn't noticed I was.

Adonis.

I wiped the makeup off as best I could before going inside for groceries.

When I passed the frozen foods section, it took all of my will power to walk past the ice cream. But I did, even though I swear the chocolate chip cookie dough sang my name like the sirens that tried to pull Odysseus' ship onto the rocks. I'm pretty sure ice cream was invented by Satan.

I made it back to my car having only bought the food I needed to eat.

When I got to my apartment, I stashed everything in the fridge. I took a couple of towels outside to spot-clean any remaining coffee left in my car. There wasn't much to do. Adonis had done a thorough job with his impromptu cleaning supplies.

Inside, I made myself a blueberry smoothie and kicked back on the couch in my living room. I was on the second story of a small building, and had an amazing view of the ocean.

I thought back to the August day I had arrived in San Diego.

When I had first rolled into the driveway of my new apartment complex, I was ecstatic. The building was beautiful, and lived up to the pictures I'd seen online.

My parents had insisted I live off-campus, even though it was my first year and I didn't know anybody. Their logic was that if I was in the dorms, I wouldn't get any studying done. I didn't know from experience, so I took their word for it, like always. That was slowly starting to change.

Ever since leaving D.C., I'd felt a growing sense of independence I'd never known while living under my parents' roof.

I had driven my VW from D.C. to San Diego by myself because my stuff took up every available inch of my car. I was glad there wasn't room for my mom or dad to come along. It was a hella long drive, but I had my mp3 player and my tunes to keep me company.

My parents had discussed flying out to help me settle in, but they were short on cash and couldn't get time off work to make the long drive. I was okay with that.

Maybe I would miss out on the glory of an action-packed college social life in the dorms, but in exchange, I would be able to study diligently in this idyllic beach environment. I mean, I could actually walk to the beach and study there. How awesome was that?

I did owe a debt of gratitude to my parents. Although I had to take out a hefty student loan to cover tuition, my parents could afford to pitch in on the apartment, taking a huge load off my shoulders.

I was all set up to take ownership of my own life.

I pulled out my books and laptop, and studied for awhile. Some time later, my phone warbled. It was Madison.

"What up, Mads?"

"So, tell me what happened with Adonis! I want to hear all the details." I had texted her about running into him at the museum while walking to my car, before the police fiasco.

"Oh, gosh. It was a disaster."

"What happened?"

I closed my eyes and pinched the bridge of my nose. "It'll probably be on the eleven o'clock news."

"What?" she shouted.

"The cops were involved. Need I say more?" I sighed.

"Wow, your car must've been super dirty from the coffee! That's why the cops came, right?" she joked.

"Okay, that was funny," I grinned. "But the real story wasn't."

"Wait, don't tell me yet. The full story demands Thai food. I'm buying. I'll be at your place in two minutes."

Madison had her own apartment a few miles up the Pacific Coast Highway. She had roommates, but wasn't into the dorm scene either. We were our very own college subculture.

We got Thai food on the boardwalk near my apartment and sat outside. The sun was low over the ocean, but the air was still warm and pleasant.

Madison wound her chopsticks into her noodles. "What happened with Adonis?"

I shook my head. "He got arrested."

Madison's eyebrows arched. "What? Creepy. You called the cops on the poor guy for flirting with you at the museum, didn't you? Harsh, Sam. Harsh."

Based on her nonchalance, any remaining fears I had that Madison harbored any sort of crush on Adonis were completely gone, thanks goodness. "No, it wasn't me. Well, it was *sort* of me. I think."

"What happened?"

"I bumped into him at my car. We were talking and the cops showed up and cuffed him and took him away. The cop told me they had a warrant for assault. I think it's because he punched that guy this morning."

"What? That's crazy!"

"That's what I thought." I tweezed a lump of Pad Thai, but my appetite was gone for the moment. I set my chopsticks down. "I don't really know what happened."

"Maybe he's an ex-con with a rap sheet. Trouble and a guy like that are BFFs. You sure know how to pick 'em, Sam."

I sure did.

"Maybe you're better off with him out of the picture."

"Yeah." But the thought of never seeing Adonis again made me feel nervous, and sort of empty. That *was* insane. I didn't even know the guy. I straightened in my chair. "You're right. I'll probably forget about him by tomorrow morning."

"That's the spirit, girl. I saw fifty other hot guys today on campus. You can forget you ever met Adonis What's-his-lame."

The only problem with Madison's logic was that I couldn't get Adonis out of my mind.

Madison dropped me at my apartment after dinner and I tried to study for awhile. I read all about balance sheets, cash flow and double-entry blahbedyblah.

But I couldn't stop obsessing about Adonis.

Was he in jail? Spending the night in some dank holding cell with a bunch of drunks, druggies, and gang-bangers? Because he had defended my honor? Shit, honor nothing. More like defending my life.

Red Face had wanted to bitch slap me for making him late this morning. If Adonis hadn't knocked him on his ass, Fatty would be the one in jail for assault, and I'd be recovering in a battered women's shelter.

I got up and made myself a drink. Seltzer water and a splash of Peach Cocktail. I leaned against the countertop in the kitchen and gazed at the fading line of light on the horizon. So beautiful. Could Adonis see the sun setting? Or did his view consist of steel bars and concrete?

I noticed my drawing pad leaning against the wall by the front door. I walked over, picked it up and flipped through it. Wow, they were terrible. The two sketches Professor Childress had drawn as examples were a million times better than mine.

I prepared to throw my drawing pad in the trash so I could focus on income statements and expenses, my true calling. But one of my later sketches caught my eye.

The sketch was just a few lines, like the professor had showed me. It really looked like Adonis. I vividly remembered him holding that pose. I was surprised I got any drawing done with his nakedness staring me in the face, but I had.

I shook my head and grinned.

I had seen Adonis naked this morning! I'd seen his guy gear! I blushed and fanned my face. How crazy was that? The question was, would I ever see any of him again? And did I want to?

Yes, of course! But also sort of no. He probably *was* in jail. Did I want to get involved with a guy like that? How many times had he been in jail already? I didn't know. I admonished myself that making such assumptions was how rumors got started, wasn't it? People conjecturing wildly about someone they didn't know.

Emo. Goth. Witch. Sorceress.

I had no right to judge Adonis based on anything other than what I'd witnessed with my own two eyes. All I knew about him was that he had helped out a total stranger, me, and cleaned my car. Did I mention he was hot?

Yes, he got arrested. But why? For punching Fatty this morning? If that was the reason, then as far as I was concerned, Adonis really was a knight in shining armor. Not some knuckle-dragging ex-con with his own WANTED poster.

It was getting late. I washed my face and got ready for bed. I changed into a lace cami and some boxers. The second my head hit the pillow and I closed my eyes, I saw twin sapphires staring back at me, full of hurt.

I grabbed one of my pillows from behind me, smashed it against my face, and screamed.

Bitch. Slut. Whore.

This had turned into a three-way suckfest. I felt terrible for Adonis. So what if he was a player? He was also a decent guy. And now he was probably spending the night in jail.

Because of me.

Tease.

I thought I'd left all my shit behind in Washington D.C.

How the hell had I managed to fuck up San Diego in less than twenty-four hours?

Suicide Watch.

Horrible images from my past flooded my mind's eye. It was always the same.

The bright flash of color. The sound. That horrible sound that echoed in my thoughts every single night. The blood.

So much blood.

And all those lies. Thousands of them.

Taylor.

Before, and after.

The ones I told myself, and the ones I told everybody else.

A vortex of discomfort spun inside my stomach, like a thousand pins and needles jammed inside me trying to poke their way out.

I teetered on the edge of insanity. But some inner spark pulled me back from the edge. No problem. I knew two time-tested methods for easing those old feelings into submission.

I threw on clothes and drove to the grocery store. Once inside, it took me a moment to ponder my options. Liquor aisle, or ice cream aisle?

Both provided an escape I had relied on many times during high school. After Taylor. When the pain inside me had become too much, and the voices too loud, I had learned how to drown them out.

Experience had taught me that I couldn't mix my poisons. Ice cream absorbed alcohol, and made getting drunk more difficult. So it was best to pick one.

I had stolen plenty of bottles of wine back in D.C. I preferred the white wines, the sweeter the better. Blushes and Rosés. were a close second. The only problem with San Diego was that it was too warm for bulky coats, and I didn't have a big enough purse anymore. I'd chucked my old grab-bag handbag when I moved out here. I was determined to leave my habits behind me, but apparently, they'd jumped in the trunk of my VW when I drove across country. I had unwittingly packed my emotional baggage with me. Not so surprising, when I thought about it in those terms. But a girl could dream, couldn't she?

My parents never discovered what a drunko klepto I had been in high school. If they had, I'm sure a full-fledged intervention would've ensued. They would've freaked. Oh well, too late now. I was nineteen, and I was the only one who could work out my issues.

Since I still wasn't old enough to buy booze legally, I settled for ice cream. I grabbed a hand basket and made my way to the frozen narcotics section.

I loaded my basket with a variety of flavors, all in pints, until it was literally full. I think I had about seventeen altogether. That should be enough.

The cashier, an older guy with thinning hair and thick glasses, had to make a comment. "You got enough ice cream?" His voice was friendly.

Mine was too. I knew how to play the part. "I'm having a bunch of girlfriends over tomorrow for movies and ice cream. Never can have enough."

He nodded and smiled and rung me up. I paid and walked to my car with my huge bag of drugs. When I got to my apartment, I shoved everything into the freezer. I barely forced them all in. That was okay, I would work my way through them fast enough.

I didn't have a TV, so I watched funny cat videos on my laptop while I dug into my first pint. Double chocolate fudge peanut butter swirl. Numbness achieved.

The thing about my jogging habit, which I had picked up two years ago to fight off the long-term side effects of ice cream overkill, was that it burned a lot of calories. So I had plenty of room for dessert on top of the minimal Pad Thai I'd had for dinner.

Countless cat videos and five pints later, my stomach was ready to burst. But I couldn't feel the pins and needles anymore. Mission accomplished.

I hadn't done this in awhile. Apparently, I'd forgotten my limits, or my stomach had shrunk. When I realized I had to pee or explode, I couldn't tell which, I stood up. My swollen belly screamed at me.

Well, I knew how to deal with that. I went to the bathroom. Peed first, just in case. Then I flushed, watching clean water fill the bowl. I casually put my hair in a ponytail and leaned over. I'd learned it was easier to do standing up. I jammed my finger down my throat and it took only a second for Mother Nature to do her thing.

My gag reflex kicked in and my stomach seized. The first gush of brownish-gray ice cream poured out. My stomach burbled, but nothing more. I flushed, clearing the bowl.

Another finger, and the second bomb dropped. I thought something in my abdomen was going to tear, and I leaned my forearms on my thighs, head inches over the bowl. Hey look, Pad Thai.

I swiped a strip of toilet paper off the roll and wiped my mouth.

I felt better. I flushed again, and rinsed my face before brushing my teeth.

I trudged to my bed and flopped down on top of the blankets.

Sleep was nowhere close, and I could tell my demons weren't ready to rest either.

I jumped out of bed and went to the kitchen. I yanked open the freezer. I'd made a good dent in my first-aid kit of frozen opium. Did I need more?

I remembered that I had made an oath to myself when I was accepted to SDU that my life was going to change for the better. Yet here I was, slipping back into old habits.

I was disgusted with myself. But I was also in pain over my botched first day, and the foundation of more than two years worth of misery that lay below the here and now.

Taylor.

I needed to do something, or else I was going to go crazy.

I slammed the freezer shut and threw on running clothes.

My demons couldn't hurt me if they couldn't catch me.

I think I put in five miles jogging the empty night streets before I walked the rest of the way home and crawled into bed, completely exhausted but still unable to sleep.

At least I didn't have to worry about fat thighs from all that ice cream still in my freezer. Because someone was going to have to eat it, for my stomach's sake.

I'd do my best to pace myself to one pint an evening. That I could handle without being forced to hit my stomach's eject button every night before bed.

Maybe I needed to buy a bigger hand bag, or dig out an old coat, so I could start swiping wine. Or, maybe between Madison and my new friends Romeo and Kamiko, I could get the line on the best college keg parties. Wasn't college all about getting drunk while still under age?

I'd have to work on that. It was too damn warm for the winter coats.

I grimaced. Fuck, I hated myself.

How was it that after leaving all the jackholes and asshats behind in D.C.—

Emo. Goth. Witch. Sorceress…

—I was still managing to make my own self miserable without

any help?

With friends like me, I didn't need enemies. Maybe all those labels were accurate.

Suicide Watch.

I really hoped I could prove them all wrong.

Even my parents.

Sam Smith, CPA.

Fuck me.

Chapter 7

I was disappointed when Adonis didn't show up for the next Life Drawing class two days later. The model was a wrinkly old man with a wrinkly old, you know.

Kamiko told me that Life Drawing classes usually had a different model every time. It helped you learn, she said. I knew it was much easier for me to concentrate on my drawing without naked Adonis five feet away.

I was even more bummed when Adonis didn't show up for the next *several* life drawing classes. I couldn't stop wondering if he was still in jail.

I hadn't seen him anywhere on campus in awhile. I'd seen Skylar, Tiffany, and various other Delta Pi Deltas around, but I wasn't about to ask any of them where Adonis was. I hoped he was okay.

I finally told everything to Romeo and Kamiko over burgers and fries one afternoon.

Romeo chewed on a fry. "I wouldn't mind being locked up with Adonis. I'd be his jailhouse bitch any day."

Kamiko stuck out her tongue. "Gross!"

"Kamiko, darling." Romeo put a fatherly hand on her shoulder. "The entire world is NOT one big cartoon, dearest. The birds and the bees have S-E-X. They do NOT talk, wear little white gloves on their hands, nor do they go on rainbow adventures looking for magical pumpkins. Just sayin'."

"I KNOW that, Romeo. But please keep your jailhouse rock talk to yourself."

"You love it," Romeo taunted.

I laughed. "Okay, you two!"

Madison joined us with a tray of fish tacos. She sure loved them. She also brought her good humor, which I badly needed. The four of us engaged in meaningless girl talk for thirty minutes.

My mood lightened considerably. What a relief. It was impossible to remain in a bad mood around the three of them. I wished I could keep them in my freezer for emergencies, instead of my ice cream. That sounded creepy, but you get the idea.

Madison dipped her last chip in her salsa. "Anyone want to join me at the beach after classes today?"

"Hells to the yeah!" I said. I had a bathing suit on underneath my t-shirt and shorts. Madison had trained me well. Between my running and my steely resolve, I'd stuck to no more than one pint of ice cream per night. Sometimes less.

Romeo wore his elegantly tailored burgundy jacket and black skinny jeans, as usual. He put his monocle in his eye and made his half frown. "Totally. I'm *so* dressed for it," he said sarcastically.

"You never go to the beach, Count Dracula," Kamiko quipped.

"Look who's talking, Coraline! Or should I say, Adventure Time's Marceline!"

"And proud out it!" They toasted each other by clinking french fries.

I laughed and picked up my drink, sipping from the straw.

"What's with the black nail polish, Sam?" Madison asked.

I folded my hands in my lap nervously, hiding the evidence. I'd been struggling to limit my nightly ice cream intake to only a pint or less. Painting my nails was the next best distraction, even if all I had was black polish, and it meant I was backsliding.

Emo. Goth. Witch. Sorceress…

I hoped nobody noticed my mouth quavering.

"You going all goth on us, Sam?" Romeo asked.

"Uh," I stammered, "no, I just wanted to do my nails last night."

"I think it looks kind of cool," Kamiko said. "Sam, you can be like, surf goth."

"Vampires don't surf, dearest," Romeo said.

"Why not?" Kamiko asked.

"Because of the sun, duh."

"Haven't you heard of night surfing?" Madison asked.

"Ha!" Kamiko blurted.

At least they'd moved the subject away from my black nails. My baggage was safe with me. As long as I kept it to the nails and didn't start wearing crypt couture again.

I promised myself I'd scrub the nail polish off as soon as I got home that night.

Two hours later, Madison and I flip-flopped down to the beach below the cliffs with our towels. I kept beach gear in the trunk of my car at all times because of our frequent beach trips. San Diego was awesome.

When we got to the beach, we stopped.

"Which way do you want to go today?" Madison asked.

"Let's try something different." We always went south. "Let's go north."

"Cool."

We found a spot away from most of the scattered beach-goers, and set up our towels. I had a great tan going after a couple of weeks of training with Madison. She'd made sure that I eased myself into it and didn't get burned. I was now brown from head to toe.

My hair was starting to lighten with the help of periodic lemon juice rinses. The rinses were a tip from Madison that had saved me from certain debt at the hands of those demons posing as colorists at the hair salons. I swear they made you sign away your soul in blood once you decided to own your blondness.

I wasn't sure how winter was going to work out in terms of maintaining my California looks, but Madison assured me there would be beach weather well into fall, and again in early spring. Why hadn't I moved here sooner?

We stripped down to our bikinis and laid out on the towels.

I almost fell asleep on my stomach, but Madison shook me to turn over. We propped ourselves on our elbows and watched the surfers and other beach goers. Something was off. "Um, Mads?"

"Yeah?"

"I think that guy's naked."

She shaded her eyes to get a better look. "I think you're right. Wait, nope. He's wearing a baseball cap. His cock's sure a-walkin'."

"Ew!"

"Look at that thing swing! It looks like a grandfather clock!"

"OMG! You did not just say that." The guy was old enough to be someone's grandfather.

"Hey, you know that old saying 'Half past the old man's ass, quarter till his balls?'"

"Gross! And it's a *monkey's* ass."

"Same difference. Do you think if he got a hard-on right now, he could use it as a sun dial?" Madison laughed.

"Wait a second." I squinted my eyes. "Does his hat say Lynyrd Skynyrd?"

Madison grinned. "Yes it does." She cupped her hands to her mouth and shouted. "Play Freeballs!"

I smacked her arm. "It's Freebird, dummy! Play *Freebird!*" I rolled onto my side and laughed.

We both succumbed to rampant giggling for several tear-filled minutes.

"What are you two fine ladies doing alone out here?" Two figures stood silhouetted against the glare of the sun. I shielded my eyes. I didn't recognize them. They looked like douches. They plopped down on our towels. "Mind if we join you?"

I frowned. "Uh, yeah."

Douche #1 didn't seem to be paying attention. I'm sure that was normal for him. He had a sloppy mohawk, and the rest of his hair had grown in about half an inch. It looked terrible. Perfect for him "You guys go to SDU?" he asked.

"We go to state," Douche #2 added. He had huge horse teeth. He was referring to San Diego State University, which I had learned was about fifteen miles southeast of SDU. It had a huge reputation as a party school.

"Congratulations," I said sarcastically.

Both of them ran their eyes all over us. I was regretting wearing a bikini. I sat up and folded my arms over my chest. Madison sat up, crossed her legs and rested her elbows on her knees. Couldn't these dummies tell they were making us uncomfortable?

"It's pretty hot out here," Horse-toothed Douche said.

"You know, this is a nude beach, right?" Mohawk Douche asked.

"Yeah." I hadn't until we saw Freeballs, but Mads and I had pretty much worked out the math on that one.

"So, why don't you ladies take your clothes off?" Horse-toothed Douche scowled, but I'm pretty sure it was his version of a smile.

"You guys are wearing swimsuits," Madison scoffed.

"I can roll with that," Horse-toothed Douche said.

My eyes widened. "But don't get any ideas!"

He stood up, preparing to push his trunks down with both

hands.

"The swimsuit stays ON!" I shouted.

He sat back down. "I was only joking," he sniveled.

"I think it's time for you guys to leave," I said sternly.

"Come on, we just got here." Mohawk Douche stroked my foot.

"Get off!" I kicked my leg rapidly until he removed it.

"Easy! No need to play hard to get."

"Get out of here, you guys." I tried to sound commanding, but the hint of irritation in my voice betrayed my uncertainty.

A feral gleam flashed in Mohawk Douche's eyes. His lips curled over yellowed teeth. "You know you want it."

"Samantha?"

I looked up into the eyes of Adonis. He held a surfboard under a tattooed arm. So did his friend, who was tall, blond and bronzed.

I guess hot guys traveled in packs. Did they grow them around here?

Adonis and his friend were dripping wet. They must have just come out of the water. How had I missed Adonis riding the waves with the other surfers? I was genuinely excited to see him. He wasn't in jail! "Hey, Adonis!"

"These guys bothering you?"

Horse-toothed Douche whipped around to face them. "Who the fuck are you?"

"Tsk, tsk," Adonis admonished with faux diplomacy. "Language, gentlemen. Language."

"Dude, we saw them first," Mohawk said.

"So what?" Adonis' surfer buddy said.

"So, fuck you, prick," Mohawk spat.

WTF? Adonis had just gotten arrested a few weeks ago. These two douches were looking for a fight. That was the last thing Adonis needed. Was my presence in his life cursing him? Probably. It wouldn't have been the first time.

Taylor.

"Easy, Jake," Adonis said to his friend soothingly. "These guys don't want any trouble, do they?" Adonis cocked his head and smiled at the douches.

"The fuck they don't," Jake growled. He wasn't quite as muscular as Adonis, but he was tall and well-built. Not the kind of guy I imagined anyone would want to get in a fight with. Jake dropped his surfboard onto the sand.

Mohawk and Horse-tooth took a moment to survey the situation. While they were both sizable guys, neither of their physiques came close to Jake or Adonis'. Both of them were soft. They were in over their heads.

Jake took a step toward them. "Get the fuck out of here, or you're gonna be spittin' teeth, fuckholes."

"Calm down, man," Mohawk whined. "We're going." He and his pal stood up quickly and scampered off.

As soon as the douches were gone, I put my t-shirt on. They'd left me feeling naked and nervous.

"You guys okay?" Adonis asked with obvious concern.

"Yeah, thanks. Again." I was genuinely relieved. I'm sure nothing terrible would've happened, even if Adonis and Jake hadn't shown up. There were too many people around.

I was relieved there hadn't been a fight. With my luck, Adonis would've put one of those douches in the hospital. He definitely looked more than capable of it. Then he'd be in jail for sure, because of me. Maybe for a long time. The last thing I wanted was for him to get into more fights because of me.

But it was nice to know someone was watching out for you. Someone with an amazing body. The way Adonis' shorts hung low on his narrow hips made me squirm. I already knew what was in them, but all I could focus on were the indentations on his hips above the waistband of his swim trunks.

"Who's your friend?" Madison asked. She eyed Jake up and down. She was in heat.

Jake held out his hand to shake hers. "Jake Stratton."

"Madison." She leaned forward with more chest than necessary. She was shameless. I couldn't blame her. Jake was pretty freakin' hot.

"Do you mind if we join you?" Adonis asked.

I chuckled. "Sure."

He cocked a dimple at me. "I promise I won't try to touch you. Without your permission."

"Perv!" I'm pretty sure I would give him permission if he asked. But I wasn't going to tell him that. I hoped he didn't ask.

He and Jake sat Indian-style on the ends of our towels. I

desperately wanted to ask him what happened with the police, but that would've been totally rude. I didn't know what Jake did or did not know, and I didn't know if Adonis would like talking about it in front of Madison either.

"How are the waves today?" Madison asked. She leaned back on her elbows, extending her legs. Her entire body was on display for Jake. He seemed to be enjoying it. He better. Madison was hot.

"Decent," Jake answered. "Got a few floaters."

"I thought I saw you drop in and carve some good ones earlier," Madison said. "You're goofy footed, aren't you?"

Jake grinned. "Yeah, that was me. You surf?"

"Totally."

I had no idea what those two were talking about. Maybe someday Mads would teach me to surf. I turned to Adonis. "I haven't seen you around campus in awhile. Is everything okay?" Foot in Mouth! Why didn't I just stand up and point at him and yell Jail, jail jail! I cringed.

Adonis was cool as could be. "Yup." His smile widened and he unsheathed his deadly dimples. "Now that I'm here with you."

I forced myself to break his gaze. So I looked at his abs. Wrong move. I clamped my mouth shut before I licked my lips, or his abs. Gulp! Help!

"What's up with the black fingernails? I don't remember those. You going goth on me?"

I folded my arms across my chest, trying to hide my hands. Why'd he have to go and mention my nails?

Emo. Goth. Witch.

Was there an ice cream truck somewhere? I needed some quick.

His smile widened as he examined my body, making me feel further self-conscious.

"I don't remember you being so tan the day we met," he said appreciatively. "It's a good look for you. Now you blend in with the locals."

I liked the sound of that! My ice cream urge faded away. "Oh, Mads has been taking me to the beach every day. I can't believe it myself. I've never been tan in my entire life."

"No? Where are you from?"

"D.C."

"That explains a lot." He chuckled.

"Be nice!" I swatted his knee. I had a valid reason for touching him. I swear it wasn't a prelude to more touching. I needed to keep him in line. As if. "What's that supposed to mean, anyway?"

"That first day I saw you, you were so fish out of water. Good thing you had a chaperone."

"Who? You?"

He nodded.

I laughed. "Yeah, right. I can hold my own."

"You sure?" He laughed.

I think in that moment I turned clinically insane. There's no rational explanation for it. I leaned forward and tried to punch Adonis on the shoulder, but he leaned back as I swung, causing me to miss. I fell on top of him.

My nose was an inch from his. I'm pretty sure he had the smallest pores known to man, if he had any at all. Up this close, his eyes were incredible. I tore my gaze away and looked at his...lips. They looked so soft, I wanted to lick them with my...

"What are you two doing!" Madison gawked. "Call the rape police! Jake, help your friend! Sam's going to have her way with him."

"Everything looks copacetic from where I'm sitting." Jake chuckled. "You need any help, bro?"

"No, I'm good. Just got this hottie on top of me threatening to slobber all over me. Nothing I can't handle."

I climbed off of him. "Quit making fun of me!" I pouted.

Adonis was confused. "Who's making fun of you?"

"You're calling me names."

"What? Hottie?"

"Yes," I whined.

"You've gotta screw loose, babe."

He called me babe. Swoon? No. Liar. I hated it when guys bullshitted me.

Adonis leaned back on his arms. His chest flexed and bulged. *Oh god.* He scrutinized me. "Yo, Jake."

"Yeah?"

"Is it just me, or is Samantha a total hottie?"

"One to ten? I'd give her a nine."

Huh? I glanced behind me in both directions. They couldn't be talking about *me*.

"I think you're going a bit far," Adonis said shrewdly. "I'd call it 8.75"

"It?" I sneered. "I'm an it? Whatever. Jerks."

They all chuckled at me.

"You should see the look on your face," Madison snickered. "You look like someone broke your dollhouse. Learn to take a compliment. You're gorgeous. Own it."

Coming from Madison, I could sort of believe it. But I was pretty sure she just wanted to build my confidence. Coming from Jake or Adonis, it had to be a ploy to get my pants off for a quick thrill.

There was no other rational explanation.

"Oh, dude," Jake said anxiously. "I totally forgot I promised to take my lady out today. She's been waiting for me for over an hour. We gotta split."

Madison smirked at me and rolled her eyes.

"All right, let's roll," Adonis said. "Take it easy, ladies." The two of them picked up their surfboards and trotted up the trail to the streets above.

"What a jackhole," Madison spat. "I should've known better. Both those guys are too good to be true."

"Sorry, Mads. If I'd known, I would've warned you. It figures." I was bummed for Madison, and I was bummed that Adonis was gone. Why did he have to keep dropping into my life only to jump back out of it just as quickly?

Welcome to my AD/HD social life. Starring Adonis, whose last name I didn't even know. Why did I bother? I was better off with him gone anyway.

Despite the speed with which Adonis came in and out of my life, I felt so much better after seeing him, knowing he wasn't in jail.

That night, I cleaned off my black nail polish before bed, and I didn't eat any ice cream at all.

I was so proud of myself.

I hoped the feeling lasted, and didn't go away as fast as Adonis did.

Chapter 8

Mid-terms were coming up quick. I tried studying with Madison in the Main Library, but it was so crowded I couldn't concentrate. We ended up at my place or her place most of the time. Romeo and Kamiko were often with us, but when it was the four of us, we barely got any studying done and ate way too much ice cream. Mmmm. Chocolate Chip Cookie Dough. I mean, it's okay when you do it with friends, right?

I was acing Fundamentals of Accounting, as well as American History and Sociology, which I was none too happy about. It was further proof that my parents were right. Studious Sam. That was me. Gag.

Life Drawing was another story. We didn't really have a mid-term. Instead, Professor Childress gave us an evaluation during office hours.

Because everyone had such a wide range of skills, it wasn't really possible to grade our work in black and white terms. There was no right or wrong way to draw. It was more about our personal progress. I liked that. We had to submit three of our best drawings from the first day of class, and three from the most recent class, for review.

I knocked on the open door to Professor Childress' office, my drawings under my arm.

"Come in, Sam." He stood up and shook my hand. Such a gentleman. His office resembled a one-room museum gallery. It was lined with dark wood bookcases full of carefully arranged art books. Various sculptures dotted his desk, the shelves, and every other horizontal surface. Hanging between the bookcases were several paintings.

The paintings were nudes reminiscent of the life drawing poses from class. They were really good. I walked up to one of them and admired it. "Wow, who did all these paintings? They're awesome!"

"Thank you." He smiled warmly.

"You did them?" I hoped I didn't sound too skeptical.

"Yes."

"You rock, Professor Childress!" Now I was brown nosing. I never got it right.

"Thank you very much, Sam. I try, but I assure you, none of these paintings came easily."

He was so humble it was killing me. "I wish I could paint as well as you. I mean draw. I've never painted anything before."

"Maybe you should try."

"Painting? No way. I can barely draw."

"If you haven't tried it, how would you know?"

I opened my mouth, then closed it. I bit my lower lip and raised my eyebrows. "I don't know, drawing's hard." Geesh, did I sound like Barbie? But it was the truth. Drawing was a struggle, unlike all my other classes.

"Yes, it is. But it gets easier, I promise."

"I wish it came as easily for me as accounting did. Need me to set up a balance sheet for you?" I grinned.

He chuckled and winked at me. "If I do, you'll be the first person I call." He laced his fingers together on the desk and looked at me over his glasses. "So, you're here for your evaluation."

"Yeah." I handed him my drawings.

He slid his glasses into place and looked them over. I was pretty sure he was going to tell me I sucked, and should withdraw from his class, rather than risk an F.

"Your improvement is exceptional. You have quickly grasped the concepts I've demonstrated during class." He leafed through the drawings. "I've seen marked progress from week to week."

"Really?" That was news to me.

"You have talent, Sam. You may not see it, but I do."

Blink. *What?*

"Have you considered seeking out an artistic mentor?"

"No."

"While you do indeed have a flair for drawing, it takes effort to develop your skills to the next level, as well as the proper guidance. Are you minoring in art?"

"No, just taking it as an elective."

"Have you considered majoring in it?"

Was he serious? "Uh, not really. I'm majoring in Accounting."

"Well, that's a bigger question for you to ponder at length. For the time being, I'd like to suggest a mentor." He grabbed a pad of paper and a pen, and jotted something down. "A mentor will expose you in more depth to a range of artistic principles we don't have time to cover over the course of a single term. Make an appointment to visit his studio. I think you will find it fascinating to see how a real artist works." He folded the paper in half and slid it across to me. "I'll contact him and let him know to expect an email from you."

I took it without looking at it. Professor Childress was beyond humble. Based on his paintings I'd call him a real artist. I couldn't imagine ever being able to paint as well as he did.

I was curious about this mentor, because if the professor didn't consider his own amazing work "real" art, I could only wonder what mysteries awaited me at the mentor's art studio.

"It's safe to say that as of the middle of the term," Professor Childress said, "you are solidly in A territory, as far as your grade is concerned. I believe you can go well beyond that."

"Beyond an A?"

He chuckled. "Well, an A is the highest grade. But I was thinking in terms of your overall potential."

"Thanks, Mr. Childress." I beamed.

He stood up and shook my hand. "See you in class."

When I walked outside. I don't think my feet touched the floor until I was halfway down the hall.

I opened the paper the professor had given me. It had a name and an email address.

Christos Manos.

Why did that name sound familiar?

I was so busy studying for mid-terms the rest of the week, I nearly forgot about the mentor. But I'd taped the note to my desk lamp so I wouldn't forget.

Friday afternoon, after my last exam, I sent a quick email out to Christos Manos. That evening, I received a reply. It contained a street address and requested, "Come on Saturday. Tomorrow. 1:00 p.m."

Where did this guy get off thinking my schedule was totally

open? I mean, it was, but still, it would've been nice if he'd asked *me* when *I* was available.

Professor Childress had called this Manos guy a "real artist" so maybe he was super busy. Maybe he had some big gallery show he was preparing for.

Snooty artists. Maybe being an artist was lame and I was better off in accounting.

Whatever, Debbie Downer. I knew I was jumping to conclusions and making rash assumptions. Professor Childress was nice. I trusted he wouldn't set me up with some jerk mentor.

What would this Christos Manos be like? I pictured someone like Professor Childress, but taller, with thinning salt-and-pepper hair and those 1950s style hipster eyeglasses, but that was a guess. I had no way of knowing. The whole thing was so uncertain.

I called Madison for encouragement, which she claimed required doughnuts, so she drove over to my place.

We walked to a place I'd discovered in my neighborhood called Thai Doughnut. They made the most amazing apple fritters ever. We bought one apiece and walked to the beach with them.

I plucked a yummy morsel off my fritter and popped it in my mouth. It was still warm. Yum! "Have you seen Jake since the beach?"

Madison had a mouth full of apple fritter. She covered her mouth with her fingers. "You mean Lady's Man?"

"Literally."

"Hell no. He sure was flirty with me, considering he had a date with his lady that day."

"Guys are dogs. I'm sure they had a double date with Adonis and Tiffany, or whatever Plastic Playmate he's seeing this week."

Madison and I had discovered that practically everyone on campus knew who Tiffany was. Apparently she liked to throw Delta Pi Delta parties on her Daddy's yacht in the harbor. And tell everyone within earshot, whether they were interested or not.

"Oh, you know what?" Madison asked, licking cinnamon glaze from her fingers. "I saw Adonis totally snub Tiffany on campus the other day."

"What? Really?"

"Yeah. I had to look some stuff up at the Main Library, and Adonis was there with a couple of girls."

I frowned and took a huge bite of my fritter. "That guy always has a harem wherever he goes. He's a total player." I grimaced while chewing on a big wad of cinnamon-sugary fatty doughiness. What did I care if Adonis was a lady's man, or who he hung out with? He was no more than an acquaintance.

"Well, from what I saw, Tiffany isn't in his harem anymore. She was totally hanging on him and he gave her the brush off. She was super pouty and stormed off. The two girls with Adonis got all snooty and catty after she left. I could tell Tiffany was crying."

"Really?" I almost felt sorry for her. "She's better off without him." She had her Daddy's money anyway, or so I'd heard.

"Well, I thought you'd like to know."

"Why would I care?"

"Seriously, Sam? You're always talking about Adonis. It's an obsession with you."

"It totally is not."

"Yeah. Uh-huh," she smirked.

Madison finished the last bite of her apple fritter and wadded up the waxed paper wrapper. We tossed our trash into one of the garbage cans along the cement pathway and strolled down to the surf to get our feet wet in the ocean. I wore flip-flops pretty much 24/7 at that point. The sun glowed gold above the horizon.

"So, tell me about your mentor. Is he, like, a serial killer? Do I need to call the cops if I don't hear from you by, like, four o'clock tomorrow?"

"Probably. I'm sure he'll turn my skin into canvas for his next painting. I'll be immortalized in some random museum for all time. Make sure you come visit and leave flowers next to wherever they put me and say a prayer for me every year."

Madison laughed. "At least then you'll be famous."

"Boring old Sam Smith," I mused, "Killed in the most artistic way possible."

"Make sure he signs the canvas."

"I'll be dead! How can I make him sign me?"

"Have him sign your breasts before he kills you."

"You're seriously morbid."

Madison rolled her eyes. "What?"

"He's probably super nasty looking."

"Then all the more reason he'll sign your chest."

A mottled brown dog with floppy ears came barreling down the beach toward us, chasing a frisbee. The dog jumped in the air and caught the frisbee right in front of us, nearly bowling us down.

"Come here, Lady! You almost killed those two!" Jake Stratton said while jogging toward us.

"Hey, Jake!" I said.

"Come here, Lady." Jake squatted on the wet sand. The dog ran up to him with the frisbee. "That's a good girl." The dog was trying her best to slobber all over Jake. "Who's a good girl? You're a good girl," he baby talked.

Madison looked at me, surprised. "That's Lady?"

"I guess we were wrong about him," I murmured. "The few guys out there who aren't dogs *have* dogs. That's why we can never find them."

Madison kneeled down next to Lady and Jake. She smiled at him. "Hi."

"Hey."

"This must be your dog, Lady?"

"Yup." Jake ruffled Lady's ears.

"She's beautiful. What kind of dog is she?"

"A german shorthaired pointer."

Lady nuzzled against Madison. "She's so friendly!"

"She has good taste," Jake said to Madison.

Jake and Madison exchanged a long smile.

Sigh. Now everyone was falling in love except me. Whatever. I was probably better off single.

But good for Madison. She was a total catch. Lady the frisbee dog had caught her for Jake.

Maybe I needed to get a frisbee dog.

Chapter 9

I woke up early Saturday morning and did laundry, which consisted mainly of bikinis, t-shirts, and shorts. It was almost November. Was this what fall was like in San Diego? I could get used to this.

When I finished my laundry, I had a light lunch, threw on a sun dress and comfortable sandals, then drove to the address of Christos Manos. It was only a couple of miles away from my apartment.

The house was larger than I expected. It was nestled in a grove of trees. The architecture looked custom, but older. Not a modern McMansion. The exterior was stained wood, not painted or stuccoed. It had multiple stories, but wasn't boxy. It was sprawling. Old-school beach chic. It was beautiful.

There was a pickup truck full of spare wood and tools parked in the driveway. A guy was up on a ladder, working on the house. I think he was replacing shingles. I grabbed my backpack full of drawing supplies and got out of my car. It seemed like no one was home, except for the work guy. There were no other cars parked in the driveway.

Maybe the work guy knew where Christos Manos was. I walked up to the ladder. "Excuse me, sir?"

Work guy hammered on a shingle. Wham, wham, wham. He had chiseled arms covered in tattoos.

"Hello?" I asked between hammer blows.

He stopped and looked down at me.

"Adonis? Oh my god! What are you doing here?"

"Hey, Samantha." He climbed down the ladder and leaned against it on one buffed arm. He wiped his hair out of his eyes and cocked his trademarked grin. All of his arm muscles flexed and relaxed in a mesmerizing pattern. He must've known what he was doing. He could he not?

"So, uh, are you, like, working here?"

"Yup."

"Are you a handyman or something?"

He didn't answer. His shirt was dirty and sweaty. The answer was obvious.

I really wanted to grab his shirt material and dig my fingers into it, then pull it over his head and rub my hands on his sweaty... *Jeezus Pleezus, someone call Animal Control on ME!*

My heart raced. I wanted to fan my face, but self control won out and I pretended like it was no big deal. "Um, do you know where I can find the guy who lives here? I'm supposed to meet him here at one."

He smirked and cocked his head toward the courtyard entryway. "Inside."

"Thanks." I knew I was supposed to walk away at that point and knock on the door, but I couldn't. I kept staring at Adonis. My smile widened. His did too. I liked that.

He raised his eyebrows expectantly. When I didn't respond, he shook his head, smiling, and walked to his work truck. "The doorbell doesn't ring itself."

Oh. Right. Doorbell. I was here for the mentor. I inwardly rolled my eyes at myself and walked up to the elaborately hand-carved front door. I pressed the doorbell. After a minute, no one answered. Was he home? Or running an errand?

"Press it again," Adonis said. "He's here."

I did. A few minutes later the door opened. An older man stood before me, nothing like I expected. Tall, handsome, silver hair cropped short, broad shoulders, and impossibly blue eyes. "Can I help you, young lady?"

"Uh, are you Christos Manos?"

"No."

Crap. That wasn't the answer I was looking for. Was I at the wrong house? I checked the street number I'd written down and compared it to the house number over the door. Nope, this was the place.

Suddenly nervous, I turned to Adonis for help. Maybe he knew what was going on. But Adonis was leaning into the passenger door of his truck, doing something or other.

I turned to face the old man. "I'm supposed to meet Christos

Manos, the artist, here at one o'clock. I'm pretty sure this is the right place." I felt like an idiot. The old guy clearly wasn't sympathizing with my confusion.

He drilled me with his eyes. His brows knit into a frown. "Christos!" He hollered. "You playing tricks on this poor girl?"

What? I whipped around again. Adonis stood behind me, a fist on his cocked hip. He looked sort of like Michelangelo's statue of David, or one of those sexy firemen calendars. He grinned at me. Dimples.

I think I started ovulating ahead of schedule. "Wait. Are, are *you* Christos Manos? I thought your name was Adonis?"

Adonis' grin spread wide over his exquisite white teeth. He stepped closer to me. I felt warm all over. I think I was even sweating between my toes.

"Adonis?" the old man chuckled. "What lies have you been telling this poor girl, Christos?"

Lies? I should've known. Total class-A jackhole player. I pivoted back and forth between the two of them.

"Adonis is his middle name. Around here, he goes by Christos."

"I'm confused. Who are you?" I asked the old man.

He extended his hand. "I'm Spiridon Manos. Christos' grandfather." We shook. His smile was warm, kind, and genuine. I liked this man. Adonis, on the other hand…

I twirled and smacked Adonis on the arm. "Jerk!" What an arm it was. I think I might have hurt my hand. It felt like hitting a tree trunk, except smooth and lickable. I imagined it would be pleasantly salty if I were to taste it right then. I swung at him again, trying to cover up my desire.

Adonis backed up, easily dodging my attack.

I was irritated. "What am I supposed to call you, huh?"

He grinned, and danced beyond my reach. "You can call me whatever you want."

"How about jerk?"

"Except that." He laughed.

"How about butt face?"

"Maybe not that."

I raised my eyebrows. "I've got a long list. Wanna hear the rest?"

"I've got time."

Amused, Spiridon interrupted our duel. "I warned my son

Nikolos not to name my grandson Adonis, even if it was only a middle name. But he and Christos' mother were firm. I believe it's been somewhat of a self-fulfilling prophecy ever since." Spiridon smiled. "But around here, he's just Christos."

I sneered at Adonis. "Pleased to meet you *Christos.* What a beautiful name you have *Christos.* Is that what all the girls call you?" I wasn't making any sense.

"Actually, none of them call me that."

"Seriously?"

"Yeah. But you can." He winked at me.

Huh? Hold on a second. Was I getting special house privileges all of a sudden?

Spiridon wrapped his arm around Adonis' shoulders. "Perhaps we should offer the young lady something to drink inside before you both start swinging?"

I shot Adonis a warning smirk as we walked into the house.

The interior was unbelievable. More natural wood. Open space, stylish lines, large rugs, exposed beams. Incredible.

The living room was filled with numerous paintings. Huge landscapes in all manner of weather and lighting conditions. They were amazing. Several reminded me of that painting of the cloud-covered coastline I'd seen in the museum at SDU, when I'd bumped into Adonis that day. Wait, had that painting been done by Adonis' grandfather? It must have. I wanted to find out for sure. "Mr. Manos, did you paint all these paintings?"

"Call me Spiridon." He stopped and put his hands in the pockets of his shorts. He gazed up at the paintings. "Yes."

"You're an amazing artist."

He sighed. "I was."

That was strange. "I think I saw your painting at the San Diego University Museum."

He replied instantly. "Shrouded Paradise?"

"Yeah! That's yours, isn't it? It's unbelievable, like you could climb into the picture frame and it would be real!"

His head drooped and he sighed heavily. "That was a long time ago. Follow me." He abruptly turned and left the room. I followed him into the kitchen. Adonis trailed behind.

Spiridon opened the fridge and pulled out a jug. "Fresh

squeezed lemonade? I made it this morning."

"That would be great, thank you."

He poured three glasses. "I don't believe I got your name?"

"I'm Samantha. Samantha Smith. People call me Sam."

"Pleased to meet you, Sam." He handed me a glass.

It tasted marvelous.

"What brings you by the house? Not my grandson, I hope." He winked at me. Spiridon handed a glass of lemonade to Adonis, who leaned casually against the doorframe (I was still thinking of him as Adonis more than Christos). His body language reminded me a lot of Spiridon's.

"Actually, yeah. My life drawing professor at SDU recommended Adonis, er, Christos, as a mentor." It was going to take some effort to stop calling him Adonis.

Spiridon guffawed. "Mentor? Which jackanapes at the university thought *that* was a good idea?"

Was my coming here a bad idea? "Professor Childress?" I suggested tentatively.

Spiridon folded his arms casually across his chest and leaned against the kitchen counter, his own lemonade dangling from one hand. "Childress, huh?"

"You know him?"

"Walt? You could say that. Walter Childress and I go back almost forty years."

Was that a good or a bad thing? I couldn't tell. I glanced over at Adonis. He was inscrutable and seemed content to listen. Did he know the story behind his grandfather and Professor Childress? Hard to say.

Spiridon smiled longingly. "I haven't talked to Walt in years." He took a swallow of his lemonade. "So, Walt thinks my grandson can mentor you?"

"Yeah, that's what he said."

He narrowed his eyes. "You're an artist?"

"Oh, gosh. Not really. I'm majoring in accounting. I just took Life Drawing for an elective." I suddenly felt like a fraud around an amazing artist like Spiridon Manos. It was probably time for me to go, so I could give my teenaged fantasy about being an artist a decent burial.

"If Walt sent you here, he must have seen something in your

work."

Really? Now I was totally confused.

"I won't keep you two from your meeting. If you want any more lemonade, it's in the fridge." He put away the jug and walked out of the kitchen.

I turned to Adonis, I mean Christos. I was still getting his name wrong in my head. "You didn't tell me you were an artist."

He grinned. "You never asked."

"And what's up with the name? Adonis? Really?"

"It's my given name. What do you want?"

"It's your middle name. Who goes by their middle name?"

"Lots of people."

"But, why?"

"When I graduated high school, I wanted to reinvent myself."

I could understand that. I didn't have a cool middle name to work with. It was terrible.

"What's your middle name?"

Great. "It's stupid."

"I'm sure it's great."

"You'll laugh. I don't want to say."

"Come on, you can tell me. I'm sure it's fine."

"Promise you won't laugh?"

"Promise."

"Anna."

He raised an eyebrow. "Samantha Anna Smith? It sounds like an echo."

"You promised you wouldn't laugh!" If it wasn't for those dimples, I would've thrown my lemonade in his face. And, it tasted really good, so I didn't want to waste it on this jerk.

"Let me get this straight. Your initials are S. A. S.? Sass?" He grinned. "Maybe I should call you Sassy."

"Come on, Christos," I begged. "Don't make fun."

"I'm not," he smiled.

"Yeah, but you have that stupid smile on your face."

"You know you like it," he said slyly.

"What, your dumb smile? You look like a donkey." Not really, but I wouldn't admit it.

He laughed. "I'm inclined to go with stallion, or quarter horse."

"You would." I was smiling now. I couldn't help myself. I was also standing closer to him than I realized. Had I moved? I suppose I had. My body was doing all kinds of things I was not aware of. I could no longer be held responsible for my actions.

Christos shifted against the doorframe. "You ever been down to the Del Mar race track?"

Every movement he made was illegally sexy. I hated him. "Race track? I'm not really into cars."

"It's horses. Thoroughbred racing. My family has a membership."

"What, do you bet on the ponies? Have a bookie?"

He tossed his head back and laughed. "I have placed a few bets in my time. But no, it's more upscale than that."

"Like private boxes and Sunday brunches with guys in white tuxedo jackets and gloves serving mimosas or mint juleps to old women with more plastic surgery than a wax museum?" Generally, I didn't like anything that had to do with exclusive clubs of any kind.

Bitch. Slut. Whore.

"I take it you had a bad experience?"

"No." I lied. He had me pegged. My nose tilted up snootily.

"Okay." He smiled shrewdly, unconvinced. "Anyway, I go to the track to study the horses. My dad used to take me down there when I was a kid, showed me how to draw the horses. They're beautiful animals."

"Your dad? Is everyone in your family an artist?"

"Pretty much."

"Does your dad live here too?"

His face darkened. "No."

Had I asked something I shouldn't have? I took a sip of my lemonade so I could avoid saying the wrong thing again. It was my specialty, after all.

Chapter 10

"You ready for some mentoring?" Christos asked abruptly. He finished the last swallow of his lemonade.

"I guess so, yeah." I was finally thinking of him as Christos, although I wasn't sure if I liked that.

"Cool. Let me grab something." He walked out of the kitchen and returned a minute later holding a box of of crayons. The big kind with tons of colors. "Okay, let's go make some art."

I wrinkled my nose. "With those? Aren't crayons for kids?"

"Are you saying kids don't make art?"

"Well, I mean, not *real* art."

He raised his brows. "Really? I hope you never tell any kids that. I'd hate to see their sad faces when you break it to them that their refrigerator drawings are not art. Come on, let's go." He led me outside.

"I didn't mean it that way!"

He smiled back at me as he held the front door for me. "After you."

"Such a gentleman."

"Yep."

"Where are we going?"

"To make some art."

The road downhill from Christos' house led toward the downtown area by the beach. I kept glancing at him, wanting to say something, but all he did was smile back at me. I sort of liked it.

We turned onto a walkway that led to the town library. "What are we doing at the library? I thought you said we were going to make some art?"

He held the door for me. "I did. And we are."

"I don't understand."

"You will." This way. He led me through the library to one of the meeting rooms. The door was open and a ton of little kids were inside. There was a sign taped to the door that said "Drawing with Christos 1:30pm."

"After you," he said.

I walked in the room and Christos followed. When the kids saw him, they went crazy.

"Christos!" they all shouted.

I felt like a deer in headlights. What the heck was I supposed to do? I jumped when I felt Christos' hand on my back.

He leaned and murmured into my ear. "Follow my lead. You'll be fine."

He walked to the front of the room and I joined him. Being in front of this many people, even if it was kids, made me nervous.

Christos cracked a huge grin. "Hey everybody!"

"Hi Christos!" the kids chorused.

"Say hello to my friend Samantha!" He motioned toward me.

"Hey Samantha!" they all said.

I blushed from head to toe.

"Who wants to draw today?" Christos asked.

"We do!" they cheered.

I noticed that the kids all had blank paper in front of them. Buckets of crayons were interspersed between them on the tables.

"All right. Does everybody know how to draw a cloud?"

"Yeah!" they shouted.

"Pick out a color, any color, and start drawing!"

The kids were excited as they dug through the crayon buckets and picked colors.

Christos was about to step away from me when I hissed at him through gritted teeth. "What do I do?"

"Help."

"What does that mean?"

"You know how to draw a cloud, don't you?"

I rolled my eyes. "Of course."

"So help them draw clouds." He winked at me. "But don't be too hard on them. Don't tell them what they're doing isn't art," he smirked.

I wrinkled my nose and flashed a sneer at him. I knew better than to tell kids something like that. Was he trying to make a point? I sort of got it, sort of not.

Christos and I walked around the room, helping the kids.

Some kids made yellow clouds, some green; clouds that looked like scribbles, clouds that looked like rectangles. It didn't matter to them. The children had so much fun, and they projected their glee so freely, it permeated my critical insecurity.

I had a blast. I wasn't worried about anyone doing anything "correctly." A very different vibe than my Life Drawing class at SDU. There was no pressure.

Over the next hour, Christos had them add the sun, their home, their families, their pets, or anything they wanted. One boy added a dragon brushing his teeth; another added an airplane with a frog for a pilot. A cute little girl with pigtails drew herself riding a unicorn jumping over a rainbow. I hadn't done anything like this since grade school. Why had I ever stopped?

At various points, I watched Christos with the kids. He had as much fun as they did. They obviously loved him. He complimented every one, told them how wonderful their drawings were, no matter how good or bad an adult might have considered them. He was a natural.

One little boy asked Christos about his tattoos. "Why do you have drawings on your arms?"

"Because I love art so much, I draw on everything I can. Even my arms!"

"Does your mommy make you wash them off?"

Christos chuckled. "No, she doesn't make me."

The boy rubbed a finger across Christos' tattoos. "That's good. I bet they're hard to erase."

"They are."

"I have a really good eraser at home, if you want to borrow it," the boy said enthusiastically.

"Thanks, Benji. I'll keep that in mind."

Was this the same guy I'd met on campus? The ladies man? Maybe it was fitting he had two names. A split personality wasn't out of the question with Christos Adonis Manos. The good: Christos. The bad: Adonis.

I would have to remain on my guard with him. *Or should I say, "them?"* Because this Christos guy seemed too good to be true. I wondered how long it would take for Adonis to pop back out.

"Time's up, everybody," Christos said at the end of the hour.

"No!" the kids groaned. Many of them hunched over in abject

defeat.

"Don't worry, I'll be here next Saturday."

"That's a million years from now!" one girl pleaded.

"You can make it that long, Emily."

Emily sighed like she was sighing her last breath.

We said goodbye to the kids and walked out. One of the librarians was waiting for Christos. She was gray haired and very grandmotherly. "You always do such a wonderful job with the children," she beamed.

"Thanks, Mrs. Elders."

"We're so lucky to have you." She turned to me. "Who's your friend?"

Why did I like it so much that Mrs. Elders called me Christos' friend?

"This is Samantha. Meet Mrs. Elders."

We shook hands. "Pleased to meet you."

"Are you going to come back with Christos next time? I peeked in earlier. You were a natural."

"Oh?"

"Yes, the two of you are a terrific team. You make a great couple."

I blushed again and stared at my toes. I was so overtaken by the harmless statement, I forgot to check for Christos' reaction.

When I did, he was already cracking his customary grin. "Thanks, Mrs. Elders."

"Say hi to your grandfather for me."

"I will."

We walked outside, into the San Diego sun.

"What now?" I desperately hoped this wasn't the end of our first mentoring session.

He held up his box of crayons, and some blank paper he'd taken from the library. "Now *you* get to make some art."

I smacked his arm lightly. "I thought we just did."

"We helped. Now you get to incorporate what you learned from the kids into your own art."

I wasn't sure how that was supposed to work, but I was game.

We walked down to the boardwalk and went to a coffee shop with outdoor seating. The people working the counter obviously knew Christos, especially the teenaged girl working the register. She fawned over him.

We ordered drinks. I ordered an Italian soda. He ordered an iced tea, and insisted on paying for both. We sat down at a table right on the boardwalk. Hundreds of people of all ages walked, rollerbladed, or bicycled by. Was this October? With weather like this, I was never going back to D.C.

Christos opened the box of crayons and offered it up to me. I selected one. "What do I do?"

"Make art."

I hesitated.

"Don't think about it. Do what those kids did. Remember, there are no rules."

He picked a color out of the box and drew a random shape, then filled it in. He picked another color and made another random shape around the first one. Then he picked a third color and did the same.

I could do that. "Can you hand me a piece of paper?"

"Use mine."

"What?"

"Draw on mine. We're making a work of art together."

I had never done that before. It sounded like fun, but I was afraid my part wouldn't be very good.

He stopped drawing and looked at me through his lashes. "Go ahead and draw, Samantha. There's no way to do it wrong."

His eyes were a force of their own. In this instance, they didn't ease my nerves. They heightened them.

"Relax. There's no grade. No one's going to tell you it isn't good enough. We're just coloring."

"Like third grade?"

"Yup." He grinned, and picked out another color. "Shapes and colors. No rules."

I started coloring.

We sipped our drinks and added to our communal drawing shape by shape. When our drinks were empty, our drawing was done. I sat back and looked at it. It was a collection of seemingly random shapes, lines and colors. But it had an order to it, and I liked it.

He raised his eyebrows and smiled. "See? Art."

"That's art?" I was skeptical.

"Are you trying to tell me it isn't?"

"Well, sort of."

He laughed. "I'm going to have to take you to look at some abstract art."

"Isn't abstract art the kind were everybody says 'My kid could do that.'?"

Christos frowned and smiled at the same time. "Don't tell my dad that. He'll knock your teeth out."

"Your dad hits women?" I joked.

Christos rolled his eyes. "No. But he'd probably throw you in the nearest swimming pool if he heard you trashing abstract art."

"Why?"

"That's what he paints. Abstract."

"Oh." I was surprised by Christos' drastically different demeanor in regard to the topic of his dad. When I'd mentioned him back at the house, Christos had seemed tense. Now he was enthusiastic. I guess everyone had mixed feelings about their parents, or anyone they loved. "Did I see any of your dad's art at your house?"

"You mean my grandad's house?"

"Yeah."

"No. But you might have seen some of his work at the SDU museum."

"Oh. Maybe I did."

"Do you remember that huge painting of the brown and gray squares, with the accents of bright red and orange?"

"You mean the one that took up an entire wall?"

"Yeah. That's my dad's."

"Oh. Is your dad in San Diego too?"

Christos face tightened. "Somewhere." He swallowed some iced tea.

"Hey, Adonis!" A gorgeous girl wearing a sports bra, lycra shorts, pads and rollerblades spun to a stop on the cement boardwalk next to our table.

"Hey, Paisley," Adonis smiled.

"Where have you been! I haven't been over in forever!" She leaned across the railing and hugged Christos. Then she kissed him on the corner of the mouth. The kiss lasted longer than a hollywood peck, but it wasn't making out, either.

Did I mention Paisley had a perfect body? The kind of body famous actresses hired for the butt close-ups? I'm talking Stunt Butt and Leg-Double perfect? Yeah, I hated her. Total bitch.

"I've been busy," Christos replied.

Paisley turned to me. "Hi, I'm Paisley." She offered her hand.

"Sam." I shook, doing my best to disguise my ire.

She glanced at the drawing. I wanted to cover it up. I felt stupid all of a sudden.

Paisley looked directly at me. "What are you guys doing?"

"Uh, coloring," I mumbled.

"That's awesome! Did you do this?"

"We did," I said, a trifle defensively.

"I love it! I totally love coloring." She eyed Christos. "Why haven't you ever taken me coloring, Christos? It looks like fun!"

Did someone have a fly swatter for Paisley?

"It's for school," Christos offered. "I'm teaching Samantha about abstract art."

"Oh," Paisley said, confused. "Sounds like fun?" She looked at me.

"Yeah, Chr—I mean, Adonis, is a great teacher." I felt like I didn't want to share his name with her.

Paisley's eyes gleamed and she chewed her perfectly plump lower lip. "Yeah he is!"

Why did I think Paisley was referring to something other than coloring?

"Sorry you guys, I'm in the middle of my work out. I've gotta blade!" She hugged Christos again and pressed her cheek against his. "It's so good to see you Adonis. You should totally call me."

"Good to see you too, Paise."

Paise? Gag.

"Did you need my number again?"

"I've still got it."

"K. Nice meeting you, Sam. See you guys later!" She bladed off. Her ass looked perfect as she pumped her perfect legs. She wasn't a bitch, but I still hated her.

I turned to Christos. The corner of my mouth smirked. "Who's Paisley?"

"An old friend."

"I bet."

Christos chuckled. "Jealous?"

"No! Sort of. She has an amazing body. I mean, I'm not gay, but that girl has a swimsuit catalog body."

"Yes, she does." Christos leaned back in his chair and clasped his hands behind his head. His muscles flexed magically.

I don't think he was trying to turn me on, but he did anyway. I threw a crayon at him. "Jerk."

"Me?"

"Yes, you!"

"Because I know Paisley?"

"Yeah!"

"How does that make me a jerk?"

"It just does." I folded my arms and pouted.

"I've never taken Paisley coloring before. Does that make you feel better?"

Amazingly, it did. "I'm sure she doesn't have time to color between her twenty-four-seven workouts."

"That is truer than you realize." He unclasped his hands and rested his muscled, tattooed forearms on the table top. "Wanna do another drawing?"

"Yeah!"

"Let me grab you another soda. Same thing?"

"Yes. Please!"

We finished our second drawing. It was as much fun as the first. After, we walked up the road to his house.

We stood in his driveway, near my VW. I had been with him for a long time today. I'm sure he had plans. With Paisley, or another one of the supermodels he knew intimately. But I was reluctant to leave.

"You hungry?"

"A little."

"Want me to make you a snack?"

"Sure!"

We went inside to the kitchen. "Take a seat. This will take a few minutes. Want something to drink?"

"I'm good."

He proceeded to pull out a food processor and various

ingredients. He whipped them up in the food processor one by one. Then he opened a can of garbanzo beans, and whipped them in. When it was finished, he scraped everything into a small bowl, and placed the bowl on a plate with triangles of flat bread. "You like hummus?"

"I don't know. I've never had it."

"You will in a second." He dipped a piece of bread into the hummus and handed it to me.

I took a bite. "Yum, that's really good! What kind of bread is this?"

"Pita bread. Have as much as you want." He grabbed a plate out of the refrigerator and peeled the plastic wrap off. "Dolma?"

I stared at the plate. They looked like a bunch of green poodle turds, or something the cat vomited up. I grimaced. "Uh, no thanks?"

"You've never had one, have you?"

"No, and I'm not about to start."

He popped one in his mouth and chewed with obvious pleasure.

I almost gagged, but didn't want to be rude.

"They're really good."

"Whatever you say."

He held one up to me. "Try it. You'll like it."

"Do you have a stomach pump handy?"

He chuckled. "It's good."

I looked at him doubtfully.

"Try it. I promise it's good."

"Promise?"

"I'm not lying, try it."

I leaned forward to take a bite. Was he feeding me? Normally I would consider that the height of romance. But he held a green monkey turd in my face. I sniffed experimentally. Was that olive oil? It made me think of international drug mules swallowing balls of hash wrapped in plastic, coated in olive oil for easier swallowing. And pooping them out afterward. I almost hurled up my hummus.

He laughed. "It's grape leaves filled with meat and rice and spices. It's good, seriously."

"I need a glass of water first. For a chaser."

"Let me get you one." He filled one at the tap and set it down on the table. "Whenever you're ready."

I gulped and cleared my throat. He held one of the green turds again for me to bite. I winced as I gingerly touched my teeth to it. I was afraid to put my lips on it. I tried not to inhale, afraid of what I'd smell. When I bit down, he pulled the remaining half away. I chewed. "Hey! This is really good! A little slimy, but good."

"See?" He popped another one in his mouth.

"Did you make these too?"

"Yup. Family recipe."

"You're quite the chef."

"That's what the ladies tell me," he taunted.

"You mean like Paisley?"

"I've never cooked for Paisley."

"Really?" I was surprised.

"We could never seem to find the time for cooking. In the kitchen anyway." His lids lowered as he mentally reminisced.

I shouldn't have asked.

"Paisley's wild." He chuckled to himself. "She's a good girl, but wild. Sort of a tornado. In a good way."

I pictured myself smashing a dolma thing into his face. Give him a dolma tornado. Since they weren't made of pooh after all, I don't think it would've bothered him. But I didn't want to start a food fight.

"You're so cute when you're jealous." He grinned.

"I'm not jealous!"

"Your frown says you are."

"I'm so not frowning!"

"Want me to get a mirror?"

"Eat another dolma." I picked one up and really did shove it at his mouth. He happily opened up to eat it.

This took me off guard, and I pulled my hand back, but he leaned forward. He closed his mouth around the dolma and his lips slid over my fingers. I felt at least 1,000 volts of electricity shoot up my arm. My heart raced and my breath caught.

"Mmm, tasty." he murmured.

Was he referring to the dolma, or my fingers? Based on his wicked grin, I'd go with fingers. I needed to change the subject before he licked my fingers, or any other body parts of mine, again. "So, Christos. Are you a student at SDU?"

He sat back in his chair, munching on his treat. He held up a finger while he chewed. When he finished, he spoke. He was so well-mannered. "Yeah. Graduate. Fine art."

"You're a graduate student? How old are you?"

"Twenty-two."

"Did you go to SDU for undergrad?"

"Yeah. Sort of a family thing. My dad went, and my grandfather has taught classes there."

"Is that how your grandfather knows Professor Childress?"

"Yup." He popped another dolma in his mouth. How much could this guy eat?

I waited for more of the story about the connection between Professor Childress and Spiridon Manos, but I wasn't getting any.

I dipped a slice of pita into the hummus. It was yummilicious.

I watched a grin spread on Christos' face. He stared at my lips and licked his.

"What?" My cheeks broiled.

"May I?" He spoke softly, yet I felt his deep voice vibrate my chest. He leaned forward, licking his lips again.

"May you what?" I was suddenly scared and thrilled. We sat at the corner of the table, so his face was less than a foot from mine. His eyes devoured me. They darted between mine and my lips.

I froze. OMG! Was he going to kiss me?

He reached up with a gentle hand and caressed his thumb across my lips. Oh gawd, I was about to slide out of my chair onto the floor.

"Hummus." He showed me a streak of hummus on his thumb. Then he licked it off, savoring the taste.

I think my heart turned to mushy hummus while watching his tongue glide over his thumb like that. Why couldn't he have licked the hummus directly off my lips, instead of his thumb? Shudder.

Christos stood up, put the remaining dolmas in the fridge, and rinsed our dishes in the sink.

How did he manage to make his every move so entirely sexy? Even his politeness? He was the sexy expert. A regular sexpert. I scoffed internally.

"I should probably get back to work," he said.

"Work?"

"In my studio. I've got some paintings I'm working on."

"I'd totally love to see them!"

"Next time."

Next time? I liked the sound of that. "I'm sorry, I'm being selfish. I'm sure you've got lots of important things to do."

"Come by next weekend, same time, and maybe I'll show you." He smiled.

"It's a date! Er, I mean plan." How desperate did that sound? Stupid.

He smiled at me with his totally confident grin.

He walked me out to my car. I almost told him I had a great time, but that would've sounded too much like date talk again.

He opened my car door for me and held it. I was about to get in, then stopped. I turned to face him. Screw it. I was going to say it. "I had a really great time today."

He smiled that mile-wide smile. "Good. Art should be fun."

He was so close to me, I was grateful the open car door stood between us. Otherwise I think I would've fallen all over him like a thirsty vampire. He made it hard for a girl to maintain her decorum. I needed to think of something witty to say to break the tension. "Yeah." D'oh! That was all I had?

Was he leaning closer to me? Was he about to send me a kiss, special delivery? I leaned back. Did he lean more? No, I think the Earth tilted, thrusting me in his direction.

Then the planet did collapse and everything crumbled beneath my feet. My heart raced and IT came crashing back around me.

Emo. Goth. Witch. Sorceress.

Bitch. Slut. Whore.

Suicide Watch.

It was a moment like this one that had started everything in motion two years earlier. The disaster, the tragedy, the pain.

Tease.

Christos' face tightened with concern. "Are you okay? You went white just now."

Taylor.

I nodded my head, but my throat locked and I couldn't speak.

"Do you need to sit down inside for a minute?"

I shook my head and cleared my throat. "I need to go." I grimaced up at him apologetically.

"You're sure? Are you okay to drive?"

"Yes," I croaked. I sat down in the car and pulled on the door.

He released it. "Sorry," I whispered.

He stood with hands low on his hips, watching me back out of the driveway. Confusion knotted his features.

I made it about three blocks before pulling onto a side street and parking. I cried my eyes out and sobbed until I felt sharp pains in my ribs every time I coughed out more buried pain.

I don't know how long it went on, but it was awhile. When I calmed, I checked my face in the visor mirror. I looked like a wreck. My eyes were swollen and red. That set me off crying again, I don't know why.

When I knew I was finally finished, I drove home. It took everything I had not to dive into the freezer with salad spoons and go through all my remaining ice cream.

Instead, I crawled into bed and slept for hours. I woke up around midnight and made a sandwich. After I ate it, I took a shower. I stood under the hot water forever. I expected it to run out at some point, but it never did. Eventually, I climbed out and went to bed.

Chapter 11

The next morning, someone banged on my front door. I dragged myself out of bed and checked the peephole. It was Madison. I yanked the door open.

"What?"

"Sam! I thought you were dead!"

"Huh?" I opened the screen door and let her in. She breezed past me with a paper bag in one hand and a drink carton with two coffees in the other.

"I called you at least forty times last night. I was sure you'd been serial killed."

My phone was on the coffee table. I picked it up. "How many texts did you send?"

"I don't know. Five thousand?"

"At least."

"Okay, so you're not dead. That's good." She grabbed me by the arms. "Did he rape you?" She looked half serious, half joking. The perfect blend of pick-me-up. Madison always knew how to cheer me up.

"No, my virtue is intact."

"Okay, that's out of the way. Coffee." She thrust the carton toward me. "Yours is the one in front." I took it. "Doughnuts." She thrust the sack at me.

"Apple fritters?"

"Of course. I got three. In case we wanted more than one each."

"You're the best, Mads."

She sat down on the sofa. "Spill it, bitch. What the heck happened yesterday?"

I sat next to her and sipped the coffee. Totally what I needed. Tons of cream. I opened the bag and pulled out a fritter and started picking at it.

"Less eat, more talk," Madison commanded.

"You're never going to believe this."

"Was he like, totally old and gross? Mentors usually are. Did he tie you up in his basement and you barely escaped with your life?"

I had noticed that Perfect Paisley, Tiffany, and Skylar had all called Christos by his middle name. Adonis. The only people who called him Christos were his grandfather and the kids at the library. Well, and Mrs. Elders, the librarian. But all of his Hot Babes in Waiting called him Adonis. It felt sort of special to call him Christos. I don't know if he felt the same way. But I didn't want to spoil the magic by telling other people, even Madison. It was a like a birthday wish I didn't want to jinx. "My mentor is Adonis."

Madison blinked. "Who?"

"GQ biker hottie?"

"What?"

"Blue eyes?"

She shook her head.

"Come on, Mads. You know who I'm talking about."

"That's not possible. Mentors are never the hottest guy in the state, if not the entire west coast."

"Yes. Adonis."

Her doubt finally crumbled, replaced by crazy excitement. "That's insane!"

Madison's enthusiasm was addictive. All of my pain from last night washed away on the irresistible tide of her optimism. "Yeah, I know, right? Freaking Adonis."

Madison tore off a chunk of apple fritter. "What'd you guys do? I need details."

I told her all about my day with him.

Madison sipped her coffee. "Geez, it sounds like you guys had a date, not a mentoring session."

"I know." I didn't want to say it out loud, but if Mads did, I wasn't going to stop her.

"Maybe you and me can double date Jake and Adonis."

I liked the sound of that. "Have you called Jake since we saw him at the beach?"

"Yeah, totally. I'm going out with him tomorrow. We're going to surf in the morning then take Lady to Dog Beach and throw frisbees for her."

"Wow, you guys are moving fast!"

"We're just hanging out. No big whoop."

"Okay, but don't forgot to make me your maid of honor."

"As if," she scoffed, "We're not moving *that* fast."

"Sure, Mads. Just don't go running off to Vegas without me. I expect you to throw the bouquet directly to me. Got it? Otherwise, I'll cut a bitch."

Madison giggled. "I'll make sure I hand it to you."

"You better. I'm sharpening my switchblade right now."

As happy as I was in that moment, I felt twinges of my old pain chewing away at me beneath the surface. Would it ever let go? Or would it pull me back under, back into blackness?

Emo. Goth. Witch. Sorceress…

If it wasn't for the apple fritter in my hand, I would've gone for the ice cream in my freezer.

By Sunday night, I was thinking all about Christos again. I couldn't get him out of my head. I dreaded waiting an entire week to see him. How was I going to concentrate in class while pining for him?

It turned out I didn't have to. I bumped into Christos all over campus. We had lunch together almost every day. Madison, Romeo, and Kamiko, or some combination of the three of them, joined us. They all really liked him. He was always cracking jokes, and remembered all sorts of personal details about each of them.

But he remained somewhat of a mystery to all of us, including me. Oh well, he was so damn close to perfect on the outside, he had to at least have one flaw. Nothing wrong with a little mystery, right?

I hoped that was all it was. Books and covers and judgment, and all that. What lay beneath his beautiful exterior was practically a complete unknown. Could be buried treasure, right?

Or Fool's Gold.

Time would tell.

One thing I did know for sure was that fewer women were hanging all over Christos. I don't know if it was because he spent so much time with me and the gang, and we were a natural deterrent, or if there was some other reason. I didn't have a way to find out.

I was rounding the corner of Fillmore Hall on Thursday afternoon when I bumped into Tiffany Kingston-Whitehouse. Literally. She was flanked by two random members from her squadron of interchangeable Fembots.

"Hey! Watch where you're going, stupid bitch!" Tiffany snarled.

Her minions sneered and gave me a pair of "As if" looks.

Great.

Tiffany examined her chest. For once, she didn't seem to be wearing a Delta Pi Delta t-shirt. "You almost made me spill coffee on my sweater, stupid bitch."

"I'm sorry," I said automatically. But the operative word here was "almost." Her sweater was spotless.

Chin down, examining herself, she brushed away non-existent coffee droplets. When she was satisfied her sweater was blemish free, she looked up at me. Her eyes widened in recognition, then narrowed just as quickly. "You," she hissed.

Me? Goodness, she remembered? I was impressed. She still didn't know my name, but I was okay with that.

"*You're* the slut."

What was she talking about? I thought I'd left this bullshit in D.C. I hadn't even gone out on a date with anyone since I'd moved to San Diego. Other than Christos Mysterios Manos, the only guy I knew on campus was gay. So, how the hell could I have earned a slut reputation?

Tiffany seethed. "I told you to stay away from Adonis."

I suddenly remembered Madison telling me about Christos snubbing Tiffany in the Main Library recently. Was that what this was about? Did she think I was competition? She was wrong, because I wasn't dating Christos. Christos was my mentor. Nothing more.

Whatever anger or pain Tiffany was dealing with over her discord with "Adonis" wasn't my problem. I didn't want to be a bitch, but she wasn't going to suck me into her personal drama. "Sorry for bumping into you. I'm late for class." I tried to step around her and her royal guard.

"Don't walk away from me while I'm talking to you!" she growled and grabbed for my t-shirt.

Her guardswomen gasped, whether at my insolence, or Tiffany losing her cool, I didn't know.

I dodged, but Tiffany caught a piece of my shirt. *Whoa, this chick is crazy!* I yanked my shirt out of her hand and kept walking. I'd had the impression that Tiffany was the sort of girl who let nothing ruffle her feathers. What had Christos done to her? And how the fuck did I get squished in the middle of it?

"Stupid whore!" Tiffany shouted at my back.

Bitch. Slut. Whore.

I'd trained myself to ignore those words for two years. I wasn't going to fall apart for some inconsequential speck like Tiffany Queenbitch-Jerkhouse now.

"Come back here!" she shouted.

I never looked back.

On Friday night, the day before my next mentoring session with Christos, I couldn't sleep. I kept imagining spending the day with him. What would we do this time? Would he wipe more hummus off my lips? Lick my fingers? Lick something else? Everything I thought of made me shiver with gleeful anticipation.

Unable to sleep, I jumped out of bed and went through my closet, considering outfits for tomorrow. My entire wardrobe covered my bed before I gave up.

The best strategy was to wait until the last second tomorrow morning. That way I wouldn't have more time to waffle on what to wear, thereby further wrinkling everything.

In the morning, I jolted awake. I tried doing homework until it was time to go, but ended up calling Romeo instead. We chatted for awhile. I usually called Madison, but I knew she was out surfing with Jake and his buddies. Again. Those two were turning into a done deal.

It was a tad chilly. It was fall, after all. At the last second, I threw on standard San Diego fall weather wear: a t-shirt, jeans, and sneakers. I drove to Christos' house and arrived a few minutes early.

There was a black Mercedes convertible in the driveway. I didn't recognize it. Christos' Ducati leaned on its kickstand.

I rang the doorbell. No one answered. I tried again. Nothing. Had I arrived at the wrong time? I checked my phone. Nope. It was five till one. I tried knocking. No answer.

I sat down on the door step and waited. At five after, I got impatient. I can be like that. I paced the driveway. I rang the doorbell. No answer.

At ten after, I considered leaving. But I had looked forward to seeing Christos all week. I wasn't scaring off that easily.

Maybe you couldn't hear the doorbell in the whole house? It was pretty big, and not modern enough to have a doorbell wired into every room.

I peered through windows, feeling only vaguely like a Peeping Tammy, But hey, I was supposed to be here.

Most of the windows on the ground floor at the front of the house revealed empty rooms. I didn't see anybody. Where was Christos? Was Spiridon home? Was the Mercedes his?

I wandered around to the side of the house and found a latched gate. *Should I open it? Why the heck not?*

I quietly pressed the thumb latch and opened the gate slowly. Why was I being so quiet? Was I sneaking? No, I was investigating.

I tip-toed down a cement path. I heard voices inside the house. A man and a woman's. Then male laughter, followed by female giggling.

I saw a small window. I peeked in. I was so bad. I was looking in on a bathroom.

Tiffany Kingston-Whitehouse, Her Royal Bee-yotchness, walked into the bathroom. Completely naked. That girl sure had a killer body. She closed the door behind her.

I ducked down before she could see me. WTF? I thought Christos had blown her off. Her bitchy behavior toward me on campus was proof of that. So why was she at his house? Naked?

And why did Christos associate with such a terrific bitch like her? The real question was, why did I care? He was only my mentor, not my boyfriend.

I heard the toilet flush through the wall. Had they just had sex? Maybe they had. It didn't matter to me if he was sleeping with her again. Or back together with her. Or whatever he called his relationships with his flock of floozies.

I didn't want to think about it anymore. I wanted to get the hell out of there.

I jogged in a crouch toward the gate, like a commando. I was on Mission: Get The Fuck Away From This Man-Whore's House Before I Do Something I Regret.

I didn't bother to close the gate behind me. I glared at the Mercedes that I assumed was Tiffany's. It was as shiny and black and as impressive as Adonis' stupid motorcycle. The two vehicles in front of me matched the two assholes inside the house. I seriously considered doing something to Tiffany's car. Did I have time to pee on her front seat?

"Samantha!"

I whipped around. Adonis. Shit. There would be no peeing. I wanted to call him a slut and a player at the same time. A Slayer. Because that's what seeing naked Tiffany in his house had done to me just now. But Slayer reminded me of Buffy. I liked Buffy. Not this jackhole.

It had only taken a week for Christos the Nice Guy to be replaced by Adonis the Jackhole. Like Jekyll and Hyde.

"Did you just get here?" he asked.

"Ah, yeah, a minute ago," I stammered.

"What were you doing around the side of the house?"

Caught. "Uhh, I thought I saw a gopher."

He frowned skeptically. "We don't get a lot of gophers around here."

"You can never be too careful. Once they get a foothold," I shook my head dramatically, "they're a bitch to get rid of." Why did it suddenly seem like the gopher metaphor referred to Tiffany? It didn't make much sense. She didn't need to dig for gold. She had her daddy's already.

"Have you been hitting the crack pipe, Samantha?" He raised his eyebrows and grinned at me. He stroked his chin thoughtfully. His forearm muscles serenaded me. Stupid muscles.

"No, no crack." Yet. I'm sure I could find a guy who could sell me some before dinner. I was going to need it. I hurried toward my car. I was getting the flock out of there.

Tiffany stepped into the doorframe next to Christos. She was fully dressed and held her purse. When she saw me, her smile decayed into a scowl. "What are *you* doing here?"

Great. Now she was cutting off my hasty escape. "I'm, uh, I had a meeting." Why not say it? Make her squirm. She had already thrown down the silk gauntlet. I wasn't afraid of her. "With Adonis."

Tiffany looked at Christos. Her brow creased with bitch-like perfection. "You didn't tell me *she* was coming over."

I could totally hear the judgmental italics when she said the word "she," like I was sewage. I'm sure Tiffany practiced thinly veiled insults in front of the mirror every morning before starting her day.

"I thought you said you had a student?" she asked Christos.

"I do. Her."

Tiffany's eyes flicked between me and him. "Oh."

"Time for you to go," Christos said.

Tiffany scoffed. "Okay already." She clopped to her car on her ankle-strap wedges and passed a few feet from me. She dished up two scoops of fake smile with a dollop of battery acid on top. After climbing in her car, she blew Christos a kiss and a wave before driving off.

"Sorry, I was running late. You ready to see the studio?" Christos asked me innocently.

"Is that what you were just doing with Tiffany? Showing her the *studio*?" Who was adding bitchy italics to her words now? Was I fourteen, or what?

"Something wrong?"

"I keep forgetting you manage the Bunny Ranch. My mistake."

He scoffed, but said nothing.

"I should really be going." I opened the door to my VW.

"I thought we had a mentor session today."

"Like your mentoring session with Tiffany?"

"Huh? I'm not mentoring Tiffany."

"Oh, really." My words dripped with bitchiness. I sounded worse than Tiffany. But I was on a roll. My emotions shifted into overdrive, and my jealousy turbos kicked in. Yes, I was crazy.

Christos smiled innocently. "Am I missing something here?"

"I saw Tiffany in the bathroom. Naked. Is that your idea of mentoring? Do I get naked for my second mentoring session? Or the third?"

He folded his arms across his broad chest, leaned against the doorframe of the house, and smiled at me. "You pick."

"You're a dog." I was furious.

He was amused. "You're a snoop. Gophers?" He arched his brows. "Really?"

"Mentoring? Really?" I said snidely.

"I told you, I'm not mentoring Tiffany."

"That much is obvious. I don't call it mentoring either. I call it—" I clamped my mouth shut. I didn't want to say it.

"I think you skipped the jumping part and took a bullet train straight to your misinformed conclusions, Samantha. You wanna see what we were doing?"

"What, did you shoot video?"

"Hardly. Come inside. I'll show you."

I opened my mouth. Closed it. "You're not going to make me take my clothes off, are you?" I growled.

"Only if you want me to." He smiled and lowered his lashes seductively. Stupid dark lashes.

"You're not helping."

"C'mon. I'll show you." He turned and walked inside, leaving the front door open.

As much as I seriously considered bailing, my curiosity was piqued. I'd heard what it did to cats, but I wasn't a cat, so I was pretty sure I would be safe.

Christos stood on the far side of the living room, waiting for me. "This way," he said.

I followed him through the house to the back. The studio was entirely walled by windows. Even the wall between the studio and the house had windows in it.

Christos gestured a hand into the room. "Welcome to the studio."

It was everything you would expect in an amazing art studio. Easels of various sizes, paintings on the easels and the walls, jars of brushes, those little wooden artist mannequins, cabinets with drawers of paint, blank canvases, supplies galore, art books. It was overwhelming.

My anger fizzled and transformed into awe. "Wow, this is *your* studio?"

"It was my grandpa's, before he stopped painting. He lets me use it now."

I walked around the room, looking at the paintings on the easels. They were totally different from Spiridon's landscapes in the living room. Christos' art was all human figures. Mostly female nudes. Why didn't that surprise me? I smirked at Christos, who stood beside me as I examined one of his paintings. "You sure like to paint naked women."

"I love feminine beauty. Does that bother you?"

I couldn't argue that these women weren't beautiful. But there were so many of them. Did his entire life revolve around naked, unobtainably beautiful women? Women he'd slept with? Because the painting I was staring at was clearly Paisley, his rollerblader friend with the perfect body.

"Is this your trophy room?" I blurted. I slapped my hand to my mouth. Why had I said that? I sounded like a jealous bitch.

"Would it bother you if it was?" He asked slyly.

What he did with his free time wasn't any of my business, no matter how much it annoyed me to know he spent it with all these perfect women. "No, I—I'm being rude. Sorry."

"That's okay. Doesn't bother me."

I walked to another painting. My anger rose. This really was a trophy room. The half-finished painting in front of me was of Tiffany. Nude. I wanted to hate it. But I couldn't. The painting in no way resembled the Ice Queen Bitch I'd witnessed outside. She looked elegant, even demure. "Is this…?"

"What I was doing with Tiffany? Yeah."

I looked at the easel. It was surrounded by various items: a palette covered in messy smears of mixed paint, brushes soaking in jars, a waste basket full of paint-stained paper towels. "You were painting her?"

"Not *on* her," he winked. "On the canvas."

I ignored the innuendo. "It's amazing. She looks so… vulnerable."

"She is. Beneath her bullshit and her money."

"It's really good," I said sincerely.

"Thank you," he said humbly.

That was a surprise. I had expected his cockiness, some sort of gloat-worthy response. Not humility.

"I try to paint what lies beneath people's facades. Their core self, when they're not trying to project their usual image."

"You just want them to take their clothes off," I joked sarcastically.

"It goes beyond that. Do you feel different when you're wearing makeup versus no makeup?"

"Well, less so since I moved to San Diego. I see a lot less makeup here than in D.C. But I know what you mean. Back east, a woman without makeup is only half dressed."

"Exactly. It's part of your public identity. Few people ever walk out in public stripped of all artifice. When I paint a subject in the nude, there is very little for them to hide behind. You'd be surprised by the transformation most people go through when they pose for me."

Okay, there was a lot more to Christos than I imagined. He had depth, compassion, and he was a natural with the kids at the library. And yes, I admit it, I had jumped to conclusions when I'd assumed he and Tiffany were having sex earlier. He had probably been painting her, like he said.

I looked at the unfinished painting again. It was so real. I reached out to it and almost ran my fingers over it, as if I would feel her skin, and not the paint and canvas.

"Be careful, it's still wet. It'll take several days to dry, and a couple more sittings to complete."

I lowered my hand. "She looks so different. Like she's not a bitch."

"She isn't, when no one else is around."

Why did hearing that make me suddenly jealous? Like Tiffany and Christos shared some kind of secret intimacy that he and I did not? Did she see into him like he saw into her? I didn't know. But if she did, that meant she had access to him in a way that I did not. Which meant she was in a position to take Christos away from me. Not Adonis. She could have *him*. But I really didn't want Tiffany stealing Christos. *I* wanted him.

No, I didn't.

Yes, I did.

Christos stepped toward me and gently cupped my chin with his hand. He turned my face until I was staring into his eyes.

OMFG.

I nearly drowned in the blue oceans behind his dark lashes. My breath stopped in my throat. Gulp. He glanced at my lips. He was so unbelievably handsome. My mouth quivered. The gigantic studio had become entirely too small for the two of us.

I glanced at the Tiffany painting. Was it staring at us? No, she was looking downward. Why was I looking at the Tiffany painting?

My eyes slid back to Christos' sapphires. I fell into them. My whole body started to shake. Was it fear? Desire? Both?

A look of tremendous compassion settled onto Christos'

features. Something that had been locked shut deep inside me began to open for the first time in years. Warmth spread from my abdomen out to my entire body. I wanted to fall into his arms.

He gently brushed a stray lock of hair that had fallen from my ponytail and tucked it behind my ear. "When I look at you, I see a young woman frightened of her own beauty."

Gag. Frightened? Yes. Beautiful? No. Total poseur pickup artist. Whatever had begun to open inside me slammed shut. I hated it when guys fed me lines. Still, he held me powerless in his grasp.

"Most women maximize their beauty. You minimize yours, like you're avoiding it." His eyes penetrated me.

He was right about one thing. I was avoiding a whole hell of a lot. On a daily basis.

Tease.

His hand slid down my cheek and along the curve of my neck, leaving a trail of warmth, yet I shivered. He ran his thumb delicately across the ridge of my clavicle, out to my shoulder. A pleasure of lightning raced up the back of my neck, then bounced down my spine to my pelvis.

I literally jumped.

I pulled free of his mesmerizing touch, and hurried over to the next painting, trying to escape. My heart hammered and the cyclone in my stomach spun the butterflies out of control, sending them straight to Oz.

"I can tell that you're hiding something inside," he said softly.

I felt his deep voice drilling past my defenses. I whipped around and stared him down.

Taylor.

"Something that has wounded you deeply."

Stop! Emergency brakes! I did the only thing I could think of. I threw buckets of sarcasm at the problem. Not only did Christos have laser beam Superman eyes, he had X-ray vision too.

I needed to head him off at the pass, or I was going to collapse and shatter into a thousand pieces when I hit the floor. "Who writes your pickup lines for you? Do you have a full time staff? You're not wearing an earpiece while Cyrano feeds you dialogue, are you?"

"Did I hit a nerve?" he asked, bemused.

"Hardly. You sound so corny, I can't take you seriously."

He eyed me shrewdly while draping his arm over the easel with the Tiffany painting. Like he had his arm around her. Like he owned her. Suddenly, that didn't bother me so much anymore. He could have her.

"I think it's time for a change of venue. You ready?" he asked suggestively.

"What?" For a second, from the way he was hanging on the Tiffany painting, I thought he meant he wanted to paint *me* nude. I was so not going to do that. "I don't think so," I scoffed.

He frowned. "The kids? They're waiting for us at the library."

"Oh! That." Oops. "Yeah, okay."

We walked outside, and down the hill to the library. I was still shaken by Christos' probing questions. But the moment we walked into the room full of kids and crayons, their glee trampled my anxiety instantly. Their joy was nuclear.

When we finished with them, Christos and I walked back to his house. He showed me some of the finer points of figure drawing on a drawing pad in the studio, using a selection of charcoal pencils. Although Professor Childress was always helpful in Life Drawing class, Christos had a way of making everything so obvious. His drawings were amazing, and effortless.

After he explained some new drawing concepts, he modeled for me, so I could practice what he'd just taught me. I was disappointed that he was fully clothed, but he did all these wacky, clownish poses. I laughed so much, it was hard to focus on the drawing. It was totally fun. Whenever it was just me and Christos, things always were.

We took a break after a couple hours and had a snack. Tortilla chips and fresh guacamole. Made by Christos.

He dipped a chip in the bowl and loaded it with a mountain of guac. "You did some great drawings today. You learn fast."

"Really?"

"Yeah. You're picking up the idea behind gesture drawing nicely. You've got an eye for it."

"Thanks."

"I think good gesture is a hallmark of artists with real talent."

"Oh?"

"You have real talent." He smiled at me.

I blushed, and ate a chip.

"Now you just need to work at it."

Professor Childress had told me the same thing. Maybe it *was* true. I smiled at Christos sheepishly.

We went back to his studio for another hour, until Christos said it was time to go.

Despite all the competition hanging around his studio in the form of his trophy paintings (I couldn't help thinking of them that way), I didn't want to leave. I felt like I was in Rembrandt's studio and the master was giving me private lessons.

Outside, I lingered at my VW in the driveway. I gazed into his smoldering eyes through his thick lashes, hypnotized. Again.

"Hey," he said, "Jake's throwing a Halloween party tonight. You wanna come with? I'm sure Mads will be there."

I cocked my hip. I couldn't believe she hadn't told me! I would have to lecture her about it later. "You know about Mads and Jake?"

"He hasn't shut up about her since we met you guys at the nude beach."

"Those two are perfect for each other," I smiled.

"Look, I've got a ton of work before the party. You want me to pick you up?"

I eyed his motorcycle cautiously. "I can drive."

"What, you don't want to ride The Duke?"

I shrugged my shoulders. Had he named his motorcycle? Such a guy.

"All right. We'll take my car. Where do you live?"

I gave him my address.

"I'll pick you up at eight."

Was this a date? No, I was getting way ahead of myself. Again. "Maybe you should have my phone number? In case there's a change in plans?" I couldn't believe I was asking him to ask *me* for my phone number. Wasn't it supposed to be the other way around?

He smirked and pulled out his phone. We swapped numbers. I had Christos' phone number! I refused to jump for joy.

So I melted instead, and not from the warm weather. I was going to be nothing but a puddle in about ten seconds.

"Something wrong? You look woozy."

"I'm good," I choked.

He smiled. "All right, I'm heading back inside. Pick you up at eight."

Chapter 12

When I got home, I was brimming over with excitement about my awesome day with Christos. I wanted to call Madison and share all the details with her. I also needed to read her the riot act for concealing state secrets about Jake's party that night. I was in such a good mood.

I was about to dial Madison when my phone belled. It was my parents. There went my mood. It deflated into cautious optimism.

"Hello?"

"Sam?" My mom Linda said tentatively.

"Hey, Mom." I was super excited about my exploration into art, and the things Professor Childress and Christos had both told me about my talent and my progress. But I would have to work up to it and frame it just right, otherwise my parents would freak and tear my optimism to shreds.

"How are you?" I heard my mom pull the receiver away from her mouth and holler, "Bill! Pick up! She finally answered her phone!"

I heard another line in the house click open. Yes, my parents still had a land line in the house with several phones. I tried to get them to use Skype so we could video chat, but they always managed to find an excuse for not opening up an account. I told them it was free, but always the same story about needing to upgrade the computer. Whatever.

"Sam! How are you! How's college?"

"Great, Dad."

"How's the accounting going? I bet you've got all A's."

"Yeah." Or something like that. I wasn't entirely sure about Fundamentals of Accounting. It wasn't exactly heating up my panties. Life Drawing, on the other hand…

"That's great news!" my mom said. "I always knew you would be a whiz at it. You're so good with numbers."

"You're laying the groundwork for a dependable career, darling," my dad said. "There will always be a need for accountants. It's the safest path. You'll be assured a job for the rest of your life. I know you will excel in business, Sam."

"Thanks, Dad."

I rolled my eyes. I swear I'd had this exact conversation, or pieces of it, with *myself* about a hundred thousand times since I'd started classes at SDU.

I realized at that moment, that my parents' middle-class belief system was firmly entrenched in my own head. It was a rampant virus that had taken hold of my brain. Or maybe some sort of creepy symbiotic thing. It wasn't killing me, but it fed off of me and ate away my courage and sense of adventure on a daily basis.

I wanted to cry. I never dreamed of being an accountant when I was a little girl. Who ever did? But I'm sure my parents were right. Accountants *could* always find work. I sighed.

The problem was that my parents were solidly middle class. My family wasn't so poor that all we had was our love for each other, or so rich that all we had was our money. Instead, we had a little bit of love and a little bit of money. But never enough of either. What we did have in surplus was a cautious sense of responsibility toward both. Great.

My family was so busy doing the right thing, we forgot to love each other passionately. But all the responsibility in the world didn't make the bills go away, and it sure never felt like love to me. We had the worst of both worlds.

"How are your other classes?" Mom asked.

"Fine." I pinched the bridge of my nose, holding back tears.

"What are you taking again, besides the accounting?" Dad asked.

"Sociology and American History." I didn't want to talk to them about art anymore. I was pretty sure they would spoil it somehow, no matter what I said. Then I wouldn't be able to hold back the tears. I hated crying in front of my parents. They were always quick to offer good advice. Cold, logical, useful advice. Silly me for wanting more.

"That's only three classes," Dad said. "Weren't you taking four?" Sharp as always.

"Yeah."

"Well," Mom pressed, "what's the other class?"

They were going to pry it out of me. May as well get it over with. I steeled myself for the worst. I was always good at holding in my emotions around them. They'd taught me how. "Life Drawing." I hoped they'd think that was some sort of Life Science. I should've known better.

"Drawing?" Mom sounded like someone had shoved a cup of poop under her nose and asked her to sniff it.

"I thought we talked about this," my dad said, clearly disappointed.

I bolstered my sarcasm and covered my pain with it. Good thing I didn't have my parents on a video call. I didn't want them to see the horrid face I was making. Plus, I mimed holding a hangman's noose around my neck. I'd get a lecture from Mom about my attitude for sure, if she'd seen me.

"Talked about what?" I sighed. I was stalling. I knew what they meant. But it took me a few seconds to completely deaden my emotions. I stared out my living room window at the sunset. Why did I have the sinking feeling that when the sun dropped below the horizon tonight, my dreams were going to go with it forever?

My parents' responsible, persistent prodding was dragging my dreams into oblivion.

"What happened to Micro Economics first term?" Dad asked. "So you could get it out of the way? You know you need Econ for your Accounting major."

I sighed. "I have to take electives too. I wanted to take art."

"But we talked about this, Sam. Leave the electives until fourth year, when your upper division classes are at their worst. That's the smart move."

"I don't know. I guess I wanted to do the art now. Explore a little."

"Explore?" my mom asked, her voice ripe with concern. "We didn't talk about exploring, did we, Dear?"

"Not that I recall," my father answered ominously.

It was like they were telling me it was a foregone conclusion that I'd never step outside of the box they'd drawn around me years ago.

Groan. I'd fought this battle many times, and always limped away the loser. But in the past, it had always been on their turf, in their house, where they made the rules. I was in college now, in my apartment. I was tired of giving in.

My eyes scanned my living room, searching for assistance. They landed on my drawing pad. I kneeled in front of it and flipped to the last page. I saw Christos' drawings next to my own. I could tell how much I'd already improved in just a few short weeks. I remembered Christos' encouraging words. They suddenly gave me new hope and new resolve.

"Can you change Life Drawing to Econ?" my dad asked.

"It's too late in the term, Dad!" I said with a mixture of confidence and a hint of whiny, teenaged uncertainty. "I can't add a class now!"

"Watch your tone, young lady," my mom cautioned.

"Yes, ma'am."

For a moment, I wanted to plead with my parents about how important drawing class was to me. I had good reason: Christos' and Professor Childress' compliments. That was valid proof, wasn't it? My parents should be as excited as I was, shouldn't they?

But I knew full well how the conversation would go. They would pick away at my fragile hope and enthusiasm like vultures until both were gone. I shook my head and rubbed my temple with one hand. I needed an aspirin. Or a glass of cyanide.

"You'll take Econ next term, right?" Dad prodded. "She should take Econ, don't you agree, Linda?"

Why did I feel like a marionette, and my parents were pulling my strings, trying to make my mouth move?

"Sam? Did you hear what your father said?" Mom asked.

No. No I wouldn't take Econ next term. Screw them. I was finally discovering that maybe I didn't have to be boring old Sam Smith, CPA. Maybe there was an uncharted path that waited for me in life.

"Sam?" Dad asked.

"Sam, are you there?" my mom asked.

"Sam? Are you there?"

"Sam? Answer your father."

My parents were nudging me like they always did. Like sheep dogs nipping at my heels until I got in line with the other sheep and bleated my way toward boredom and security, herding me inside the pen with all the other lost souls.

"You'll take Econ next time, right Sam?" My dad asked.

"I guess." I told myself it was a defensive lie to get them off my back. I hoped I could stick to my guns. But I felt myself slipping as they bored into me with their responsible logic.

"You can take more electives senior year," Mom said. "You can even take art. But please take your father's advice. Focus on the economics and accounting classes now. You'll thank us later when you're taking all those upper division classes. I remember how hard my major was."

My mom had been an office manager since the day she went back to work when I was six months old. She hated her job, but said we needed the money. I wanted to ask her if I would thank her if I ended up stuck in a job I hated when I was her age.

"I guess," I mumbled.

When had my parents become my jailers? I felt like I had been suffering from Stockholm Syndrome ever since serious talk of college had started two years ago. I hadn't agreed with many of their decisions along the way, but somehow I'd let them make most of them for me, simply to avoid further incessant pestering.

The only reason they'd even allowed me to go to faraway SDU was because the business school was so highly ranked for undergraduates. If I had told them about all the drama I'd endured during junior and senior years—

Bitch. Slut. Whore. Suicide Watch.

Tease.

Taylor.

—they probably would've forced me into therapy and a college close to home. I'd be stuck in their cocoon of conservative choices for the rest of my life.

"…so your mother and I told Fred and Donna that they would have to take the downstairs bedroom at the condo this winter," my dad droned.

How long had my parents been talking about who gave a shit what? I didn't know.

I let them bend my ear until they told me they had to go to bed, what with the three hour time difference.

"Good night, Sam," my dad said.

"Take care, Sam," my mom said.

There was a pregnant pause while they awaited my response. It widened into an infinite gap. The distance between their world view and mine. They were on the far side of a giant chasm, trying to tell me what to do. The only problem was I felt like they were encouraging me to jump into this huge, hellish chasm that was my future. Carved into the rocks at the bottom were the words:

"Here Lies Sam Smith, CPA.

She was responsible.

R.I.P."

I wasn't ready to take that plunge. I couldn't let myself. I knew the fall would entail a long, slow, miserable death.

The pregnant pause had stretched into genuine discomfort. I again thanked my luck that we weren't on video.

"Goodnight, Mom. Goodnight, Dad."

As always, not enough love, and not enough money. Right in the middle of the road. Nausea bubbled up the back of my throat. I swallowed it down and hung up.

Fuck this shit.

I didn't have time to call Madison after getting off the phone with my parents. I'd have to lecture her at the party. Besides, my good mood and desire to share had been vampired out by Mom and Dad.

I shifted my focus to getting ready for tonight. I had only a couple of hours.

My apartment was sloppy and needed a once-over. And I had no costume. What the hell was I going to wear? I could go as a beach bum. I had that costume down pat.

I did have some of my old clothes from D.C., but I didn't want to fall back on something ambiguously gothy. In San Diego, it might have worked as an actual costume, but it was my last resort.

I'm sure if I'd owned a pair of bunny ears or angel's wings, I could've gone in my underwear. What was with slutty near-nakedness being the official costume for most women on Halloween? I didn't think I had the body to pull it off anyway, so scratch that.

I brainstormed while I cleaned. I could cut some eye holes in a bed sheet. But who outside of grammar school went as a ghost? As I scrubbed my toilet, just in case Christos had to use it, I considered going as a maid. Could I dress up as *Mrs.* Clean? I had a hoop earring and a white t-shirt, but I didn't want to shave my head.

As the clock ticked down, my brain ran out of storm. I showered and jumped into jeans and threw on a metallic print V-neck blouse. A touch of eyeliner and mascara and I was good to go. Nobody would fault me for looking nice, would they?

As I slid my sandals on, I heard rumbling outside. Why did I assume it was Christos? I opened my front door, I saw a muscle car pull into the parking lot. It was navy blue and had two white racing stripes running over its length.

Christos saw me and waved.

I grabbed my purse and glanced at my somewhat clean apartment. All that trouble and he wasn't going to see it. Maybe later? When he walked me to my door? Not bloody likely! I locked my door and trotted down the stairs.

Christos held the passenger door open like a valet. He wore a white t-shirt, dark skinny jeans, and boots. "Your chariot awaits, madam."

I blushed. No one ever held so many doors for me like Christos did. I slid into the seat. "Where's your costume?"

"I'm wearing it."

"Me too."

"What are you going as?"

"Can't you tell? I'm the cool guy who gets run out of town by the cops at the end of the movie because of my rebellious ways. What are you?"

"The girl that goes with him, seeking adventure?"

He nodded approvingly. "If the cops catch us, I'm going down with guns blazing." He closed the door.

"Do you have a gun for me?"

"In my pocket." He smirked.

"Okay, way too much innuendo for me. I didn't wear my rubber gloves, so I'm not touching it."

"It?" he asked suggestively.

"Your comment, perv! Get in the car!" I giggled.

He climbed in the driver's side while I admired the interior. It was in perfect condition, but it was obviously a classic car. "Wow, Christos. Nice car. What is it?"

"Sixty-eight Camaro."

"Is it fast?"

"Not as fast as my bike. But I'll see what I can do."

"Oh, that wasn't a request!"

He backed the car onto the street and revved the engine. "Hold on." He winked.

"No, wait!"

Tires squealed and I was pushed into the bucket seat. "Jesus Christ!" I'd never been in a car this fast.

He braked for a stop sign. He was chuckling.

"Do you know where we're going?" I asked. "I don't know where Jake lives."

"I do." He floored the car again.

I never knew a car could pop a wheelie. Leave it to Christos to expose me to new things!

I'm pretty sure at some point all four wheels were off the ground during our drive. But I couldn't say for certain because most of the time I had both eyes closed.

Terror can do that to you.

Christos explained that Jake lived in a huge house near the beach with four of his surfing buddies, and two of their girlfriends. Parked cars filled the street out front.

Inside it was crowded. I was relieved that almost no one wore a costume. I loved how casual San Diego was every time I peeled back another layer.

Christos seemed to know half of the people on a first name basis. Everyone fist-bumped him and patted him on the back. I felt like I was with a world-famous rockstar.

We found Jake and Madison standing together. Madison was up on her tip-toes, whispering into Jake's ear. Neither of them wore a costume.

When they saw us, Jake turned to Christos. "What up, bro!" They clasped hands and did some sort of complex elbow bumping routine. There were so many fluid movements, I'm sure they studied it at Julliard.

Madison and I hugged, with no excess choreography necessary.

"You brought Adonis!" Madison said, sipping from her red plastic cup. "Lucky girl," she winked.

Jake and Christos were busy talking to a group of guys.

I smiled broadly and smacked Madison's arm. "You are such a

traitor, Mads!"

"What?!"

"How could you not tell me about Jake's party?!"

She laughed. "Down, girl! I just found out today. Jake told me about it this morning when we were surfing. He said it was a last minute thing. I was going to tell you when I called you this afternoon. Didn't you check your phone?"

"Oh, uh, no. My parents called to—" eye roll "—lecture me. Then I had to clean my place before the party."

"Clean your place? It's not like the party's at your apartment."

"In case you-know-who came inside." I nodded toward Christos.

"You've got it bad, girlfriend."

"What's that supposed to mean?"

"Nobody cleans for a boy unless it's love."

"I'm not in love with him! He's my mentor!"

"Yet."

"What?"

"In love. Yet."

"You are mentally ill, Mads."

"Never mind that." I leaned over and whispered in her ear. "Adonis totally told me Jake talks about you all the time."

"OMG! He does?"

"Who's in love now?" I tilted my head back and leveled my best superior-than-thou smile at her. "Get that bouquet ready. And I'm not wearing some stupid tangerine or fuchsia colored bridesmaid dress. Pick a real color."

"How about pastel! I love pastels!"

"Okay, girl. Leash it. You're not at the altar yet."

"Vegas is only a five hour drive. Don't tempt me, Sam!" She beamed the joy of being in love. I so envied her.

Christos and Jake's ears must've been burning because the two of them turned back to face me and Madison.

"You guys need brews?" Jake asked.

Christos looked at me. "Samantha? What are you drinking?"

"Nothing with Rufis in it," Madison warned.

"I don't need Rufis, Mads," Christos said confidently. "Girls faint when they see me two blocks away."

"That is *so* gag!!" I shouted.

"When Freud coined the term Superego, I think he had Adonis in mind," Madison said.

Jake swung an arm around Christos' shoulders. "That's my boy!"

"Where are the brews, man?" Christos asked him.

"Out back."

"Let's go grab some beverages, Samantha."

Madison stayed with Jake. I waved at her. "See you guys later."

The backyard was huge. People crowded the wood deck that surrounded a big pool. No one was swimming but it was almost warm enough if people were in the mood to get wet.

Their were two kegs next to a table covered with various bottles of hard alcohol.

"What's your poison?" Christos asked.

"Oh, I don't drink," I lied. Spending the day with Christos had left me feeling alive. Despite the downer phone call with my parents, most of my afternoon good mood remained. I didn't want to dim it with drinking.

Christos filled a cup of beer from the keg. "You gotta drink something. It's Halloween!"

"I thought Halloween was for candy."

"You want something sweet? You've got me for that." He chuckled when I eye rolled him. "How about a vodka cranberry?"

I wasn't getting out of it. One drink wouldn't undo me, would it? I could nurse it all night. I reluctantly agreed and Christos made my drink. We circulated the party while I sipped it. How many sips did it take to get to the center of a vodka cranberry? Hopefully more than one, two, three. I was shooting for at least fifty.

As I had expected, whenever I turned around, another random hot girl was falling all over Christos. I heard a constant string of female voices extolling "Adonis this" and "Adonis that."

Why did all of them have to be taller than me? I felt like a midget. I think the fact that most of his admirers wore mini-skirts and six-inch stripper platforms was part of it. But they were all so damn leggy and clearly card-carrying members of the Hourglass Figure Club. Consequently, I felt lucky to have Christos' attention for more than a minute at a time.

But it wasn't just the girls. The guys were bombarding him as well. I'd never seen so many man crushes and bromances at one time.

Everyone wanted Christos' attention. He seemed happy to oblige.

I couldn't blame him. He was having a blast, laughing and joking with everybody. I watched it all from the sidelines, stuck inside my own head.

So I turtled further into myself, my favorite destination. I'd been a certified loner for the last two years of high school. I had mapped out the territory of loneliness in depth during that time. No big whoop.

Some time later, I left Christos to his many conversations. I wandered through the house until I found a bathroom. The line was long. I waited while the people around me thoroughly enjoyed themselves. Maybe I needed to drink more. I pounded the rest of my vodka cranberry. I'm pretty sure Christos had gone easy on the alcohol. I don't think I had more than a minor buzz. Was he being a gentleman? Or overly protective? Considering his absence, I'd say neither.

I finally had my turn in the bathroom. I hovered over the bowl while I peed. So many people had used the toilet before me, I wasn't taking a chance. When I walked out, the music cranked up.

"Yay," I mumbled to myself sarcastically. "Dancing. Just what I need. Not."

I wandered into the dining room.

"There you are!" Christos said, his hand on my shoulder. "I've been looking all over for you!"

Did he miss me? Maybe he was just drunk.

"Come on, Samantha. Let's dance." He grabbed my arm.

I resisted. "Is dancing appropriate for a mentor-mentee relationship?" I quipped.

"Who gives a fuck! Let's dance!"

Yeah, he'd had a few. I wouldn't have been surprised if he was totally hammered. That didn't stop him from dragging me into the middle of a bunch of swirling bodies.

No matter how hard I tried to be a stick in the mud, Christos wouldn't let me remain stuck. He put his arm around my waist and took my hand. He twirled us around. I had no choice but to go with the flow.

"How much have you had to drink?" I said into his ear.

"I don't know, two beers?"

"That's it?"

"Yeah. I've been busy dancing. Why?"

"You just seem so, I don't know, carefree?" Christos was so cocky-cool most of the time, I guess I never imagined he could cut loose like this.

"Remember those kids we helped at the library? I try to act like them, when the moment calls for it. This is a party, after all."

He was right. I envied his free spirit at the same time I wanted to run away from it. But that's what I'd done back home. Did I have to keep doing it forever?

Maybe I could channel joy like Christos did. I didn't want to live life as a straight-laced accountant. I wanted adventure. I wasn't going to find fun by avoiding opportunities like this.

I did my best to loosen up. I twisted my hips and shook some booty. I actually started getting into it. I didn't have much dancing experience, but I managed to have fun.

Eventually, I was breathless from exertion. "I need to rest for a minute," I shouted at Christos. I motioned toward the house.

"Okay." He kept dancing.

Did that mean he was coming with me, or was I on my own? Again?

When I started out of the bustling dancing area and turned back to look for Christos, I watched the crowd swallow him up.

It was a pattern for him. Life seemed to have a hold on him in a way that no one person, and certainly no one woman, ever would.

I went inside the house, needing to get away from Good Time Christos. I ended up in the kitchen where a Quarters tournament was in progress at the kitchen table. A bunch of very drunk guys bounced their coins into a shot glass.

One of them looked up at me with bleary eyes. "Hey, babe! Join us!"

Uh, no.

The guy wearing a football jersey stood up. "Have my seat." Such a gentleman. He was as drunk as his friend, but in this moment, possibly more thoughtful than Christos.

"Sorry, I'm looking for someone," I lied. I really just wanted privacy. Where was I going to find it in this zoo?

I turned around and went into the living room. A bunch of surfer looking guys sat around a huge TV playing one of the Call of Duty games on the xBox. It somehow involved drinking while shooting things. Surprised? Nope. Men? Yup.

The surfers paid me no mind so I dropped onto a corner of the couch. A bunch of people stood behind me, chatting on and on about random stuff. I was ensconced in a cocoon of people having fun without me. Worked for me.

Some time later, I heard Jake's voice emerge from the chaos behind me. He was talking to someone. I turned around on the couch, but couldn't see him through the huge guy standing directly behind me.

"Dude," Jake said to his mystery conversationalist, who was a guy, "Adonis is flipped for that girl."

"The one he came in with? The hot one?"

I perked up. Were they talking about moi? I shouldn't have been listening. Eavesdropping always turned out badly. Okay, maybe I would listen a little.

"You mean Mads' friend?" Jake asked.

"Yeah. She's hot. Adonis hooks up with the finest chicks in town, man. He's so fucking lucky."

Hooks up? Was I detecting the birth of a rumor? Because this was how it usually started. Gossipy bullshit. I hated being the subject. Fuck.

I turned in my seat, wanting to intervene, but the gigantic guy was still blocking my view behind, and I was trapped between several of the Call of Duty tournament players. I wasn't going anywhere without yelling "Fire!" or calling in a bomb threat to 911.

"They haven't hooked up," Jake said to his buddy. I liked Jake. "He just totally digs hanging with her. Says she's some kind of natural artist. He's showing her all kinds of stuff at his studio."

"I bet he is. Showing her all kinds of stuff." I distinctly heard Mystery Man suggesting dirty deeds. "I know I would."

"No, man. Not like that. Adonis is a real artist. Have you ever seen his work?"

"No."

"Dude, he's amazing," Jake said enthusiastically. "The real deal. And he says that girl Sam has a gift. He wants to help her develop it. Be like her own personal coach and shit."

"Fucking lucky," Mystery Man said, suddenly sounding sincere and envious.

"Who? Adonis?"

"No, bro. That girl. Having someone help you out like that? Doesn't happen every day."

"No it does not."

Whoa. What? My stomach tilt-a-whirled. Jake and the Mystery Man moved away from where I sat, and the sound of Call of Duty drowned them out entirely.

Had my assessment of Good Time Christos been too hasty?

I decided to find out. I went looking for him.

Chapter 13

The obvious first place to check was the deck in the backyard. There were now more dancers tearing it up than before. I was surprised the cops hadn't shown up yet due to all the ruckus.

I circulated through the writhing bodies, searching for Christos. Drunk college kids surrounded me. I could smell alcohol in the air. Was it in everyone's sweat? How much had people drunk? I bet the kegs were empty and the alcohol table was cleaned out.

I felt stupid strolling normally through the crowd while people danced around me, so I put my arms up in the air and tried to rekindle some of my dancing enthusiasm from when I was shaking it with Christos earlier. Several guys tried to dance with me, but I kept moving. They were too drunk to successfully fondle or follow.

At one point, I passed a guy dancing with a girl shorter than I was. She had a huge pile of dark hair. For a moment, I was stuck behind her, so I scanned the crowd for Christos. The guy dancing with Short Girl, who had a shaved head and tattoos on his scalp, kept looking at me. He was making me nervous. I did my best to ignore him while trying to peer into the crowd beyond him.

A moment later, I felt a stiff finger jamming into my shoulder.

"You gotta problem?"

I turned around and discovered Short Girl scowling up at me. The anger in her eyes took me off guard, so did her huge boobs. I think each one was larger than my head. I didn't know what to say.

"You looking at my boyfriend?"

I was confused. "Who's your boyfriend?"

"Cassandra, calm down, " said the guy with the shaved head, the one who had been dancing with her.

Cassandra went from zero to bitch in less than a second. She flashed her teeth at him. "Shut up, Emilio. I wanna know why this skank was checking you out." She turned back to me. "You eyeing my man, ho?"

Whore.

"What? No! I'm looking for my friend!"

Cassandra must have sensed my fear, because she went on the attack. "Don't be looking at my boyfriend, bitch."

Bitch.

"I'm not!" I tried to squeeze past her, but her boobs were in the way.

Tease.

"Where you going, slut? I'm not done talking to you!"

Slut.

"Easy, ladies," Christos said, suddenly standing beside us. "No reason to get all worked up."

Cassandra glared at Christos. "Who the fuck are you?"

Christos put a protective arm around me. "I'm her boyfriend. Who are you?"

Boyfriend? Had I missed something?

Cassandra didn't know how to answer Christos' question. Her face wrestled with itself. Eventually she puzzled out an answer. "Stupid bitch was checking out my man!"

Christos cocked a dimple at Cassandra. "Relax, sweetheart. She wasn't trying to steal your man. Why would she, when she's got me?"

"Yo, player. Don't be calling my lady your sweetheart," Emilio said.

The next thing I knew, Emilio and Cassandra turned to face Christos and me as a team. The surrounding dancers noticed the tension. A circle was widening around us. Great. Was I going to have to fight Cassandra while Christos fought Emilio? It would give new meaning to the phrase "fighting like cats and dogs."

"Relax, you two," Christos said calmly. "I'm not trying to take your girl, and my girlfriend's not trying to take your man."

"I see how you be looking at my woman," Emilio snarled.

"Why would I be looking at your woman when I've got my own hot girlfriend?"

"You saying my Cassandra isn't hot enough for you?" Emilio growled. "You saying your girlfriend's all that?"

What? I couldn't follow Emilio's logic.

"I didn't say it," Christos chuckled. "You did."

Cassandra turned on Emilio. She put her fists on her hips. In a low voice she said, "What did you just say?"

Emilio's eyes widened in horror.

"Nothing, baby."

"What did you just say, Emilio?"

"I didn't say anything, baby. I swear!"

"I heard you! You think this bitch is hotter than I am? You do, don't you!"

"No, Cassandra! I swear!"

"You do!"

I was dumbfounded. Christos had just turned Emilio and Cassandra on each other. Cat-Clawed Cassandra had been ready to slice my eyes out mere seconds ago. Now she had her sights set on her own boyfriend!

Cassandra erupted like a swollen volcano. She started slapping at Emilio like a psycho hyena. He ran into the crowd of dancers, all of whom had stopped to watch the drama. Cassandra chased him across the deck, hot on his heels.

Emilio dodged around a group of people standing near the pool. He tripped and plunged headlong into the water. Cassandra dove in after him without a second thought.

"Get back here, Emilio! I always knew you were a dog!" She thrashed in the water, trying to reach him. Her pile of hair clung to her head like a wet mop.

He dog-paddled away from her as fast as he could.

"Come back here! Emilio!"

The crowd laughed at the crazy duo.

"If I get my hands on you, Emilio, I'm going to cut your balls off!"

I stifled my laughter.

Christos chuckled. He smiled at me and squeezed my arm. "You okay?"

"How the hell did you do that! It was like a freaking Jedi mind trick!"

"You ever hear that old martial arts thing about using your enemy's force against them?"

"Uh, I guess."

"That chick had more jealousy than everyone in this party combined. All I had to do was point it away from you, toward her boyfriend. The rest took care of itself."

Christos cocked his chin toward the pool, where Emilio was climbing out of the shallow end while Cassandra slogged through water nearly to her neck. She was really short.

I turned back to Christos. "But I still don't get why she was so jealous. What was she so worried about?"

"Are you serious?" Christos scoffed. "When was the last time you looked in a mirror?"

I didn't follow. I shrugged my shoulders.

"You're easily the hottest girl at this party."

I laughed. "No I'm not." The truth was, Cassandra was really good looking, despite how much of a bitch she was to me. She didn't need to worry about me stealing any men.

Christos grinned and shook his head. "You need to get your eyes checked. That poor girl was totally jealous of your looks."

"That doesn't make any sense."

"It does to me."

The people around us had tired of watching the spectacle of Emilio and Cassandra dripping by the poolside, and had gone back to dancing.

"Wanna dance?" Christos asked.

"Sure."

The music suddenly changed to a slow song. Christos swept me into his arms and stared into my eyes. Had Cupid picked out the playlist?

My hands pressed lightly against Christos' rock hard chest. I had intended to put my arms up in protest, but now I felt his chest muscles flexing beneath his shirt. Wrong move on my part.

I wanted to lean my cheek against his chest, but resisted the urge. So I slid my arms around his muscled back. Another wrong move.

He pulled me close. I was enveloped in his arms, protected from everything in the world. I looked up at him. He gazed at me through his thick lashes. Hadn't we just been here earlier today?

The entire frontside of my body pressed against his. His pelvis pressed gently into mine. I started to throb downstairs. Tingling sensations fluttered out from my thighs and swam up my spine. My breasts pressed against the tops of his rippled abs. I pulled myself into him tightly. Surprised by my own boldness, I glanced up at him, expecting rejection.

He gazed down at me. A slow smile stretched across his lips. I so wanted to lick them. I think he read my mind, because his tongue slid out from his mouth and glided across his luscious lower lip.

Heat flared in my chest and flowed up to my face. I needed him to kiss me. I tilted my head back and parted my lips with a sigh. My eyelashes fluttered in anticipation.

He leaned toward me. His eyes suddenly blinked and he frowned. "We can't do this." He pulled away and released me from his arms.

"What?"

"I'm your mentor, Samantha. Not your boyfriend."

Hello, rejection. I was surprised to hear him say that after he'd defended my honor in front of Cassandra and Emilio by calling us boyfriend and girlfriend. But that was just a ruse he'd used to diffuse the situation. He hadn't really meant it.

I wasn't sure if I was supposed to be hurt or angry. Or feel nothing at all.

I wanted to run away. I wanted to stay. Then I remembered what I'd overheard Jake saying in the house. Was it possible that Christos had my best intentions in mind? That he wanted to help me become an artist, not just hook up with me like he did with all his other girlfriends?

I was disappointed on some level. I know I'd seen genuine desire in his eyes. For a moment. I wanted that fleeting feeling to last forever. But on the other hand, I'd never had someone devote themselves to helping me realize my dreams beyond an accountant's career.

Which was more important to me?

Art mentor or hot boyfriend? A career I actually wanted, or this amazing man? Could I have both? Or would a relationship interfere with the coaching?

This sucked. I can honestly say I couldn't decide. My mom would've said I wanted to have my cake and eat it too. What the hell did that even mean? Who served up cake then told everyone not to eat it? That never happened in real life. Screw you, Mom.

I wanted both.

Christos had a pained look on his face. He wasn't going to let me eat his damn cake.

"I need some air," I said, backing away. I turned and squeezed past the other couples before he could follow me.

I stumbled into the house and wandered from room to room. Tears ran from my eyes. I thought I could stop them, but it was impossible. Christos rejecting me hurt way too much.

Eventually, I found Madison. She was making out in a dark hallway with Jake.

"Can you take me home?" I begged tearfully.

Madison broke off her kiss with Jake. "What's wrong, Sam? What happened?"

"I need to go. I'm sorry, Jake. I really need Mads to take me home."

Jake and Madison exchanged a concerned look. "No problem, Sam," he said. "Take care of her, Mads."

Madison grabbed her purse from Jake's room and walked me to her car. Fortunately, she wasn't parked in by all the cars on the street.

"What happened, Sam?"

"It was Adonis."

Madison's brows cinched together. "What did he do to you? That guy is such a player. I knew he was going to hurt you!"

"Samantha!" Christos came running up to us. "There you are!"

"Get the hell out of here, asshole!" Madison glowered. "Haven't you done enough damage already?" Madison shot him a warning glare.

Christos stopped short.

"No, Mads," I said. "It's okay. You don't understand."

"Samantha, we weren't finished," he said, exasperated. "I wanted to tell you—"

"There you are, asshole!" Emilio shouted, strutting down the driveway, still damp from his dip in the pool. "Cassandra broke up with me and left me here, yo. If your ho girlfriend hadn't been up in my shit, none of this would've happened. It's your fucking fault."

Emilio had two friends with him. Both looked equally unruly and pissed off.

"Easy, bro," Christos said calmly. "I don't have time for this right now. We can work it out later."

"We're working it out now, mother fucker." Emilio stepped in and swung downward at Christos' head with a massive fist.

Christos swiftly side-stepped and grabbed Emilio by the wrist with one hand while pushing against the back of Emilio's elbow with his open palm. He pivoted and flung Emilio into the door of a parked car. Head first.

Emilio dropped like rocks.

Madison and I exchanged a look of surprise.

Emilio's two friends stopped in their tracks, shocked looks on their faces. Emilio was bigger than both of them. Neither of them were remotely as big as Christos.

"Get the fuck out of here, or you're next," Christos warned. "Take your friend with you."

Emilio groaned on the ground.

One of the friends reached into his pocket.

"Whatever the fuck you're reaching for in your pocket, stop right now," Christos growled. He advanced a step toward the guy. "Or I will break your fucking arm."

The guy stopped. "It's cool man. Just my car keys."

Christos glared at him. "Take them out slowly. With your fingers."

The guy tweezed his keys out of his pocket with his index finger and thumb. He jingled them for everyone to see. "See? Just keys."

"All right, get your shit out of here."

The two friends helped a dazed Emilio stand up. Blood dribbled from Emilio's nose. They put his arms over their shoulders and walked him into the darkness.

"What. The Hell. Just happened?" Madison asked, mouth agape.

"I have no idea," I said. I started to laugh. I think I was releasing the tension. Madison joined in. We both looked at Christos.

He shrugged his shoulders. "Don't look at me. I swear I had nothing to do with their breakup. That guy brought it all on himself. His girlfriend was a peach."

"Am I missing something?" Madison asked.

"I'll tell you later," I said.

Madison looked from me to Christos. "Are you two okay? Do I need to intervene?"

I smiled at Christos. "No, we're good. Can we have some privacy, Mads?"

"Talk amongst yourselves," Madison said, flicking her splayed fingers. "I'll be inside if you need me." She went into the house.

"I wanted to explain myself," Christos said. "Back there."

I looked at him and arched my brows. "Please continue."

"Samantha, you're a gorgeous young woman. There's no denying that."

I blushed and tilted my chin down, trying to hide. But I gazed up at him shyly from beneath my brows.

"The thing is, I don't want anything developing between us getting in the way of my mentoring you."

"It's not getting in the way."

"Not right now, but it could. I don't want that to…" He trailed off. His eyes narrowed and he peered over my shoulder.

"What?"

"Get down. Now." He shoved me to my knees.

"Christos! What are you doing!" When I recovered my balance, I twisted and saw a car stop in the street at the end of the driveway. Emilio and his friends. The windows were rolled down. One of the friends leaned out of the back seat with a gun.

Christos dove on top of me. "Get down!" We rolled behind a car on the driveway.

I heard five pops and then the engine rev. Tires screeched and the car sped off.

"Are you okay? Did you get shot?" Christos asked desperately.

"I don't know, I don't know!"

Madison, Jake, and several other people came running out of the house. They were all yelling.

"What the fuck!" Jake shouted.

"Somebody shot someone!" a random person cried.

"Sam!" Madison screamed. She ran up to me. "Sam! Are you okay?"

"I don't know. I…I think so."

"Dude, are you all right?" Jake asked Christos.

"Yeah, man. I gotta get the fuck outta here. The cops are going to be all over this place in a couple minutes."

"Okay, bro. Go."

Christos looked at me. "Are you okay?" He looked all over my body. "You're not shot, are you?"

"I don't think so."

"Madison," he said, looking right at her. "Make sure she's okay. I have to go. Now."

She nodded.

"Wait! Why are you leaving!" I cried. "You didn't do anything! They shot at us!"

"I have to go, Samantha." Obvious panic strained his face.

He stood before I could stop him and sprinted down the street to his car. I heard his tires screech, and I'm pretty sure he drove in the opposite direction of Emilio's car, At least he wasn't chasing them.

So why was he running? I gave Jake a pleading look. "Why did he leave?"

Jake shook his head. I wasn't getting any information from him.

Madison slapped Jake's arm. "What the fuck, Jake! What just happened? Why did Adonis run like that?"

Jake didn't answer. Madison started slapping at him like crazy.

"Madison! Stop!" I pulled her off of Jake. "He didn't do anything."

"It's his stupid party! You almost got shot!" Madison clapped her hands to her face and started bawling.

Jake put an arm around her and she leaned into him. He looked at me. "Are you okay, Sam?"

My adrenalin was still going, but I was pretty sure I wasn't shot. My knees felt tender, probably skinned from when Christos pushed me down, despite the protection of my jeans.

"I'll take you home," Jake said.

"I'll do it," Madison said. "Just give me a few minutes."

"You guys should go now, before the cops get here."

"You're right." The same inner confidence I'd discovered I had in situations like this took control. "I'll drive."

"What?" Madison asked through a mask of tears. "You can't drive!"

"You can't either. Don't worry, I'll be fine. Let's go." We climbed into her car and drove off.

The only thing on my mind was the fact that the only two people who had seen the shooting were Christos and myself. With him gone, I didn't want to be there when the cops showed up and started asking questions.

After Christos' arrest in the SDU parking lot at the beginning of the school year, I suspected it was for the best.

I had been right all along.

Christos really was trouble.

I drove Madison's car back toward my apartment. We didn't talk much. I think we were both in shock.

When we got close, I asked, "Do you want to hang with me for awhile at my place? Or go back to Jake's?"

"Do you want me to? I'm sure Jake's place is a nightmare right now."

"I wouldn't mind the company." I turned into the small parking lot of my apartment building.

Christos was leaning against his car.

"Oh," I said surprised. I noticed Madison scrutinizing my reaction. "On second thought, maybe I should leave you with Adonis."

I parked in my space. "Sorry. He looks like he wants to talk."

"Are you going to be all right?" She rested her hand on my forearm protectively and gave me a concerned big sister look.

"Yeah, as long as no one shoots at us," I said half-seriously. Why did I fear regular shootings were an actual possibility with Christos around? Maybe I was better off with him as only my mentor.

"You'll be fine." Madison patted my arm. We both got out and she climbed in the driver's seat.

I walked over to Christos. Madison rolled down her window when she got her car turned around. "Keep her safe," she said to Christos.

"Don't worry, I won't let anything hurt her."

"You better not." Madison waved and drove off.

As I stared into his blue eyes, the entire world fell away. In that moment, I believed the only thing that might actually hurt me was Christos.

"What happened back there?" I asked. "Why'd you run away?"

He put his hands on my shoulders. "We need to talk. Can we do it inside?"

I didn't like the sound of that. "Okay."

We went upstairs to my apartment. I was suddenly grateful for cleaning earlier. Women's intuition is rarely wrong. I let us in the front door. "Do you want anything to drink?"

"Water's fine."

I filled a glass from the water jug in my fridge.

I joined him on the couch. "So. The car chase? You didn't follow those guys, did you?"

"What? No way. I came straight here."

"You did?"

"I figured this was the next logical place to find you, after Jake's."

"You waited for me?"

"Of course." He threw back the water glass and downed all of it.

"Do you want some more?"

"Please."

I got up and poured him another glass.

"Look, Samantha. About what I said. About the mentoring." He swallowed more water.

"Yeah?" I said hopefully. All I wanted in that moment was for him to tell me he been wrong, that he could be my mentor *and* more.

"I meant it."

Fuck. I jinxed myself.

"I was going to reiterate what I've already said. Samantha, you're very talented at art. You don't see it yet, but I do. You have more potential than you realize, and I don't want anything to stop you from developing that."

I wanted to tell him it wasn't his decision to make, but I kept my mouth shut.

"I've heard the way you grouse about accounting with Romeo. And how you envy Kamiko's talent, yet she's pre-med. I think you're right about her. She could probably be a successful comic book artist."

"Yeah, she's amazing. I'd hate to see her throw away her talent because her parents wanted her to be a doctor."

"Exactly. I feel the same way about you. You can be a successful artist, Samantha. I know it. You don't have to be a comic artist like Kamiko, but there's lots of options. I don't want you to give up on your dreams, under any circumstances."

"I wasn't planning to." He was being so supportive. What was I supposed to say? "Does this mean we can still be friends?"

"Always."

"What if our friendship starts to develop into something, you know, more?" I asked hopefully.

He ran his hand through his hair. "I don't want you to get distracted. If you and I, if we...if we have anything more than a strictly platonic mentor relationship, you're not going to get anything done. I can't let that happen."

"It doesn't have to be that way, Christos."

He clenched his jaws and leaned his elbows on his knees. A black look shadowed his face. "You're not getting it Samantha. It's more than that." He stood up abruptly and circled around the coffee table.

He started waving his arms, like he was making a case in front of a jury.

"I'm a bad influence, Samantha. I'm shitty all the way around. I have a tendency to fuck things up, even when I set out with the best intentions."

Taylor.

"We all do, sometimes." I consoled.

"The thing is, I know I can help you if I'm nothing more than a mentor. I'm confident I won't fuck that up. Like teaching the kids at the library. I promised myself I would never let them down. Now, it turns out, maybe I have."

"What do you mean?"

He stopped and looked me in the eyes. His jaw worked like he was considering something. "That's another issue. Don't worry about it. It's not your problem."

Okay, now I was scared. How did you let down a bunch of kids taking a free class at a library? You had to do something pretty bad. I shuddered and held my elbows. I was getting ahead of myself.

"I don't want to let you down, Samantha. The mentoring thing I can do. For now. I know that. But beyond that, I can't make you any promises. Trust me on this. Things will get messy down the road. I don't want to drag you into the shit storm that is my life."

"What are you talking about? I don't understand." From the outside, his life seemed pretty damn good to me. Most of the time he acted like he didn't have a care in the world. Was it all an act?

"I can't go into it."

"Please, Christos. Whatever it is, you can tell me. I won't judge you."

"I hope that's true." He stared at me for a long time. Desperation darkened his eyes. He turned away.

I could tell he was hurting. I stood up and went to him.

He turned away, hiding his face.

"Christos, look at me." I reached up and placed my palm on his cheek and turned his eyes toward mine. "You can tell me anything."

He was on the verge of tears. In that moment, he looked like a wounded child. What had happened to this poor boy?

"I have a whole lot of problems you know nothing about. I don't want you getting dragged into them."

"Like what?"

He squeezed his eyes shut, holding back tears. I couldn't believe it. Christos never struck me as the type of man to cry. "Some serious shit." He shook his head, like he was trying to make his problems go away, but he couldn't. His face slowly hardened into tortured calmness, a restless attempt to force down tremendous pain. I knew the look from personal experience. Sometimes it mocked me from the mirror ten days out of ten.

"Forget about it," he said in an even tone. "I want you focused on yourself. Your life can be better, even if mine is spun out."

Without thinking, I wrapped my arms around him and hugged him fiercely. "It's okay, Christos. It's okay." I smelled his cologne, his skin, and his vulnerability. It was an intoxicating combination. My head spun.

He shook, as if the defenses he'd put up were falling again. Was it because his pain was too great to hold in? I could relate. Or was it something else?

I felt his hand cradle the back of my head and stroke my hair. He lowered his chin to my head and inhaled my scent.

I looked up at him. His expression was completely different. The sense of unrest and agony was gone. It was truly calm. In that moment, I felt his heart open to me completely. Yet I had no idea what was going on inside his head. But that didn't matter. His lids lowered. His face tilted toward mine.

He ran his hand across my cheek then slid it behind my neck. I arched my neck back and my lips parted. My eyes narrowed expectantly for the second time that night.

His eyes pressed closed and a pained expression tightened his features. He touched his forehead to mine. "I can't, Samantha. I won't do this to you."

I don't know how, but I felt his heart slam shut at that exact moment. My old vow that I would never grieve when a man pushed me away was on the verge of breaking. That scared me more than anything else. I wanted to cry.

My arms quivered while I hugged him as tightly as possible, trying to restrain my tears, trying to force his heart back open. It wasn't working. Not because I wasn't trying. He went rigid in my arms; tense, defensive, guarded.

I don't know how long I held him before I ran out of energy and my arms relaxed. He put his hands on my shoulders and gently separated us.

He took my hands in his. "Can we agree to keep this a friendly, totally platonic, mentor-student thing? And nothing more?"

I barely had the energy to speak. I had used every ounce of it trying to force his heart back open.

He waited for my answer.

I was afraid to respond. If I said yes, I was shutting a door I didn't want to close. If I said no, I feared he might leave my life forever.

Neither choice was appealing.

But something was better than nothing.

I slumped my shoulders. "Yes." I felt defeated.

After Christos left, I crawled into bed. I considered calling Madison, but I didn't think she could help. There was still too much about me she didn't know, and I wasn't prepared to tell her, no matter how close we had become. I considered a late night jog, but I was physically exhausted from the night's adrenalin drain.

I considered my stash of ice cream in the freezer, but the thought alone churned my stomach in nauseating flips and flops.

I twisted up into my covers and cried myself to sleep. At least I could mourn in private.

I repeatedly dreamt of the haunted look I'd seen so clearly in Christos' eyes when he alluded to his secret problems.

I knew all about secret problems.

Taylor.

I didn't sleep well at all.

Chapter 14

I didn't see Christos on campus the week after the party. I think he was avoiding me. When I called him, it always went to voicemail. When I texted him, he always replied back with the same message:

I'll c u Saturday. 1pm. Bring sketchbook, pencils. Wear comfortable shoes.

I suppose it could have been worse. What was with the shoes?

By the middle of the week, the separation was driving me crazy. I decided to throw myself a pity party over lunch with Romeo and Kamiko. Fish Tacos always made me feel better.

They had already heard about the shooting at Jake's party. Word was all over campus. The topic wasn't willing to die a quick death.

"I've been working up a design for a fashionable bullet proof vest for you, Samantha. Want to see it?" Romeo joked.

"So not funny, Romeo," Kamiko said.

I took a bite of my fish taco and immediately felt the tension in my stomach subside. At least food still had the power to quell my discomfort. I'd eaten through all my remaining ice cream at home over the last several evenings.

"What?" Romeo looked hurt. "She needs one! After Jake's party? Where was it, Sam? Behind enemy lines?"

"It was random, Romeo. Nobody at the party knew who those guys were. They must have crashed it."

"How many cops showed up?"

"I don't know. Mads said there were like ten cars."

"Sounds exciting."

I could tell Romeo was trying to make light of the whole thing, but it wasn't really working. "It wasn't, Romeo. They shot at us. It was not an adventure."

Kamiko threw him a glare.

Romeo's normally impish face calmed into seriousness for once.

"I'm sorry. You're right. I shouldn't be joking about this. I think in reality, it scares the shit out of me. You could've been hurt. I wouldn't want that to happen."

"It's okay, Romeo. I get it. It was pretty traumatic."

Romeo brightened again. "So, when do you see Adonis again? He seems to have disappeared."

I hadn't told them about the new boundaries laid down by Christos. They'd been pestering me for news all week. I decided to put it out in the open. "He said we should restrict our relationship to strictly mentoring."

"What?" Kamiko was shocked. "You guys make such a cute couple!"

"Not anymore. But I'm meeting him on Saturday for another session. That's all I know. Can we change the subject? Kamiko, how was the latest episode of Adventure Time?"

That was sufficient to steer the conversation clear of more talk about me and Christos.

"I've decided I want to marry Finn the Human," she giggled.

"You're perfect for each other," Romeo laughed.

Maybe if I watched more cartoons like Kamiko, I wouldn't be so depressed about everything.

No, I just needed to stock up on more ice cream on the way home.

On Saturday, I threw on whatever clean clothes were on the top of my drawers. I considered dressing to impress, but I knew Christos would see right through it. So it was t-shirt and jeans.

I wanted to maintain the formality of the relationship and honor the boundaries he'd set down. If things disintegrated, it wouldn't be because of me.

If my shirt was a little too form-fitting and the scoop neck revealed too much cleavage, it was entirely by accident. I swear.

I drove to his house and arrived early. I don't know if I was hoping for some extra social time with Christos or not. I worried we wouldn't have snacks afterward like we had before. But if I was there early, we could chat for a bit before we started. Or so I told myself.

Luckily, no black Mercedes, but his motorcycle was there. I'd feared Tiffany would be in residence again, posing for her portrait.

Now that I knew she was only there for the painting, I was okay with it. But I still didn't want to run into her.

I rang the doorbell. No answer. Loud music drifted outside. Maybe he hadn't heard. I tried knocking. There was so much bass pumping out of the house, maybe it blocked out my knocking. It was a pretty big house.

According to my phone, it was five after one. Maybe he was busy in the studio, working to his tunes, and was caught up in what he was doing.

I tried the door. It was open. I paused on the threshold, wondering if I was making a mistake.

Screw it.

I walked into the house.

The music thumped in the living room. No wonder he couldn't hear me. Then I saw the rollerblades on the floor in the foyer. Two pairs.

I crept into the living room. Christos was on top of someone on the couch. Naked. Two perfect long legs wrapped around his waist. Perfect Paisley.

I watched Christos' tattooed shoulders flexing and relaxing. His perfect ass rose and fell languorously. Every thrust stabbed my heart. My face knotted into a scowl.

Paisley released a throaty moan. She was certainly enjoying herself. "Harder," she begged.

He grunted, and fulfilled her.

Their wordless wails blended together as they worked toward conclusion. Christos' back muscles glistened and writhed.

"Yes!" Paisley cried in ecstatic release.

I was in turmoil. I envied Paisley more than I was willing to admit to myself. I should've learned my lesson not to snoop after Tiffany.

I was a slow learner when it came to Christos, and good at self-inflicted misery.

Christos groaned with intense pleasure.

Time for me to go. Why had I waited so long? Rubber-necking, I guess. Everyone stops to watch a train wreck.

Luckily, they hadn't heard me. I backed up as quietly as possible and let myself out.

Now I knew why he told me to wear comfortable shoes. So I

could bolt when I realized what an asshole he was.

I drove home. My eyes were dry. I stood by my promise to never shed tears for assholes.

What was with Christos? Make that stupid Adonis. He was available to all other women except me? I don't know what the hell they were doing on that stupid couch together, but I'm sure it wasn't mentoring. Because mentoring didn't include what he was doing with Paisley, or whoever the bitch was. Not that I cared.

Men made absolutely no sense. Was this that stupid Madonna-Whore thing? Was I some kind of sweet innocent object of purity to him? Was he objectifying me in the reverse? Did he think I was too good to touch? Meanwhile, all the whores got to really have him?

And all I got was art instruction?

I'm sure my parents would be happy to hear it. They'd probably pat him on the back and tell him what a great guy he was for preserving my maidenhood. They sure thought I was the Madonna type.

But I didn't want to be innocent and virtuous and pure. I wanted excitement in my life. I didn't want to be a whore, but I didn't want to be a virgin either.

Somebody hand me a hot poker! I was ready to kill myself.

At 1:15pm, he texted me.

Where r u? The kids r waiting 4 us at the library. Need 2 head over soon.

Shit. I forgot all about them in the hurricane of hatred I'd felt toward Christos.

A few minutes later, another text.

I don't want 2 let the kids down. They're going 2 miss u.

Why'd he have to pull the guilt card? Damn him. I texted back:

Meet u at the library at 1:30.

I got in my car and drove back to his side of town. Bastard. I was doing it for the kids, not Christos.

When I walked into the library, Christos was already in the room, helping the kids. I thought of him as Christos and not Adonis because how could I hate a guy who was so devoted to helping out children?

By the end of the hour, my foul mood had subsided. I got into helping the kids out, and had a great time. I loved how they did that.

I hadn't made up my mind what I would do afterward. Would I go back with Christos to the studio? Or go home?

When the last kid had left, it was just me and Christos. We stood on opposite sides of the room from each other.

"Are you ready to do some drawing back at the studio?" he asked.

"I should probably go." The only problem was that he blocked the door, and I had to pass him.

"Is something bothering you?" He must not have known I had seen him on the couch. "You looked all broken up about something when you came in earlier."

"I did not!" I denied. Maybe I had. Why was I shouting?

"It's about the mentoring thing, isn't it? Is that still bothering you?"

"It's not that. I should really go." I walked toward him, wishing he'd move away from the door. "Excuse me." Why did his shoulders have to be so broad? He was blocking my escape.

"Whatever it is, we can talk about it. Let's go up to the studio. I'll make you something to eat."

"Did you make Paisley something to eat?" I hissed.

"Hello, Samantha," Mrs. Elders said, standing in the doorway. "Another successful day of art class, I hope?"

"Ah, yeah. It was great." I smiled at her.

"I love how the two of you work so well together. You make a great team. The kids love you both."

A broad grin widened Christos' mouth. His dimples came out from behind the clouds.

I hated Mrs. Elders. For a minute, anyway.

Christos had walked, so I drove us up to his house.

He got out of the car. "Are you coming inside?"

"Not until you explain a few things."

He sat back in the car. "Okay."

"What the hell was that?"

"Paisley?"

"It was her, wasn't it."

He grabbed the suicide handle over the door window. His knuckles tightened to white. "Yes."

"How could you?"

"How could I what?"

"Do I have to spell it out?"

He took a deep breath. "Sam, I thought we went over this."

Sam? Why was he calling me Sam? What happened to Samantha? Now I was angry and scared. "What, me catching you screwing one of your many girlfriends? How is that part of the mentor-student relationship?"

"First of all, how the hell did you know I was with Paisley today? She left before you showed up. I was watching the clock."

How to explain that? That I'd snuck in his house, before I was supposed to be there?

"Did you walk in on us?"

Whoops. "Maybe," I said sheepishly.

"I hate to sound like a parent here, but someone has to. Normally, people knock first, or ring a doorbell. You have no one to blame but yourself on this one."

"But you were having sex with her! Weren't you?"

"So what if I was? It's my private life. Not yours. It shouldn't matter to you what I do in my spare time."

"But it does matter!" I turned to him, my eyes wet. Stupid tears. How did he do this to me? I hated him. Or the opposite.

He released the suicide handle and turned to me. "Look, Samantha, I'm sorry you saw us. I don't want you to get hurt." He touched my hand, which rested on the center console. "I so don't want you to get hurt. Ever. That's why I said what I did about only mentoring you."

I thought about that Madonna-Whore thing again. "It's not for you to decide," I argued. "If I get hurt, that's my problem."

"I don't like where this is going, Samantha."

"I don't either! In fact, I hate where it's going!" I sat back in a huff, folding my arms across my chest.

He sighed again. "Look. I've got a lot of work to do after you leave today. We're not going to fix this right now. Can we just get to work on your drawing? And talk about this another time? I meant what I said before about making your art instruction a priority. I'm not changing that."

Why did he have to be so damn handsome while sounding so reasonable?

"Fine," I pouted. "Let's go." I was settling for what I could get from him. I wasn't sure if I should hate myself for being so pathetic.

But he *was* trying to mentor me. Not get in my pants. Why did that sound reversed and mixed up to me? Groan.

We climbed out of my VW and went inside.

Christos went upstairs to change while I waited in the living room, admiring his grandfather's landscape paintings.

One of them hung over the mantle, and I wanted to get a better look. A collection of family photos on the mantle distracted me.

Some of the pictures were older and showed Spiridon with dark hair. He looked very much like Christos did now. Another photo showed Spiridon with a young man. The family resemblance was clear. The young man was obviously Nikolos, Christos' dad. I remembered Spiridon mentioning his name the day we'd met.

Nikolos held a baby in one photo. Little Christos. He smiled proudly, projecting the proud father thing perfectly.

More photos documented the years as Christos grew into a boy. His loving father always had an arm around him, or was tickling him and making funny faces. I couldn't imagine a happier pair. I saw something in Christo's dad's body language that I'd never seen in my own father. Relaxed, affectionate joy. In simplest terms, happiness.

In that moment I envied Christos' relationship with his father far more than I envied Paisley earlier, when I saw Christos on top of her. There was a chronolgy of love depicted in the Manos family photos I had never experienced in my own family.

I looked at more photos and noticed Nikolos was suddenly absent from the rest. Teenaged Christos was only pictured with his grandfather Spiridon from that point forward. What happened to his dad?

Then it occurred to me: there were no photos of Christos' mom. Not a single one.

What was that about?

"You ready?' Christos hollered. I heard him trundling down the stairs.

I felt like I was invading his privacy by scrutinizing his family photos without permission. I moved over to a painting on the opposite wall.

Christos walked into the living room wearing a tank top, surf shorts, and sport sandals. He looked like the consummate beach bum. His tan, chiseled chest, shoulders, and tattooed arms were free for the world (and me) to adore. How did he expect me to get any drawing done with him dressed like this? He was crazy, but I already knew that.

He glanced at my feet. "I see you remembered the shoes."

I wore my cross trainers. "Yeah, what do I need them for?"

"Hiking."

"Aren't we going to draw?"

Christos held up a small sketchbook and pencil. "You ready?"

"Where are we going?"

"To look at beauty." He grabbed a water bottle on the way out, and I pulled my backpack with my sketchbook out of my car.

There was a small trailhead a few blocks from the house. It led up into the hills. We hiked for about twenty minutes straight up the hill. The weather was perfect. Warm, sunny, a cool breeze. In November! San Diego rocked.

Eventually we stopped in a small clearing with a handmade wooden bench that overlooked the ocean. The back was curtained off by a variety of shrubs and small trees. Christos sat on the bench and patted the open space next to him. "Join me."

There wasn't much room. I took off my backpack and sat down reluctantly. The view was spectacular.

"This is beauty." He said it with no hint of sarcasm.

"This place is amazing! It's like a secret grotto or something. You must come up here all the time."

"I do."

Something about the view was...familiar. "Why do I feel like I've been here before?"

"Because you have."

"No I haven't," I scoffed.

"Remember my grandpa's painting at the museum?" He nodded in the direction to my left.

It had been awhile. "Uh..."

"Imagine storm clouds."

"Oh, I see it! This is where he painted that beautiful landscape, isn't it?"

"Yup. Shrouded Paradise. The weather was a tad bit worse that day."

"I'll say. It's gorgeous right now." I inhaled the clean ocean air.

"Shall we draw?" He pulled out his sketchbook.

I watched his fingers work delicately. Those hands had punched people out. They were so strong and manly, and yet sensitive. Such a contrast.

I unzipped my backpack and took my sketchbook and several new pencils out.

Christos drew with this ragged little golf-looking pencil. It seemed an inadequate tool for the job. But within a few minutes, he'd roughed out a small sketch of the view.

It looked half-finished already. "Wow, Christos. I can't get over how good you are."

He didn't respond. His brow furrowed in concentration while he continued drawing. A lock of hair dangled from his forehead. It kept bouncing, but he didn't seem to notice. I wanted to smooth it back with my hand. I shifted uncomfortably in my seat instead. Better start drawing, before I did something with that lock of hair that I regretted.

I perused the view. It really was gorgeous. I began sketching long lines, like I had been taught.

A few minutes later, Christos set his sketchbook down. His drawing was finished, and it looked amazing. He stared thoughtfully at the view.

I kept drawing.

Eventually he picked up his sketchbook, turned to a new page, and swiveled on the bench to face me. One of his legs rested on the bench. His knee brushed up against my thigh. He started drawing, glancing back and forth between his sketchbook and me.

I put my pencil down. "What are you doing?"

"I told you we came up here to look at beauty. So I'm drawing beauty." Dimples appeared.

I grinned back. "I thought you meant the view."

"The view looks good from here." He curled his lopsided smile.

What was he doing? I thought we were supposed to be mentor and mentee. Nothing more. He wasn't making this easy on me. Was he testing me? "Are you drawing me?"

"Maybe," he said coyly.

"Can I see it?"

"No," he smiled.

Without thinking, I grabbed for his sketchbook. He leaned back, out of reach.

"Lemme see!"

He chuckled, and sketched more quickly.

I tried to lean over to look, but he stood up and backed away. I followed him and tried to get behind him to see. The curiosity was killing me.

He stood at the edge of the small clearing, near a steep drop off, facing me so I couldn't see the drawing. I feinted left, then went right, but he dodged me, the sketchbook held just out of my reach.

When I stopped myself, my foot slipped and I lost my balance. It was then that I noticed that the hillside drop-off was substantial. Almost a cliff. I flailed my arms and tried to regain my footing. I twisted, trying to lower my center of gravity back onto the level ground. But I was falling anyway.

Strong arms wrapped around my ribcage. Christos pulled me into his body. I flung my arms around...his ass.

My face was right in his crotch.

My first thought was that it would be better if he simply dropped me to my death. Because I was ready to die of embarrassment. This was no way for a mentee to behave toward her mentor!

He leaned back and pulled me so that I slid up his chest. My breasts dragged across the thin material of his t-shirt. I could feel his abs. Oh, damn.

My nipples tightened in response. Now my breasts compressed against his chest. Fortunately my bra shielded my nipples from detection. I hoped. Because our close proximity was not exactly helping with my embarrassment. At least now my face leaned against his rock hard chest.

I heard his heart pounding in his ribcage, matching rhythm with mine. Was he as scared as I was? I reminded myself to breathe. Seems I'd forgotten to do it since he'd grabbed me.

I closed my eyes and inhaled. I smelled a combination of fresh laundry and man. It was exquisite. The scent seeped into my body and a tingling sensation rained down my thighs to my toes. I sighed. It was a good feeling. I thought I might take a moment to enjoy it. Squeezing my arms tightly around his muscled back, I embraced him.

I didn't want to let go.

Neither did Christos. I peered up into his eyes. He gazed back at me through half-lidded eyes. I saw distinct concern in his azure gemstones. I felt his hand stroke the back of my head. My hair was up in a pony tail, otherwise I sensed he would've run his hands through it.

"You almost fell," he murmured.

I blinked several times. "You caught me."

He slid his palm across my cheek and ran his thumb across my bottom lip. I didn't want him to stop touching me. Ever.

My lips parted and my eyes narrowed in response to the whirlwind of ecstasy emanating from his touch. I felt heat swim out from my core. My legs shook. It wasn't the adrenalin from almost falling. It was Christos. I wanted him to kiss me. Badly.

His eyes clamped shut. Sighing deeply, he touched his forehead gently to mine. "We can't do this."

I looked up at him. *Please, kiss me. Please.*

He straightened and rubbed my back vigorously, like a parent would. I clenched my arms around him. *No.* My cheek rested against his chest.

An image of his naked butt thrusting into Paisley flashed in my mind. I broke our embrace and pulled back. I forgot that the cliff was behind me.

"Be careful," he said. "You don't want to fall again." He grabbed my shoulders, pulling me away from the edge.

My eyes flashed with anger. "What would you care anyway? I'm just your student. Or mentee, or whatever."

"No, you're not. You're more than that."

"No, I'm not! *Paisley* is more than that."

"Paisley is less than that. She's a girl I see now and then. We have an agreement. We like each other."

"You *like* her?" I shouted.

"I like a lot of people."

"But you don't like me!"

"You know that's not true. I wouldn't be doing this mentoring thing if I didn't like you. And see your potential."

"I don't care about my potential!"

"I do."

I opened my mouth to shout more, then snapped it shut. Why did he insist on being so thoughtful and reasonable and concerned?

Like my parents. That wasn't what I wanted from him. I didn't need anymore parenting than I already had. Impending tears burned my eyes.

What was this man doing to me? He was making me a total wreck.

I tried to go around him, but I was caged in his arms. "Let go of me."

He backed up a step and released me.

I considered running, but I couldn't. I noticed his sketchbook lying on the ground, so I picked it up to hand it to him. It opened in my hands to the page he'd been working on. The page had been folded part way over, but I could see that he had been drawing an incredibly realistic portrait of me. And I looked beautiful. Did I look like that? Is that how he saw me? "It's so good, Christos. I look... beautiful."

"It's easy to make you look beautiful."

"Really?"

"Really."

Why was he doing this to me? It was breaking my heart. I looked into his eyes. I wanted him more than anything I'd ever wanted. But he wouldn't give himself to me.

I did the only thing I could. If he was going to drive a wedge between us, then I was going to help him swing the hammer.

A storm of cattiness boiled up inside me. I rolled my eyes at him. "You probably take Paisley and every other girl up here to draw them, just so you can get their pants off."

"I don't."

"Are you saying you don't have to take their pants off? Because all of them drop their pants for you when they walk in the door?"

"No."

"Yes," I snarled. "Tiffany and all the girls in your paintings. You don't even have to ask them to get naked. They do it so they can be in your stupid trophy room. It probably makes them feel special." Unlike me.

I didn't have time to realize how nasty I sounded. I was too busy covering up my pain.

"They're not trophy paintings," he said quietly.

I was on a roll. I mimicked his earlier words in a snide voice, "'You're seeing their true self,' or whatever bullshit you tell yourself. And them. I'm sure they eat it up with a spoon. You take the most intimate piece of them and put it on a canvas for all the world to see. That's terrible. You're invading their privacy. It's foul."

His head hung, his expression dark and heavy.

"So why did you take me up here, anyway? So we could draw the stupid view and sit on the stupid bench?"

His nostrils suddenly flared. "Stupid? Is that what you think?"

"Yeah, it's stupid. You've probably fucked every one one of your girlfriends right here on that bench."

He shook his head. "None of them," he said hoarsely.

"None what?" I was bitchiness incarnate. I didn't know how to stop myself. It was easier being angry at *him* than feeling all the hurt and rejection that was suffocating *me*. I desperately walled my pain behind anger. If I didn't, I feared I was going to run off the cliff and dive headfirst to my death. Being dead sounded easier than feeling what was killing me in that moment.

He grit his teeth. "I haven't taken any women up here. Ever."

"Bullshit!" I spat. I was horrible.

"My grandfather has been coming up here to paint for forty years. He built that bench himself. He brought my dad up here almost every day when he was a kid. My dad brought *me* up here since I was a baby. When I was two years old, my dad put me on his lap and put a pencil in my hand and taught me how to draw. Right on this bench. This place is sacred to me. No one comes up here, except family."

My eyes goggled. I stopped myself before I could do more damage with my runaway mouth. But I was afraid it was too late.

I remembered the photos on his grandfather's mantle. The shining love between Christos and his father. What happened to his father? Christos never mentioned him. Was he dead or something?

I didn't know the answer to that, but I did know I had unwittingly trampled on Christos' precious memories of his dad.

Another thought spun my mind out of control. What did Christos mean only family came up here? I wasn't his family. Why was he calling me family?

A second later, everything collided together in my head. *Oh my god.* I realized Christos was as confused and mixed up about us as I was.

He shouldered past me and stormed down the hill before I could protest.

My stomach tightened and nausea clenched my guts.

I still held his sketchbook. "Wait! Christos!" I trotted after him.

He bounded down the trail like a jungle cat. Clouds of dust billowed behind him.

I couldn't keep up. "Christos!"

What had I done?

Not only was my pain eating away at me, it was biting into Christos. I was destroying the man I wanted because I couldn't have him.

As I jogged down the hill, I hoped that I would trip and break my neck. Unfortunately, I was so overwhelmed with emotion, I couldn't breathe. I ran out of air after a short distance and slowed to a walk.

To my dismay, I made it to the bottom without killing myself. I trudged the rest of the way to Christos' house. My legs felt like lead. My heart was even heavier.

His motorcycle was gone. I climbed into my VW and drove toward home.

Chapter 15

Back at my apartment, I grabbed a spoon and a pint of ice cream from the freezer, and collapsed on my couch with my sugary contraband.

Despite all the drama in my life since college started, I'd miraculously managed to keep my binging to a minimum thus far, compared to previous years.

Tonight, I decided to relax my rules and indulge whole hog. Pun intended.

The ice cream went down so smoothly. At first, I was consumed by the intoxicating effects of the junk food. Oh, sweet surrender. But when I was half past full, I pushed away the empty ice cream carton with disdain.

Although I'd only eaten a single pint, I was disgusted with my lack of self control, not only with my binging, but with all the horrible things I'd said to Christos.

I seriously considered dashing to the freezer and chucking all the remaining ice cream into a trash bag and running it down to the dumpster outside.

But that felt as chaotic as my binging. I did my best to calm myself. I would use will-power to make a wise choice. Not heat-of-the-moment extremism.

Hands on hips, I looked around my apartment for something, anything, to distract myself. I went into my bedroom and dug through my make up kit. Found what I was looking for at the bottom.

Black nail polish. I still had some left. I never should have stripped it off a few weeks back. But that wasn't really the point. There was something therapeutic about the application process. And once it was on, you were forced to sit and do nothing until it dried.

A form of fashion-induced straight jacketing. It was the best I could come up with on short notice.

I sat on the couch and brushed black onto my index finger.

Emo.

Shut up.

Goth

I brushed polish onto my middle finger, and paused for a moment to curl my other fingers and flip myself off.

Fuck you, from me. Fake smile. Bitch.

Witch.

So what? So fucking what? I didn't care what people called me. I had problems they couldn't begin to fathom. So I armored myself behind black.

I spread my wet nails in front of me and smiled. My old friend, isolation.

The only problem with isolation was that you had to listen to the voices inside your head.

Bitch. Slut. Whore.

I considered calling Madison. She was more than likely tied up with Jake, having a good time while I drowned in bad memories.

Tease.

Besides. I didn't want to dwell on my past. I'd had enough of it.

Taylor.

Fucking shut up! I decided to willpower my way out of this.

If I was going to reinvent myself, like I'd promised myself when I enrolled at SDU, I needed to shed the black nails and the bad memories for good. At this point, my skin was golden brown and my dishwater hair had lightened noticeably from the lemon juice rinses and all the time I'd spent in the sun with Madison. I wasn't ready to throw away all my hard work.

I dug out the acetone and wiped all of the polish off. *Fuck you, black. I ain't never going back.*

I remembered I still had Christos' sketchbook. I retrieved it from my backpack and paged through it.

His drawings were amazing. Everything he drew looked so real. He was such an incredible artist compared to me.

Despair slipped in beneath my awareness. Who was I fooling? My parents were totally right about the Accounting.

After my blow out with Christos, the mentoring was probably over. How was I going to keep making progress without his extra help?

Every phone call with my parents since the last one was more of the same. Them ramming caution down my throat.

I turned to the last drawing in his sketchbook. The one with my portrait. I folded back the crease at the bottom of the page that covered everything from the chin down.

Beneath my face, Christos had drawn a cartoon body, like one of those novelty caricature drawings you get at amusement parks. He had depicted me wearing an artist's smock, and I stood in front of an easel and canvas, holding a palette of paint in one hand, and a brush in the other. Beneath my body were block letters that read "World Famous Master Artist Samantha Smith." Below that, in cursive, "You can totally do it!"

Had he meant this as a gift?

Now I felt like a complete asshole. An immature baby. What was wrong with me? Christos was so totally supportive of my dreams. He encouraged me in a way my parents never could. They worried about getting beaten down by life. He looked upward, toward the heavens, where dreams were fulfilled.

With him gone, I was lost.

I would be right back to where I was when I left D.C.

Emo. Goth. Sorceress.

Running away when my fingers got burned.

Tease.

Running away from my pain.

Suicide Watch.

Always running away from what I knew was right.

Taylor.

That name. I had tried so hard to block it out. I hated that name. It was still dragging me down. Because of the shame. Because of the guilt.

Because of the lies. The ones I still told myself every day.

I couldn't let myself think about the truth or I would slit my wrists. Literally.

Taylor.

Every time I thought of that name, it enticed me to run away from my own life.

Taylor.

Because of the one I'd ruined.

Taylor.
It was too much.
Taylor.
It wasn't my fault.
Suicide Watch.
It was all my fault.
Tease.
I couldn't let it go. The anger, the hatred, the disrespect for basic human life.
The selfishness.
Taylor.
I grabbed my purse and car keys and ran out the front door, eyes swimming with tears. I sped down the freeway in my VW, sobbing uncontrollably, hoping I would be pulled over for speeding, or spin my car out of control into the cement column of an overpass. Anything to silence the insanity boiling through my veins.

At some point, my cell phone rang. I dug my phone out of my purse one-handed, welcoming the distraction, secretly hoping it was Christos.

"Huh, huh, hello?" I mumbled through tears.

"SAM!" Romeo squealed. "Where have you BEEN, girlfriend!!!"

I broke into more sobs. It wasn't Christos like I'd hoped. I blubbered.

"Sam? Are you humping a yak? What's that noise, Sam?" Romeo chuckled. "You're humping a yak, aren't you?"

My sobs lightened and transformed into crying and laughing.

"Did you kill the yak, Sam? Did he die of auto-erotic asphyxiation? You must be pretty good in the sack, girl."

I chuckled through snotty tears. The picture he painted seemed so morbidly comical, I couldn't take it seriously.

"Necro-bestiality is a serious crime, Sam." I could hear him grinning.

I cried a coughing laugh.

"Do you need help getting rid of the body? I know a guy who knows a guy. We can sell it as deer meat. No one will know."

I giggled.

"Tell me where you are, and don't touch anything. I'd tell you to wear gloves, but I'm thinking of that scene in Fight Club where Brad Pitt opens the door naked except for yellow rubber dish gloves. You're not wearing yellow gloves, are you?"

I sniffed. "Pink."

"Pink gloves? You are such a girl, Sam. Well, I feel for the yak, but that's not the reason I called."

"Ok."

"Kamiko and I were planning on going to a snazzy art gallery opening in La Jolla tonight. It's not yak humping, but it's a close second."

I took a deep breath. Did I want to be around more art tonight?

"They have free booze at these things. So if you see another yak at the gallery, you can get him loaded and have your way with him."

"I don't know."

"There should be girl yaks there too, if that's your thing."

I laughed. "Lesbian yak sex?"

"Hey, I don't judge."

I laughed again. I was so grateful to call Romeo a friend.

"Is that a yes?"

"Yeah."

"Hells to the yeah! I'll come by your place with Kamiko around seven. I hope you're in the mood for burgers. Non-yak, of course. Beef. Kamiko insists on In-N-Out for dinner."

"All right." I wasn't sure I'd have any appetite. I still had that pint rotting my gut. But at least I'd be out of the house.

At the next freeway offramp, I turned my car around. I drove home and took a shower. I attempted to scrub away my botched afternoon. It sort of worked, but my pain was tattooed beneath my skin. It was permanent, because it was written in blood.

Taylor.

I felt a surge of anxiety and emotion tighten my ribs. No. I pushed it down. I heard Romeo's cheerful voice gong through my head. It told me to think about yak sex.

A rudimentary smile tugged at the corners of my mouth. Shielded by memories of Romeo's zany enthusiasm, I set to putting on makeup and styling my hair down.

I dug through my closet for something appropriate for a gallery opening. I wasn't sure what Romeo meant by "snazzy" but I had some cute dresses from my D.C. goth days that would double as a little black dress in a pinch. *Look out, yaks!*

Goth. Suicide Watch.

I felt my lips quiver. I was going to cry again, and I already had my makeup on. I didn't want raccoon eyes.

Did yaks get it on with raccoons? Maybe they did. I blurted out a laugh. I would have to thank Romeo later. He and yaks would be forever linked in my mind. I considered myself lucky. Or yacky.

When I added platform heels to my outfit, I spun in front of my mirrored closet doors. I looked pretty good.

Tease.

Fuck me, would I ever be free from my past?

There was a pounding on my front door. Thank god.

"Open up! Vice squad! We're rounding up all the yak sodomites!" It was Romeo. More pounding.

"All right! I'm coming!" I yanked the door open. "Where's the fire already?"

Romeo wore an all-black version of his normal steampunk attire. "Where are you hiding the yaks, ma'am?" he asked, totally serious, his monocle pinched into place by his cheek and brow.

I could only laugh.

He looked me up and down. "Nice outfit! I didn't know you could doll yourself up like this!"

"Hey!"

"Down, girl. I was worried your beach-bum friend Madison had stolen all your fashion sensibility. You've become progressively more casual since I first met you."

"What's wrong with casual?"

"Style, darling. Style. Now let's go before you turn into a pumpkin, Cinderella!"

We went downstairs and climbed into the car, were Kamiko waited. "Wow, Sam. You look hot!"

"Thanks, Kamiko. You look pretty good yourself. You've got the whole rocker chick thing down."

"I'm supposed to be Marceline from Adventure Time."

Romeo started the car and drove toward the freeway. "Did you have to go and ruin it by telling everyone you're dressed as a cartoon character?"

"But Marceline is totally cool," Kamiko protested.

"Yes, darling, but it's cosplay."

"Give her a break, Romeo," I said. Their banter was infectious. I felt better already.

"Yeah, Romeo," Kamiko said. "You're dressed like a Jules Verne character."

"How very droll of you, Walt Disney."

"Hey," Kamiko beamed, "Disney made a movie out of Twenty Thousand Leagues Under the Sea. That's Jules Verne."

"Oh, snap! Sounds like cosplay to me!" I chided.

"Who's the cosplayer now, Romeo?" Kamiko reached into the backseat and high fived me.

We stopped at In-N-Out for burgers. Inside, Kamiko danced in line, clapping her hands and saying "Strawberry shake, strawberry shake," over and over like it was Christmas.

When we finished eating our cheeseburgers with grilled onions and extra crispy twice-cooked fries, we drove to La Jolla. I'd never been before. It was very upscale. Lots of huge houses and a trendy downtown area. That's where we found the gallery.

There was a big crowd spilling out of the gallery onto the sidewalk. Most of the people were dressed in casual evening attire. I was worried I might be over-dressed, but this wasn't the SDU college crowd. This was an entirely different scene.

Romeo led us through the front doors and straight into the middle of the crowd inside, toward the back. There were so many people in the gallery, I couldn't see any of the paintings on the walls. A string quartet played in one corner, but the noise from all the charged conversation in the room practically drowned them out.

"Who's the artist, Romeo?"

"I don't know. Some guy named Christos Manos. Kamiko says he's awesome."

WTF? How had I been snookered into this? I guess I should've told everyone Adonis was Christos when I had the chance. Now I had to deal.

Was he going to be pissed to see me here? After what I'd said? I didn't want to ruin this for him.

"Professor Childress sent out an email to the class," Kamiko said. "Didn't you get it, Sam?"

"Oh, uh, I must have missed it." How could I have missed it? And speaking of Professor Childress, he was standing right in front of us, admiring one of the paintings.

"I'm glad you three made it," he said pleasantly.

Me, Kamiko, and Romeo said hello and shook his hand nervously. It was weird seeing your professor in the real world. But he didn't seem to mind.

"I hate to say hello and goodbye," the professor said, "but I have to meet my wife for a late dinner. She's been to so many of these things, they all blur together for her."

"Oh, no problem," I said.

"But stay and enjoy the paintings. It's not every day a master artist has a showing at a San Diego gallery."

When he left, we worked our way to the back of the gallery to a bar that had a bartender serving drinks. Romeo got in line.

"I'm not twenty-one," I hissed.

"Neither am I," Romeo said. "Act older."

"How am I suppose to do that?" I wasn't used to actually ordering it, just five-fingering it.

"Act confident, like you're getting food at In-N-Out."

"What, like ask for a to-go cup?"

"No, silly. Like you do it every day."

"Vodka tonic," Romeo said to the bartender. The bartender made the drink and handed it to Romeo without a second thought.

I guess drinks were free?

"What would you like, miss?" The bartender asked.

I saw wine bottles. "I'll have white wine, thanks."

He poured me a huge glass.

"Next!"

Yup, drinks were free. Who knew? Art galleries were awesome.

Kamiko ordered while I stood next to Romeo and took several gulps of my wine. I needed to numb the confusion hammering my head. How could I possibly face Christos after what I'd said earlier? I wanted to hide.

Kamiko grabbed me and we walked around to look at the art, sipping our drinks.

Maybe we wouldn't see Christos.

The paintings were obviously Christos' work. Lots of beautiful women. But none of them were nudes. They were all clothed elegantly and posed in various impressive outdoor locations at various times of the day. Morning, sunset, night time. They all had cards on the wall next to them. The card had the name of the painting and a price. The prices ranged from $5,000 for the small ones to $25,000 for the larger ones. Many of them had red dots on the price tag.

"What do the red dots mean?" I asked.

"It means the painting has already been sold," Kamiko said.

My accounting brain took over. We'd looked at over a dozen paintings already. I added up an estimate in my head, then multiplied it by the remaining paintings in the room. "That's like five-hundred grand in paintings!" I whispered.

"The artist usually gets about half, sometimes higher, depending on how big of a name they are."

"Oh, okay, so it's only a quarter million dollars for the artist?"

Even Romeo seemed impressed. "Gosh, Kamiko, maybe you should delicately broach the subject of becoming a gallery painter to your parents. I know doctors make a lot of money, but..." He trailed off, chuckling.

"I've never done oil paintings," she said. "Not seriously, anyway. I don't know if I could do work this good."

For once, I didn't think Kamiko was being falsely modest. She was good, but Christos was on an entirely different level.

I suddenly wondered what Christos had been talking about, telling me how shitty his life was, when he told me he could only be my mentor. From everything I had seen about his life so far, he was blessed. Kissed by Lady Luck at every turn. What problems could he possibly have? It didn't make any sense to me.

We moved to the next painting.

Oh no. Tiffany Kingston-Whitehouse-Presidential-Suite, Queen of the Delta Pi Deltas, stood in front of it. She frowned when she saw me. "Hello, um...what was your name again?"

"Sam."

"That's right," she fake smiled, "I was just gonna say."

Uh huh. Sure she was.

"How do you like my painting?"

I turned to Kamiko and Romeo, hoping for an explanation. How could this be Tiffany's painting? They looked as confused as me.

I re-examined the painting. It was signed by Christos. The painting itself was of a huge deck behind a mansion. A blond woman in a bikini was stretched out elegantly on an expensive chaise, one knee up, staring out past an infinity pool into the distance.

"Adonis, I mean Christos, did a great job capturing Daddy's pool, don't you think?" Tiffany gloated.

Daddy's pool? I think the confusion glowed like Las Vegas on my face.

"This is my backyard," Tiffany clarified.

Oh. Great. Good to know. Could we leave now? Or would that be rude? I couldn't decide whether I envied Tiffany more for her obvious wealth, or the fact that Christos had painted her twice. How much time did she spend with him? A lot more than I had, or probably would be in the future. I sighed internally.

"I swear I went through twenty swimsuits before Adon—I mean Christos, helped me pick out that one. Do you like it?" she prompted.

It wasn't so much a question, but more of an order. How did Tiffany make it so easy to despise her? "It's great, Tiffany." It was, but she wasn't. Total bitch.

Kamiko and Romeo nodded silently. Kamiko was examining her drink. Romeo glanced around, scouting for an escape route.

"I told Christos to make sure I didn't look fat."

I took a closer look at the painted image of Tiffany. It didn't have the same honesty and demureness of the nude in Christos' studio. "It makes you look great." Like a bikini clad robot.

"Thanks," Tiffany giggled uncertainly. I could tell she was worried about what I thought of the painting. She probably worried what everyone thought of it. "Daddy already bought it. He insisted on it."

I glanced at the card next to the painting. The red dot was there. $25,000. Wow. Tiffany's family wasn't worried about money, that much was painfully obvious.

"My Dad wants Christos to sign the back of it to me. But I told Daddy that it should be made out to both of us, since he's paying for it. It's going to hang in our yacht."

Who hung paintings in yachts? Oh how I wished she'd shut up. She was killing me. "That's great, Tiffany."

Kamiko pulled my arm. "We should see the other paintings, don't you think?"

"Yeah. Sorry, Tiffany. We just got here and my friends really want to see everything. There's so much to look at."

"Oh, I know, right?"

I gave her a half-hearted pity wave and we soldiered onward. I felt like I'd just stepped out of a minefield. Why did every conversation I'd had with Tiffany seem so dangerous? I hoped I never found out. I wondered what her friends thought of her. I felt bad for them.

She started talking excitedly to the next group of people to stop in front of her painting. She acted like the painting's private hostess. Gag.

Once we'd given Tiffany a wide berth, we stopped at another painting.

"Do you like what you see?"

I turned to face a man I didn't recognize.

"Uh, yeah." I stammered.

He was young, but slightly older than me, probably in his late twenties. He was tall, tan, very handsome, and wore an expensive-looking satiny button-down shirt with the cuffs rolled back, and slacks. He had a long, broad shouldered, slender swimmer's body. He offered his hand. "My name is Brandon Charboneau. My father owns the gallery, but I'm overseeing the opening tonight."

I shook his hand. His hazel eyes were rather amazing, and coordinated perfectly with his chestnut brown hair. Whew, someone turn up the AC! Otherwise I would be forced to stealth-swoon where I stood.

"Charmed. And you are?"

"Oh, Samantha Smith. People call me Sam." I think my eyes sparkled, but I did my best to play it down.

"It's a pleasure to meet you, Sam." Damn, he was smooth. His voice reminded me of chocolate mousse, or some other kind of dessert, or maybe velvet. Oh boy. "Who are your friends?" He turned to Romeo and Kamiko.

Romeo was in love. I couldn't blame him. Brandon was male-model hot. Romeo fawned and blushed while introducing himself. "Hi. Romeo Fabiano." He blushed so hard, his ears turned red. Someone turn off the burner under Romeo! He was coming to a boil!

"Pleasure," Brandon smiled, but shook Romeo's hand with a

firm, manly handshake. I think that turned Romeo on even more.

Kamiko was nervous for the first time since I'd met her. Her voice quivered. "My name's Kamiko Nishimura. You have a wonderful gallery, Brandon. I'm sorry, should I call you Brandon, or Mr. Charboneau?" She giggled like a song bird. Poor thing. She didn't know what to do when she wasn't in love with a cartoon.

Brandon laughed politely. "Brandon will do fine, Kamiko. And thank you. We work hard to make Charboneau Gallery a special place."

This guy Brandon was very classy.

"Have you had a chance to enjoy the artist's work?" he asked me directly. His hazel eyes were as enchanting as his fine features.

"We just got here, but yeah, it's really good," I sipped my wine, trying to hide my nerves.

"Christos is a talented young artist. He has a perceptive eye and a confident hand. His work is far beyond his years, but with a pedigree like his, that's no surprise."

"Pedigree?" Somehow, that made Christos sound like a show dog. I didn't like that.

"Ahh, perhaps you mistook my meaning," Brandon said tactfully. "The Manos family name carries a lot of weight in the international art market. Spiridon and Nikolos both have established themselves as celebrated painters. Christos follows in their footsteps. Although they have paved the way for him, every artist must prove themselves. Christos is well on his way, I should say." I couldn't tell if this guy was *trying* to sound dashing and gentlemanly, or if he actually talked this way all the time.

"Yeah," I said. For some reason, after Brandon's words settled in, they rubbed me the wrong way. I suddenly felt like I needed to stand up for Christos, like this Brandon guy was viewing Christos as some kind of commodity or asset for him to manipulate. "Christos is really good. His paintings are beautiful."

"As are you, Sam. Can I call you Samantha? It seems so much more elegant and fitting, don't you think?"

Why was this guy trying so hard? "Sam's fine." Despite his beauty, he made me uncomfortable. I glanced at Romeo and Kamiko, wondering if they'd noticed the change. Nope. Both remained hypnotized by Brandon's beauty.

"You should consider sitting for Christos," Brandon said to me.

"He's always in need of beautiful women to pose for him."

"Oh, I don't know. I, uh…" I shot Romeo a pleading "bail me out" look.

Romeo was busy sipping his drink while sneaking ogling glances at Brandon.

I elbowed Romeo, catching him off guard. He sputtered his drink all over his hand and choked down a swallow. He coughed a few more times, which served to draw attention away from me. "Oh, she couldn't. Sam's dance card is usually full."

Dance card?

"You see," he continued, "Sam doesn't like to hold still for long periods of time. Poor circulation. Hence all her dancing." Romeo looked around for some place to wipe his wet hand. Finding none, he smeared it conspicuously across his pants. He made a sniveling, apologetic face.

Everyone gawked at Romeo, even Brandon. Brandon's gawking was the most subtle, but his raised eyebrows were a dead giveaway.

Romeo blundered forward like a court jester. "Sam wouldn't do well posing for hours at a stretch while being painted. Reminds her of mannequins." Romeo flashed his teeth nervously. "She, uh, had a traumatic experience, uh, in her childhood. Trapped overnight in a department store. Can't bear to go inside shopping malls ever since."

I exchanged an eye roll with Kamiko. Well, at least Romeo had come swashbuckling to my rescue, even if he did trip over his sword while pulling it out of the scabbard.

"Do you want to look at some of the other paintings?" Kamiko asked. "I know I do."

"Great idea, Kamiko." I edged toward her.

"Well, thank you for coming to the gallery." Brandon smiled suavely. "If you're interested in anything you see, let me know. Here's my card." He handed me a business card for the gallery.

Interested? The paintings were a tad bit out of my price range. In fact, they were on the other side of the galaxy from my price range.

Brandon gazed into my eyes again. As hot as he was, something about him made me increasingly uneasy. The business card was already in my hand, and his fingertips brushed mine. I don't think he wanted me to call him about the art.

"Pleasure meeting you, Samantha," Brandon smiled suavely.

Romeo yanked me by the arm. "Let's go, Sam! Lots more to see! Paintings everywhere!"

Kamiko took my other arm and they led me into the crowd. I couldn't help glancing over my shoulder. Brandon was still smiling. He slid his hands casually into his pockets and mouthed the words "Call me."

"You know in cartoons—" Kamiko started.

"Now is not the time for cartoon talk!" Romeo interrupted. "We need to escape!"

"That's what I was going to say!" Kamiko pleaded as we wormed through the crowd. "You know the part when the snake starts charming some poor mouse, saying all kinds of nice things, but he really wants to eat the mouse? That's what Brandon was doing to Sam!"

"Do you mean G-rated eating or X-rated eating?" Romeo asked lasciviously.

"Gross, Romeo!" Kamiko grimaced.

"Hurry up!" Romeo cracked. "We better get away before Brandon lassoes Samantha with his serpent!"

"Okay, you two," I admonished. "Enough antics. Back to the art."

We blundered past a group of silver-haired ladies in designer evening dresses. They stood in a circle, talking to someone, laughing and giggling demurely.

"Oh, Christos," one of the women said, "you are just like your grandfather. You look like him too. If I was a few years younger, I'd chase after you myself."

"Thank you, Mrs. Moorhouse. If you weren't married to Mr. Moorhouse, I'd take you up on that offer," Christos flirted.

Between the shoulders of the silver hairs, I saw Christos, holding a glass of champagne in his hand, talking up all the women. He wore a long sleeve shirt that hugged his body tightly. It showed off his muscles while hiding his tattoos.

"The apple doesn't fall far from the tree, does it girls?" Mrs. Moorhouse asked. The hen party clucked in response. "When are you going to paint me, Christos?"

"When my skills have developed to the level required to capture your elegant and timeless beauty. I have a lot to learn."

Mrs. Moorhouse blushed. "Will someone bring me a fainting couch? I'm about to expire."

Christos grinned at her. Or should I say Adonis. He was workin' it tonight! I knew he was probably being charming to sell paintings, but it was gag-worthy all the same.

"Where is Spiridon, by the way?" Mrs. Moorhouse asked. I was wondering the same thing myself. Wouldn't Spiridon come out to support his grandson at a big event like this?

"My grandfather had to leave early. He wasn't feeling well."

"I'm sorry to hear that. Give him my best when you see him, will you?"

"I'll do that Mrs. Moorhouse."

"And say hi to your father the next time you see him. We all miss him."

Christos' jaw clenched, but he forced a smile at Mrs. Moorhouse. "I'll do that."

I squeezed around the group of women and pulled Romeo and Kamiko with me.

"Hey!" Romeo whispered in my ear. "I think Christos is your buddy Adonis!"

"I think you might be right," I said dryly.

"What's with his secret identity?"

We were far enough away for us to speak normally. "That's what I'd like to know."

"I can't believe Christos Manos is Adonis," Kamiko gasped. "He's super hot, *and* an amazing artist?!"

"I thought you were only attracted to cartoon men," Romeo quipped.

"Well, considering Adonis looks like a super hero from a comic book, I'm okay with it." Kamiko sipped her drink, which was lemon-lime soda, to hide her bashful smile. "He's like ten times hotter now."

"Because he looks like Superman?"

Kamiko stamped her foot. "No, stupid! Because he's a great artist! Do I need to punch you?"

Romeo folded his arms over his chest. "What, and cause a scene?"

"I'll do it." Kamiko raised her fist menacingly.

"Great! Because I love scenes!" Romeo giggled. "More drama,

more drama!" He devolved into snickering.

I felt a hand slide down my lower back. For a second, I thought it was Brandon and he was pulling that cartoon snake charmer trick like Kamiko had talked about. I turned around. "Oh, hey Adonis! Er, Christos."

Kamiko and Romeo both said hello.

I had been afraid Christos wouldn't want to talk to me. Or ever see me again. I glanced at his eyes, but saw only warmth. What a relief.

"Hey Samantha." He smiled down at me, taking in my outfit. "You're beautiful tonight."

I covered my gaping smile with my fingers. "No I'm not."

Christos stood next to me. His hand wasn't on my back anymore, but he leaned slightly into me, like we were a couple on a date. He nodded toward Kamiko and Romeo. "What brought you three out to the show?"

"Professor Childress sent out an email," Kamiko answered. "What were you doing art modeling for our class when you're selling gallery paintings?"

"Don't be rude, Kamiko," Romeo admonished.

Christos chuckled. "It's okay. I owed him a favor. His model cancelled at the last minute."

"Lucky for us," Romeo said bashfully. "Oops! Did I say that out loud?"

Christos took it in stride. "Have you guys seen the sculpture garden outside?"

"No!" Kamiko said. "There's a sculpture garden here?"

"Yeah, out back. I can show you."

"I totally want to see it!" She sounded like she was ordering strawberry milkshakes at In-N-Out.

"Christos probably needs to stay inside and talk to the people," I said.

"I need a break." he said. "Let's go take a look."

We all followed him outside. The sculpture garden was surrounded by hedges strung with white Christmas tree lights. The sculptures were all of ballet dancers.

"I'm glad you guys came out," Christos said. "It gets a little old at these things, being on all the time. One wrong word, and you piss off some Daddy or Mommy Warbucks, and you lose a huge sale."

"We know what you mean," Romeo drooled.

How the hell did any of us know what it meant to make several hundred thousand dollars in an evening? Or to worry about screwing it all up? Christos lived on another plane of existence from the rest of us mortals.

"I like being able to bullshit with you guys. Hey, Samantha. Can I have a swig of your wine?"

"A swig? You make it sound like a communal pig trough."

"Then you won't mind if I drink some," he grinned.

"Yeah, sure." I offered him the glass.

He drank several long swallows, then handed me the glass.

As I processed the ramifications of this huge gallery show, I realized I was somewhat confused about Christos' background. "So, Christos, why are you even at SDU?" I gestured at all the art in the room. "I mean, as a student? You seem to already have an art career."

"Yeah, school's sort of a formality at this point. But this is my first big solo gallery show."

Kamiko's mouth dropped. "Your *first* show? How come the prices are so high?"

"Well, because of my name. And because they're good." He cocked his ever-egotistical Adonis grin.

There was no denying it. He *was* amazingly talented.

"But I've sold a bunch of pieces over the years in various group shows. People have been waiting for my first show for awhile."

Brandon Charboneau walked up, somewhat flustered. He had that possessive look on his face I didn't like. "There you are, Christos. You have guests inside. They all want to spend a few minutes with the artist. Can you spare a moment for your adoring patrons?"

"See what I mean?" Christos whispered in my ear. To Brandon, he said, "Yeah, no problem." He waved to us. "See you guys later." Christos walked off with Brandon. I saw Brandon lean in close and say something pointed into Christos' ear. Christos jerked away and frowned at him. That was strange.

"Well, there's more paintings inside," Kamiko said. "I want to see the rest of them. You guys coming?"

"Yeah."

We all went back inside. Kamiko was in artist's heaven looking at the paintings. She pointed out all these little details about the compositions that I and Romeo had missed. The way the edge of a cloud would circle right into a women's head, pulling your eye down her body. Or the way the shade from a tree made the image of a person pop out from the background.

I was fascinated by all of it, and tried to soak up as much as I could.

After awhile, I despaired that Kamiko knew so much about art, and was so much better than me.

Christos was better than all of us combined, and came from a family of artists who had connections in the business.

How the hell was I ever going to be anything more than an accountant?

Sam Smith, Pipe Dreamer.

Sigh.

At some point, I wandered off by myself while Kamiko and Romeo talked to some of the other people in the gallery. I think Romeo was crushing on a young hipster guy he'd just met.

I finished my wine, and got more. I definitely had a good buzz going.

Brandon walked up next to me and put a red dot sticker on the placard beside me. The price for this one was $18,500.

"Hey, you," I said.

"That's the last of them. We sold everything."

I covered my mouth and stifled a hiccup. "All of the paintings sold?"

"Yes, they did." Brandon smiled proudly, almost like it was his accomplishment.

I didn't like that one bit. Why was that?

"I already called my father to tell him the good news," Brandon said as he slid his hands in his pockets, still facing the painting.

"About the paintings?"

He turned his head to look me up and down. "That, and I met an amazing woman tonight, one that rivaled the beauty of Christos' paintings." His eyes gleamed.

Was he doing that snake charmer thing Kamiko talked about? I kind of liked it. "Thank you, Brandon. Maybe you can sell me tonight, and put a red dot on me too." Boy, I was at least two sheets to the wind. Maybe not three, but close.

"No one here has that kind of money," he smiled slowly.

"Not even you?" I flirted.

"No, not even the richest man on the planet."

"Isn't that Bill Gates? He's pretty rich."

"Well, I wouldn't let him buy you. No matter how much he offered. Beauty like yours can never be bought."

"That's sweet, Brandon." Yeah, those were snake charmer eyes. He ran a gentle hand down the side of my arm.

Chills swirled under my skin and jumped across my chest, ricocheting between my breasts. I realized my breath had stopped. I giggled and took a deep breath. How drunk was I? I must've had more wine than I realized.

Screw it, snake charmer be damned. Brandon was hot. And I was single. I giggled at him coquettishly.

"Hey, Brandon," Tiffany said. Where the F had she come from? She had radar, I was sure of it. She looped her arms around Brandon's neck. She stood on her tip-toes and kissed his cheek. Then she glared at me. I was waiting for her to hike her skirt and mark her territory. "Hey," she said to me dismissively.

"I was just telling Sam here that I'd sold the last painting," Brandon said.

"That's awesome, Brandon." She seemed genuinely excited. "Now you and me can go out and celebrate!"

Great. Tiffany had already warned me off Christos. Now she was laying claim to Brandon? Did she date both of them, or just not want me to have either, so she could pick and chose?

"I have *got* to go to the ladies room," she bitched. "I've been standing in front of that painting of mine for two hours in these heels. Pardon me, you two." She smiled her false smile and pranced off.

"My apologies for her behavior," Brandon said. "Tiffany tends to be a bit high strung."

"She seemed pretty comfortable with you. Do you guys have a history? Or is it a story still in the making?"

Brandon chuckled and shook his head. "Yes and no."

I repressed a smile.

"Tiffany and I have known each other since childhood. Our

fathers are good friends. In recent years, she's hinted several times that she and I should date. But I value my relationship with my father too much to put him through hell. And I wouldn't want to jeopardize my father's relationship with Tiffany's dad."

I guess Tiffany wasn't the polished picture of perfection she liked to present. I secretly hoped Brandon would pull out a shovel and start digging up more dirt about her, but I wasn't going to come right out and ask. But if he wanted to use just a teaspoon, I'd take that.

"Tiffany and I have always been," he raised his eyebrows suggestively, "and will continue to be, nothing more than good friends. Therefore, I'm entirely single. Are you?"

I looked into his dreamy hazel eyes. "Yes," I nodded. He was so fricking handsome and refined. And from the sound of it, he'd given Bitchany the stop sign long ago. Whoopee!

"Hey, Brandon," Christos said as he patted Brandon's shoulder from behind.

"There you are, Christos!" Brandon faced him.

For a moment I couldn't tell if Brandon was actually excited about Christos' sudden presence, or slightly disappointed.

Christos glanced at me, but directed his question at Brandon. "How are sales?"

"Everything's sold. Congratulations," he grinned. "I was looking for you to tell you the good news. Well done, my friend."

Brandon shook his hand vigorously.

"I'm glad to hear it," Christos said. "I'm all out of sell for tonight."

"You were working it tonight. Mrs. Moorhouse needed a bib, she was drooling so much."

"One of those lobster ones," Christos joked. "She was ready to dig into me with a knife and fork."

Brandon chuckled while he scanned the main room. The gallery was still half full of people.

"Well, I'm stuck here until everyone's gone so I can close up the gallery, but I thought I would ask Samantha here if she wanted to get a drink after I locked up?" He gave me a hopeful look.

Did I see Christos' nostrils flare when Brandon called me Samantha? I think I did.

"Oh man, I'd already told Sam and her friends that I'd take them out for drinks tonight," Christos lied casually. "They're all student artists at SDU and wanted to talk shop with me after the show. I promised them weeks ago."

He had told me no such thing. Had he told Romeo or Kamiko? He couldn't have. Kamiko said she just found out about the show.

One of Brandon's brows lifted casually. "You don't say."

"Yeah. Sorry, man. Sam and I should probably head out. It's getting late."

Brandon and Christos exchanged a tense look.

Did I sense a rivalry here? Between the two of them? Over little old me? This was too much. All they needed were some shooting irons and some cowboy hats. Then the survivor could claim his prize. Men. I wasn't anybody's prize. But it sure was exciting.

The real question was, how did I manage to put myself in the epicenter of epic drama everywhere I went?

"Pardon me, I didn't mean to interfere with your plans," Brandon said pleasantly.

"Yeah, I don't want to keep her out too late. I know Sam has a busy day tomorrow, so we should probably go."

Christos didn't know what I had planned for tomorrow. But that was fine with me.

I sighed apologetically. "Yeah, I can't stay out too late tonight. I've got a really busy schedule," I mimicked.

Brandon smiled at both of us. "I understand. Have a terrific time, you two. Please say your goodbyes to the guests before departing, Christos. Mrs. Moorhouse is still here."

"I'll do that," Christos assured.

Without warning, Brandon took my hand and kissed it. "It was a pleasure meeting you tonight, Samantha." He lowered his lashes and gazed at me through hooded eyes. Snake charmer.

Christos tugged on my arm. "Good night, Brandon. I'll call you tomorrow and we can go over the sales from tonight."

"Excellent idea. Have fun, and good night."

Chapter 16

It took me a few minutes to round up Romeo and Kamiko while Christos gave his goodbyes. The two of them were in the sculpture garden.

"Where were you! We've been looking all over for you," Romeo said.

"I thought Mr. Snake Charmoneau had gotten you," Kamiko said.

I giggled. "I think I would've been okay with that."

"Whorish bitch! You're taking all the good men," Romeo joked.

I laughed. "Poor Romeo."

"We should go," Kamiko said.

We walked back through the gallery, out to the street.

Christos was waiting outside. "Hey, you guys. Ready to go?" He cocked a brow expectantly.

"Oh, uh…" I looked at Christos. "You were serious?" What happened to him being only my mentor? I almost blurted it out loud, but didn't want to say it in front of everyone. I'd look like as much of a bitch as I had on the hillside by Christos' house. "Did you still want to get drinks?"

He cocked his grin. "Of course. I have to celebrate my sell-out show with somebody."

"Can they come?" I motioned toward Kamiko and Romeo.

"Of course."

"Drinks?" Romeo said. "Nobody told me anything about drinks!"

"I'm pretty tired, Romeo." Kamiko said. "I'd sort of like to go."

"Party pooper. Didn't you set up your TiVo to record whatever show that's on Cartoon Network that can't be missed?"

"Yes, but I'm still tired. I'm sorry."

"Fine, we can go. Sam, you coming?"

I spread my hands, shrugged my shoulders and gave Christos a non-committal look.

"I can give you a ride," Christos offered.

I turned to Romeo. I noticed the wheels turning in his head as he surveyed the situation. He abruptly put his hands on Kamiko and turned her around, pushing her down the sidewalk. "We've really got to be going. Poor Kamiko is half-asleep already. You guys have fun without us! Good night!"

They were gone, before I could protest.

I turned to Christos. "Romeo's crazy."

"I like that guy. Shall we?" He motioned down the street. "There's a great bar around the corner from here."

A pained look twisted my face. "I'm only nineteen."

"My mistake. At least you're legal," he smirked.

"I'm sure it wouldn't have stopped you if I wasn't."

"I do have *some* boundaries," he smiled.

"You sure?" I quipped.

"Please, Samantha. I'm not a criminal."

An image of him being handcuffed and stuffed into a police car flashed in my mind. From the look that passed over Christos' face, I'm pretty sure he was thinking the same thing.

"There's some coffee shops in Pacific Beach that stay open all night. We can go there."

"Okay."

He motioned. "This way,"

We walked.

"So, uh, where's your car?" I asked.

"Car? Right here." We stood in front of his black motorcycle.

"What? This?"

"Yep."

"Oh, I couldn't." I pulled my cell phone out of my tiny clutch purse. "I better call Romeo before they leave."

"Don't worry. I brought an extra helmet." He held it up.

"Oh, no that's okay. I'd rather not."

"You worried?"

"No, it's just that—"

"You're worried."

Hell yeah I was worried!

"You'll be fine. I'll go slow."

If my mom and dad knew I was about to climb on a motorcycle, driven by a guy covered in tattoos, they'd ground me all the way from Washington D.C. "I really can't."

"Come on. If you hold on tight, you'll be perfectly safe."

Hold on? To what? Him? This was going in a dangerous direction quickly. I was least worried about the accident part of the equation. It was the holding part that made me nervous. He handed me the helmet.

"Put your hair up in the helmet, or else you'll spend all night getting the tangles out."

I knotted my hair in a bun and squished the helmet on. He straddled the bike.

"I can't get on." My dress was too short and my heels too tall.

He climbed off and in one swift motion picked me up by the waist and lowered me onto the back of the bike. How strong was this guy? He lifted me like I was a kitten. I yanked my dress down and shoved the hem under my crotch. This was the wrong outfit for a motorcycle ride.

He climbed back onto the bike and started the engine. It thrummed between my legs.

"Hold on tight."

Um, my nearly non-existent dress and panties where all that stood between me and him. Good gracious, this was close quarters. I made sure my crotch was at least two inches from Christos' butt. "Where do I put my feet?"

"On the pegs."

I found them beneath me. My heels hooked over them nicely. The only problem? My two inch gap between me and his hot butt was now a single inch.

"Get a good grip."

"What?"

"With your arms."

I reached around. "Where do I put them?"

"Around my waist."

What? I couldn't do that!

"You don't want to fall off, do you?"

"No." I wrapped my arms around him. I had two choices. Chest or abs. Neither was exactly what I'd call platonic. I settled for high abs. It was farther from his package. Why did I have to go and use that word?

He reached behind me and pulled me into him, obliterating my one-inch safety gap. I don't know how I was going to keep my dress tucked beneath me.

"I don't want you sliding off."

Good to know. The front of my pelvis pressed against his buns. Oh gawd. I was touching his buns. With my hips and thighs. I hadn't signed up for this. Check please! Time for me to go.

He revved the engine. "Ready?"

"No!"

He laughed. "As long as you hold onto me, you'll be safe. I promise."

"Promise?"

"Cross my heart. You can trust me, Samantha. I'll always keep you safe."

What did he just say? Was he talking about the motorcycle ride? Or something more.

"Don't worry, Samantha. I'll keep it below the speed limit."

What he failed to tell me was that he would accelerate to the speed limit faster than the speed of light! Holy shit!

My arms locked in a death grip around his ribs. I squeezed my thighs around his waist as tightly as possible.

When we slowed for a red light, I was breathless. "Uh, are you sure you're not going too fast?"

"Never passed twenty-five."

Until we were on the freeway. When we hit the onramp, I think booster rockets popped out the back of his motorcycle. I swear we were going two thousand miles an hour.

I had heard that speed was sort of like orgasm. I'd never really had a big orgasm on my own. Just little ones. Whatever this speed thing was, it was way bigger.

I don't know if it was the way my knees clutched Christos' sides, or the feel of his abs beneath my arms, or the fact that the bike vibrated between my legs and my lady parts were right on the seat. But all of it sent me over the edge into uncharted waters. What concerned me most though, were the uncharted waters possibly leaking through my panties. Holy crap, this motorcycle was fast.

At one point, I felt the distinct desire to let go. I freaked out, imagining myself flying off the back of the motorcycle and sliding skin-first along the freeway.

That quickly ended any potentially orgasmic thoughts I'd been having.

I also believed that I had not yet breathed once since we got on the freeway, so I took a moment to inhale deeply. I felt Christos pat my hand reassuringly. Did that mean he'd taken a hand off the handle bars? Jesus, he was crazy! Thankfully, he released my hand.

Eventually I noticed we weren't passing any cars. So our speed was probably no more than sixty five or seventy.

I made the mistake of glancing down at the blacktop screaming by. If I were to take my peep-toed heels off the pegs, or if they were to accidentally fall off of their own accord, my toes would be literally ground right down to my ankles.

Okay, I want to officially go on record here and say that anyone who rides motorcycles in a dress and heels is schizophrenic, or worse. I absolve myself from guilt, because I hadn't realized what I was getting myself into.

At one point, Christos accelerated and switched lanes. He did it expertly, but I'm pretty sure I peed my panties. Of course there was so much wind, it probably blow dried my pee right off the seat. I could tell that my dress desperately wanted to fly up behind me, but I wasn't going to give a bra and panty show to the other cars on the road. I willed my dress to safeguard my humility. Thankfully, it obeyed.

Pacific Beach was only a few miles from La Jolla, but I'm pretty sure the ride there took at least five hours, or five seconds. I couldn't tell which. They say speed is relative. But I did know we were going excruciatingly fast, even if we mostly did the speed limit.

I heaved a sigh of relief, but luckily not my dinner, when we got off the freeway. We made it to the coffee shop unharmed.

He parked the bike on a side street and turned it off. I didn't let go.

He flipped up his visor. "You okay back there?"

"I think I have frost bite." It was warm, but wind chill had done its damage. My fingers felt locked together, although that could've been the adrenaline.

"Then a hot drink will be perfect." He waited. "You can let go now."

"Gimme a minute. I want to make sure we've stopped moving."

He laughed. "I told you you'd be safe. But if you want to hold on for awhile longer, I don't mind."

I had to repress the urge to run my hands all over his sexy chest. But I restrained myself. I let go and he climbed off. I pressed my dress down quickly. I had been too scared at all the stop lights to let go of him and fix it.

"You okay? You look like you need to hit the ladies room."

"I think I did, on the freeway."

He chuckled. "I thought I felt something wet on the seat. I just didn't think it was pee." He winked at me.

"Okay, gross!" He may have been right. I was so ashamed. Okay, okay, ladies. I exaggerate. The seat was dry.

Once again, he picked me up easily and set me down on the ground in one fluid motion. "How much do you weigh?"

"You can't ask a girl that!"

"I was going to say fifty pounds. You're a feather."

"I'm not anorexic! But thank you for the compliment."

He grinned. "Coffee time."

We walked to the main street and found the coffee shop. It was called Xanadu.

A rowdy crowd of big, rough looking biker guys blocked the entrance. A row of Harleys were parked next to them in the street. I supposed this was a regular hang for them.

"'Scuse us, guys," Christos said, flashing the bikers a smile.

The bikers fell silent and eyed Christos warily. I suddenly felt nervous, like the amount of testosterone in the immediate vicinity had multiplied beyond acceptable levels of safety. I waited for them to start pounding their chests while hooting and hopping around.

Then they noticed me. Great.

"Hey, babe," said a guy with tattoos on his forehead and huge spikes through his earlobes. While I liked tattoos, too much of a good thing was exactly that. This guy was frightening. "Where you going so quick? Stay and talk with us."

"Easy, dog," Christos said with a welcoming smile. "The lady and I are going inside for a drink."

"Who you calling dog, dog?" Ear Spikes snarled. He didn't seem interested in friendly conversation. "If I wanna talk to your lady, I'm going to talk to your lady."

I watched Christos' brows lower and bunch aggressively. His jaw muscles flexed repeatedly.

Okay, I knew Christos knew how to handle himself in a fight. I'd seen him in action the day I met him. But there were six guys this time, and they were all pretty big. One of them was so huge and hairy, he looked like Bigfoot. Six on one only worked out for the best in movies.

"Let's go," I whispered. "We can go somewhere else."

Christos stared down Ear Spikes while talking to me in a low, dangerous voice sharp with malice. "We don't need to go anywhere else because these guys are not going to bother us." It was clearly a threat.

"Oh yeah?" Ear Spikes scoffed. "You sure about that, Easy Rider?"

I didn't get the reference but I knew we were in way over our heads.

Christos stood his ground. "I'm sure," he hissed.

My knees started to shake at that point. I glanced around, looking for help. I couldn't believe our luck. At that moment, a police car slowed to about one mile an hour right next to us on the street and buzzed its horn with a brief bark.

All the bikers swiveled to look at the squad car like a bunch of prairie dogs sensing danger. They knew when it was time to hide their heads.

"Shall we?" Christos asked, gesturing into Xanadu with a broad smile.

I worried that if we went in, and the bikers were still outside when we left, there would be trouble later, and the chances of the cops showing up like the cavalry twice in one night were low.

But Christos didn't seem at all worried. He was as calm as could be. Oh well, college was about trying new things. Danger was one of them. I hoped I wouldn't regret it. "Okay."

We walked in together.

Inside, Xanadu was fairly crowded for a Thursday at midnight. College age kids filled many of the cramped tables. The decor was something out of a West Indies trading company. I loved it.

We got in line and ordered hot spicy chai. I didn't usually go for caffeine at midnight, despite my tolerance. I really wanted an

Italian soda, but I was too damn cold. The chai was served in tall glasses too hot to hold comfortably.

Christos found a table against the wall, which had a bench. We set our motorcycle helmets on the bench and I felt like we were the cool couple that rode everywhere on a motorcycle together.

The guy to our right had a pile of textbooks and a laptop open in front of him, and wore headphones. The two middle-aged women on the left frantically discussed vacation destinations.

All the same, we talked low. I asked about the gallery show, but Christos played it down like it was no big deal. I couldn't tell if it made him uncomfortable, or if he was being humble.

"I heard you say your grandfather came earlier. I would've said hello if I'd seen him."

"No worries. He likes to leave before the crowds arrive. But trust me, he made sure everything was tip-top before he left. He's had a gallery show or twenty in his career. I'm surprised Brandon didn't kick him out sooner for micro-managing."

I could tell Christos appreciated his grandfather's attentiveness.

"What about your dah—" I stopped myself mid-sentence. I remembered seeing Christos' jaw clench when the subject of his dad came up with Mrs. Moorhouse at the gallery.

He took a sip of his tea. "What about my what?"

I lifted my tea to my mouth to cover myself. I blew on it. "Boy, this tea sure is hot."

"My what?"

"Whew. Hot tea! I think I need some ice cubes." I glanced around the coffee shop. "You think they have an ice maker around here?"

"Finish your question. Please?"

I met his eyes. For a second, I expected to see tension, or the face I'd seen when he yelled at me on the hike today about his dad and grandfather and the family bench. But I saw only sorrow. "Uh, well, I was going to say 'your dad.'"

"Yeah, that's what I thought." He grimaced.

This was obviously a sore subject that needed Novocaine. "Do you not want to talk about it? We can totally talk about something else, if you want."

"It's okay. I don't mind."

I sipped my tea. What was I supposed to ask now? I felt like an idiot, like I'd purchased a one-way ticket to awkward. "So, uh, did your dad come earlier, like your grandfather?"

"No." He traced the woodgrain in the table top with his fingernail, like he was waiting for me to continue.

"Where is your dad?"

"Around."

"Does he live in San Diego?"

"Yeah."

"Do you ever see him?"

"Rarely."

"You said he was an artist, right?"

"Yeah."

"Where are all his paintings?"

"New York. Private collections."

I wished he'd just tell me so I didn't have to play twenty thousand questions with Greg Gregarious' brooding brother Tony Taciturn sitting across from me.

I drank my chai, needing something for strength. And warmth, which I wasn't getting from Christos.

I sensed he wanted to talk about his dad, but sort of didn't. I could certainly relate. "We can talk about something else. It's really okay."

He stared at the table top. "My dad hasn't been around much for a long time." He took a swallow of chai and slammed his cup on the table. It was final punctuation to the discussion of his father.

I changed the subject. "So, what's up with Tiffany? She's seems to show up everywhere you do." Boy, was I smooth. From one drama bomb to the next.

Christos smiled. "Ahh, Tiffany. She's a piece of work. I've known her for a long time. Her family knows Brandon's family. My family knows Brandon's family. We all bump into each other."

"She was all about your painting of her at the gallery."

He shook his head. "Tiffany likes to own things. It makes her feel better about herself. Especially if she has something that no one else does. It makes her feel special."

"Is that why she wants you?" Whoops. Could somebody pass the sugar? I needed it for my foot. Mmmm, toe jam.

"She wants me, but she's never going to own me." Christos

grinned. His Adonis grin. The one the ladies loved. "The trouble with Tiffany is, once she gets what she wants, she gets bored. Then she wants something else. Her father's money distracts her from dealing with her shit."

"I wouldn't mind being distracted by my own yacht and mansion."

"You say that now, but have you ever had either?"

"No."

"So how would you know? Grass is always greener." He sipped his tea.

"So you've never dated her?"

"Hell no. She doesn't want *me*. She wants the idea of me. I can tell. I could always tell."

"What about slept?" I blurted. Why was I purposefully walking over hot coals? I needed my head examined.

"With Tiffany?"

I tilted my head back proudly, prepared for the worst. If I was going to play with fire, I was going to act like I liked it. I nodded.

"Nope."

"No? Really?"

"Tiffany's a one way street."

Why did that sound hookerish? I had no idea what he meant, but I was afraid to ask.

When we finished our teas, I felt much warmer. It could've been my blood flushing through my body as I realized that Christos and I were chatting it up like a couple of friends at a coffee shop. Or a couple. I mean, if he was only my mentor, shouldn't we have been talking about art and only art?

Not his love life?

"I should probably get you home," he said.

No! I didn't want the evening to end. "I need to use the ladies room."

He stood and picked up the helmets. "I thought you peed everything out on the ride over," he joked.

I swatted his arm. "No, silly. That wasn't pee." What the heck was I saying? How did Christos send me from platonic to X-rated so quickly?

"I'll wait for you out front."

I walked to the back of the coffee shop, and found the lone restroom, by the back door. It was in use. I waited patiently.

The screen door leading outside opened and a bearded biker dude walked through. I recognized him from out front earlier. I had forgotten all about those biker guys.

This guy was the Bigfoot looking guy that made me most nervous. Every piece of his clothing was covered with studs or patches or chains. He stopped when he saw me.

"Hey, pretty thing." With the beard, frizzy long hair, overly hairy arms, and gravelly voice, he was certainly related to, if not descended from, the actual Bigfoot. "Where's your man?"

He didn't waste any time getting down to business. I stifled a gulp. "In the bathroom," I lied.

"Lucky me."

I rolled my eyes. He loomed toward me. Where was my bear trap? "He'll be right out," I warned.

Bigfoot didn't appear worried. "What's your name?"

"Waiting."

"Waiting?"

"Waiting for you to go away," I gave him a scowly head bob.

He didn't seem much for brains, but he was persistent. I tried the bathroom doorknob. I knocked. No response. Was it locked and I needed a key from the front?

"I thought you said your boyfriend was inside."

"He is." I knocked. "Uh, Adonis, hurry up!"

"Wanna go for a ride on my Harley?"

"No," I scoffed. I folded my arms across my chest protectively. Why did I feel like a field mouse all of a sudden? I turned my back to him.

I looked around for my quickest exit route. Because of how the hallway turned, I couldn't see the main room of the coffee shop, so I couldn't see Christos, or anyone else. I couldn't motion anyone for help. Bigfoot stood between me and the back door. Was it time for a rape shout?

"Your hair is pretty," Bigfoot mumbled. I felt him stroke it.

I lurched away. He grabbed for my shoulder. This was about to turn into a Lifetime movie that I didn't want to star in. Shit.

Bigfoot lumbered toward me.

Christos exploded out of nowhere and slammed Bigfoot back

against the wall. Christos remained at the ready, crouching in a fighter's stance. Bigfoot recovered his footing. He was huge, a full head taller than Christos. He swung a mammoth fist at Christos. Christos dodged easily.

Undeterred, Bigfoot pulled out a huge knife as casually as if it were his wallet. His face was bland. He eyed Christos like this was business as usual.

Someone was going to get killed.

Bigfoot lunged, knife first.

Christos slipped around it and somehow managed to steer the knife right into the wall. It lodged deeply in the sheet rock. Bigfoot yanked on it. It was stuck.

Christos ducked and launched his entire body upward in a powerful spiraling motion, rocketing his fist into Bigfoot's jaw. Bigfoot staggered back, dazed. His eyes blinked, but he stayed on his feet. He leaned against the wall behind him.

Christos moved in on him, firing punches to Bigfoot's face and gut. Amazingly, Bigfoot swayed drunkenly forward, swinging his hairy paws.

Christos side stepped and clobbered Bigfoot on the side of the head. The giant man went down on all fours, then reached into his leather jacket. I worried what sort of arsenal Bigfoot had hidden inside. He could easily have a gun.

Christos twisted in a tight overhand arc, firing a fist straight down into the back of Bigfoot's neck, connecting at the base of the man's skull. Bigfoot's arms and legs flew out, flattening him into the cement floor face-first. He was out cold.

One of the Xanadu employees, who wore an apron, walked around the corner. "Is everything all right back here?"

This scene did not look good. I remembered the cops putting Christos in handcuffs. I couldn't let it happen again. That was my cue. I grabbed Christos arm. "We have to go, now!"

He looked at me, brows furrowed, lips a tight stripe over his teeth. He was still in fight mode.

"Come on!" I pleaded.

His nostrils flared and he flashed clenched teeth.

I put my palms on his chest. His thick pectoral muscles spasmed, but he calmed a moment later. I pushed him out the back door.

I glanced behind me and noticed our motorcycle helmets. Christos must have dropped them when Bigfoot was about to turn me into the Missing Link. I darted for the helmets.

The employee with the apron stared at me, bug eyed.

"Don't mind us." I snatched up the helmets and went outside.

Christos grabbed my arm and held a finger to his lips. In a strained whisper he said, "We have to get the fuck out of here." He grabbed my hand and pulled me down the alley behind Xanadu.

I glanced over my shoulder and saw Bigfoot's buddies standing in a circle in the parking lot behind the coffee shop, next to their motorcycles. Had they been waiting all this time for me and Christos to leave? My stomach sank.

Christos took his helmet from me and put it on while we crept quickly down the alley. I put my helmet on too. "Move it," he hissed. He grabbed my hand and pulled me toward the side street where we'd parked.

"Hey!" one of the bikers shouted. "That's him!"

Oh shit.

Good thing I jogged regularly. We ran as fast my slow ass could keep up with Christos. I could tell he wasn't going his full speed, but I went mine.

He swept me up and onto the motorcycle the second we were close, then swung on and revved the engine.

Just as Christos turned his Ducati around in the street, the biker gang poured out of the alley onto the sidewalk. "Fucker's getting away! Get your bikes!"

They turned and ran back toward their Harleys.

Oh fuckity shit.

Were these guys going to chase us?

I didn't have a second to think about it because the engine between our legs screamed and we rocketed down the street and leaned into a corner so far over, I thought the bike was going to slide out beneath us, but it didn't.

Christos took dark side streets and ran stop sign after stop sign. I was going to die in an accident or a motorcycle gang murder. I felt Christos' heart pounding in his chest. It thudded as fast as mine. Perhaps he feared the same dire end.

I vaguely thought I heard the sound of Harleys behind us, but Christos' Ducati was plenty loud with the amount of insane accelerating he was doing, so I couldn't tell for sure.

One of the cross streets we passed had a huge bump. The bike caught air as we went over it. I literally came up off my seat and slammed down. I would've flown of the bike if I hadn't been clutching Christos for dear life with my arms.

I couldn't count how many stop signs we ran. I'm pretty sure it was all of them.

When we got to the freeway onramp, he floored it, or whatever you do on a motorcycle. We were going way faster than on the way to Xanadu.

Going around the curving onramp was like riding an insane roller coaster, but not fun at all.

We were going so fast on the freeway, the cars around us seemed to literally be standing still. How was it possible that the cars, which had to have been going sixty-five mph, seemed motionless?

Fortunately, Christos expertly wove the bike in and out of the deadly obstacle course. Once we cleared the pack of cars that had been near where we entered the freeway, the bike's engine screamed and we took off even faster.

I'd never gone so fast in a vehicle on the road in my entire life. Over Christos shoulder, I saw the lane lines flying at us in a literal blur.

When the freeway curved, we started to lean. I chanted in a quivering voice, swept away by the wind, "Ohgod, Ohgod, Ohgod."

I slammed my eyes shut and prayed I wouldn't die. There was nothing sexy about this ride. It was scary as hell.

Half way home, he slowed down to a reasonable speed. He glanced behind us repeatedly, no doubt checking for the biker gang.

My heart pounded. Could a nineteen-year-old have a heart attack? I was very close to it. Every cell in my body wanted to run away from the danger closing in on me, but there was nowhere to go on the back of the moving bike.

Besides, my legs and arms were wrapped around danger. And I wasn't letting go of him.

I was crazy for sure.

When we arrived at my house, Christos leaned the bike on the kickstand like it was no big deal. He helped me off. My legs were rubber.

He picked me up and carried me upstairs, cradling me like a baby. I leaned my cheek against his shoulder. I was safe.

At my door, he asked, "Keys?"

I opened my tiny clutch purse. I can't believe I hadn't lost it on the motorcycle. I fished out my key and handed it to him.

He opened the door and carried me over the threshold. I didn't mean it that way, I meant through the door. It's not like we'd just been married.

He laid me down on the couch and sat next to me. "You all right?"

"Fine." I was traumatized.

He stroked my hair out of my face. "It's tangled. Sorry I didn't give you time to put it up in your helmet."

"It's okay." I felt dreamy. My adrenalin was probably all used up for the year.

"I should go."

"No, don't, please," I whimpered.

"It's late. You should sleep."

He stood. I grabbed his wrist with both hands. "I don't want to be alone. What if the bikers come?"

I saw gears turning behind his eyes.

"Ok," he said reluctantly.

I felt his powerful arms slide beneath me. He picked me up.

"Where are you taking me?" I asked.

"To bed."

My chest seized for the fortieth time that night.

Tease.

"Don't worry. I'll crash on the couch."

I don't know if I felt relieved or disappointed. He sat me on the edge of the bed and took my heels off. I felt like Prince Charming was doing the glass slipper routine.

"Do you have boxers or a t-shirt or whatever? To sleep in?"

They were on a folding chair in the corner, but I was too tired to get them. I waved my arm toward them.

He picked them up and held them out to me. "I'll go outside so you can change."

"No, don't go."

"Okay, I'll turn around."

I tried to pull my dress off, but I felt so completely sluggish, I couldn't seem to figure it out. "Help," I mumbled, my dress half over my head.

I felt the dress slip over my head. I was wearing nothing but bra and panties. In front of Christos. If I hadn't felt so exhausted, I might have done something I would regret. I gave him a sleepy smile.

He held out the t-shirt. "Arms." He slid it over my head. I felt like a little girl. I dropped my arms.

"Aren't you going to do that bra through the sleeve trick?" he asked.

"I'm too tired."

"Front or back?"

"Huh?"

"The clips, or whatever."

"Back."

"That should be easy."

"I bet you say that to all the girls," I chuckled.

He smirked a dimple at me. The next thing I knew, Houdini had my bra undone and I felt the cups fall away.

"You can do the rest. Unless you want me to do it for you."

I did, but I wasn't saying anything. I fished it out through my sleeve and held it out to him like a, well, like I'd hooked a fish.

"What am I supposed to do with that?"

"Hamper."

He took it and tossed it in, then faced me, fists on hips.

I felt my nipples harden. Crap. No hiding them under my cotton shirt. I crossed my arms over my chest and giggled. Was I drunk? I'd had no more than two or three glasses of wine at the art gallery a few hours ago. But I was, because of Christos. He was intoxicating.

"Do you want the panties off?" He held up the boxers

Why did Christos saying the word panties make me want to take them off and hand them to him? It was probably a regular thing for him.

Christos was so confident, so relaxed. He never had to try to do anything. He just did. With no effort. So unlike...*him.* I shivered.

"You cold?"

I shook my head and frowned. "No. Just tired."

"Okay, no boxers. Under the covers, Bonnie."

"Who?"

"You know, Bonnie and Clyde?"

"Oh. Because we're like two outlaws on the run from the long arm of the law?" I smiled. I liked the sound of that, totally romantic.

Christos smiled. "Yep."

"And Bigfoot," I giggled.

"Who?"

"The guy who tried to run off with me into the mountains to make caveman babies? Back at Xanadu's?"

"Yeah," he chuckled. He bent over and picked me up again. I put my arm around his neck. My un-bra-ed breast pressed against his rock hard chest. My nipple was pencil eraser rigid at that point. He had to have felt it.

He set me gently at the top of the bed and pulled the sheet and thin blanket over my legs. I held my hand on his shoulder the entire time.

He straightened to stand, but I clutched his shirt in my fist. "Stay with me." I wasn't drunk. I was high as a kite.

"Couch. Mentor, remember?" He smiled the warmest smile I had ever seen. His thick eyelashes enhanced the depth of his blue eyes. He dimpled his panty dropping grin.

Not helping. Boldness swept over me and I sat up before I could think through my actions. I threw my arms around his neck.

"Please. Sleep with me. I don't want to be alone tonight."

He caressed my cheek. "You won't be alone. I'll be on the couch."

I resorted to blatant manipulation. I pouted.

He smiled slyly. "Not gonna work. Couch, me. Bed, you." He leaned forward and kissed my forehead. "Good night."

Reluctantly, I released him and laid back down. He pulled the covers up to my chin. Christos Manos tucked me in! I think I fainted before he was able to turn out the lights and close the bedroom door. He left the door open a crack.

I fell into sleep the second he was gone.

Chapter 17

I woke up to whimpering.

At first, I thought I was still dreaming. It came from the living room. I slid out of bed and tip-toed to the bedroom door.

Christos mewled on the couch. "No, I didn't, stop. Please don't. It wasn't, they aren't…" He was mumbling. He sounded boyishly afraid.

Without hesitation, I went to him.

I kneeled beside the couch. His back was to me. "Christos," I whispered.

"Wha—?"

"Christos, wake up. You're having a nightmare." I leaned toward him. I wanted to comfort him, but was afraid I'd startle him. I touched his shoulder. He twisted toward me, startling me. His eyes popped open.

Even in the near-darkness, they seemed to glow. It must have been the moonlight streaming through my living room. It was ghostly. He looked haunted.

For a second, I thought he didn't recognize me.

"Samantha," he murmured. His face softened. He reached out and cupped my cheek.

I leaned into his hand. "What were you dreaming about?"

"You don't want to know."

"I do."

"It's better off if you didn't." His face darkened suddenly and he pulled away.

"Christos?" I squeezed his arm. "You can talk to me about it. Christos? It's okay. Whatever it is, you can tell me. I won't judge you. I promise." And I meant it.

Bitch. Slut. Whore. Suicide Watch.

Tease.

I knew what it was like to be judged.

He sat up on the edge of the couch, elbows on his thighs. His head hung low.

I sat next to him. I stroked his knee. "It's okay."

"You are so good to me," Christos whispered.

That was news to me. I thought I'd been mainly a total bitch to him.

He slid the knuckle of his finger affectionately across my cheek. I inhaled a quivering breath. His knuckle tugged at my lower lip. My exhale stopped short.

"You're too good for me," he said. His face knotted painfully.

I wanted to shout, *No I'm not!*

He hung his head between his fists and started to shake with silent sobs.

I kissed his hair gently over and over again. "It's okay, it's okay." I wrapped my arms around him. "It's okay, Christos. I'm here."

He leaned into me, then threw his arms around me and squeezed. He cried for awhile, I don't know how long. When he was finished, I stood and took his hands in mine. "Come to bed."

He hesitated.

"Just sleep." I led him to my bedroom and we crawled into my queen-sized bed. I wrapped myself around him. Hearing his heart thump beneath my ear, I felt completely safe.

For the first time in two years, nothing that led up to Taylor, and all the names and horrid labels and shame that came after—

Emo. Goth. Witch. Sorceress.

Bitch. Slut. Whore.

Tease.

—seemed to matter anymore.

I wished I could feel that calm and peaceful forever.

I feared that Christos was a dream, and morning would steal him away from me forever.

But I slept so peacefully beside him, it almost didn't matter.

Sun peeking through my drapes and the smell of eggs and toast woke me up in the morning.

Was I still dreaming?

I heard dishes in the kitchen.

That meant last night hadn't been a dream! Unless some Breakfast Bandit was on the loose in my neighborhood, I was pretty sure I was safe.

I had to pee, but was afraid that if I moved, I'd break the spell, and all of this really would disappear.

Luckily, a few minutes later, Christos walked into my bedroom holding a plate of steaming eggs and a glass of orange juice. He was down to his shirt and boxers. He looked stunning. Because he was in my bedroom, in his PJ's.

"You didn't have any trays. I considered dragging your kitchen table in here, but I thought that'd wake you up," he joked.

"It's perfect." Everything really was.

He sat on the edge of the bed and handed me the plate. "Knife and fork."

I took them and he set the OJ on my night table.

"Where's yours?"

"Kitchen. I'll go get it."

He returned and sat on my bed. We ate together.

"I would've made bacon or sausage, but couldn't find any in your freezer. But I can tell you like your ice cream."

A nervous smile stretched my face tight.

"Who has nine pints of ice cream?" he asked.

This subject needed to be changed quickly. It was then that I noticed the gigantic pile of scrambled eggs on his plate. "Do you have enough eggs?"

"Huh? Not really," he smirked. "Let me know if you need any help with the ice cream. I'll make quick work of it after these eggs." He plunged a forkful of steaming eggs into his mouth and grinned while he chewed.

Problem solved. Subject avoided.

"Are you still my mentor?" I asked before forking some eggs into my mouth.

He reached over and took a swig of my OJ. I liked that we were sharing it. "Of course. Why wouldn't I be?"

"Because of all those nasty things I said yesterday on the hike."

"It's okay."

I could see that it was only sort of ok. "I'm really sorry. I was being a bitch. I don't know why."

"You're forgiven." He chewed on some toast.

When we finished eating, he took our dishes away. I heard him washing them in the sink. I snuck into the bathroom to pee and change into fresh underwear. When I came out of the bathroom, he was lying casually on my bed, hands behind his head.

I really liked the look of him on my bed.

"What?" he smiled.

"Nothing." I sat down next to him, and scooted over until my hips were against his. I wasn't so bold as to cuddle with him like I had during the night.

"What are you doing today?"

"I don't know. Homework?"

"Bummer."

"Don't you have mentoring things to do?"

"Nope. I sold a shit load of paintings last night. I don't have anything on my calendar. For weeks." He cocked a grin.

I sneered at him. Same old Christos. "I totaled the numbers up in my head. You made a pretty penny. Kamiko said you'll get half?"

"A bit more. Fifty five percent."

"Holy crap, Christos. I think you can exit graduate school whenever you want."

"Yup."

"So why don't you? Don't big name artists end up going to L.A. or New York, or someplace like that?"

"Oh, there's some charity case at the university I'm helping out," he said magnanimously.

My first thought was Professor Childress.

"Yeah, she's totally into art and shit, and still needs a mentor."

"Christos!" I smacked his chest, which felt like granite. I think I hurt my hand. "Ow! What are you made of? Marble?"

He chuckled. "So you want some mentoring today?"

"I don't know, I've got accounting and sociology homework up the butt."

"Why don't you leave the boring classwork where it is currently, up your butt, and let's have a field trip."

"You are so bad! Asking me to blow off schoolwork!"

"Hey, I'm your art mentor. Not your accounting mentor. What's it gonna be?"

I smiled at him questioningly. I hadn't missed a class all quarter. Despite a rocky start, I now had A's in all my classes. I could spare a day off, right? "Ok. Who showers first?"

"Ladies first." He grinned.

I hoped out of bed and into the bathroom. I shut the door but didn't bother to lock it. I was disappointed he didn't try to come in. He was a total gentleman. Of course, when the suds ran down my naked body, I couldn't help but imagine his hands sliding down my skin instead.

When I came out of the bathroom in a t-shirt and boxers, toweling my hair, he sat on my bed, reading my accounting textbook.

"There's some good stuff in this book. I might have to borrow it."

"You like accounting?"

"Someone's going to have to manage my money. I may as well know what they're doing with it."

When he put it that way, it didn't sound so bad. I nodded, brows arching.

He smiled at me. "You're pouting at me again."

"I wasn't pouting!"

"You were, just now! You looked totally cute."

I threw the towel in my hand at him. "Go shower."

He didn't bother to close the bathroom door. I was so not going to walk right in. I considered it about, oh, a dozen times, but finally opted out.

He came out a few minutes later, towel around his waist, hair damp and mussed. He had the perfect five o'clock stubble, having not shaved that morning.

I really, really, really times ten, wanted to jump him. It would be so, so easy to pull his towel off. Not that I hadn't seen, *ahem*, his goods, already. But not in private. Not in my frickin' bedroom!

"What's with your 'Fearless' tattoo?" I asked.

"Just what it says."

"Duh. I was hoping for some elaboration." I motioned a big circle with my arms.

"It means 'Don't be afraid to take risks, go after what you want in life, otherwise regret will consume your soul, and you'll kick yourself on your death bed.'" He winked. "I would've tattooed the whole thing, but I didn't think it would all fit. My shoulders aren't that broad."

I made a sarcasm face. "There's something to be said for brevity."

He darted his eyes toward his crotch and thrust his pelvis at me. "Who you calling brief?"

I rolled my eyes and Oed my mouth. "You are triple bad today, young man. Get dressed before I call the cops." I threw his t-shirt at him and walked out of the room.

When he came out of the bedroom, we walked down to my car together.

"Wanna take my bike?"

"No way am I going on the Suicide Ride any time soon, cowboy. We'll take my VW. Where are we going, anyway, Mr. Mentor?"

"On a time machine."

"What? You're joking."

"Nope."

"Then we're definitely taking my car. I won't risk falling off your bike and getting stuck with the dinosaurs or something."

Two hours later, we pulled into the round-about entrance to the parking lot at the Getty Center in Los Angeles.

We had to take a crowded tram up to the hilltop museum from the massive subterranean parking garage below. Tourists were everywhere, even in November. Southern California seemed like a perpetual vacation to me.

The view from the top of the hillside was incredible. You could see all of Los Angeles. The museum was immense, and made of huge cut stones.

When we reached the main entrance to the museum proper, Christos held his hand out like a butler.

"Welcome to the time machine." He flashed his dimples at me, as always, but in a gleeful boyish way I'd never seen on him. I could tell he loved this place.

"Is this what you meant last night when you told Brandon I had a busy day today?"

He grinned. "I suppose it is. So come on, the ancients await our presence."

Christos guided me around the museum, starting with ancient greek statuary and art. We worked our way forward in history. He had so many stories to tell about the artists who'd made the paintings and sculptures, like he knew them personally. It was obvious he lived and breathed art.

I was overwhelmed by it all. At one point, we stopped in front of a painting by Rembrandt Van Rijn that I recognized.

"This painting is nearly four hundred years old. But if you look at it closely, you can clearly see the brush work. If you know what you're looking at, you can understand exactly how Rembrandt laid down his oils. It's the closest thing anyone will ever get to a Youtube video of something that happened in the 1600s."

"Are you saying it's like one of those how-to drawing videos they have? But from four hundred years ago?"

"Pretty much. If you know what to look for." He smiled at me like he'd just showed me his secret stash of buried treasure.

"Wow, that's amazing, Christos." He had a way of making everything amazing and fun.

After we left the galleries, we had a snack in the outdoor cafe. It overlooked the west side of Los Angeles and the Pacific Ocean beyond. It was beautiful.

A cool breeze blew through my hair. "I love this place," I said over a bite of kiwi-covered fruit torte we'd bought at the snack bar. "I never want to go back to Washington D.C. Who needs presidents when you have the Pacific?"

"My sentiments exactly."

When we returned to the underground parking lot, Christos asked, "Mind if we stop in Beverly Hills? I need to hit up a gallery on Rodeo Drive and do some glad-handing with the owner."

"Beverly Hills? Mind? Hell no!"

We drove down Sunset Boulevard, passing tons of mansions and dozens of trendy clubs. It was unbelievable. We finally arrived in Beverly Hills. The actual 90210 Beverly Hills. Was I going to see movie stars? I'd never seen one in real life.

No movie stars, but plenty of expensive cars and expensive clothes.

The art gallery, called Spada, was immense. The paintings were just as big. Some canvases looked twenty feet wide and ten or more feet tall. They were abstract, colorful, and chaotic.

A really tan middle-aged guy with super white teeth, expensive slacks, and a silk dress shirt walked up to us from behind a huge circular desk in the middle of the gallery.

"Franco! I didn't expect to see you here on a Sunday!" Christos said.

"Hey Christos!" Franco chuckled. The two men hugged and clapped backs. "Good to see you, young man! I heard about your show last night. Selling out already! You're dad would be proud."

"Well, it was only two-thirds pre-sales. I had to schmooze most of the evening to close the rest of them."

"Two-thirds?" Franco scoffed. "What a tough night you had," he said sarcastically. "Who's your lovely lady friend?"

I blushed.

"This is my friend Samantha. She's an artist. Samantha, meet Franco Viviano."

"Oh, artist, huh?" Franco sounded impressed. I blushed more. We shook hands. "If Christos is shopping you around already, you must be amazing. He has an eye for talent, am I right?"

Oh crap, how was I supposed to respond to that? I was in way over my head. "Uh, thanks?"

Franco laughed a gravelly laugh. "She's as modest as you are. Well, make sure you give me first crack at her paintings, Christos. I'll get her top dollar.

"I'll do that." Christos wrapped his arm around me and squeezed me affectionately.

Holy crap! What the holy hell? What the what WHAT? I'd never painted in my entire life!

"And it won't be any of that chicken feed Charboneau pays." Franco cocked his head at Christos. "You're going to bring your next show up to L.A., right? Your dad's never complained about sales with me."

"Not at all," Christos agreed casually.

I think Franco's smile had suddenly turned shark-like. I glanced at Christos. He didn't seem phased. This was Christos' world for sure.

"Have a look around you two," Franco said. "I need to oversee an installation in Brentwood in about thirty minutes. But the gallery will be open until four. It was a pleasure meeting you, Samantha."

Franco walked into the back. An assistant, a gorgeous woman in her twenties, took over the desk. I imagined she was one of Franco's saleswomen. She looked like she could be a movie star, or a model, but I'm pretty sure she wasn't.

"Hey, Victoria," Christos said, waving at the beautiful assistant.

Victoria waved back. "Good to see you, Christos!"

"Wow, Christos," I marveled. "You know people everywhere we go!"

"Ahh, it's nothing. My dad's been selling through Franco since the nineties. I've known the guy for years. Franco's been to my grandad's house a bunch of times. He's always bugging him to paint again."

"How come your grandfather doesn't paint anymore, if you don't mind my asking?"

"It's a long story. Some other time?" Christos flashed an uncomfortable smile. The story would have to wait.

We looked at the paintings in the gallery. They were all abstract, very different from the realism in the Getty Center.

"This is the kind of work your dad paints, right?"

"Yeah, pretty much."

I walked to the next painting. "Where are the price tags?"

"This is one of those 'If you have to ask, you can't afford it' galleries."

"I couldn't afford anything of yours! How much does this stuff cost?"

"A lot more."

"Well, like how much?"

"Add a zero on the end of everything I sold last night."

My jaw dropped. "What?"

He nodded. "Yup."

"These artists make in the millions?"

"Tens of, sometimes."

"Holy bank heist, Batman! That's a fortune!" I realized I was talking too loud, and hunched my shoulders, peeking around to see if anyone was giving me the stink eye. Luckily, the gallery was almost empty on a Sunday afternoon. Victoria didn't seem to notice.

"Don't worry, Boy Wonder, I'll protect you from the evil gallery owners," Christos smirked.

I suddenly felt like both of us had spent far too much time around Kamiko and her cartoons. I laughed and leaned into Christos.

"Let's hop in the Batmobile and round up dinner," he suggested.

"Wait, you're letting Robin drive the Batmobile, Batman? Has that ever happened?" I gasped.

"Stop the presses, it's about too." He winked at me as we walked to my VW.

After leaving Rodeo Drive, we drove east, away from the setting sun, and ended up on Melrose Avenue.

I saw all the boutiquey shops and restaurants. Tons of people were walking from store to store wearing chic outfits and the trendiest shoes. I wanted to do a stop and shop so badly, but I knew once I got started, we'd never leave. I couldn't subject poor Christos to clothes and shoe whoring. We were doing the mentoring thing, right?

I reluctantly waved goodbye to Melrose Avenue. Next time.

We ended up back on Sunset Boulevard, and Christos directed me where to park.

I turned off the car. "Where are we?"

"Silver Lake."

"What's here?"

"Dinner."

We walked up to a gate in a cement wall abutting a hillside.

"This is it." He opened the gate for me.

"Where's the restaurant?"

"Upstairs."

I climbed the steps and he followed. There were so many steps, I was out of breath by the time we reached the top.

A hostess stood at her podium. "Table for two?"

"Yup," Christos answered.

"Right this way."

We walked into a dining room. A gigantic tree came up through the floor in the middle of the room. I looked up, and realized there was no ceiling. Just artfully arranged canvas tarps. I saw the twilight sky above.

The hostess seated us by a railing that overlooked an incredible view.

"This place is like a giant tree house! It's awesome!"

Christos held my chair for me. "Pretty cool, huh?"

"When you said dinner, I was thinking fish tacos or something."

"We can get those if you want. There's a place a couple miles from here in Los Feliz that has the tastiest fish tacos you will ever eat."

"Oh, no, this is fine." I smiled and picked up my menu. I wasn't giving this place up for fish tacos.

"Get whatever you want. Dinner is on me."

"Oh, no, I couldn't." Most of the items on the menu were affordable. I could spare the cash. But I wanted to maintain the "just friends" boundary Christos had drawn.

"Don't sweat it, Samantha. After my gallery sales last night, I can afford to buy you dinner."

"Yeah, but, I don't know. Do friends buy friends dinner?" I asked reluctantly.

"When friends make buckets of cash, yes they do." He toasted me with his water glass. "To selling art."

I raised mine and clinked. "To selling art."

"Your art." He took a swallow.

I choked on my water. "I'm not selling any art!" I sputtered.

"You heard Franco, he's ready and waiting to sell your paintings."

"I thought you guys were joking! I don't have any paintings!"

"So? That just means you'll have to paint some."

"I don't know how!"

"Your mentor does." He smiled smugly. "It's a simple matter of proper instruction, which I will be happy to provide."

Christos was doing that thing again where it was like a foregone conclusion that I was a successful artist, and the money and accolades were ready and waiting to roll right in.

I considered myself extremely fortunate to have him in my life, even if he was no more than a mentor.

The waiter came by and Christos ordered bourbon, neat. He was promptly carded, but he was twenty-two, so it wasn't a problem.

"Would you like anything to drink, Miss?" the waiter asked.

I wanted to get a drink too, but I was S.O.L. on that front. "Iced tea?"

"Excellent." The waiter walked off.

"You can share mine," Christos said.

"Oh, they won't let me, will they?"

"What're they gonna do, send the cops in and get me for contributing to the delinquency of a minor?"

I didn't like the idea of Christos tempting fate anymore than he already did. I didn't want to inject more drama into his life. He had enough on his own, that much he'd made clear. I just didn't know what his drama specifically was.

When the bourbon arrived, Christos encouraged me to taste it.

I glanced around. No one was going to notice in the busy restaurant if I took a sip. "My throat is burning! It tastes like gasoline!" I reached for my water. "How can you drink that stuff? Is it some man thing?"

Christos chuckled and took a swallow of his bourbon. "What can I say? I like how it tastes."

I would stick to wine in the future.

We ordered appetizers and entrees, and everything was wonderful. The sun had set and the city lights twinkled beneath the twilight sky.

The temperature had dropped, and I didn't have a sweater. When I shivered and hugged my arms, Christos found the waiter to light one of those gas heaters with the metal umbrella things on top.

"You warm enough?" He was so thoughtful.

"Now I am. Thanks for dinner, Christos. And everything else. I've had a wonderful day." I wanted to tell him how romantic everything was, but I didn't want the mentor-student lecture again.

"Me too."

He paid the bill without letting me see it.

We drove home and chatted about the art at the museum, Spada gallery, the tree-house restaurant, and all the shops I wanted to visit on Melrose next time.

It was so easy talking to Christos. He was genuine friend material, without a doubt. And the perfect mentor. So why did he have to be so damn hot? *And* make himself off limits?

I'm pretty sure Christos could've been a torturer during the Spanish Inquisition from the way he was treating me, pulling my emotions in every direction, stretching them to the limit.

Not that I wasn't enjoying it some of the time.

Did that make me a masochist?

Ahhh, who cared. You couldn't live life without getting a few bumps and bruises, right?

Taylor.

Chapter 18

It was late when we got back to my apartment. Christos walked me upstairs.

"You want a drink or anything?" I asked.

"I should probably go. Don't you have classes tomorrow?"

"Yeah. And homework to catch up on. My mentor made me blow it off," I smiled. "I'm going to be super busy for the next couple days."

"No problem. I'm sure I'll see you around campus. And we'll meet next Saturday for more mentoring?"

"Yeah!" I loved that we had a regular schedule now.

"Maybe we'll try some painting next time?"

"Oh, I don't think I'm ready."

"It's never too early to start. My dad put a paintbrush in my hand when I was four." He got a faraway look in his eyes. "All I remember is I managed to get paint on our dog. Beans was white, and the paint was red, and I thought I'd cut him open or something."

"Your dog's name was Beans?"

"Yeah. It was easy for me to say. Anyway, my dad was totally cool about the whole thing. I was freaking out, thinking Beans was bleeding to death. My dad cleaned him off, but I remember bawling the whole time. My dad kept reassuring me Beans would live."

"Wow, if I'd gotten paint on the family dog, I can only imagine my mom would've had a heart attack and my dad would've told me I was killing my mom with worry."

Christos looked at me thoughtfully. "I'm sorry."

"It's okay. It's how I grew up, I guess. You really love your dad, don't you?"

Christos face contorted with a maelstrom of conflicting emotions. "Yeah," he said quietly, lowering his eyes.

I couldn't leave him like this. "Let me get you a drink. Come inside." I opened the door and pulled him into my apartment by his arm.

I made tea for both of us, and joined Christos on the couch. I made sure to leave a respectable twelve inch mentor-student gap between us. Not that I wanted to.

"When was the last time you saw your dad?" I felt like I was prying, but I also sensed he needed to talk to someone about it.

He sipped his tea. "Months ago. He doesn't leave his house much."

"Do you visit?"

"He doesn't like visitors much anymore."

"Anymore? What happened."

"My mom happened."

I remembered she wasn't in any of the photos on the mantle at Spiridon's house. I wasn't going to pry. What if she was dead? I was afraid to ask. I sipped my tea.

"When she left my dad, he was crushed. My grandfather freaked out. He did his best to talk her out of it, but she wasn't having any of it. I freaked out too. I was ten at the time. My whole world fell apart."

I set my tea down and put my hand on his shoulder.

He stared at his hands, which knotted into fists. "You know how they say when the parents divorce, kids often blame themselves? I can tell you that's true. I begged my mom not to leave. I did everything I could to help cover up my dad's drinking, thinking that would change her mind." His knuckles were completely white and his hands quivered.

Drinking? His dad was an alcoholic?

"I tried throwing away his stashes, but he always bought more. I'm sure my parents fought about it plenty before my mom gave up. I heard them yelling all the time behind closed doors."

"Was your dad violent?" I asked timidly.

"Mostly no. He was the sweetest drunk you can imagine. Still is. But every once in awhile, he'd go off. Tear his paintings apart, make a mess of his studio. He was scary as hell when he was like that. But he never turned his anger on me or my mom, or anybody else. He just beat himself up."

I stroked Christos shoulder. He was obviously in agony. "I'm really sorry."

"Thanks." His face was bright red and his eyes dripped silent tears, like he was trying as hard as he could to hold them in, but he had so much pain, he was overflowing.

I slid over until my hip rested against his and hugged him fiercely. I had no idea what to say. How can you fix pain that big, that old? It was bigger than any person should ever have to endure. But it was there. Inside Christos. Eating him alive. I felt helpless.

I started crying too.

Taylor.

I knew about infinite pain as well.

Christos was taken aback by my tears. He reacted by wrapping his arms around my waist and pulled me into his chest in an intimate hug. It took me completely by surprise, but I didn't resist. I blended my body into his, chest to chest. He pulled me until I sat on his lap.

He sobbed convulsively while cradling me in his lap.

I was aware of his warmth, his scent, and his openness. Unlike last time, it didn't shut down after a quick taste. It flowed powerfully between our hearts. A connection beyond words, something eternal, something sacred.

Something entirely human and loving.

Something entirely new to me.

I cried harder, my own pain mixing with his. Our emotions amplified each other's. We were communicating without words, sharing the hurt and emotional trauma we'd both held inside for far too long.

Tears poured out of me. For the first time, I found a release valve for my sadness. The volume of it was larger than I had ever imagined. I realized in that moment that my repressed sadness was the source of the constant tension I felt brimming under the surface of my skin for over two years.

The shame.

Bitch. Slut. Whore.

The guilt.

Tease.

The sorrow.

Taylor.

For over two years, I'd avoided facing what had happened back *then*. I'd tried distracting myself with ice cream and alcohol, too much jogging, and countless bad decisions, but none of it helped release my pain. It had merely distracted me temporarily. Like clockwork, the pain of my hidden sadness, shame, and guilt always reared its head with a vengeance.

I really had believed I could shed my painful past by simply moving to San Diego and turning myself into a California beach girl. I thought by changing my outside, I would change my inside too. But it hadn't worked.

The internal scars hadn't healed. New clothes and a tan only covered them up.

But now, something *was* changing. I felt it deep inside me as I clung to Christos and his emotions poured through me. His release was cleansing my infected heart, washing away my old pain.

Our sharing of emotion was activating a natural healing mechanism. I began to sob more deeply and more profoundly than I ever had in my entire life. I shook with spasms of tortured release. My heartache was beyond anything I'd ever imagined possible. It was titanic.

I was afraid the pain would tear me apart.

Let it.

I wailed.

Christos gripped me tightly, positioning me so that my cheek nestled in his shoulder. He kissed the top of my head repeatedly, soothingly, affectionately.

"Samantha," he whispered in a voice so tender, I couldn't believe it had come from this intensely masculine man. "Samantha."

I shook with fresh sobs. He stroked my hair and kissed my forehead, showering me with affection, acceptance, and understanding.

Without the aid of any words, I felt my pain draining on its own. I had never been able to figure this out on my own. I had thought holding it in was the answer. But it wasn't.

The process wasn't about talking it out, either. It was about feeling it out. Feeling Christos' pain had triggered mine. I think I felt so safe with him, that I was finally capable of letting down my defenses. The simple sharing of Christos's pain had summoned my own, in a good way.

In release.

I couldn't have done it with any other person on the planet. Not my friends, not even my parents.

No one made me feel this safe.

This loved.

Terror swept through me. Warning sirens screamed in my heart. I was too open, too vulnerable. I was in danger. I needed to shut down or I was going to get hurt worse than I ever had been by my pain from my past.

The closest I had been to such thoughts for another person before Christos had led me toward heartbreaking disaster.

Tease.

No, I couldn't allow myself to feel love *from* Christos. It was dangerously close to allowing myself to love *him*. I was deathly afraid of where that would lead me.

"Let me up!" I panicked. I pushed away from him with both arms.

"What?"

"Let me go! I need to get out of here!"

He was so surprised, he released me and I jumped up. I didn't know where to go or what to do. I was trapped. I needed to get away.

I yanked the front door open and ran outside as fast as I could. I rushed down the balcony stairs, into the parking lot, and ran right out into the street.

My neighborhood was very quiet, so I literally ran down the middle of the empty road. Had there been any cars, I wouldn't have noticed until they ran me over, which I hoped would happen.

"Samantha! Come back! Samantha! Where are you going?" Christos' boots pounded the pavement behind me. He caught up before I made it to the next block.

He fell into step beside me. I didn't look at him. I was barely able to see through my tears. I tripped on a pothole and went down.

Christos caught me in his arms and we stumbled to a stop. He held on to me tightly. "Shhh, shhh, shhh. It's okay. I've got you."

A fresh storm of sobs poured out of me. He hugged me in the middle of the street. I held my arms stiffly at my sides, head turned away, trying to shield myself, trying to escape from Christos' kindness.

"I won't let go, Samantha," he whispered. "Let it out. I promise,

I won't let go."

His words should have been freaking me out even further. But they didn't. The simple act of his chasing me and catching me when I fell had comforted me in a way I couldn't understand. I wrapped my arms around him and hugged back.

Slowly, my feelings transformed in a crazy direction. Sadness yielded to its polar opposite. I felt authentic, unabashed joy, in a way I couldn't remember having before. I started to laugh. I tried to stop it, suddenly mortified, afraid Christos would think I was crazy.

But Christos laughed with me. We were laughing together. Standing in the middle of the street like fools. We both laughed so hard, we released our embrace, and stood leaning shoulder to shoulder like the two oldest pals in the history of the world.

The belly laughs continued until I was wheezing, and we both calmed into giggling. I don't know how long it lasted.

When we were both quiet, he rubbed my back until I stood up straight.

We looked into each other's eyes, both of us smiling widely. It took about three seconds for another wave of laughter to double us over, hands on knees.

When we calmed again, Christos said, "We should get back to the apartment. I left your door wide open."

We returned, and I washed my face in the bathroom sink. My eyes were totally red.

Christos stood behind me. "You look fine," he said.

His eyes were pretty red too. I guess it was okay.

We sat back down on the couch, facing each other.

We were both still giggly. When our eyes met, another round of laughter shook us. sending us rolling onto our backs on the couch.

We sprawled at opposite ends, draped over the cushions like two spent lovers. Staring at the ceiling, I sighed audibly. He sighed too. His voice was so damn manly and rich.

That got me thinking entirely inappropriate thoughts. I pulled my feet under me and sat up straighter.

He was still sprawled, and grinned at me.

Screw being careful. I crawled over to him and snuggled up against him. "Can friends and mentors cuddle?"

"Looks like it." He chuckled.

He stroked my hair gently. "I'm going to have to get you down to the studio and get you started with the paints next weekend."

"I promise I won't use red," I joked.

"Don't worry, Beans went to the dog beach in the sky a long time ago. He's probably rolling around in every color of the rainbow. Got it all over his fur." Christos chuckled.

"He looks like one of those rainbow unicorns, I bet. There's this one on Adventure Time that probably looks just like him." I felt stupid talking to Christos about Kamiko's cartoons. The truth was, I had now watched several episodes of Adventure Time in her dorm room while hanging with her and Romeo between classes.

"I know a guy who works on Adventure Time."

"What do you mean?"

"A buddy of mine works on the show. He's one of the storyboard artists."

I slapped my palms on his chest and sat up. "What? Do you seriously know, like, everybody?"

"Only in the art world." He gave me that smug smile of his. "He came down for my gallery opening."

"Kamiko would freak if you told her that!"

"If I'd known, I would've said something. I can set it up for them to meet, if you want."

"OMG! She would be so in love with you if you did that."

"Let me know, I'll make it happen."

"You're like the coolest guy ever."

"So they say."

I slapped his chest one-handed. "Ass." I laid back against him, stroking his chest. His muscles were so defined, deliciously ridged and curved. I made circles, pressing down with the heel of my hand. I slid my hand down to his abs. I couldn't help myself.

"You might not want to do that," he murmured.

"Why not?"

"Mentor, mentee?"

"Who thought of that word mentee, anyway? It sounds like manatee. It makes me sound like a blubbery sea cow."

"You are far from blubbery."

"Really?"

"You're about as far from being a cow as rainbow unicorns are from reality."

I snickered.

"I really should paint you nude sometime."

"No way. You only paint super hot women."

"Yup."

A pregnant pause vacuumed all the air out of the room.

"Are you saying I'm super hot?"

"Yup."

"Liar."

"Nope."

I propped myself up on my elbow and smiled at him. "You're totally just being nice. Between your paintings and my, uh, unexpected visit when you were with Paisley, I've seen more of the women you've been with than I ever cared to. They all have perfect bodies. I'm not even close to them."

"I'm the artist here, I'll make that call."

"But you haven't seen me naked!"

"I saw you in a bikini at the beach. It was pretty obvious."

"That's right! I almost forgot!"

"Why do you think I wanted to mentor you so bad?" He smiled mischievously.

"You are such a perv, Christos!"

"Why, because you're hot, and I like it?"

"You, you like it?"

His face twisted into a smirk. "Are you insane? Of course I like it. I'm sure every guy who gets a good look at you likes it. Why do you think so many guys hit on you, Samantha?"

"I don't know, because guys are dogs?"

"While that may be true, and I'm not pointing any fingers here, I'm somewhat picky. If you hadn't noticed."

"Yeah, I've noticed all your super model cohorts. Guys are so damn shallow."

"Why, because we go after the best looking women we can find?"

"Exactly." I flopped onto my back. I wasn't the women he 'went' after, so that automatically disqualified me. He was bullshitting. "If I was so hot, you would totally be all over me right now."

"That can be arranged."

My heart stopped. No, seriously, this time it actually stopped. I don't know for how long. Not like an hour, or even a minute, but it seemed like forever. "What," I coughed. "What did you just say?"

"I said, that can be arranged."

I stared at the ceiling, afraid to move, like I would break the spell. "I thought we were mentor and student, or mentee, or whatever."

"Thus far, yes." A sly smile slid across his lips.

I really wanted to lick those lips.

"Well, what are you going to do about it?"

"Anything you want."

A pulse surged up my entire body and bounced back down. What did he mean by anything? Did he mean *anything* anything? Judging by the way his eyes smoldered, I think the standard definition was in effect.

He crossed his chest on top of me. His nose was an inch from mine. "You have no idea how long I've wanted to do this."

"You're right, I don't. You've acted like I was the least desirable woman on the planet most of the time."

"I had a professional responsibility to adhere to. But we can change that." He slid his thumb across my lower lip.

Oh, shiver.

He kissed the tip of my nose. I didn't think that would be sexy, but it was. Incredibly. He kissed one of my cheeks, then the other, then each corner of my mouth, as if he was anointing me with a blessing of some kind. Maybe he was.

"I don't know if you realize this, but your lips are exceedingly luscious," he murmured. His mouth hovered over mine. I smelled his sweet breath. I'm glad I served us mint tea!

"How luscious are they?"

"This luscious." He brushed his lower lip across my mouth. It was slick and wet. A quiver shot up from my sex to my head. A soft moan whispered from me.

He flicked his tongue across my upper lip. Oh, wow. He tickled me with gentle almost-kisses for I don't know how long. I was sailing over the moon. My body flushed with heat.

I felt his fingers stroke my cheek, slip down the line of my jaw, caress my neck, and dance across my chest. The gentlest feather touch from his fingertips slid down my cleavage. I wanted him to rip my t-shirt off right then.

Then his hand was on my waist. Fire flared in my belly as it worked down to my hip. His thumb teased the tops of my jeans, probing the seam between my t-shirt and the waist band of my panties, were the thinnest strip of skin was exposed completely to him.

More shivers spasmed through my body, emanating from my core. My eyes squeezed shut as the pleasure overwhelmed me. I squeezed my knees together, not to prevent his access, but to hold in the incredible energy that he had stirred inside my body with the faintest touch. I wanted to hold on to that pleasure as long as I could.

I had made out with a couple different boys a bunch of times in high school, but nothing approaching this. And Christos and I hadn't even joined our lips together in a full kiss.

His soft touches continued along my collar bone, then alternated back to my waist, where his thumb slid across to my other hip.

I was so distracted by his touch that I almost missed the moment his lips first pressed all the way into mine. When I felt the wetness of his slick lips, he had my full attention.

All previous kisses were but ripples on a pond. This was crashing forty-foot waves, the perfect storm of kissing. The intense energy flew through my body and heart, spiraling out in every direction. My thighs quivered and my pelvis throbbed while my mouth burned with hunger fulfilled.

I reveled in the experience of his kiss. One moment gentle and yearning, the next desperate and forceful. I could feel him wanting me and wanting me to want him.

He was both confident and uncertain. It seemed so unlike him. Was the confidence the Adonis part of him, and the uncertainty the Christos part of him? I had never seen him behave timidly with any of his women friends, but I felt it now. The vulnerability. That seed of self-doubt and insecurity. Was he afraid of rejection too? Like a normal human being?

That drove me wild. I opened my lips and his tongue slid into my wetness and circled my own, the tip of his dancing against the tip of mine. I needed him inside me. Like this, like…what was I thinking?! I was getting way ahead of myself!

I pushed my palm to his chest. "Wait," I breathed, "a second, just a…"

Tease.

He pulled away.

I feared anger would suddenly disfigure his beautiful features. But no, calmness, warmth, and openness emanated from him like sunrise.

"What's wrong?"

A voice sprung up in my mind, *"You're not mad at me, are you?"*

And that inevitably led to...

Taylor.

No. No, no, no. It was happening again. Horror seized my heart.

Christos frowned. "Do you want me to stop?"

"Yes. No. For a second. I need to catch my breath." I sat bolt upright, ready to run from the couch because I was convinced Christos was going to explode and go ballistic on me any second.

"Samantha?"

He never called me Samantha. Always Sam. There was a soothing note in Christos' deep baritone voice that calmed me instantly.

"Are you all right? Something's bothering you. If you want to stop, give me the word. We don't have to do this."

Did he mean the kissing, the mentoring, or everything? I started to panic. I didn't know if I was afraid he would leave, or afraid he would stay. And what would happen if he *did* stay?

"If it's something else, Samantha, I can go home. If that will make you more comfortable."

"I, no. Don't leave. It's just that, when I kissed you, I..."

"Did I hurt you? I kind of got carried away." He grinned. "I sort of lost my equilibrium for a minute there, when my tongue went in your mouth. I've never been so, I don't know, so swept away. Just from kissing."

"You too?" I blurted like a little kid. I was immediately embarrassed and hid my face in both hands.

"It's okay," he chuckled. "Yeah, me too. It was pretty awesome."

"I thought you were totally into, like, sex with your hot girlfriends. How could kissing do that to *you*?"

"I don't know. But it did. I'm sort of not surprised."

"Really? Why?"

"Because you're different."

I lowered my hands, wanting to hear more. "How?"

"You have this feisty spirit. You just barrel into things."

I wrinkled my nose. "That makes me sound clumsy."

"No, not like that. You jump into things, try new stuff without worrying about the consequences. You went to college on the other side of the country where you didn't have a single friend. That takes courage."

I didn't want to admit that in this case, courage equaled running away.

"And you took an art class."

"There were plenty of girls drooling all over you that first day of class. It's like they knew you'd be there," I scoffed.

"Maybe they did. But you didn't. You were there to learn how to draw."

"I suppose you're right." I smiled.

"And you're totally hot."

"Stop!" I covered my blushing cheeks with my hand.

"Your eyes are twinkling." He smiled warmly.

"Are they?"

"Like diamonds."

"Hey, that sounds like lyrics from Twinkle Twinkle Little Star. You are way too corny, Christos!" But I sort of liked it anyway.

"How I wonder what you are," he grinned.

"Up above the world so high," I answered.

We both broke into soft chuckles.

"Nerd," I said.

"Hey, what can I say? I hang out with the crayon kids at the library every Saturday. Their musical tastes have rubbed off on me."

How did this boy manage to wash away all my pain and fear so easily?

He was a godsend.

He was Christos.

I don't know when we fell asleep on the couch. But I woke up in his arms.

He was staring at me through his dark lashes.

"What are you looking at?"

"You."

"Don't. I probably look like death."

"You look like life."

I opened my mouth to object. Closed it. He kissed my forehead gently. I could only smile and hug him tightly.

"It's late. You should go to bed. I should go home."

"No. Stay."

His eyes narrowed thoughtfully and he sat up. After a moment, he stood up.

"Where are you going?" I didn't want him to leave.

He bent over and picked me up. "To sleep." He carried me into my bedroom. "With you." From the soft, sleepy tone of his voice, I knew all he meant was sleep, like last night.

At some point, we had kicked our shoes off when we were on the couch, but I still had my clothes on. So did he.

He stood in front of me and pulled his shirt over his head. No matter how often I saw him, once the shirt was off and the abs came out, I melted. He was certifiably perfect.

He unbuckled his belt and slid his jeans down.

My eyes widened.

"You ever see a deer caught in headlights?"

"No." I frowned. "Random?"

"I have. Just now." He chuckled. "Don't worry, the boxers stay on."

"What happened to commando?"

"That's for summer. When it cools off, I wear the boxers for warmth."

"Geez, in D.C. people wear long underwear."

He pulled the legs of his jeans off each foot. "How about you? Sleeping in your clothes?"

"Of course not."

"Want me to help?"

My eyes popped at the thought of what that might lead to. But he'd done it the night before. Why not twice? "Okay."

"T-shirt and panties again?"

"I guess."

"You want your boxers? Where were they again?"

"No, not really."

He cocked his head. "What are you saying, Samantha?"

"I don't know." I rolled my eyes. Because I didn't know.

"You want the shirt off?"

"Yes." I smiled coyly.

He pulled it over my head. I liked being undressed by Christos. I needed to work on making it a daily habit, if at all possible. I was down to bra and panties now.

"You gonna sleep like that?"

I never slept in my bra. "Okay." I really didn't want my shirt on.

We laid down on the bed together. Skin to skin, for the most part. Was I going to be able to sleep like this? Probably very little. I was okay with that.

"Wait, the lights!" I hopped up, dashed into the living room, and turned everything off. I dove back into bed, right on top of Christos.

He wrapped his arms around me. I pecked him on the lips. "Good night."

I rolled off him and snuggled myself into his form-fitting side.

I was right about the no sleep thing. I could hear his heart beating. It helped lull me, but about twenty minutes later, my boobs were screaming for me to take my bra off.

T-shirt or naked. Which was it going to be?

I reached behind my back and unhooked the strap. It popped free.

"You okay over there?" Christos asked.

"Yeah, just a second." I sat up and gave him a cocky smile in the near darkness. "Get those dollar bills ready, boys!"

"Hey, I can't see shit with the lights off!" The only light in the room was the faint glow from the bathroom nightlight.

"It's extra for the light show," I said slyly.

"My wallet's full."

"And other things, I'm sure." I giggled. Who was running my potty mouth all of a sudden?

He reached over and snapped the nightstand lamp on.

"Hey!"

"I'm not missing this for the world."

"Fine." I shrugged my bra down until I felt it teasing against my nipples, which were now completely hard. I lowered my chin and batted my eyelashes comically, pretending like this was all a big joke.

I considered wiggling my shoulders until my bra fell off, like a trashy stripper, but I had *some* class. I let gravity pull my bra gently free. I held it up in one hand like a prize, then let it drop to the floor behind me.

Now it was Christos' turn for his eyes to goggle.

"Fuck me."

"We're not having sex, Christos!"

"I wasn't talking about sex. I was emoting."

"Emoting?"

"Expressing the emotional explosion of awe that is pounding in my chest right now." He took my wrist and I gasped, but he was only placing my palm over his heart, which really was pounding. "Yeah. That. Because of those." He flicked his eyes at my breasts.

"You like them?"

"'Like' is an inadequate word for what I'm feeling at the moment."

"I always thought I had weird boobs. You really like them?"

"I'd really like to lick them."

I covered them instantly with my forearms. "Okay, sleep time. Lights out, campers!"

I twisted and turned the lamp off, then fell into his arms. Thank god for my panties and his boxers.

I laid my torso across his. My bare breasts were actually touching his thick pectorals. His soft chest hair tickled my nipples.

This was not helping the sleep thing any.

I crossed my knee over his thigh. That's when I felt this huge thing in his boxers pressing against my leg. I flinched.

"Sorry," he said sheepishly. "I can't help it."

Oh my god, how large was he? His manhood was burning hot under his boxers, and I felt the thickness of him pressing against my thigh.

"I'll reposition, hold on." He reached down and pulled himself over to the other side of his boxers. "Better?"

Yes, no? Yes, no? Yes? No? I couldn't decide. "Uhhh..."

"You know, this is entirely your fault," he snickered. "Why don't we try and sleep."

As if.

Despite my doubts, Christos behaved admirably. I was pretty sure if I was any of the other girls he'd been with, we'd be having sex right then. But he didn't try any orchestral maneuvers in the dark, not that I would have necessarily rejected his advances. But nothing happened.

And strangely, I didn't feel like a slut. Or a tease. I'd never been this completely naked with a boy, or man, ever before. But it felt so natural. So normal. So wonderful.

How lucky was I?

"So," I whispered while gently stroking his silken chest hair, "how come you always call me Samantha, when everyone else calls me Sam?"

"Because, Sam seems so plain and boyish. You are the opposite of both. You are all woman, and a fascinating one at that."

I could live with that. "Why, um, did you kiss me, and break the mentor code?"

"The tattoo."

"Huh?"

"Fearless?"

"Oh." Still not getting it. "Huh?"

"I've only got one shot at life on this planet, as far as I know. Or anyone else knows, for that matter. And there's only one of *you* on this planet, Samantha. That much I know for certain, beyond all doubt. I've been really lucky to have met a ton of women in my life already. But not a single one has torn away my armor like you have. No woman has ever seen me cry. Except maybe my mom, when I was a kid. But none of the women I've dated or been with have ever seen what's beneath my surface. I've always hidden it."

I was nearly speechless. "Why?" I whispered in the darkness.

"I think because, deep down, I never trusted any of them."

Okay, now I was speechless.

Believe it or not, some time later, we both actually fell asleep.

I was caught in a terrible dream. But it was real, because I had lived it. Or a version of it.

I was being chased by a terrible presence. A dark thing that wanted to hurt me. A thing that had already hurt me countless times. A thing that had snuck inside my body and fed off of me every night for over two years. No matter how hard I tried to exorcise the thing, it always came back, haunting me, stalking my dreams, twisting them into nightmares.

"Samantha."

I thrashed, trying to get away.

"Samantha."

It was going to devour me if I didn't escape.

"Samantha."

But it was *still* inside me. I feared it couldn't ever be exorcised.

"Samantha, wake up!"

I jumped and flailed in the darkness.

"Samantha," Christos whispered. "It's me. You were having a nightmare."

"Oh, Christos!" I hugged him and cried into his chest. "Hold me."

He wrapped his arms lovingly around me and stroked my hair. "It's okay, Samantha. I'm here. You're safe."

I did feel safe. In his arms.

When my crying subsided, he kissed my forehead. "Who's Taylor?" he asked.

I shot up to a sitting position, terrified. "How do you know that name?" I gasped.

"You were whimpering it over and over again in your sleep."

Oh no. What else had I said?

"I heard you saying 'Taylor' last night, too," he said quietly. "When I was on the couch, before I dozed off. You were talking in your sleep for a long time."

"Oh my god, what did I say?"

"Most of it was gibberish, but you kept saying Taylor."

"Is that all I said? Taylor?"

"Yeah, as far as I could tell."

I breathed a huge sigh of relief. "Good."

"Good? You don't sound good at all."

"I need ice cream." I jumped out of bed, threw on a t-shirt, and went into the kitchen. I grabbed a pint and when I closed the freezer, Christos was standing right there.

"Want to talk about it?"

"No." I grabbed a spoon from the dish rack. "Want some?" I felt like such an enabler, not that Christos was in danger of over eating. He ate like a horse.

"Sure."

We sat on the couch and shoveled ice cream together. I couldn't tell if he was eating at a normal pace, or trying to eat all the ice cream before I ate too much. I wasn't going to ask. I was busy inhaling creamy release.

"Do you think if you eat enough ice cream, it will take the pain away?" Christos asked innocently.

How the fuck did he know that?

"You can't fix emotional damage with sugar, you know."

Okay, he was reading my mind. "Do you have like ESP, or something?"

"No. But its pretty obvious what's going on. Your freezer could stock an ice cream parlor. Who keeps that much ice cream on hand?"

I was so caught red-handed. I expected to look at my palms and see wet red paint glistening on them. If Beans the Dog had been around, I would've wiped my hands on him to get rid of the evidence, distracting Christos from using his ESP action.

Christos dug out a huge chunk of ice cream loaded with chocolate chunks.

"Hey, that's mine!" I jousted spoons with him.

"I'm happy to share," he chuckled.

Why didn't I feel ashamed when Christos was seeing right through me? He was some kind of modern day medicine man or something.

"Want to talk about Taylor?"

"No."

"Did Taylor hurt you?"

"No. Yes. Stop asking questions! I need more ice cream!"

"Let me get it for you. What flavor do you want?"

"Are you enabling me now?"

"No, I'm hungry. I'm pretty sure I can work through the rest of what's in your freezer tonight."

Damn him. Why did he have to make indulging in my vices so freaking enjoyable?

"You better not eat all my ice cream!" Somehow, I didn't really care if he did. Being with him, like this, made me not want it that much.

He returned with Coffee Mocha Fudge Suicide. It wasn't *actually* called that, but you get the idea.

"Tell me about Taylor."

"Some other time, please, Christos?" I begged.

He looked up at me. His eyes were so damn blue. I hated his eyes.

"All right, but one of these days you should really talk it out. I'll be there for you when you're ready, okay?"

I took a bite of ice cream and mushed it around in my mouth. "Ogay," I said through the ice cream blob on my tongue.

He leaned forward and kissed the tip of my nose. "Mmm, it tastes so much better when I eat it off your skin."

I looked cross-eyed at the tip of my nose.

He chuckled. "That's a good look for you."

"Did I have ice cream on my nose?"

"Until I licked it off."

"Maybe I should put ice cream on the rest of my body."

"Anywhere you want, I will lick it clean."

Gulp. And I wasn't swallowing ice cream. I jammed another spoonful in my mouth.

I actually stopped eating before I felt remotely close to bloated. Although I didn't need the extra calories, at least it hadn't been a full-fledged binge. I had Christos to thank for that. It didn't take long for me to forget the ice cream. And Taylor.

We ended up pulling out my laptop and watching clips of Adventure Time online. Christos thought the show was hilarious. I couldn't decide whether or not to curse Kamiko for introducing me to it. Then again, I was watching cartoons with Christos. I couldn't complain about that!

When I was tired, and the sugar high had worn off, we went back to bed. I slept soundly until morning.

Chapter 19

Christos went home Monday morning, and I went straight to school. I didn't have time to get coffee.

I was pretty groggy because I hadn't slept nearly as well as I'd hoped. Sleeping with Christos' arms around me was difficult, to say the least. But it was worth it.

I'd have to power through class on adrenalin and memories of Christos.

On my way to Fundamentals of Accounting, Madison nearly bowled me over, knocking me into two students who scowled at us like we were the bane of their college experience. I nearly dropped my drawing pad, but now that I kept the pad clipped to the clipboard, it was easier to keep a grip on it.

"Sam!" Mads screeched comically while hugging me. "Where have you been!

"Hey, Mads!"

She shoved a coffee into my hand. "I bought you this on the chance you weren't dead in a ditch somewhere."

"Thanks, Mads." I swigged the liquid crack caffeine. "You have no idea how bad I need coffee right now. Oh, and the *perfect* amount of half-and-half."

"*Half* half-and-half, right?" She winked.

"You got it."

"You have some 'splainin' to do, chickie-boo. I texted you all weekend and you totally blew me off. Jake told me Adonis was going surfing with us Sunday morning, but he never showed up." She arched her brows theatrically. "You wouldn't happen to know anything about that, would you?"

I couldn't hide my smile.

"You do!"

"What can I say? You've been so busy with Jake on the weekends, I had to find a distraction."

"Man distraction?"

I shrugged my shoulders.

"I call bullshit! Don't try to hide it from me, girlfriend! I have informants everywhere. I finally talked to Romeo Sunday afternoon and he told me you went out for drinks with Adonis Saturday night, after some gallery show?"

"*His* gallery show."

"Who? Adonis?"

"Yeah. And his name's actually Christos." I figured since Romeo and Kamiko knew, Mads should too.

"Really," Madison said, flabbergasted. "He's an artist AND hot AND rides a motorcycle AND is super nice?"

"Yeah," I said shyly.

She frowned. "He didn't get you shot at again, did he?"

I repressed any comments about the Bigfoot attack in the back of Xanadu. I was pretty sure getting chased by a crazy biker gang was not what one thought of when imagining the ideal man.

Madison scrutinized my face. "Whatever drama there was, Sam, I don't want to know about it." Was she reading my thoughts? "But you can tell me all the juicy good parts after class," she smiled.

We walked into the lecture hall together. Another mind-bending session of accounting principles. I did my best to not think about Christos. I was lucky I had a laptop and not a notebook. Otherwise, I probably would've spent the entire class doodling sketches of his beautiful body in the margins of my notebook, instead of actually taking notes.

After accounting, Madison and I went to the Student Center to meet up with Romeo and Kamiko.

"Hey, Sam!" Kamiko smiled.

Romeo ran up and threw his arms around me. "We thought you were dead!" His voice shook with fake sobs. "Madison called Sunday and told me you had been abducted by aliens. Did they probe your behind?"

"No butt probes," I giggled. "Sorry, Romeo."

"What about man probes? You *did* leave with Christos, girl. Don't try to deny it! Tongue or schlong probe? Which was it?"

Madison and Kamiko blurted out laughter, exchanging horrified stares.

"Subtlety, thy name is not Romeo," Kamiko mocked.

Romeo shot her dirty daggers. "You *so* want to know what happened, Kamiko. Even though Christos doesn't have a cartoon penis."

Everyone was shocked into silence.

"What?" Romeo protested. "We all saw his cock months ago!"

"I didn't!" Madison protested.

"Kamiko has a great drawing of it in her clipboard, if you want to see what you missed," Romeo sneered.

"Okay! No!" Madison blushed. "General verbal details will suffice. Measurements are not necessary! Sam? Care to tell us what happened, before Romeo spoils the mood?"

All eyes were on me. They wanted answers. "We sort of spent the night together."

"Which night?" Kamiko demanded.

"Saturday."

They nodded appreciatively.

"And Sunday," I said bashfully.

"Schlong probing, ladies and gentlemen!" Romeo said triumphantly. "There's no other possible explanation."

Madison snapped her fingers. "That's why you didn't have coffee this morning! I should've known!"

"We didn't, you know." I blushed. "There was no probing," I shot a warning glare at Romeo. "We just slept together," I said timidly.

"You are such a LIAR!" Romeo shout-whined.

Madison cocked her head thoughtfully. "I'm going to say the evidence weighs in favor of the prosecution."

Kamiko nodded. "It's okay, Sam. People do have non-cartoon sex now and then." She leveled a dirty look at Romeo. "If they didn't, there wouldn't be any newborn baby cartoonists and animators!"

Romeo rolled his eyes and stuck his tongue out at Kamiko.

"I swear, I didn't have sex! No probing of any kind!" I didn't mention our kissing tongues. Did that count?

They all cocked their heads doubtfully.

"Aren't we late for class or something?" I pleaded.

"We want details, darling," Romeo demanded, folding his arms across his chest.

"Yeah," Madison chimed in, "we're not moving an inch until you dish some dirt."

"Okay, okay! There may have been some nudity involved. But that's it! I promise!"

"What say you, the jury?" Romeo asked.

"All right, Sam. We'll let you off the hook. For now," Madison sighed. "But come lunch today, you're taking the stand, and swearing on bibles."

"Fine, I'll tell you guys more over lunch. Now can we go?"

"See you guys at lunch," Madison said before walking to her next class.

Romeo, Kamiko and I went to Life Drawing together, drawing pads in hand.

We made it to class with time to spare and set up. I was now comfortable in this environment and started warming up with sketches from my imagination on my drawing pad. Such a difference from the first day when I thought I was a complete poseur.

"Who do you think the model is today?" Romeo asked.

"I hope it's Genesis," Kamiko said. "She's got those super long legs and wasp-waist that looks totally anime."

"Yeah, she does great poses," I said. "I think she must be a dancer." Genesis was by far the best model we'd had, and she'd posed on three separate occasions already.

"Okay, class! We have a treat today," Professor Childress said. "We're going to have two models posing together. This will be a unique opportunity for you to study how the lines of one figure flow into the other."

Two models? At the same time? I was a little worried. It was hard enough drawing one at a time.

"Don't worry about finished drawings," the professor said. "Focus on long lines and the basic gesture."

Okay, I could do that. I really liked the gesture part.

A minute later, Genesis walked in. Cool. Her poses would be awesome. I wonder if the other model would be a dancer too? I think one of our other models, Zoey, was also a dancer. Maybe it would be her.

Genesis undressed and started with one minute poses on the

dais in the center of the room. Her hair was up in a tight dancer's bun.

Where was the other model? I didn't have time to worry about it. I started sketching. It was such a wonderful feeling to realize that I'd made a lot of progress in only a couple of months. I had a confidence, due in part to Christos' instruction, that I'd never imagined myself capable of. I really enjoyed drawing.

I was so into it, almost missed the knock on the door. Professor Childress walked over and opened the door a crack. He whispered to someone in the hallway, then closed the door again. Who was he talking to? The other model? I guess the model would have to wait until Genesis took a break.

After twenty minutes, Genesis put on a silk robe and walked around the room. When she got to my pad, she stopped. "Wow, nice drawings. I remember your work from the last class. I can tell you're getting better super fast."

"Thanks, Genesis! That's sweet."

"What's your name?" She offered her alabaster hand.

I shook it. "Sam."

She smiled warmly. "Nice to meet you, Sam. You drawings have a natural flow to them. Really nice."

"Do you draw?"

"I have, but it's a struggle. I think dancing's my calling." She smiled. "But I can tell your calling is drawing."

I blushed. She smiled, then walked around the room, looking at the other student's work.

Professor Childress unlocked the door and went outside. I was chatting with Romeo and Kamiko when the professor returned.

With Christos.

Why was Christos in drawing class?

"Our second model was a little late, but here he is, as promised. Everybody remembers Christos Manos?" the professor asked.

The two flamingo girls, Hourglass and Breasticles, who had been in class since day one, were still here. They both started preening the second they saw Christos. I was surprised they didn't drop the class weeks ago, when Christos didn't come back. I guess they really were taking the class as an elective, even though they were bitches.

Wow, why was I so worked up all of a sudden? I think it was the fact that Hourglass licked her lips when she looked at Christos. Yes, bitch for sure.

Christos stepped onto the dais and stripped. I didn't have a reaction anything remotely like I'd had last night, or even the first day of class.

Christos was naked. In front of a room full of people, half of which were girls. Two of which were the preening flamingos, both of whom where busy flipping their manes of hair at the man who had spent the night in *my* bed. And one very naked Genesis, who looked like a super model and was now standing completely naked next to Christos.

W. T. F.

"We'll start with one minute poses, so let's see something dynamic," the professor said.

Genesis briefly conferred with Christos in a low voice. Although her tone sounded business like, did she have to shove her nose in Christos' ear?

Christos nodded.

Genesis took Christos' hand in hers and they leaned back from each other, counter-balancing each other's weight.

They were naked. And they were holding hands.

I believe at that moment I completely lost the ability to draw. The sensible solution would be for me to pack up and walk the F out of the room.

Okay. Pause. Breathe. No, I wasn't going to be that way. It's not like they were holding each other in their arms.

Okay, fine. I started drawing. Then they changed poses. And they were holding each other in their arms.

My charcoal stick snapped in two in my fingers. I had to dig out another one.

Romeo glanced at my pad. "We're not drawing the invisible man and woman," Romeo hissed. "Put some lines down, Sam."

I glared cruise missiles at him.

His eyes popped. "Sor-*ry!*" he whispered.

To be fair, the pose had a very ballet vibe to it. Not porn, or even R-rated love scene. But stylized and classical.

Maybe I could do this.

Christos leaned over, supporting Genesis in his arms. Her back arched dramatically, her head turned elegantly to the side, and her arm extended into delicate outstretched fingers.

If I didn't know better, I'd say they had practiced this routine together. But when? I was with Christos most of the weekend. Hadn't he spent Saturday preparing for his show? Or had he slithered off to be naked with Genesis? I'm sure they knew each other. How could they not, considering how fluidly they posed together?

I frowned and looked at my drawing pad. All I had was black scribbles. They looked angry and spiteful. Was I jealous?

Duh.

Christos and Genesis changed poses again. Now his arms were around her waist in another ballet-style pose. I glanced over at Hourglass Flamingo and she was literally chewing on her lower lip. All she needed to complete the ensemble was to massage her own breast or shove her fingers down her pants. Grrr.

Oh my god. I secretly eye-rolled her for that, shook my head in disgust, and fumed.

I had two choices. I could either stab Hourglass Flamingo in the eye with a pencil, or stab Genesis in the heart with one.

Why was I being so possessive? I mean, it's not like Christos and I were dating. He'd spent the night at my house. We'd kissed. We'd slept naked together. Now he was naked and practically on top of Genesis. Crazy voice: *why would I have any reason to be angry?*

I inhaled deeply, trying to pull myself out of my bitchward spiral. Genesis had been super cool to me during the break, and she didn't even know me. Plus, she was obviously focused intently on her pose. She wasn't drooling over Christos like Hourglass Flamingo was.

I exhaled my anger.

Christos was also focused on what he was doing. His pose was part of a complete story that the combination of his and Genesis' body language told together. His head was turned away from Genesis, and he stared at the floor, forlorn. He appeared to be pulling her by the waist in a direction opposite the way she wanted to go. Genesis appeared completely open and surrendered in Christos' arms, yet a certain confusion tightened her features, as if she were contemplating escape.

They were distant in their closeness. She tried to flee while he pulled her into the unknown.

Two lovers united, yet in conflict.

It felt annoyingly symbolic and relevant to what I was feeling right at that moment. When I made this connection, I set to drawing and scribbled down some lines.

I finally appreciated the beauty of the pose. My lines were no longer black and angry, but light and flowing.

The poses continued for twenty minutes. I realized Christos never looked at me the entire time. I wasn't sure if I should be offended and hurt, or impressed by his professionalism. Because Genesis and Christos made an amazing team.

When they finished, Genesis put on her robe and Christos pulled on his jeans. He glanced around the room. Moment of truth. Which way was he going to go?

He nodded at Hourglass. She swooned. Bitch.

Then he turned and walked over to my easel. "Surprise." He smiled broadly.

Romeo leaned in front of me and shook Christos' hand before I could offer up any bitchiness. I think I was grateful.

Kamiko joined us.

"Hey, guys," Christos said to all of us. "Good to see you."

"Hey, uh, Christos," Kamiko said. "Your gallery show was awesome! Your paintings were amazing."

"Thanks, Kamiko." He smiled.

Christos leaned over and kissed the corner of my mouth. "Hey, Samantha." His eyes held mine. I admit this made me hot all over.

"Hey, Christos," I choked out stiffly. I was still somewhat defensive.

"Did you manage to get our dear Sam home safely on Saturday?" Romeo asked.

Christos' grin widened further. "You could say that."

"I hope she wasn't a burden," Romeo quipped.

"Not a bit. She's too easy on the eyes for that." He stroked my arm with the backs of his fingers. "How'd your sketches turn out, Samantha?" He walked around my easel to get a good view.

I was embarrassed for him to see the angry blacks stabs of charcoal that were my first drawings of him and Genesis. I was pretty sure that he, as an artist, would figure it out. All I had to do was not show him that page. I turned to the last page of drawings.

"I really want to see the first couple we did," he said innocently.

"They had a lot of dynamic energy. I'm curious how you handled it." He reached to turn back the pages.

I stopped him and smoothed the page back down. "Oh, um, my charcoal broke on those. They're terrible." I gave him a guilty grin.

"Okay," he said strangely. "How about the others?"

Those I was willing to show.

"Nice, Samantha. Your gestures are better every time I see them. I really like what you did with Genesis' hips in this one. Simple flaring lines. Really captures her narrow waist."

I wanted to ask what *he* did to Genesis' hips during that pose, since he had his hands on them. But I bit down on my words. I was determined not to be a jealous bitch. "Thanks."

Genesis slowed as she came by. "Great work, Sam. I love that one on the bottom right!" She crinkled her nose and smiled, but kept walking. I'd half feared she would come up and drape her arms around Christos, but she hadn't.

The timer beeped, signaling that the break was over.

"Five minutes poses, please," Professor Childress said.

Christos and Genesis undressed and posed on the dais.

"Too bad Madison isn't here to see Christos," Romeo whispered.

I rolled my eyes. "You're such a slut, Romeo," I hissed.

"I know, right?" He smiled with no hint of guilt whatsoever.

I sighed. I was a bit calmer now, and focused mostly on the drawing. Because the poses were longer, the models had to assume more relaxed stances.

During the second pose, Christos looked directly at me. I saw him smirk ever so slightly. I met his eyes, suddenly determined to make him crack a smile completely.

I pouted my lips seductively. I lowered my lashes and casually slid my fingers toward my cleavage.

He widened his eyes and cocked his head a quarter of an inch. He shook his head minutely, as if to say, "Stop what you're doing." His raised eyebrows clearly warned, "Or else."

I gave him an "Or else what?" head cock.

He rolled his eyes and lowered his gaze to the floor. That wasn't the effect I was going for. I was bummed. But I could tell he was struggling to hold back his grin. His face reddened.

I had him. He was about to break. But then he took a deep

breath and released it slowly. He raised his eyes to mine and stared at me stoically.

I glanced around to make sure no one was watching me. Everyone was busy drawing. I narrowed my eyes again and caressed my stomach with my fingertips. I bit my lower lip. I slid my fingers across the bottom of my breasts, tickling them through my shirt and bra.

Then I saw Christos twitch. I mean it. His...probe. It twitched again. Oh shit! What had I gone and done? I hadn't thought this through! Whoopsie me!

Christos' eyes widened in full panic. I froze. He was pleading with me. His cock grew ever so slightly. Shit!

"Oh my god," Romeo moaned in a throaty whisper. He looked at me, and saw what I was doing to Christos. "Whatever you're doing, Sam, don't stop..."

Holy crap! I was turning Life Drawing into Romeo's Spanktime Theater! I may as well have grabbed Romeo and Christos both by the cocks and started tugging! I was crazy!

I blushed beet red and hid my face behind my drawing pad, afraid to witness the carnage. I imagined the morality police knocking down the door any second. Hordes of cops waving billy clubs and offended old biddies in church dresses would stampede through the room.

"It's okay to start drawing at any time, Ms. Smith," Professor Childress said dryly over my shoulder. He raised his eyebrows and smiled at me over his glasses.

Caught.

When the professor walked away, I leaned against my drawing pad, burying my face.

At some point, I got a hold of myself...not the way you're thinking! And went back to drawing.

Christos seemed to have recovered. His face was blank, his member at rest.

Thank god.

A minute later, Christos and Genesis changed poses. He made sure his back was to me.

It was for the best. I could not be trusted. D'oh!

Believe it or not, I made it through the rest of class actually drawing. I was really happy with the results.

Genesis and Christos were great together. Not too great, I hoped. I couldn't decide if they had a history or not. Knowing Christos, probably. But did it matter? No.

After the final pose of the class, when they were both dressed, Genesis said to Christos, "Good to see you again, Adonis." She smiled wide. Were her eyes glimmering? Pupils widening?

Shit. At least she was calling him Adonis. Maybe she *didn't* know him that well. Or, she knew Adonis TOO well. Grrr.

I'd been watching her nipples like a hawk during the later poses, looking to see if they hardened at any point, but I couldn't really tell. I have to admit, I partially did it to avoid further virtual foreplay with Christos.

"You too, Genesis." Christos smiled at her.

Was he flirting?

"It's always a pleasure working with you," she said. "It's nice having someone who can handle the more intense poses."

"Totally," he smiled.

Okay, this was too much. I gave Romeo a "Can you believe those two?" sneer.

Romeo shrugged his shoulders, confused. I glanced at Kamiko. She was packing up her stuff. Even the preening flamingoes weren't paying attention to Christos and Genesis.

Was it just me? Was I all bent out of shape over nothing?

"I do a lot of modeling in town," Genesis said to Christos, "and people are always looking for couples poses. If you're interested." I wasn't sure if she was suggesting anything, but I certainly didn't like her use of the word "couple." Or the phrase "if you're interested."

"Thanks, Genesis." Christos said smoothly. "I totally appreciate the offer, but my schedule's pretty full up now. I've got to finish work on my next gallery show. I'm not going to have time for modeling."

"Oh, no worries. Thought I'd ask." Genesis smiled at him professionally.

Okay, maybe she wasn't angling for my man, I mean Christos.

"If you need any models for your new paintings," Genesis said, "Give me a call."

What! I flexed my claws at my side.

"I will," Christos said politely.

"You have my number, right?"

"Yup."

Crap, he *did* know her. How well was the question. Or should I say, how intimately? How big of a mess was I getting myself into? Was I stupid for falling for Christos Adonis Manos?

"Take it easy," Christos said to Genesis in goodbye. Then he walked over to me, not giving Genesis a second thought.

"Hey, Samantha." He smiled at me seductively. "Want to get lunch?"

I felt trapped, certain my jealousy was uglifying my face. My eyes darted around the room. The first thing I noticed was the distinct look of disappointment on Hourglass Flamingo's face because Christos was talking to me. She packed up her drawing equipment and marched out of the room with her pal Breasticles. Okay, that was a good sign.

"Let's get lunch," Romeo said, referring to himself, Kamiko, Christos, and me.

Christos awaited our consensus.

"Sounds good," Kamiko said. "Come on, Sam."

I guess the decision was made for me.

"Okay," Romeo smiled like an imbecile. He was so in crush with Christos, but him I didn't worry about.

I texted Madison to meet us at the Student Center.

While the four of us waited in line for fish tacos, Romeo and Kamiko argued about the finer points of the newest episode of Adventure Time.

"Missed you," Christos said quietly, his eyes burning into mine. He stroked the corner of my mouth with his thumb.

Electrical current jolted from his thumb down my spine. I was still thrown by his naked posing with Genesis.

He leaned down and kissed me softly. The electricity intensified into bolts of lightening that shot down between my legs, hitting my core in pulsing jerks.

"Can you guys at least sneak into a restroom?" Romeo joked.

Kamiko giggled. "So romantic, you two!"

Christos broke off the kiss slowly, our lips dragging apart in slow motion. Oh god, I needed a moment alone after that.

Romeo's face screwed up thoughtfully. "Doesn't she look like a zombie right now? Like Christos drank her life blood and turned her into a zombie?"

"That would make Christos a vampire," Kamiko corrected.

"You're confusing me, Kamiko," Romeo said. "Can you explain that in a language other than Klingon?"

"Zombies don't drink life blood, duh. They infect you with zombie virus. Vampires drink life blood."

"Ahem, nerd," Romeo coughed.

Christos chuckled. "I'm going to have to agree with Kamiko on this one, Romeo. Besides, I prefer to think of myself as a vampire. Much sexier."

"Zombies can be sexy, too," Kamiko said. "Sexy Zombies are totally in right now."

"Nerd alert!" Romeo shouted. "How do you *know* these things?!" Romeo's overly dramatic, humorous personality got the best of us. Even Kamiko joined in with our laughter.

We ordered our food and sat down together.

"So, you two dating, or what?" Romeo asked, munching on tortilla chips.

"Okay! Subtle alert!" Kamiko jabbed.

"Admit it, Kamiko, even you want to know what's going on between Sam and Superhunk here."

Madison walked up with a tray of food and sat down. "What'd I miss, you guys?"

"I was just asking the lovebirds if they had any bow chicka bow wow wow to report," Romeo said casually.

My eyes popped open.

"Did you forget your Ritalin this morning, Romeo?" Kamiko gawked. "Show some manners!"

"I think porno movie music is the soundtrack to Romeo's life," I said.

"Yes!" he hollered without hesitation.

We shared a laugh.

"So, come on, you two. What's your official status?" Madison asked.

I was holding up a fish taco, about to take a bite. I didn't know what the hell to say. So I passed the buck. "Christos? Care to answer that?" I sounded perhaps a tad more snide than I intended. I blamed nude posing with Genesis. Sue me.

He chuckled while chewing food. Everyone stared at him, so he felt pressure to hurry up and answer. He sipped his drink to wash it down. "Well, I'm not much for labels."

I didn't like the sound of that. I think I saw Madison rise up in her seat an inch or two, as if ready to spring. *Go, Mads! Tear his balls off!* If she didn't, I would, in about five seconds.

"Labels tend to under-deliver. They're like sound bites. What is dating, anyway?" he smiled.

Why was he smiling? I didn't like where this was going at all. My stomach seized in response.

He continued. "Dating for one couple may mean something entirely different than it does for the next couple. I mean, some married couples have open relationships." He sipped his drink.

I sank in my seat. *Here it comes. Male justification for doing whatever the fuck the man wants while leading the woman down the primrose path.*

"If you want some sound bite, like 'we're exclusive,' that's not my style." He sipped his drink again.

I glanced at Madison, Romeo and Kamiko. It seemed all their jaws hung as slack as mine. Was I receiving some kind of blow off? In front of my best friends?

"I prefer a clear description of the facts at hand," Christos said confidently. "Samantha is the most beautiful woman I've seen in my entire life. She's also possibly the coolest."

Huh?

"More than that, I feel this amazing connection with her that I've literally never felt before. The kind of connection that you didn't know was possible until you felt it for the first time. The kind of connection that probably comes along once in a lifetime, if you're fucking lucky." He smiled at all of us. "And we all know I'm fucking lucky." He flashed his cockiest smile. "But I'm not stupid, either. There's no way I would take the slightest chance of screwing things up with Samantha. All other women have ceased to exist for me." He leaned back in his chair, lacing his fingers behind his head proudly.

Everyone at the table was utterly silent. I saw a fleck of tortilla chip slide down the corner of Romeo's chin. All of our jaws were at full hang.

"So, call that whatever you want," Christos said as he leaned forward and popped a chip in his mouth. "I don't have a convenient word for it."

I don't know if you can swoon with your mouth drooping completely open like an idiot, or not. Doesn't it require the back of the hand to the forehead and a huge, girlish sigh? Technically, yes. But I can say with confidence that at that moment, all of us were swooning. Even Romeo. I saw it in his greedy eyes.

Christos merely grinned at us, and ate another salsa-covered chip.

Romeo sputtered, and shook his head violently. "So, does that mean the ugly-bumping is in full swing?"

Christos laughed deeply. "No, not yet." He leveled a probing look at me through lowered lashes. "Sam's in charge of that department."

I. Uh. Wait. What? Slow down. Swoon? Faint? Suffocate? Fall over dead of embarrassment and giddiness? I was completely confused. What the hell-all had he just said? I needed to go back and review the crime scene tapes.

Madison broke the silence. "Oh my god, Sam. That was some kind of Shakespeare sonnet or something."

"I wouldn't go comparing him to the Bard," Romeo observed dryly, "but I think I'm wet."

Kamiko grimaced. "Eww, Romeo. You never told us you went through with the sex change operation."

Kamiko delivered the line so perfectly, and it was so out of character for her, everyone in the group erupted in belly laughter. I think the gravity of what Christos said enhanced the releasing affect of Kamiko's joke. Especially for me.

I still couldn't completely process the fact that Christos had publicly declared the essence of the same sincere sentiment he had conveyed to me in my apartment.

"So, anyway," Madison said, "you guys dating, or what?"

Everyone laughed again.

"Did you hear something, Samantha?" Christos asked.

I was confused. "Huh?"

"I thought I heard something just now, but since all other women have ceased to exist, I wasn't sure." He pecked me on the cheek.

"You mean Mads?"

"Who's Mads?"

Madison chuckled. "This one has potential, Sam."

Chapter 20

That evening, Christos came over. We had dinner together, and he spent the night. There was some kissing before bed, but mostly we were so busy talking about all kinds of things, joking around, and having fun, we were both worn out when we hit the sheets.

I really liked that. There was no pressure from Christos for things to always end up physical. My experience with dating in high school had been all about fending off the gropers.

Not with Christos. He simply wanted to be with me.

We also hung out Tuesday and Wednesday evenings. When I wasn't studying for my other classes, Christos gave me extra drawing instruction. I would have loved nothing more than to drop all my classes and study art full time with him, but that was pure fantasy.

I wasn't an art major, and probably never would be.

But I made sure to enjoy every moment I had a stick of charcoal or mechanical pencil in my hand.

Thursday night, we stopped at Christos's house to pick up something. He didn't tell me what it was.

Spiridon was in the living room reading when we came in. "Christos! I thought you'd disappeared! You haven't forgotten your grandfather, have you?"

Christos smiled lovingly at Spiridon. "Sorry, Pappoús. I've been super busy. I'll be right back. I have to grab something from the studio." He left the room.

Spiridon smiled at me. "Have you stolen my grandson, Samantha?"

I smiled. "No, Mr. Manos, I mean Spiridon. He's stolen me." I noticed he was calling me Samantha now. Had Christos been talking to him about me?

"The way Christos talks about you, I thought you might have." He smiled.

There you go.

Christos walked back into the room. He held a gift-wrapped package with a bow and offered it to me. "For you."

"Oh, Christos! You shouldn't have. It's not my birthday or anything."

"So? Open it up."

I removed the card and read it. It said:

"Samantha—

You are more than you realize. Discover how far you can go by exploring your passions. Dream big. Don't let anyone stop you from fulfilling your wildest desires. Be Fearless.

—Christos"

My eyes watered. I smiled at Christos. "Thank you, Christos. This means a lot."

"You're welcome, Samantha." He gave me a big hug. "Don't forget to open the rest of the present."

I tore the wrapping open. It was a box of 96 Crayola Crayons. The kind with the sharpener in back. After the crayon drawing we'd done together, and working with the kids at the library, it was the perfect gift.

"Remember I told you that you needed to start painting?"

"Yeah?"

"Start with crayons. Start putting color into your sketches. A little at first. By the time you start working with actual paint, you won't be wondering about what to do with color so much."

I threw my arms around him. "Thank you Christos. I—" I almost blurted out something I would've regretted. "You're, amazing Christos." I pulled away so I could look him in the eyes. "You really are."

He held me by the waist and touched his forehead to mine. "You are too, *agápi mou.*"

I frowned. "What was that word you used?" It sounded like gibberish.

"Nothing."

"Was that a Greek word?"

Christos pulled back from our embrace.

Had I said something wrong? I glanced around and noticed Spiridon's eyebrows were raised high. I saw Christos exchange a look with Spiridon. My eyes darted between them. "Am I missing something here?"

Neither were going to answer. Spiridon's eyes dove back into his book. He placed a bookmark in it and closed it. "Do you two want dinner? I was about to make some."

"You never told me you spoke Greek," I said to Christos.

"You never asked."

"What did you say?"

He shrugged his shoulders.

Spiridon stood up and walked over to Christos. He put an arm around his grandson, clapped his shoulder, and led him out of the living room.

"Join us, Samantha," Spiridon called from the kitchen.

I followed, crayons in hand, totally confused.

Christos and his grandfather whipped up a pile of Greek cuisine. They worked together like a well-oiled team, joking and elbowing each other affectionately during the entire process. I had never seen behavior like this between anyone in my family. I envied Christos the bond he shared with his grandfather. I wonder if things had been like this with his dad as well?

When dinner was finished, I did the dishes. Spiridon tried to help, but I refused. "You guys did enough already. Sit down while I clean."

"Thank you, Samantha. She sure is considerate, isn't she, Christos?"

"The best," he said.

I hid my blushing smile by focusing on the dishes.

"Has an amazing ass, too." Christos said.

I turned around and gawked. "Christos! You shouldn't talk like that around your grandfather!"

Spiridon chuckled. "My grandson is very forthright, Samantha. He says what he feels. You can't slight him for his honesty."

Christos arched his brows. "See? I'm just being honest."

I had definitely never had anything approaching a conversation like this with my parents. I couldn't imagine telling my mom about Christos' amazing abs in front of people, or alone with her in private. We never talked about guys and feelings and romance. We talked about dating rules and birth control and curfews.

Had I been born into the wrong family?

Spiridon said goodnight and retired to the upstairs of the house, which I still hadn't seen.

Christos and I went outside.

He looked up at the night sky. "Full moon out tonight. It's super bright."

"Yeah." I gazed up at the glowing silver ball.

"Wanna see something awesome?"

"Okay."

Christos led us to the trailhead we had used to go up to his family's private view before.

"Isn't it sort of dark? Don't we need flashlights?"

"Can you see the trail?"

"Yeah, I guess."

"Then we don't need flashlights. Come on."

"Is this more of your 'Fearless' stuff?"

"I hadn't thought about it, but I guess it is." He smiled back at me.

We hiked up the hill, the trail a pale line in the darkness. My eyes slowly adjusted and I could see enough to avoid tripping. When we reached the lookout, I was out of breath.

I worried about being up here with him again. The first time, which I'd feared would be the last, I had been a total bitch. I prayed I wouldn't crap-stain things tonight.

Christos was already sitting on the bench. I was warm from the exertion. I sat next to him and he automatically put his arm around me while I snuggled against his side.

Then I looked at the view. "Oh my god. It's beautiful."

The moon reflected off the Pacific Ocean. Scattered clouds floated past the giant silver orb, outlined in thin lines of pure mercury. The black waves were capped with flickering silver tinsel. I felt like I was viewing a window into an alien world. Everything was familiar, but limned with magic by the haloed moon.

"I always preferred this place at night. Everything's so quiet."

"I've never seen anything like this. Thank you, Christos."

"Anything for you, Samantha." He pressed me into his side with a firm hug, then went back to gazing at the view. It was worthy of long, silent contemplation. Words couldn't do it justice.

Eventually, the warmth of our exertion wore off. I shivered.

"You cold?"

"Yeah, a little."

"Let me warm you up." He reached over and pulled me onto his lap so that I faced him. Because of the seat back on the bench, there was no place for my legs to go. I was forced to straddle him with my legs wide apart, knees high, feet resting on the bench.

I felt his hardness pressing through his jeans against my softness. I mean, right where everything was supposed to go. Only the thin barrier of our clothes stood between me, him, and completion. His shaft strained against me. I worried that all my body weight was pressing down on it, and I didn't want to hurt him. "Are you comfortable like this?"

"How's this?" He pulled me forcefully toward him. It startled me, but I liked it. I gasped as my chest pressed into his. My ass thrust out behind me and he grabbed the bell of my hips with both hands. My hands were on his chest.

"Better?"

"Yes," I murmured.

"I've been wanting to taste your lips all through dinner. I couldn't stop staring at your mouth while you talked to my grandfather."

"I noticed. You seemed quieter than usual."

He snickered. "I had good reason."

I leaned forward and kissed him softly. He responded with a low groan and slid his tongue into my mouth, searching for mine. We mingled them together and I indulged in the wetness of it all.

When I moaned and deepened our kiss, he squeezed my ass in a hypnotic kneading motion. Every time he squeezed with his powerful fingers, jolts of pleasure fired out from my center. I was instantly wet and antsy. I felt like my jeans were a chastity belt. Maybe that was okay, under the circumstances. I wasn't sure I was ready to go beyond making out.

Not that I was disappointed with what we were doing.

He startled me by grabbing one of my breasts through my t-shirt. He massaged it gently. I writhed every time his fingers contracted. If he didn't stop, it was very possible I was going to come.

Eyes closed, I threw my head back and released a long, uninhibited moan. No one could possibly have heard me on the remote hillside. I felt free to let it all out.

Christos shuddered and growled at the sound of my pent up pleasure. In response, he thrust his hips up into me. It was hard but good, like a huge bucking bronco beneath me. I didn't realize I liked it hard.

Tease.

I felt my throat suddenly constrict in terror. I froze. No, not now. I didn't want to think about that now. I tried to bury it under the same old mountain of avoidance I'd used in the past. Where was my ice cream?

"Samantha? Did I hurt you?"

I opened my eyes and leaned my forehead onto Christos'. Sliding into his gaze, my pain fell away. The voices in my head calmed. "I'm okay. Don't stop."

He tipped his head up and kissed me deeply. His tongue was ecstasy in my mouth. I ground my core down on him. He moaned greedily. I knew he wanted more. But did I? Was I ready? I was afraid to find out.

He lifted up my t-shirt until my bra and breasts were exposed. With both hands he squeezed me through the satiny material. He lapped the crease between my cleavage until it was slick. His tongue dipped lower, below my bra. Then he literally picked me up by my ass so he could run his tongue down my navel, to the tops of my jeans.

He was unbelievably strong.

I was intimately aware of how his powerful fingers pulled me apart. Down there. Another flood of energy swirled out from my core and climbed up to my breasts.

He lowered me to his lap, then slid the tip of his nose tickling up my cleavage. He brushed his fingertips across my ribs then thumbed my nipples through my bra. I needed more. My bra was in the way.

He pulled back. "I need to see your breasts. Please."

Was he asking permission? "Yes."

He unhooked my bra and folded it upward. "Oh my god, they are so perfect from this angle." He dove at one of my nipples with his ravenous mouth. His tongue circled the tip, hardening it until it was tight and erect. I quivered down to my toes. I wrapped one arm around his neck and placed the other on top of his head, digging my fingers into his thick hair. I had never experienced pleasure like this. I made a stifled "uh, uh, uh," sound. I was falling over an edge into a deep abyss.

Previous experiences had led me to believe foreplay was no more than some tingles, maybe a little tickle between the legs, and a lot of spit swapping. This was a trip to another dimension. An infinite world I'd never explored.

He switched nipples and a new fork of lighting shot from my core to the top of my head. I whimpered. He squeezed my other breast in response and thrust his hips up into mine powerfully, slowly, persistently.

He grunted, unfulfilled. I didn't want him to be left wanting. I felt like I was having all the fun in that moment, and he was a caged lion, begging release.

"Oh, Christos," I moaned.

He hissed and looked up at me, his face tightened in a feral snarl. "You. Are. So. Fucking. Hot. I want to be deep inside you. Right now."

I was torn with indecision, and my thoughts took over, blocking out sensation.

I didn't remember Christos talking like this to Paisley. Admittedly, I'd only spied on them for a minute or so, but he hadn't sounded so...hungry. Was it just me?

"Samantha, I need you more than I've ever needed any woman before. Like you are the only woman who has ever walked this earth, the most feminine, womanly, gorgeous creature that has ever existed. I'm a man starving without food, and you are my sustenance. I'm dying of thirst and your are purest water. I'm suffocating without you. You are oxygen to me, Samantha. Without you, I cannot breathe. I'm going to die if I don't take you in with every breath I draw." He inhaled deeply.

His talk of taking me in made me want to take *him* in. Deep. All the way in. Then I would rain all over his manhood, quenching his thirst, igniting his fire.

I jumped at the thought. Oh my god, when did I get so slutty? I stifled a giggle.

"What?" I could hear amusement in his voice.

"Nothing, it's stupid." I hung my head to the side so he couldn't see the smile on my face.

"Nothing you say is ever stupid." He sounded so earnest.

I looked into his eyes, a warm, inviting smile on my face. "That's way I luh—" I stopped myself short. My throat caught, and I coughed twice. I had almost said it. Again. Whoops. Can't go doing that! It was way too soon!

He wasn't bothered by it. "What?"

"I was going to say, that's what I *like* about you so much, Christos. Everything you say is like the most supportive, genuine, wonderful thing one person could possibly say to another."

"Oh, I thought you were going to drop the L-bomb on me." He grinned, dimples blazing in the pale moonlight.

I dropped my head until it pushed into his chest. I was trying to hide, but there was no place to go. Not that I wanted to escape his hold on me.

"Back to what you were thinking back there, when I was talking all romantically about you being my oxygen. Which I meant, by the way. What were you thinking?"

I twisted my head against him. "Uh uh."

"You can tell me. I won't laugh."

"I'm embarrassed."

"It's okay, Samantha. I'm sure it's fine."

"Promise?"

"Promise."

"When you said you wanted to take me in with every breath, I thought that I wanted to take *you* in. Inside." I couldn't believe I was saying it. "Into, you know, into me."

"Ahh. I see. Yeah, no. That's fine. No complaints from me on that front." He kissed the top of my head. "Someone's got a dirty mind."

I smacked my fist against his chest. "I do not!"

"It's okay. I like dirty just fine."

Bitch. Slut. Whore.

My brows knit together. "I'm not a slut, Christos." I sounded more harsh than I intended.

"I know you're not. When did I ever give you that idea?"

This was going into territory I didn't want to think about. "Let's forget it, okay?"

"Hey, look at me." He lifted my chin with gentle fingers until our eyes met. There was that earnest, caring look again. "Whatever you want to do, Samantha. Remember, talking dirty, thinking dirty, is totally okay. I happen to like it quite a bit." He grinned.

"Really?"

"Yup. I almost came in my pants when you said you wanted to take me inside. You."

"Nuh-uh."

"So uh huh." He smiled wide.

"I love you, Christos." Oh shit. The words slipped out, I couldn't stop myself! I clutched him in my arms as tightly as I could, afraid he'd throw me to the side and run down the mountain like last time. At the same time, I wanted to run away myself.

Who had I become in that moment? I hadn't said the word love to anyone since...*him*. After *him*, I thought I might never say it again. To anyone.

But I just had.

My head was starting to spin. I pulled away from Christos. He wouldn't let go. I rolled my t-shirt down without bothering to hook my bra.

"Easy, Samantha. Where are you going?"

"I need to go. Now. Let me go!"

"Okay." He released me.

I swung my legs onto the dirt and ran down the trail. Now the situation was reversed. I was the one running away in total emotional agony.

I jogged down the hill slowly, unsure of my footing in the moonlight. I heard Christos close on my feels. He didn't try to overtake me.

When we reached the street, he ran beside me. This running away thing was becoming a bad habit with us.

"Something's wrong, Samantha. Do you want to tell me about it?"

Hell no! I ignored him and kept running. I wanted to get away and jump into a vat of ice cream and eat my way out. Or jump off a cliff. Shit, I should've done that when I was up at the hillside bench.

"Talk to me, Samantha."

Why did he have to be so fucking understanding? Why couldn't he let me rot away in isolation? Why couldn't he let my pain chew me to shreds in private? "Go away," I sobbed.

I was trying to run, but I was crying now, and it was impossible to breathe. A cramp knifed my side and I stumbled to my knees.

Christos was instantly beside me. "You okay?"

I leaned on my hands and sobbed. Tears and snot and drool poured from my mouth.

"I can't, Christos. I just can't," I bawled.

"Can't what?" he asked softly, a gentle hand on my shoulder blade.

"I can't be with you. Like that."

"Like what?"

"Like, you know. With you inside me."

"That's okay. Whatever makes you feel safest and most comfortable. Are we going too fast? We sort of jumped into things."

That wasn't at all the answer I was expecting. I sat back on my heels. "No, it's my fault. I wanted it. But I didn't realize what I was doing."

"What are you saying? Should we go back to the mentor-manatee thing?"

"Yes. Wait, did you just say manatee?"

"I did." He grinned.

I started laughing, then crying. "Oh, Christos!" I threw my arms around him. He hugged me tightly. I sobbed for awhile, then calmed. "Are you calling me a sea cow?"

"Yes, I am." He laughed softly. "You have eight teats and need a milking. But your milk is salty because you drink sea water, so no one buys it. Then Aquaman, the underwater dairy farmer, has to sell you for hamburger meat."

"What?" I cry-laughed.

"It's all I could think to say. Sorry." He kissed my cheek gently. "Why don't we go back to my grandfather's and have something hot to drink."

"Okay."

The next thing I knew, he swooped me into his arms and carried me to the house. It was three blocks. He held me like I was weightless.

After our tea was ready, we crept into the backyard. The view was incredible. Not as breathtaking as the bench, but pretty nice. We cuddled together in a chaise lounge next to Spiridon's pool. There was a small glass-topped table next to the lounger, where we placed our tea and saucers.

"It's so funny your grandfather has a pool and he's like five blocks from the beach."

"Yeah, he's got it pretty rough. The benefits of buying in early. He's been in this house since before I was born."

"It's really nice. I've never even seen the whole thing. How big is it?"

"I think it's six bedrooms, give or take a ton of bathrooms, an office, a study, an art library, the studio. But enough of the small talk. What happened back there? I felt your heart go from wide open to locked behind a bank vault."

"How can you feel my heart?"

"I don't know, I just can."

"Do you feel the hearts of all the women you've been with?"

"Now that you put it that way, I can tell you exactly why I know when you're heart is opened or closed."

"How?"

"Because I've never felt it before."

"That's ridiculous. You're telling me none of the many women you've slept with had open hearts?"

"If they did, I never noticed. But yours is wide open with me. I can't not feel it. It's like an earthquake every time you open up. So what closed it down tonight?"

I leaned over and picked up my tea, stalling.

"Like I said before," he encouraged, "you can tell me anything. Get it out, let it go. As long as you hold it in secret, it gnaws at you. I know."

I wanted to believe him. But I feared that if I told Christos the truth, he would judge me. Push me away and end our relationship on every level, even the mentoring. Why wouldn't he?

Once he knew how terrible I was beneath my suburban college student, accounting major exterior, he would be horrified. Because I was horrified. Of *myself*.

I was scum, for what I did.

If Christos thought he had hidden shit, he had no idea. My guilt and shame had been killing me slowly for over two years.

I searched my brain for a worthy change of subject. "Hey, what was that word you called me before dinner? When you said it, your grandfather looked like he'd seen a ghost or something."

"Maybe he had."

"That doesn't make any sense. What was the word?"

"It was two words. Agápi mou."

"So what's it mean? Why's it such a big deal?"

"It means 'my love.' I haven't said the word love in over a decade. And my grandfather knows it."

Huh? *Processing, 404 not found. Web page does not exist.* What the hell? Did that mean he had called me his love two hours ago? He had snuck it under the radar! "Hey! You tricked me! Here I am, freaking out that I blurted out the L-word, and you already said it! No fair!"

He chuckled and hugged me affectionately. "Is that a problem?"

"No, but, I mean, what the hell! You could've let me off the hook a bit sooner!" I was pretend mad.

"Sorry," he grinned.

"So why haven't you said the word love in so long?"

"That's another story. You need to tell me yours. About Taylor."

The fact Christos had secretly called me his love gave me courage. I prepared to drop my bomb. I hoped it wouldn't obliterate my growing relationship with this amazing man.

The only person who knew the whole story about Taylor was *Him.* I was about to cross a line I never thought I would.

I took a heavy breath. It hitched spasmodically when I released it. "No. This story is about Damian."

"Who's Damian?"

"A terrible person. A mistake. Let me begin at the beginning." I sipped my tea and nestled into Christos' arms.

I was going to need all the support and cuddling I could get if I was going to tell this story for the first time. To the man I'd said "I love you" to less than thirty minutes prior.

The man who called me *his* love.

OMG, I was so confused in that moment.

"Damian Wolfram was the worst mistake I've ever made," I said quietly.

"When I was a sophomore in high school, I fell in love with Damian, a senior. He was easily the hottest guy in our school. All the girls were in love with Damian. He was smooth, popular, rich, and captain of the lacrosse team. His parents were loaded, and being with Damian meant country club access and high society on the arm of a total hottie. What teenaged girl didn't dream of such things?

"If I'd known better, or been more mature, I might have realized Damian wasn't the golden boy he portrayed. He had a dark side. But I ignored it. I lied to myself and told myself that his short temper was okay. It was sexy. Every girl likes a brooding bad boy, right?"

I grinned at Christos.

"Bad boys are not all created equal," he replied confidently.

"That's for sure." I sipped my tea and continued.

"In the beginning of our relationship, I turned a blind eye every time Damian got angry. There was a thrill to talking him down when he was mad. It was like I could control him. I could tame him. It gave me a sense of power. I thought I was the only person who could soothe this big, muscly guy who was super dangerous when no one else could. I thought it was the sexiest thing in the world.

"I can't remember how many times I stopped him from jumping into a fight by kissing him or holding onto him. I thought I could control him. But that was a fantasy.

"I couldn't control him. Unless I ignored my own feelings, and blocked out the fact that his behavior horrified me.

"Damian was a terrible person. A bully. Not the kind of friend I would ever want. But I told myself he was the kind of lover that *every* girl wanted. And he wanted me. I was high on his craziness. But I came to realize he wasn't crazy. He was selfish. He was spiteful, and he was terrible."

I turned and gazed at Christos' magical blue eyes. I placed my palm on his cheek. "When I met you, Christos, I thought you were just like Damian. I was afraid that you would be a total womanizing asshole. But you're not. You're different. There's a gentleness in you. Every time I've seen you get violent, it was to protect me. But you never provoke anyone, you never start anything. You just finish it."

"I was protecting *you*."

I felt a tremendous sense of pride well up in my chest. I wiped a tear from my eyes and sniffled. "You are a good man, Christos. I'm so lucky."

"Me too," he whispered.

"The night I started to see through Damian's facade was the night I had planned on losing my virginity to him. But I didn't lose it that night. That night, he took something far worse. He took my innocence. Because I let him. I didn't have the courage to stop it.

"We had been dating for six months at that point. Damian had been pressuring me to have sex for awhile. I never told him I wanted to wait because I didn't want him to know I was a virgin, but he figured it out on his own. We made out plenty, but I had to stop things from going further so many times, it was obvious.

"The thing is, Damian wasn't my first boyfriend. I'd made out with other guys before. I was sixteen.

"Anyway, we were together for six months. My parents got to know him. They loved him, thought he was terrific. I don't think they ever saw the dark side of him that I knew so well.

"Looking back, I'm surprised I didn't break up with him. But the problem was, dating Damian Wolfram was like dating the King of England. Every girl in my high school was either jealous and wanted to sabotage my relationship, or wanted to be my best friend, just so they could be close to him.

"The guys were just as bad. Everybody wanted to sleep with whoever King Stud was dating, meaning me. I loved the attention. I excuse my stupid behavior because of teenaged hormones."

"I remember those," Christos chuckled. "I think I still have some leftover."

"You're so bad." I swatted his arm.

"I hate to disillusion you, but I'm pretty sure those guys at your high school wanted you mainly because you're hot."

"Yeah, right," I dismissed.

"It never ceases to amaze me, Samantha, how the hottest women I know have the lowest opinion of their own looks. You take the cake."

I gazed at him silently for a long time. He stroked my hair. "Thank you," I murmured. I sipped more tea, then continued my story.

"So, after six months of pressure from Damian, and constant talk from my girlfriends about how much sex everyone in my high school was having, I decided I didn't want to be left out of the conversations any longer. I mean, how bad could it be? Just about everyone on the planet had sex. Why was I making such a big deal about it?

"One afternoon during class, I texted Damian that I was ready.

He knew exactly what I meant. We were in luck because both his parents and mine would be out that night. We decided to use his house, because it was huge, he had his own private bathroom connected to his bedroom, and if his parents came home early, we'd have plenty of advance warning when they walked into the house.

"He tried really hard to make it special. He'd bought me flowers and cooked me a fabulous dinner in his parents' kitchen. He had dug up recipes on the internet, and made everything himself.

"When we finally made it up to his bedroom, with time to spare before his parents got home, everything was perfect. He had set up candles and had the perfect playlist on his iPod. The setting was more than a teenager could hope for. No fumbling in the back of a cramped car with foggy windows like most of my friends. Maybe it was too perfect, I don't know.

"We fell onto the bed and started making out. For whatever reason, I wasn't feeling it. I have no idea why. I didn't know how to tell Damian, so we kept making out. When he tried to take my dress off, I stopped him.

"Maybe it was all the anticipation. Maybe he'd tried too hard to make everything just right. Maybe we'd waited too long and I should've slept with him months before.

"But it never occurred to me once that deep down, I knew Damian was not the right person for me to lose my virginity to. But I couldn't admit that to myself in the moment. I had been denying the truth for too long.

"So I told myself that I wasn't ready for Damian *that* night, that I just needed more time to get used to the idea. I remember folding my arms across my chest protectively. Damian asked me what was wrong.

"That was when everything took a nose dive."

Chapter 21

THREE YEARS EARLIER...

At Damian Wolfram's house.

"What's wrong," Damian asked.

"I'm sorry, Damian. This is my first time. You know it is. You told me we could wait until I was ready. I guess I'm just not ready," I said regretfully. I gave him a sad smile. I knew he'd be disappointed. I worried he'd be angry. And I knew exactly how explosive he could be. "You're not mad at me, are you?"

Damian rolled off of me and laid face up, staring at the bedroom ceiling. He didn't say anything for a long time.

"Damian?"

He sighed deeply. Several times. That was how the tantrums started. Like he was building up a head of steam.

I was afraid to move. He slapped the bed with his hand. He was mad. I stroked his arm. "I'm really sorry. I know how hard you tried to make all of this special."

I rolled my knee over his legs and cuddled up next to him. I squeezed his arm and tried to calm him. "Don't be mad. We'll do it next time. I promise."

"What next time? Who said there was going to be a next time?"

I was confused. "I love you, Damian." It wasn't the first time I'd told him. I started saying "I love you" after about three months of dating. He'd never said it, but all my girlfriends had told me not to pressure him. "Of course there's going to be a next time. We'll have plenty of chances to make love. Just not tonight, okay?"

I looked up at him. He tilted his chin down and scowled at me. "If you loved me, we would be having sex right now."

There was a coldness to the way he'd said those words that shocked me. I suddenly doubted every kind word he'd ever said to me.

"If you loved me, you would already have your dress off." There was venom in his words. Not love.

I rolled away from him until my back faced him. I hugged my elbows to my chest and pulled my knees up. He didn't love me. That much was clear. I wondered if he'd ever come even close to loving me. I started to cry quietly. Why hadn't I seen it sooner?

"Quit being such a baby. Do you want to have sex or not?"

That made me cry harder.

He sighed petulantly. "Shut up. I don't want to hear it."

I choked back a sob.

"Put up, or shut the fuck up!"

I sobbed freely. Part of me wanted to turn to him and tell him how angry I was, how much he was hurting me. But Damian always had to be the angriest person in the room. I knew it was pointless. I slid my legs off the bed, looking for my heels. "I want to go home."

"You want to go? I bought flowers. I made you dinner. I set up my room to make everything special. I held up my end of the deal. Why didn't you? Huh? What's wrong with you?"

I slid my heels on one at a time. I stood up, grabbed my coat, and draped it over my shoulders. I picked up my purse and folded my arms protectively across my breasts. "Please take me home."

He jackknifed off the bed. "You want to go? Now? Fuck, Sam, you're the worst fucking girlfriend I've ever had."

"Please."

He slammed his fist onto his dresser, rattling everything on top. "What the fuck, Sam! We're supposed to have sex tonight! You're not going anywhere!"

I looked at him. He was gearing up for a titanic tantrum. I couldn't deal with it. "I'm going downstairs. Please take me home. Or I'll call my parents."

That triggered him. "Fuck you, Sam! Fuck you! Fine! Go downstairs. I'll drive your fat ass home!"

Normally, I always let Damian win the "who's the angriest" contest. But that night, my anger flared bright. "I don't need you, Damian! You're nothing special!"

"Not special? I'm the only thing special you've got, honey." The way he said "honey" didn't sound like a term of endearment. "Once I'm gone, say goodbye to the lavish lifestyle. Go back to the monotony of your parents' boring-as-fuck middle-class lifestyle."

I bit back tears. On some level, I knew he was right. My parents *were* boring. They had boring jobs and boring lives. Damian's entire family was like some Fortune 500 cover story.

I'd be lying if I said his behavior surprised me. It was just more of what I'd already seen. "You make it sound so bad, Damian. Maybe I'm the one who's special, and you're the monotonous one." Points for me.

"You're nothing, Sam. Without me, you're nobody. You and your boring fucking family. I'm all the spice you have."

I turned my back to him and walked downstairs as quietly as I could. I heard him banging around in his bedroom while I waited in his parents' gigantic foyer, near the elaborate etched glass double doors.

I thought about how such a beautiful mansion could contain such a terrible person. Both were beautiful on the outside, ugly on the inside.

A few minutes later he trotted down the stairs. He'd changed into a t-shirt and sweats. "Let's go," he growled.

I held one last shred of hope that somehow he'd calm down and we could spend the rest of the evening watching a movie or something. Anything. I just didn't want to end it like this. "Damian, please, can't you understand where I'm coming from?" I pleaded.

His eyes flashed and his anger stabbed into my heart. "It's too late for that, Sam. Maybe you can give your virginity to some night cashier at a convenience store. We're through."

I was stunned. I stared at him blankly.

"Outside." It was a command. "Get in the fucking car already!" He opened one of the etched glass front doors in the foyer. "Go!"

I'm surprised he didn't shove me, or boot me in the ass on my way down the slate front steps. I walked stiffly toward his BMW, across the crushed gravel roundabout, and climbed in. I clutched my coat tightly around me, wishing it was some kind of magical, emotion-deflecting armor. I didn't want to feel any more of the anger scorching off of Damian.

He jumped in the driver's seat and slammed his door. While jamming his key in the ignition and revving the engine, he gave me a final glaring sneer.

The only thing running through my head was that I was surprised he didn't make me walk home.

PRESENT DAY.

"After that night, my heart was broken. I couldn't believe the young man I thought I'd loved could be so hateful."

Christos was silent, his eyes lowered. Was he going to say anything?

I waited, and waited. Dread crawled into my stomach and took root.

When Christos still hadn't spoken, I panicked. I think he felt my tension. His eyes narrowed in a combination of pain and I think revulsion. It was in that moment I realized the infinite power of words. They had transformed the man who had been holding me lovingly in his arms mere seconds ago into a complete stranger.

Christos didn't know me. He never had. He only knew an idea of me, a thin slice of the whole rotten pie. Would it have helped if I'd told him everything sooner? Or would he still turn away no matter when he found out? I started to cry. Me and men were not slated to work out in the end.

"What a total fucking prick," Christos whispered. "He was no King Stud. He's King Douche. How could he do that to you?"

"Wuh, what?"

"If that asshole were here right now, I'd feed him his teeth. You deserve so much better than that, Samantha. That guy was heartless."

I wept tears of relief and hugged Christos. He tucked my head into his chest and comforted me.

After sitting in silence for awhile, we went inside and put our teacups in the sink, then drove back to my apartment.

It was late, so we undressed and climbed quietly into bed. When the lights were out and Christos' arms were around me, I kissed him briefly. "Good night, Christos. I love you," I whispered.

"I love you too, *agápi mou*."

"So, um, I know you don't like labels, but what *would* you call us now? Are we dating?"

"I don't think there are words big enough or grand enough to describe what we're doing. The first one that comes to my mind is supercalifragilisticexpialidocious. After that, I run out."

"Isn't that from Mary Poppins?"

"Yeah. I loved that movie when I was a kid."

Everything about Christos was unexpected. He always surprised me. "I never pegged you for a Disney fan."

"Why? Because tough guys don't like cartoon musicals?" I could tell he was dimpling in the darkness by the sound of his voice.

"Yeah."

"I defy all stereotypes," he said proudly.

"That you do. But is it possible for you to abide by one stereotype?"

"Which one did you have in mind?"

"The one where we agree to be exclusive?"

"You mean you don't want to see other people, and you don't want me seeing other people?"

I worried that he had to ask for clarification. Didn't everyone know what exclusive meant?

I think he sensed my unease. "Don't worry, Samantha. There's is only one perfect woman for me on this planet, and you are her. I want you, and only you. You are my one and only."

I sighed audibly. "I can live with that."

"Good, because you have all of me."

"I love you Christos. I love you very much."

"I love you too, *agápi mou*."

"No matter what?"

"No matter what. I hope you feel the same way about me."

Did I detect a note of doubt in his voice? The slightest strain? Was I missing something? Was there something Christos wasn't telling me? Or was I imagining things?

I felt sudden trepidation. Not because of that hairline crack of doubt that had suddenly appeared in my perception of Christos.

But because of what I hadn't told him.

All the parts about the Damian story I had left out. Everything that had happened *after* I'd gotten in Damian's car. The parts of the story I was afraid to tell even Christos because I was so ashamed of what I'd done. The ones that proved beyond all doubt that I was a terrible person.

The ones that if Christos heard them, he'd surely run away as fast as he could.

The part of the story about Taylor.

The next morning, I woke up feeling pretty good. The night

before had been very cathartic, even if Christos didn't know the whole truth. I drove him to his grandfather's on the way to campus so he could get his motorcycle. The sun was just beginning to peak over the hills to the east.

"Are you going to be our secret drawing model again today?" I asked while we still sat in my car.

"Sorry, I've got actual work to do," he grinned.

"Are you saying having Genesis hanging nude all over you wasn't work? Because it was fun?" Did I sound jealous? Geez, it never stopped with me.

"Are you still worried about that?"

"Sort of." I felt so immature.

"Look, I agreed to model for Professor Childress weeks ago. I seriously didn't think you'd mind. I mean, you are so much hotter than Genesis anyway."

"I am?"

He shook his head. "Didn't I tell you that the hottest women are the most insecure? You probably look in a mirror and imagine it does funhouse mirror tricks that make you look like the elephant woman."

I was afraid to answer lest I incriminate myself.

"See! I was so right! You do think that way!"

"Hey." I felt like he was making fun of me.

"Let it go, *agápi mou*. You mean so much more to me than looks anyway." He kissed me gently on the corner of the mouth.

"You mean it?" I pouted.

"Yes. I love you. No one else. If it really bothers you, I can decline the couples posing, or even solo posing. It's not like it's my job. It's up to you."

I shrugged my shoulders. "Can I get back to you on that?"

He ruffled my hair. "Yes, *agápi mou*. Now you better go, or you're going to be late for class."

Why was it that now that I had Christos, all I could think about was losing him? That wasn't very fearless of me. I'd heard about self-fulfilling prophecies, and thought I might want to work on my insecurity. Otherwise, I might ruin things myself. "I love you, Christos."

"I love you too, Samantha." He leaned over and kissed me deeply, tongue and all, before getting out of my VW.

He waved when I started the engine.

"Bye!" I waved as I drove off.

I forgot all about Christos posing naked with Genesis on the way to campus.

Because all I could think about was the nasty things Christos' tongue made me feel between my legs every time he slipped it in my mouth.

I joined Madison for Fundamentals of Accounting, again without coffee. After class, we walked to the Student Center to buy coffee at Toasted Roast.

We got in line, I groaned when I noticed Tiffany Kingston-Whitehouse and two of her Delta Pi Delta cronies ahead of us. I did my best to ignore them while I chatted with Madison.

When Tiffany and Company had bought their coffee and were on the way out, they passed right by me and Madison.

"Oh," Tiffany said when she saw me, as if discovering dog shit on her shoe. "It's *you*."

"Why are you talking to the riff-raff, Tiff?" the brunette Delta Pi Delta asked. "You might catch a social disease."

The other crony cackled.

"Oh, you know," Tiffany said. "It's impossible to look away from a freak show."

"You're just mad because Christos came to his senses and booted your ass to the curb for someone better than you!" Madison said defiantly.

Tiffany glared at Madison as if she had just uttered a beheadable offense to the queen. "Better than me?" Tiffany scoffed. "Your *friend* is so nothing, I will not even address her directly," Tiffany said to Madison, without looking at me.

Wow, Tiffany and Damian would be perfect for each other. Maybe he could beat some sense into her. *Did I just think that? Oops.*

"Who's Christos?" the brunette crony asked.

Tiffany rolled her eyes with bitchy perfection. "She's talking about Adonis, dimwit."

"Oh," Brunette said, chastised.

"Don't worry, Whatever Your Name Is," Tiffany said, addressing Madison. "*Christos* will come to his senses soon enough. He's not going to waste his time with a Plain Jane like your nobody *friend* forever." She tilted her nose up and stalked off, but not without jerking a slosh of coffee out the top of her cup that came dangerously close to splashing all over my long-sleeve white sweater.

"Hey!" I shouted.

"You missed, bitch!" Madison hollered.

Tiffany walked away, hips cocking from side to side in exaggerated runway model fashion. Her perfect blond hair swayed perfectly. She threw her arm over her head and flipped us off without looking back, her many bracelets jingling around her wrist.

Her two cronies fell into step on either side of her and turned to give me and Madison a pair of glaring stink eyes and fisted middle-finger bird flips.

"Total bitches," Madison said.

"Groan," I said.

"Is douche the appropriate term for female douches? Or is that just for dudes?" Madison pondered.

"Houches?" I suggested, saying it like "hooshes."

She giggled. "Sounds too much like Hoochies. I would go with Couches. Sounds more like the C-word."

"Couches it is."

"Couches!" Madison hollered after them, even though they were long gone.

That night after classes, Christos and I ordered take out Thai Food and ate dinner at my apartment.

We sat on the carpet around my coffee table, doing crayon paintings with the box of Crayolas Christos had given me as a present. Opened boxes of thai food and half empty plates surrounded us as we worked.

I was filling in a teal blue ring on the corner of our joint picture. "You owe me a story about why you haven't used the word love in such a long time."

"That's right," he said quietly. He nodded his head while scribbling down a blur of fuchsia crayon on his side of the page. "But first, I'm pretty sure you can't do crayons right without ice cream. Don't you think?"

I winced. My stupid Costco-sized supply of ice cream still taunted me every time I opened my freezer. I hadn't replenished it in awhile, but I was loathe to just throw it out. "I, uh, guess?"

He went to the kitchen. "I'll spoon some out." He clattered around in the silverware drawer, then returned with two modest bowls of Mint Chocolate Chocolate Chip.

I could do that without guilt or disgust.

As we ate our ice cream, Christos told me about the new paintings he was preparing for his next show. I think he was dodging the story he owed me, but he was so enthusiastic about his current project, I didn't want to stop him. I also realized I was completely enjoying my ice cream like a normal person and not someone in love/hate with junk food.

How did Christos manage to set me so at ease?

I set my empty ice cream dish down and leaned back against the foot of the couch. "It sounds like you're going to be super busy painting and with your graduate studies. How are you going to find time for me?"

"I'll find time. If I have to take a quarter off from school, no one's going to care."

"That's crazy! You can't take time off from college for a girl, Christos." I sounded like my mom. Why was I being Ms. Sensible all of a sudden? Probably the latent affects of responsible parenting.

"I just had a sell-out gallery show. I made a ton of cash. And that's good for SDU's reputation. They'll work with me." He spooned ice cream into his mouth.

"You sound so confident."

"Well, considering all that my grandfather and dad have done for the university, they basically owe us."

"Really? How?"

"Oh, my grandfather helped found the art program. That's how he knows Professor Childress so well. And my dad donated so much money to keep the program cutting-edge, it's not even funny."

For a minute, he sounded vaguely like Damian. I didn't like that at all. Like his family's money bought him privilege. Was I disgusted, or perhaps jealous? I wasn't sure. But I did know that Christos was very, very different from Damian. Unless he was a master at deception.

Damian wasn't much for disguises. He was too angry to hide it. Maybe Christos was somehow worse, and I couldn't see it yet? He *had* managed to dodge my question to him about not using the word "love" twice now.

I didn't want to think about it, so I grabbed at the most available thing to say. "Wow, your family is really involved with the university. I think my dad sends a hundred dollars to his alma mater every year, but that's about it."

Christos was coloring again. "When my dad's art career exploded, he had money coming out his ears. Money doesn't solve everything but it sure helps."

"What do you mean?" I asked, picking up a tangerine crayon.

"My dad is an abstract painter. Shapes, colors, textures. He wanted to do realistic art, like my grandfather. But my grandfather had the market locked up at the beginning of my dad's career. Everyone compared Dad's landscapes to my grandfather's. At the time, no one was buying much in the way of figurative art, you know, with people in it, other than portraits. My dad didn't want to do that either. Sure, painting famous people pays pretty good, and you gain a certain notoriety from it. But it's still essentially a job.

"So he looked at what was selling, and it was the abstract stuff. My dad understood that abstract art was fundamentally about emotional expression through pure composition, without the use of narrative."

"I don't get it," I interjected, feeling somewhat ignorant.

"Narrative art is recognizable things: people, buildings, landscapes, historical events, etc. Abstract uses none of those elements. Remember what I said about Kandinsky way back at the museum on campus?"

"Uh…"

Christos smiled indulgently. "Abstract art is about exploring pure emotion. Things like, 'This shape makes me angry. This color makes me sad. What happens if I put the two together? How do I feel when I look at the painting?' That kind of thing."

"Oh, I see." *I guess.*

"Anyway, my dad totally got it, and went nuts, cranking out canvas after canvas. And guess what? They sold. Worldwide. Any serious collector has one or more of my dad's paintings in their private collections. It was really ridiculous for awhile. My Dad became an art celebrity. He could shit on a canvas and sell it for a million at his peak." Christos set down his crayon and picked up his bowl of ice cream.

"What about now?" I asked, dumbfounded. I'd never known anyone first or second hand that was remotely as wildly successful as Christos' father. It was like listening to a story about some heroic greek god that was recorded on stone tablets and passed down from generation to generation to wow the crap out of people. People who would never ever meet the fabled hero of the story. Like it was only make-believe, to inspire them. But this story was real. I'd seen enough proof to know.

"My dad still sells. When he bothers to paint. But he drinks too fucking much." Christos set his ice cream bowl down with a disgusted look on his face. I could tell it wasn't the ice cream that was bothering him.

"Why would your dad drink if he was so successful? I don't get it."

"Because he hated what he was doing. Deep down, he didn't give a shit about abstract art."

"But why? If it paid so well and made him famous?"

Christos looked completely miserable. It didn't make sense to me. "Wait till you're as successful as he is, then you'll find out," he grimaced.

"I'll never be that successful," I scoffed. "*You* might, Christos. I'm just hoping to keep a roof over my head and have a car that runs."

"You have to dream bigger than that, Samantha. Look at my situation. I'm already making money. You could too."

"I don't think so. You have so much more skill than me. Maybe in twenty years. If I stick to it." My voice dropped into a muddled, depressed tone. I couldn't hide my true feelings on this topic.

"Why do you think I wanted to keep mentoring you?" he asked, as if the answer was obvious.

"I don't know. Because you love me?"

"No. Because I believe in you." He put a reassuring hand on my shoulder. "I believed in you long before I knew I loved you. I saw your raw talent." He cracked a dimpled grin. "And I knew you were fucking hot. Why *wouldn't* I want to mentor you?"

That was way too many compliments in a row. Something spun in my chest and butterflied my stomach. How could he be so sure about me when I had so many doubts about myself?

Heat raced through my body. My eyelids fluttered and I think I moaned when I simply meant to exhale. How did he do this to me, every time?

Crap, he was distracting me again. I clamped down my lust and drilled him with my gaze. "Christos, you still haven't told me about why you haven't said the word 'love' in so long. I told you about Damian. You have to uphold your end."

"I was getting to that." He stood up and took a deep breath. Then he started pacing my living room, like he was running away from the truth, but he had nowhere to go except to let it out.

"The last woman I told I loved them was my mom. I told her pretty much every day, right up until the day she left my dad.

"I remember my dad begging her over and over not to leave because he loved her. I can hear his voice in my head, pleading 'I love you, Vesile, I love you. Don't go, my love. I need you.' My mom ignored him and walked out the front door of our house.

"I hated her so much for leaving, I swore I would never make the mistake of telling a woman I loved her. Not even my mom."

Christos looked like he was reliving the moment. I wanted to touch him, to comfort him, but I felt like he needed space. I sat on the couch, elbows on my knees, clasping my fingers in front of my face.

"After that," he said, "I tended not to trust any women. I avoided them. But when puberty hit, I had to make some sort of peace with women, because I felt that need for them, that yearning I couldn't ignore.

"I made a vow that I wouldn't let a woman get close to me like my dad had with my mom. It was too dangerous. I saw firsthand how it destroyed him, and the hurt my mom left with *me* was devastating. I wasn't going to invite more pain in by loving someone like my dad had loved my mom.

"So every time one of the girls I was seeing mentioned love, I shut down, or played it off so we could hook up. I felt like shit, but I didn't care. I wanted release, and they wanted it too. But it's all I could give them. It was an escape from my pain.

"My broken heart never healed. I saw love as a prison, a place you willingly entered and shut the bars on yourself. A place where you risked being beaten without warning by the cruel people who trapped you inside."

Christos exhaled deeply, slumping over.

The way he said it sounded so awful. I couldn't wrap my head around it. "Do you still talk to your mom?"

"Rarely. When I turned eighteen, I didn't have to visit her if I didn't want to. And you can bet I fucking didn't, after the way she tore my family apart. She moved to New York shortly after that. Then it was easy to avoid her."

Silent tears dripped from his eyes. He wiped them away with his forearm.

"Oh, Christos, that's terrible." I stood and hugged him and kissed his cheek gently. I couldn't imagine his pain. I don't think I was close enough to my parents to feel so terrible about losing them. Then again, I still had both. I didn't know how I would feel if my mom left my dad. "Why did your mom leave, if you don't mind me asking?"

He laughed through tears. "The funny thing is, it wasn't the drinking. Remember I told you how successful my dad was? And how miserable?"

"Yeah?"

"My mom helped build his career. Believe it or not, my mom's name, Vesile, means 'flood of fame' in Turkish. She was half the reason my dad got so famous. She could sell his paintings like no one else. The only problem was, the more successful my dad got, the more he hated himself for becoming something he never wanted to be. You couldn't blame my mom. She thought it was what he wanted. But my dad never admitted his own truth to *himself*. My mom was just trying to help."

"Oh, Christos. That's tragic." I released him and he began pacing again.

"I know, right?" He wept openly and continuously. "My mom loved my dad, and helped him the best way she could, but my dad was self-destructing the entire time. I didn't understand what was going on, I was just a kid. But I figured it out over the last few years, talking to my dad about it, and every now and then, my mom."

"Do you see your mom at all?"

"Not really. Maybe once a year. If that. It's still so uncomfortable being around her."

"Have you forgiven her?"

He stopped pacing and looked at me like I'd just announced the cure for cancer. He blinked.

"You haven't, have you?"

He hung his head. "No." Tears dripped from his eyes, falling to the carpet.

"If you're right about your dad, then you have to forgive your mom. I don't know if your mom felt like she had become the source of your father's misery, or the cause of his drinking, or what. But I'm sure she felt terrible."

"I never thought of that. All I could think about was the fact that she left. She broke up the family. Even if things were bad."

"Maybe she was trying to save the family, by giving your dad space?"

He looked at me hopefully, then shook his head. "I don't know, Samantha. It makes logical sense, but that doesn't help my pain any."

"Come sit with me." I patted the couch cushion. He sat down and I hugged him. "Maybe this will help." I kissed his cheek, kissed the corner of his mouth, his temple.

He wept for a long time as I kissed him and caressed him quietly.

"I love you, Samantha. I really do."

My breath caught. Those words now carried new weight. Considering all that he had told me about his mom, it took everything I had to keep breathing. I was too stunned to respond.

After awhile, he stood up. "I need some fresh air."

I followed him onto the balcony and leaned on the railing with him, watching the ocean. You could faintly hear the surf crashing on the distant shore.

Neither of us spoke. It was enough to be shoulder to shoulder, enjoying the view. Eventually, we went back inside.

Christos plopped down on the floor where he had sat earlier. He picked up a crayon and started working on a new crayon painting.

I sat down and started one of my own. We worked for awhile in pleasant silence.

He set his crayon down. "Let me see how yours is coming along," he said.

I handed it to him. "It's not very good."

"This is really nice, Samantha." I could tell he was analyzing it closely. "Do you see the way you have this shape flowing into the one next to it?" He traced the line with his extended pinky.

"Yeah?"

"Did you do that on purpose?"

"No."

"That's what I mean about talent. You're unconsciously organizing things in a way that naturally leads the viewer's eye through the picture. This is pretty advanced stuff."

"Really?"

"And you're doing it without even realizing it."

"I am?"

He smiled. "Yeah, Picasso, you are."

I smiled.

He smiled back at me, his dimples flashing. "You're driving me crazy with that luscious smile of yours, *agápi mou.*"

Shiver. Between his dimples and the way he said that phrase in his accented Greek, he literally sent jolts between my legs that lit up my nipples.

He crawled around the couch like a stalking lion and brushed the tip of his nose across my cheek, then licked a slick line down to my mouth. He kissed me passionately, then nipped my lower lip with his teeth. He pulled back enough for me to see his feral eyes. He looked like a hunter and I was his prey.

Oh, shit.

He leaned in and kissed me forcefully. I responded. Our tongues twisted together, fighting for dominance. I thought I could subdue him until he stroked my neck with his fingertips, then slid his powerful hand across my chest. He had me.

My breasts responded instantly, nipples hardening against the inside of my satin bra. He pushed his chest into me until he was on top of me, mounting me, kissing downward, drinking the heat from my mouth. His tongue pushed and prodded against mine, sinking down into my mouth over and over again.

I moaned and writhed beneath him. He slid his palms up my cheeks, then behind my head, grabbing a fistful of hair. His other hand thrust between my legs and he leaned his weight onto it. His wrist pressed into the front of my pelvis. I felt his fingers press up against my wet folds through my jeans. I tilted my hips down onto his fingers, sending shivers into the dense knot of nerves between my legs, just above the heat of my opening.

I wanted him so badly I was shaking with desire.

He shifted and lowered me back onto the carpet, then pushed the coffee table away from us with a powerful arm, giving us plenty of room to writhe.

His wrist was still between my legs. I squeezed my thighs together, resisting. But he was too strong. His forearm pried into the cleft between my legs and dug into the denim of my jeans. He kissed me deeply, swallowing my moans.

"I love you, Samantha. I want to make you come until you scream. I want you gasping for air. Gasping for me. Make me your oxygen, Samantha. Tell me you'll die without me."

"Yes." I wasn't even sure what I was agreeing to. I didn't even care. He could do whatever he wanted.

He unsnapped my jeans.

I squeaked and froze.

He suddenly slowed, toning down his energy almost instantly. I was a second away from freaking out. I thought he was going to yell at me.

"Do we need to stop?" he asked calmly. "I don't want you to be afraid of any of this. I want you to be one hundred percent sure you want it."

I wasn't sure what *it* was. "Ahh," I said uncertainly.

"I can stop any time you want me to, *agápi mou*. Just give me the word."

"You mean, like, a safe word?" I asked in a shaky voice. I was half nervous and half felt like a complete baby.

"Yes," he smiled.

"How about grapes?"

"Okay, grapes will work. Shall I continue."

"Please." Did I sound like I was begging? *Oh, who fucking cares!* I was about to shout "Take me, Christos!" or "Grapes!" But since I wasn't sure which would actually come out of my mouth, I kept it shut.

Christos was calmer now, but he flowed with it. He reached down and unzipped my jeans one link at a time. I thought it would take at least a month until he finished. Each languorous tick-tick-

tick of my zipper sent a tiny spark into my core. Oh god. I was going to explode like a time bomb as soon as the timer hit zero.

When the zipper was open all the way, he peeled my jeans down my hips until they passed below my ass. He lifted my hips completely off the ground so he could get the jeans down to my ankles. He left the jeans on, binding my legs together. No going back!

Grapes? Anybody have any grapes?

I was down to panties, bra, and t-shirt. He leaned forward and rolled my t-shirt up until my breasts were nearly out. Then he carefully pulled each one free of the cups and licked my nipples thoroughly.

Boom. I was writhing from the sensation within two seconds. I lost track of time as pleasure burned through my entire body. The next thing I knew, his tongue glided down over my navel, where he swirled it around gently. It was like he was eating me out, but using my belly button. I felt my clit spasm every time his tongue made a complete rotation.

Oh god, if my navel felt this good, what would the real thing be like?

His tongue slid down to the hem of my panties. He licked across the border of skin and cotton, from one hip bone to the other. His tongue dipped under the panties, the closest any tongue had ever been to my private parts. I was melting with the warmest pleasure imaginable. Liquid ecstasy dripped from my center.

"More?" he asked quietly. "Or grapes?"

"No grapes. *Please,* no grapes," I moaned desperately.

"Is that yes grapes or no grapes?" he smirked.

"It's don't stop, winemaker!"

"Who's whining?"

"Shut the fuck up, Christos! Don't stop!"

He chuckled as he twisted his fingers into the waistband of my panties and pulled them down, exposing the most intimate part of me to the air. He exhaled his hot breathe onto my core. Yes, he was my oxygen. Oh god. His tongue flicked across my drenched folds. Once. Just once.

I shivered with cold fire as a blazing hail storm of ecstasy tore through my body. My very cells pulled in every direction at once. I was going to implode while exploding.

He lifted my legs and pushed my knees toward my chest, opening me up. Then he laid down on the carpet, his face directly in front of my opening. He lowered my jeans-bound legs over his head.

"Grapes?" he asked softly.

"Don't stop," I begged in a husky whisper.

The tip of his tongue slid up and down the crevice between my wet flesh.

Oh shit, it was too much. I never wanted it to stop. His tongue stroked my clit repeatedly, lighting me up. Every circuit in my body tingled with intense pleasure. Each stroke against the cluster of nerves between my legs caused me to buck against him, but he held on, forcing the pleasure into my body. It felt so fucking good, I was gasping in short, tight breaths, as if the pleasure was electrocuting me, tightening every muscle in my body to the point of total contraction.

He was relentless. I thought the pleasure couldn't possibly intensify until he plunged his tongue inside me.

My fingers splayed, my toes pulled back. My legs stiffened over his muscled back, my thighs squeezed against the sides of his head. My arms shook and danced.

He wrapped his arms over my thighs and buried his face even more deeply between my legs.

Oh fuck, it was too much. I couldn't take it. The pleasure was overwhelming. It was going to undo me. I wanted it to last for eternity.

Then he inserted the tip of his finger inside me. Oh. My. God. He slid it up and down my opening, teasing me. Then it went back inside my core. Deeper. Just a tiny bit, then back out. Then deeper still. My pleasure began to build even more intensely. I didn't think it was possible. Until it slid still deeper, penetrating me.

The tension in my arms and legs built to a final peak. I was rigid, every muscle in my entire body completely contracted. My back arched, I pushed down with my denim-bound legs, forcing my pelvis into Christos's face.

His tongue continued to swirl, coaxing me toward the edge of insanity. His finger filled me up, probing, circling, stimulating me. My entire consciousness was gathered between my legs. Everything else ceased to exist. All I knew was the electric effect of his powerful tongue and his plunging finger.

When I thought my body couldn't possibly contain any more pleasure, a power deep inside me began to build. A heat so hot, I was going to combust. It sparked off in my core, then swirled in a thick blaze throughout my stomach. Tendrils of fire pulsed up to my breasts and throat. The inferno spread down my legs like wildfire. A fireball exploded upward and uncoiled in my throat, then sank down my entire body, to my toes. I suddenly felt completely and totally relaxed. But the molten pleasure in my body had not subsided. It had transformed, intensifying beyond all measure, emanating from between my legs in a steady current of infinite bliss.

Christos' face was embedded deep within my whirlpool of pent up sex, drilling, caressing, plunging, coaxing, stoking, igniting. I breathed deeply, repeatedly, and the fire in my being expanded ever further with each breath, consuming me entirely, filling the room, then spreading beyond the walls to encompass the entire planet. I was channeling some infinite fountain of pleasure that existed beyond the bounds of normal reality, summoning a flood of ecstasy into the world.

Christos was unrelenting. He forced his power into me. I pushed my hips against him one last time as my body tensed for final, total release.

I breathed, in and out, in and out, in and out, until my chest was full of energy. The massive ball of pleasure restrained inside me finally broke free. I screamed. I screamed so loud I thought the planet would split beneath me. I screamed again, and again, and again.

Then I was thrashing as the sphere of energy inside me exploded a second time, against my will, shattering me in a million directions of infinite pleasure at once. I left my body.

Time stopped.

I don't know for how long.

Forever. An instant.

I don't know.

When time resumed, I began to breathe again, slowly at first, panting deeply. Christos' head gyrated lazily between my legs. I was numb to the sensation now. I was warm, pleasant pleasure from head to toe. There was no more intensity that could go into my body, or release from it.

I was completely relaxed. I had no idea anyone could ever be *this* relaxed.

I think at that point, it was safe to say:

First. Orgasm. Ever.

Hmm, maybe that was an understatement. I mean, I could've sworn I'd given myself one or two orgasms in the past. Oh, no, no, no. Not even close. Those had been like firecrackers. This was a super nova. This was the end of the universe.

How about:

First. Near death experience. Ever.

"Grapes?" Christos mocked.

I grabbed his hair with both fists and laughed deeply, freely, like I don't think I ever had before. Total, joyful, ecstasy.

"Grapes," I said, still laughing.

"I so fucking love you, Samantha."

"I so *going down* love you, Christos Manos."

We chuckled together. I lifted my legs over his head and twisted them to the side. He snaked up my body and pinned me with his eyes.

His face glistened with my wetness. He cracked his dimples out like a pro, then leaned in and kissed me.

I tasted myself, and I tasted good.

I was so fucking dirty, and I loved it.

Chapter 22

That night, I slept like a log. There was no way you could've woken me up. If the apartment were to catch fire, I trusted Christos to carry me outside to safety while I snored.

The next morning, Christos made me breakfast in bed again. It was a good thing, because after last night's 10.0 Richter quake between my legs, I wasn't sure I could stand up yet.

After breakfast, we showered separately. Christos told me he had a special surprise and we needed to get moving.

When we were dressed, I asked what the surprise was.

"You'll find out when we get there. You're going to need a sketchbook. Do you have an extra one I can borrow?"

"Actually, I've got yours."

"I forgot all about it!" He smiled and pecked my cheek. "Hey, sorry for ditching you that day at the view," he said quietly.

"Don't worry about it." It seemed ages ago. So much had transpired since he'd left me at his family's bench up at the view with me thinking I'd destroyed everything between us.

He opened his sketchbook and carefully tore out the caricature drawing he'd made of me as a master artist. "This is for you." He smiled.

I took it from him with two hands, admiring it again. "It's so good, Christos. I'll treasure it forever."

He grinned, somewhat abashed. "And so true. You're destined to be great, Samantha Smith. I know it."

When he said it, I totally believed him. I hugged the drawing gently to my chest and stifled fresh tears. After a moment, I carefully set the drawing on my bookcase. "Okay! So, what are we doing today?" I asked.

"Lion or Stallion?"

"Huh?"

"Pick."

Was he talking about himself? If that was the case, both applied. "Both?" I grinned.

"You have to pick one."

"Oh, I don't know." Although Christos was most definitely a stallion in every respect, after the way he devoured me last night, I think the safe answer was, "Lion?"

"I was hoping you'd say that. Lion it is. Do you want me to drive?"

"Sure!" I handed him my keys.

We hopped in my car and drove to the freeway. He took the southbound onramp.

Twenty minutes later we took the Washington Street offramp and drove through neighborhood streets, then suddenly pulled into a huge parking lot.

"Where are we?"

Kids and families were climbing out of cars.

"The San Diego Zoo."

"No way! I love the zoo!"

We walked to the entrance hand in hand. For the first time, I felt like we were on an official date. Christos had a membership and a guest ticket, so we got in free.

"How often do you come here," I asked.

"Whenever I want to draw the animals. Maybe once a month?"

"This must be totally boring for you then," I said, unable to hide my disappointment.

"What do you mean?"

"You've been here so many times, there's nothing new."

"I've never been here with you, have I?"

My pouty mouth widened into a smile. I leaned against him and tip-toed up to kiss his cheek. He turned and our lips met.

"Come on, there's a lot to see. And I don't want to miss something." He dragged me through the main entrance by the hand.

He wasn't kidding. The zoo was enormous. He knew his way around and we cut through tons of animal exhibits. I wanted to stop and enjoy it all, but he wouldn't relent.

We ended up near a large cage with a crowd of a dozen people around it. It seemed anti-climactic compared to what we'd passed on the way there.

"What is it?" I asked, somewhat confused.

"Feeding time. Get ready."

The next thing I knew, a huge black panther hopped up from nowhere, onto a tree limb.

"Oh, wow! He's beautiful."

A zookeeper narrated as an assistant hung a huge hunk of meat from a rope that dangled in the center of the cage. The zookeeper talked about jaguar eating habits while the assistant yanked on the rope and the chunk of raw flesh danced around the panther.

The zookeeper explained that they made Mbwana the jaguar work for his food to give him exercise.

Mbwana was beautiful and powerful. His eyes darted as the meat swung and jumped at the end of the rope. He padded from the tree branch onto the roof of his sleeping hut. He crouched down, his head dipping liquidly, timing the trajectory of the meat. He lunged suddenly, launching through the air at the hunk, hooking it with one paw. The assistant yanked on the rope, trying to snap it from Mbwana's grasp.

Mbwana swiped at the chunk with both enormous clawed paws and pulled it into his chest. I could see every muscle in his body flexing magnificently while he pulled against the rope. The assistant was almost powerless to resist and let go of the rope. Mbwana took his kill into his den and had breakfast.

"That was awesome!" I couldn't believe it. I'd been maybe five feet away, just on the other side of the cage, the whole time. "I've never been so close to a black panther before!" My eyes were beaming. "Is this what you meant by lions?"

"Yup."

"What would've been stallions?"

"The horses at the Del Mar track."

"Oh, what? We missed the horses?"

"Next time." He hugged me to his side.

After that, we casually strolled the zoo, enjoying all the exhibits. We found the tigers and lions as well. My favorite exhibit was probably the baby pandas. They were totally, ridiculously cute. If Kamiko had come, I imagined she would've spent the entire day watching them.

Christos pulled out his sketchbook at various exhibits and explained the basic differences between drawing people and animals. He was so damn good at it, but he encouraged me to draw stick figure animals, much like how I had started with people the first day of Life Drawing. I had a ton of fun.

Everywhere we went, Christos knew people. He talked to the zookeepers, who knew him by name. He talked to the guys who drew caricatures for the customers. The caricature manager told Christos he had gone by Charboneau gallery to see Christos' paintings after the opening. The manager then introduced Christos to the other artists, one of whom Christos already knew. Christos was a local celebrity. It never ceased to amaze me how well connected he was.

We had an early lunch, and made it back to his grandfather's house in time to walk down to the library for Drawing With Christos with the kids.

It was an amazing day all the way around.

The next week was Thanksgiving week. Classes flew by.

Madison, Romeo, and Kamiko all talked about their four-day weekend plans. They were all driving or flying home to see their families, as were most of the kids on campus.

I, on the other hand, would remain in San Diego. My parents didn't have money to fly me home for Thanksgiving *and* winter break, so we opted for winter break. Thankfully, Madison invited me to her family's house on Thanksgiving day so I wouldn't be completely alone the entire long weekend.

When I talked to Christos on Wednesday, he invited me to his grandfather's house for Thanksgiving dinner.

"We're having people over all day long. I would love to have you, so would my grandfather."

"Oh, I'm sorry, Christos. Madison already invited me to her parents house in Huntington Beach. I said yes. She asked me like a week ago."

"That's cool."

I couldn't tell if he was disappointed or not. "You could come with me to Mads' house. I'm sure she wouldn't mind. She made it sound like there was plenty of room."

"I sort of have to help out my grandad."

"Let me check with Mads, I'm sure she'll understand if I can't make it." I was torn because I was forced to chose between my best friend and Christos.

For all intents and purposes, even though Christos and I hadn't confirmed the boyfriend-girlfriend label, I felt like that was the category we fell into.

Weren't boyfriends and girlfriends supposed to do holiday things together?

I mean, I'd even gone to Damian's parents for Thanksgiving dinner fairly early in the relationship. Afterward, we'd gone to my parents house for dessert. We did the reverse for Christmas. And that was stupid Damian.

"Maybe you can do both," Christos suggested. "Hit up Mads then drive to my place? Or vice versa?"

"Yeah!" Only Christos wouldn't be with me. Unless. "Can you come?"

"I wish. We're making a lot of food, and people will be coming and going all day long. I need to help play host. The Charboneau's will stop by, as will the Kingston-Whitehouses."

"The whos?"

"Brandon's family, the guy who runs the gallery?"

"Oh yeah." Handsome Brandon. The snake charmer.

"And Tiffany's parents."

"Oh." Why did I not like the idea that Tiffany would be alone at an all-day party with Christos? It sounded very dangerous to my love life.

Christos chuckled. He must've picked up on my anxiety. "Don't worry, *agápi mou*. I love you. You don't need to worry about Tiffany. I know how to draw boundaries. But I have to schmooze her parents. They're big art buyers. They've known my family forever."

I rolled my eyes at myself. "I'm sorry. I'm being totally immature. I love you, Christos."

"It's okay, *agápi mou*. I love you too. Look, what time is Madison's thing?"

"They eat at two."

"Perfect. Eat with them, then come over to our house in the evening. We'll be serving food into the evening."

"Okay!" At least I didn't have to disappoint Madison. Hopefully I wouldn't have to worry about stupid Tiffany. She was such a rude bitch.

Christos spent the night before Thanksgiving at his grandfather's house because there was so much to do to prepare, and Spiridon really needed his help.

I woke up in an empty bed for the first time in days. It was very lonely. I missed Christos already. At least I'd see him in about twelve hours. I could handle that.

I moped around my apartment for awhile, then walked down to the beach. I strolled along the surf, enjoying the sunrise. It was so beautiful. I couldn't believe this was fall weather. The temperature was cool, but not cold. The sky was clear blue and cloudless.

I went back to my apartment and called my parents around noon, east coast time.

"Hello?"

"Hey, Dad. Happy Thanksgiving!"

"Well, hello, Sam. Linda!" he shouted away from the phone, "our long lost daughter is calling again!"

My mom picked up. "Sam! It's been weeks since we've heard from you! Is everything okay?"

"I'm fine, Mom."

"Then why haven't you called or answered emails? We were getting worried."

They hadn't heard from me because I didn't really want to tell them I was in love with an amazing man, an artist, and I wanted to be an artist too. How was I going to explain all that without a lecture and threats of coming out to stage an intervention on my behalf? Groan. "I guess I've been super busy studying, so I forgot. Sorry."

"That's okay, Sam. As long as you're all right, that's all that matters."

Why did I think that wasn't exactly true?

"Your mother is right, Sam. We care about you."

Yes, they cared, but what about the love part? I was ready to cry already.

"How are classes going," my dad asked.

"Classes are fine, Dad." Fuck. I really was born into the wrong family. My life was evolving into something neither I nor my parents could've ever predicted. And I knew they were the last people on earth I could tell about it, share it with, or rejoice with. I would have more luck telling a random stranger about my new excitement than my parents.

"Have you signed up for classes for next quarter yet?"

"No," I lied.

"You'll sign up for Micro Economics, like we discussed back when, right?"

"Yes," I lied. I dropped onto my couch and pulled my knees to my chest.

Not that it was hard to lie to my parents. They never knew why I broke up with Damian. They had pried and probed, but I gave them some vague story about things not working out. My mom had said that these things happened with teenage romance. That was about it. No consolation, no hugs, no commiseration. Just reassurance that I would get over it. Thanks, Mom. My dad had been disappointed because he always thought Damian seemed like such a nice guy. My parents were clueless sometimes.

"How are you grades?" Dad asked.

"Fine," I sighed.

"We're sorry you couldn't be here with us for Turkey Day," my mom said.

Sorry? How about: *We miss you.*

Groan. My parents were either worried or sorry. I sighed again, more heavily this time, and held the phone away so they wouldn't here me.

"Do you have any plans today," Dad asked.

"Yeah, I'm going to my friend Madison's parents in Huntington Beach. It's close."

"Oh, that's nice, Sam. It's good that you're making friends."

"We were worried about you, over the last couple of years," my mom said. "It seemed like all of your high school friends disappeared for no good reason, so that's good news."

Worried. Good news. Ugh. If they only knew how bad things got after Damian. If they only knew how I'd lied in their faces every single day the same way I'd lied to everyone at school, and even myself. They had no idea how miserable I was back then. They had no idea what happened to…

Taylor.

Nobody knew. Not even Christos.

I was close to sobbing. I held it back "Mom, Dad, I have to get ready to go to Madison's."

"Okay, Sam," my mom said.

"We'll see you at Christmas," Dad said.

"But call us before then, okay?" Mom suggested.

"Okay."

"Bye!" they said.

"Bye."

I ended the call and hugged one of my couch pillows tightly, burying my face as I shook with muted sobs.

Taylor.

I drove up to Huntington beach after I calmed down, showered, and dressed.

The drive took ninety minutes and there was little traffic. The nearly empty road was nothing compared to the traffic jam between campus and my apartment the night before. It seemed like everyone was leaving San Diego for Thanksgiving weekend on Wednesday evening.

The Lockhart house was a modest three-bedroom stucco home only blocks from the beach. It was warm and charming.

Madison ran outside as I walked up the driveway. She actually wore something other than beach attire for once: a V-neck sweater and slacks. Her hair was down for I think the first time ever, and she wore makeup. She was beautiful.

"Look at you, Mads. All dolled up!"

"Sam!" She threw her arms around me. "So glad you could make it!"

Jake walked up behind her. "Hey, Sam. What up?" When Mads and I finished hugging, she wrapped a loving arm around Jake. They looked so happy together.

"Come inside," Madison said. "I want you to meet my family."

Madison's parents looked like well-groomed beach bums. I liked them immediately. Her dad was making margaritas while her mom oversaw the turkey, the stuffing, and the other All-American Thanksgiving dishes.

After Madison introduced me to her parents Wayne and Barbara, her dad handed me a freshly poured margarita. "Taste this, Sam. Does it need more tequila?"

I goggled at Madison. My parents never would've handed me alcohol while I was still under age.

Madison nodded, giving me the okay.

I sipped carefully. "It's good!" I didn't know what else to say.

Madison dragged me by the arm to her sister's room, which was covered with boy-band posters and too many pink things.

"This is my sister Piper. She has no life beyond texting."

Piper laid on her bed, knees up, ferociously texting away on her phone. "I heard that," she said while texting.

"Say something to Sam, Piper."

"Hey, Sam," Piper said, still flicking buttons.

"She'll emerge when she smells my mom's banana bread," Madison said.

"Heard that!" Piper said.

It turned out that Piper was not as addicted to texting as Madison suggested, but she didn't come out of her room until the banana bread came out of the oven.

Piper was funny and cute and so fifteen. She reminded me of me, before I got involved with Damian. Innocent, carefree, happy. I hoped she stayed like that for a long time.

The six of us sat down to early dinner together. It was a blast.

Madison's family were so much fun. They all cracked jokes and had endless humorous stories about family vacations, sporting events that Madison or Piper participated in, and boating trips to The River (wherever that was).

Madison's family had their own language of love and connectedness that was completely alien to me. I envied Madison in a way I could never communicate to her. She had what probably every girl in America wanted. A normal, loving family upbringing. She was so lucky. I hoped she realized it.

When dessert came out, Madison stopped everyone to make an announcement. She stood up in her seat, her hand resting on Jake's shoulder. "I just wanted to take a moment to give thanks, because that's what we're supposed to do today, right?"

Everyone nodded.

"I want to thank my parents, because they're totally awesome, for everything they've given me. You're the best. I love you guys." She grinned at them.

Barbara Lockhart teared up instantly and nodded. "Thank you, Madison. I love you, honey."

"That's my girl," Wayne said proudly. I could tell he barely held back a tear of his own.

"And thank you, Piper," Madison said. "Even though you're annoying sometimes, and I wish mom and dad would take away your phone. I still love you, and couldn't imagine a better sister."

Piper rolled her eyes bashfully.

"And thank you, Jake, for being the best boyfriend ever. I love you." She leaned down and pecked his cheek, then hugged his neck.

Jake blushed through his tan. He turned to Wayne. "Is it okay if I kiss your daughter, in your house, I mean?" Jake asked sheepishly.

"Go for it, son," Wayne said. "But keep the tongue to a minimum."

Everybody cracked up. Jake stood and kissed Madison deeply.

"Gross! Too much tongue," Piper joked.

What about me? I suddenly felt left out. Like always.

In the past, whenever I'd shared Thanksgiving dinner with my parents, I'd somehow felt left out, like something was missing, even though the family was together. But I never knew *what* was missing. Until now. Because I was seeing it firsthand in the Lockhart abode. They had this emotional bond, this heartfelt connection that my parents knew nothing about. I privately envied Madison for having the family I never would.

I sipped my margarita. I wanted to down it and ask for three more, but I had to drive to Christos' soon.

"And last but not least, I want to thank you, Sam, for being my new BFF." Madison held up her margarita to toast. "Let's raise a glass, everybody, to Samantha Smith. The bravest girl I know."

Everyone at the table picked up their glasses. I shyly raised mine.

"Sam came all the way out to California from Washington D.C. to make her way in life." Madison smiled warmly and looked me directly in the eyes. "Samantha, I can't tell you how much better you make my experience at SDU. I miss my parents and my sis every day I'm away from them, but you give me a home in San Diego. I don't think I could do it without you, girlfriend." She toasted the table. "To Sam!"

"To Sam!" everyone echoed.

I was going to cry. Screw it. I let my tears flow and raised my glass. "Thanks, guys."

Madison walked around the table to where I sat next to Piper and gave me a huge hug. "I love you, Sam. You are *so* the bestest BFF ever."

I sniffled back tears and returned Madison's hug. "I love you too, Mads."

That turned out better than I expected.

Silly me.

When I left Madison's house around five o'clock, I thanked everyone profusely. I texted Christos that I was leaving, but I never heard back from him. He was probably busy.

I was at Christos' by six-thirty.

The driveway at Spiridon's house, which was normally empty, was crammed with cars. I had to find parking on the street. I sort of felt second-class after the royal treatment I'd received at Madison's.

Oh well, Christos did warn me that it was going to be crowded.

I walked into the house because the front door was unlocked. There were people everywhere. The crowd was all ages: babies, toddlers, teenagers, parents, grandparents. I wandered through the house looking for Christos or Spiridon. I found Spiridon in the kitchen, overseeing food. He had a catering team helping him out. The caterers wore black and white, and hustled like crazy.

"Sam!" Spiridon said when he saw me. "Grab a drink, grab some food! We've got plenty."

"Do you know where Christos is?"

"I think he's on the deck."

Spiridon was so busy, I left him alone. "Thanks, I'll find him."

I walked outside to the backyard, which was just as crowded as the inside. After I'd circulated through the throng, I still hadn't found Christos. Frustrated, I went inside and grabbed a glass of wine. I downed it in four swallows. I grabbed another glass and tipped it back.

"Hey, Samantha! There you are!" Christos had a platter of hors d'oeuvres in one hand. He hugged me to his side with one arm and pecked me on the lips. "Sorry, this place is a madhouse. The caterers couldn't keep up, so I'm helping out. Do I make a good waiter?" He seemed distracted.

"Yes, you look good," I smiled. "As always."

His energy changed and his smiled widened. "I missed you all day, *agápi mou*." He leaned toward me and kissed me slowly and deeply. There was only the hint of tongue, but it felt so welcoming.

I sighed. I felt better already, and it wasn't the wine.

"I've got to keep moving. People are about to go cannibal if I don't get them food. Dinner hasn't even been served yet. I hope you're hungry!"

"Yeah. Okay, go do your thing."

"Are you going to be okay by yourself?"

"Yeah," I smiled. "Now go, feed the barbarians!"

"I love you, Samantha." He spun and the crowd swallowed him up.

For the next two hours, I saw only glances of Christos. He always tipped me a wink, or blew me a kiss. But I don't think we exchanged more than a dozen words.

I made idle conversation with several people, but everyone always seemed to drift away to other conversations, or to get food and drink. I saw a number of faces I recognized from Christos' gallery show. I even saw Mrs. Moorhouse, the matron who had asked about Spiridon and Nikolos, but I didn't talk to her.

I was basically in it alone.

Wandering from room to room, I finally saw most of the house for the first time, except for the upstairs, which was closed off. I think that's where Christos and Spiridon's bedrooms were.

I was strolling down a hallway after using the bathroom when I bumped into the first familiar face in an hour.

Brandon Charboneau was studying a painting hanging on the wall, probably one of Spiridon's, by the look of it. "Hey, you," he said warmly when he saw me, flashing his hazel eyes with impeccable charm.

"Oh, hey Brandon. How are you?"

"I'm good. Enjoying the evening?"

"It's wonderful," I exaggerated.

He leaned against the wall and swirled his wine. "What have you been up to, since the gallery show? I haven't seen you since then, have I?"

"Uh, no. I've been busy with school. And, other things." Why didn't I tell him about Christos and me? Maybe because I'd had more wine than I could remember? That was my defense, and I was sticking to it.

"Did you ever do a portrait sitting for Christos?"

"No, I totally forgot to mention it." Like I was going to go into the reasons why I hadn't asked Christos to paint me nude.

"You really should. He is fully capable of doing justice to your exquisite beauty on canvas. I doubt any other living artist would be up to the task."

I blushed. "Thanks, Brandon. I just don't think it's my thing."

"That's too bad. It would be a magnificent painting. Botticelli had his Venus. Da Vinci had his Mona Lisa. Vermeer had his Girl with a Pearl Earring. I would paint you myself, but I'm not an artist. So, if I had to chose someone to immortalize your timeless beauty, I would chose Christos. You should give it serious consideration, Samantha."

To say I wasn't flattered would be a lie. He was comparing me to three of the most famous women ever painted. What girl didn't want to be the muse of a famous artist, revered by millions of people for hundreds of years? It was only somewhat magical to think about. Somewhat.

His hazel eyes seemed to flare like falling stars that slipped past my defenses and pierced into me.

Snake Charmer! Kamiko had been right all along. I blinked and shook my head, trying to force back my buzz and reclaim cold sobriety.

Brandon leaned toward me. How had he gotten so close? He must also have vampire abilities, including hypnotism and teleportation.

I backed up a step, but with the wall behind me, there was nowhere to go.

Brandon lowered his face toward mine.

"Samantha, there you are!' Christos said. "What are you guys doing back here?"

"Hey, Christos," I said. *Phew, that was close.* I wished I hadn't drunk so much wine.

"Hey," Brandon said casually. "I was just telling Samantha that you need to paint her portrait for your next show. I can't think of a better artist, with enough talent to capture her beauty, than you."

Christos' eyes danced between us suspiciously, analyzing the situation.

Then he pinned his eyes on me. I expected to see anger poking out around the edges of his customary easy-going smile. I did not. I saw a conspiratorial shimmer. Like we were on the same team. *Phew,* again.

"I don't know, Brandon. I think Samantha may be too beautiful for even me to paint. I wouldn't want to screw up perfection."

"I'm sure you could pull it off," Brandon said dryly.

"Maybe you're right," Christos said in his traditional cocky style. "Maybe I am the only one who can capture beautiful Samantha."

I smiled at him, enjoying our private joke.

"Tiffany's here," Christos said to Brandon without breaking our gaze. "You should say hello to her."

"That I should. I wouldn't want Her Highness to feel neglected."

"Nope." Christos still held my gaze, never looking at Brandon. "Don't forget to freshen your drink. The bar's still open."

"Okay." Brandon took the hint. "Samantha, it was a pleasure seeing you again. Christos," he nodded, then walked off.

"I'm going to have to put a leash on that guy," Christos joked.

I anticipated, at the very least, a mild lecture from Christos for being alone in a dark hallway with Brandon. If it had been Damian, it would've turned DEFCON 1 in two seconds flat. I searched Christos' eyes. I saw only amusement. So be it. Christos was awesome. I smiled. "I'm sure Tiffany will take care of him for you."

"You're right. Leave the dirty work to the queen of dirty deeds."

"That's an understatement."

He cocked his head inquisitively. "Did I miss something?"

"No."

He skimmed my jawline with gentle fingers, then kissed me on the lips.

"I hate to kiss and run, but my grandpa still needs help."

I couldn't hide my pout. This was the first private moment we'd had all night. Some Thanksgiving. I rolled my eyes at myself. I was being such a baby. "Okay. How late are you going to be?"

"At least till one a.m. The caterers stay until then. I may have to stay later."

"Really?" I whined.

"Sorry, Samantha. It's a tradition."

"Okay," I sighed.

He kissed me again. "All right, I'll see you later. I'll be around here somewhere."

He walked off, and I was alone again.

I wandered the party for another hour or two. I saw Tiffany hanging on Brandon. He did his best to keep her wandering hands off, but she was insistent. I actually felt bad for him. I remembered what Brandon had said at the gallery about the relationship between his family and Tiffany's, and his commitment to not getting involved with her. Poor guy. Tiffany exuded desperation and was unrelenting with her grabby hands. I don't know why. I'm sure she could find some available guys somewhere. She was more than beautiful enough. Maybe she had worked through all the eligible bachelors already, like Christos had said.

The party was still crowded, and I really didn't know anybody that I wanted to talk to. My buzz had worn off by that point, and I didn't feel like drinking anymore. That was when the loneliness really set in.

I remembered how intimate things had been at Madison's house. Their loving energy was unbelievable. It wasn't grand, it wasn't exciting. It was grounded and connected. This huge party was chaotic and noisy and disconnected. I was hoping to spend Thanksgiving evening with Christos and his grandfather and maybe a few other people. This seemed like a big social event.

Then I remembered the phone call with my parents. That was the complete opposite of this. Too quiet. Too cold. Too nothing. I'd always dreaded Thanksgiving at my parents' because it was so exquisitely uncomfortable for no apparent reason.

Now that I had a bit of perspective, I could draw distinctions. Somehow, I wasn't surprised that just like The Three Bears, one was too hot (Christos' extravaganza dinner party), the other was too cold (my parents' house), and one (Madison's family), was just right.

Was I still in the wrong place?

Was I in some honeymoon phase with Christos? As we spent more time together, would I discover that he was too busy with family commitments and social gatherings like this? Too busy to make time for me?

Was his grandiose talk of my art career and selling paintings at galleries pulling me into a world I didn't want? A world that was the direct opposite of my family's, but equally bad?

No, that couldn't be true. Christos was devoted to me. We spent more and more time together, and it was mostly just the two of us. I couldn't imagine a better boyfriend.

And the way he handled Brandon's advances? Because it was pretty damn obvious Brandon was trying to snake charm a kiss out of me. Christos had caught him. But Christos was so easy-going about it. So unlike Damian.

Christos always managed to do the right thing by me. Christos was as close to perfect as I could possibly imagine. He had been so honest with me about everything. He had told me about his mom and dad and his deepest, most private pain.

I was the one with the problems. Because I was still lying to him. I held back the worst part of myself because it was too awful to share. Christos would hate me if he knew the truth.

The truth about Taylor.

Sadness and loathing swept over me. I was disgusted with myself. Christos was laying his heart bare to me and I was holding back. I didn't deserve him.

I didn't deserve anybody.

I made my way to the front door. I needed to go home and be alone and sort things out.

I heard Christos call my name as I dashed out the front door. He was trapped behind the crowd of revelers. I ran to my car and drove home before he could stop me.

I didn't want him to find out how horrible I was.

Taylor.

For the remainder of the Thanksgiving weekend, I avoided my apartment and Christos. I searched online for the location of the biggest mall in San Diego, and hit it up when the sun rose.

It was easy to get lost in the insanity of the Black Friday shopping madness. I was distracted from my pain and inner turmoil by the rush of greedy gift buyers.

Despite the whipping activity that surrounded me at the mall, it wasn't enough to completely quell my need for a fix.

I bought a huge Cinnabon on Friday and indulged in the warm, sugary goodness by myself. It was only a temporary reprieve from my shame and guilt over lying to Christos.

Christos texted and called me a thousand times or more. I

couldn't blame him. I was blocking him out for no obvious reason. He probably wondered why we weren't enjoying the long weekend together.

But I couldn't explain it to him. It wouldn't make any sense if I tried. Because I wouldn't be telling him the whole truth. I'd be covering up the story of Taylor with a fabrication of weak excuses. Christos deserved better than that.

He deserved someone better than *me*.

When I went home that night, I tried to study, but it was impossible. I went to bed early.

Someone knocked on my door around eleven. It had to have been Christos. Madison was still in Huntington Beach at her parents', and Romeo and Kamiko were both out of town.

The knock came again. I remained in bed, in the darkness, alone.

"Samantha? Are you home? *Agápi mou?*"

He must've known I was home. My car was parked outside.

I felt terrible for ignoring him. I dug my face into my pillow and sobbed until he stopped calling for me and went away.

I couldn't decide if I felt worse because I was blowing him off, or better because I was setting him free.

Chapter 23

Saturday was almost a repeat performance of Friday. Shopping all day at a different mall, dragging myself home in the late afternoon to attempt studying, and to eat some ice cream. Ice cream had become my go-to food group in the last two days.

There was a note taped to my door from Christos. It read:

"Please call me, Samantha. I love you. Christos."

I felt like total shit reading it. I folded it carefully and tucked it inside my sketchbook in the apartment.

I couldn't focus on my books and notes. I was going to screw up my grades on finals if I couldn't concentrate.

I considered going to the Main Library on campus, thinking perhaps the public environment would force me to study, but I knew it would be abandoned for the remainder of the weekend. I suspected my sense of loneliness would be amplified while in that public emptiness, so I stayed home. It was much easier to tolerate my loneliness while in the privacy of my apartment, close to my ice cream.

I woke up early Sunday morning. I showered and dressed quickly, intent on more shopping. Something told me Christos might stop by. If he came looking for me again, I didn't want to be in my apartment.

I grabbed my car keys and opened my front door. I almost tripped on the lump on my doorstep.

Christos lay there under a blanket. He looked frozen. His ice blue eyes peered up at me. "Samantha, what happened?"

"How long have you been here?" I choked out the words.

"I couldn't sleep, so I came by around four-thirty this morning. Your car was still here. So I went home and got a blanket and came back."

"You look like you're freezing."

"Somewhat."

"Come inside, you idiot. It may be San Diego, but it's not that warm, silly."

He stood up and stretched a kink in his back. His spine popped in about twenty places.

"You've been there for almost four hours?"

"Yeah."

I made him hot tea and pulled a blanket off my bed.

He sat on the couch, swaddled up, sipping tea. "I wanted to say goodbye to you Thursday night, but you left before I could stop you."

"Uh, yeah," I said guiltily.

"I was going to tell you to crash in my bedroom upstairs."

"You were?"

"Yeah. It was crazy on Thursday. Worse than most years. Me and grandpa were slammed. We bribed the caterers to stay later. Paid them double overtime to help out."

"Wow, that's huge."

"I think it's due to my gallery show. All of a sudden I'm a somebody. The Manos family lineage continues. All that shit."

"You're family sure seems blessed."

"I don't know if that's the word I'd use. Definitely don't use it around my dad." He sipped his tea. "So what happened to you? I tried calling and texting, but you never answered. I was worried something was wrong."

I sighed heavily. "Yeah. That. How to explain."

"Whatever it is, you can tell me. I won't hold it against you. I love you, Samantha, *agápi mou*."

Shit, he wasn't making this easy. I'd been thinking about what to say for two days. I knew it would eventually come to this. Looking into his eyes, everything I'd planned to say now seemed wrong. But I didn't know how else to put it. He was waiting for an answer.

"Christos, you and I are heading in two very different directions. Your career is already in the stratosphere. I've got student loans to worry about, and no matter what you say about how talented I am, I can see that I'm nowhere close to where real artists are at. I've taken on a lot of debt, my parents are spending their savings to help pay for my college, and I can't let them down. I can't keep focusing on the art when I know it's not going to pay my bills until way down the road, if ever. I need to focus on what's right for me now."

Christos looked at me like I was speaking a foreign language. "What about your talent? And the mentoring?"

"Maybe I have talent, maybe not. Even you said I have to develop it. I don't know if I have the time to do my art and an accounting major."

"Of course you do," he smiled.

"It may seem that way to you. You can take time off from school at a whim. Your family has tons of money. Mine doesn't. I need to focus on getting through school as fast as possible, so I can find a job and settle down. Then maybe I can find someone and have a family."

I sighed deeply, realizing how much my words matched my parents' philosophies. They would be so carefully proud of me.

I thought about Madison, and what her family had. Her parents were totally middle class. But unlike my family, hers had the love that I was missing.

Life and love weren't about tons of money and achieving the Manos family's stellar level of success. Christos had said it himself: the money had torn his mother and father apart. I didn't want that happening to me and him. I needed to stop things before circumstances turned our love into hate five or ten years from now. It was the safest path for us both.

I didn't want to risk *ever* hurting Christos. He'd been through enough already, and I wouldn't chance adding more pain into his life. Not when he still didn't know the real me.

Taylor.

No need dragging him into my shit.

"I'm totally confused," Christos said, frowning. "This doesn't sound like you, Samantha. I feel like I'm talking to a totally different person than the one I've gotten to know over the last several months."

That's because he didn't know the truth. He didn't know the real me at all.

Taylor.

Christos knew someone else. He knew my facade.

He shook his head. "Are you breaking up with me?"

"Yes." My hair hung around my face in a curtain. I couldn't look him in the eyes.

He put his hand on my wrist. "Samantha, look at me, *agápi mou.*"

Why did he have to keep saying that? I peered up at him from beneath my lowered brow. I could barely face him.

His face tensed and struggled with emotion. "I get it, Samantha. I understand what's going on. It's like my parents. You don't want it happening to us. I get it. You're afraid." His tears were flowing now.

Shit, he was right about that.

"Samantha, you have my heart. I'm not afraid to love you. I won't let fear of getting hurt stop me from taking a risk on you. I will throw away all the money and success if it means keeping us together. I couldn't live with myself if my career pushed you away. I'll never let that happen to us, *agápi mou*."

I was crying now too. He was breaking down my resistance. How could I argue with what he'd just said? I couldn't. But I didn't have to.

Because of Taylor.

Christos' face opened in total vulnerability. He took my hands in his. "Can you be fearless too, Samantha? Can you take a chance on me?"

I so wanted to. I wanted to believe his career wouldn't get in the way. I wanted to believe I could become an artist too. Maybe we could have some little house somewhere, and paint for the rest of our lives, raising a family, without all the bags of money and celebrity obligations.

I was crying hard. Christos hugged me tightly, whispering warmly into my ear.

"I love you, Samantha. I love you."

But he didn't, because he didn't know me. I was a fucking liar! *Taylor.*

I don't know how I managed to extract myself from that moment. I think I made some vague promises to Christos that we would talk about it more. I told him I needed to study for finals, which he respected.

The next three weeks consisted of very little Christos and lots of ice cream and studying. I was miserable.

Madison knew something was wrong with me, and kept prying, but I wasn't telling her the truth either. I knew how to hide it quite well. I told her I was stressed about finals, my parents, etc. She bought it. I laid the same line of bullshit on Romeo and Kamiko.

Now I was lying to everyone. My parents, as usual. My best friends, who deserved better. And the man I loved, who had given me his heart.

All I could give them were lies.

But wasn't that how I'd lived for nearly three years?

Somehow, I managed to make it to finals week without exploding from ice cream overdose. I didn't have anymore mentoring sessions with Christos. I told him I was too busy, and apologized about the kids at the library. Luckily, they took a break from lessons for most of December, so I missed only one weekend. I felt terrible for them. How many people could I manage to let down altogether? The list was growing.

The final exam for Life Drawing consisted of Professor Childress giving everyone detailed evaluations of our most recent work during office hours. He encouraged me again to consider a double major in art and accounting, or at the very least, a minor in art.

I wasn't sure how either would go over with my parents. I dreaded bringing up the topic with them over winter break.

On Wednesday of finals week, I sped through my Fundamentals of Accounting exam. It was so easy. I knew I had aced it. My parents would pat me on the back when they saw my grades.

I waited for Madison to finish before turning in my booklet, so we could walk out together.

"How'd you do?" I asked her after we walked up the stairs of the lecture hall and went outside.

"Okay, I think. I'm hoping for an A, but I can't say for sure. You tore it up. I saw you whip through the questions."

"Yeah," I said with no sense of accomplishment.

"Want some lunch?"

"Okay."

We walked outside the building that contained our lecture hall and onto the cement pathway.

Christos leaned against a tree on the opposite side, waiting.

Madison looked at me. "Rain check on lunch?"

"Uh, I guess?"

"You should talk to him, Sam. I know he's been all whacked since Thanksgiving. Jake told me Christos is miserable."

"Jake knows?" I whined.

"Of course. Jake and Christos are totally close. Why wouldn't he?"

"Shit," I hissed.

"I don't know what's going on, Sam, but something doesn't add up. You and Christos are perfect for each other." She looked at me, waiting for a response. "What's really going on?"

I couldn't tell her. I couldn't tell anyone.

"Whatever it is, Sam, I don't need to know. But Christos does. You *have* to talk to him. I'll see you later." She walked off, leaving me stranded, twenty feet away from Christos.

I couldn't bring myself to cross the chasm between us. Because fucking Taylor held me back.

Christos broke the barrier, walking despondently toward me, stopping a few feet away. "Hey."

"Hey." I felt like a shitheel douche prick-stick to the asshat power.

"I miss you, Samantha."

He wasn't saying agápi mou anymore. I didn't know whether to feel relief or loss. Who was I kidding? It was deep, painful, agonizing loss.

"I'm dying inside," he said earnestly. "Having you torn away from my life is like having my skin peeled off. We crossed a line a few weeks ago, you and I. I dropped all my defenses for the first time in forever, maybe for the first time ever. I was living life honestly, giving my true self to the world. No bullshit, no facades."

His face quivered with intense, barely-restrained emotion. But he wasn't letting it stop him from pouring it all out. "Samantha, when you dropped out on me, I was in so much pain, I can't begin to describe it. It's like you had become my armor. You protected that vulnerable person I had allowed myself to become from the sharp edges of the world. I knew I could put my old armor back on, my old habits. But I didn't want to. I still want what we had. I want to live freely, open to the world. I don't want to hide afraid behind protected, dishonest behavior. I want you, Samantha. I love you, and I want the love I know you have for me. Above all else, that's what I want."

Why was it that all I could notice while this man poured his heart out to me was the fact that groups of students were passing by, possibly listening in on what he was saying to me without fear of judgement?

Because I was a fucking liar, and he epitomized fearless honesty.

I turned on my heel and walked away from him.

"Samantha?" He followed close behind. "I'm not giving up on you. I need you, and only you. I will wait for you, *agápi mou.*"

I started to run. I was crying. I needed to get away.

Taylor.

I ran into the first women's restroom I could find and locked myself in a stall. I bawled for a long, long time. I'm sure whoever came into the restroom heard me crying. I didn't care, as long as I didn't have to look anyone in the eye.

When I finally went outside, Christos was gone.

Possibly forever.

That evening, I packed my bags before bed and showered. I had a six a.m. flight the next morning back home to D.C., care of the Ronald Reagan Airport. I called Madison to confirm she could still drive me, even though it was butt fuck early. She said of course.

I slept like crap that night. No surprise there.

In the morning, when Madison texted me she was outside, I grabbed my bags and locked up my apartment. It was dark outside.

I didn't see her car anywhere.

A '68 Camaro pulled into the parking lot.

Christos.

Madison was a traitor.

I got another text from Madison.

Is he there yet?

I texted her back furiously.

Treason is punishable by death. Where r u?

Snuggled under my covers

Get over here, now!

U better go with Christos. U don't want to miss ur flight. C u after winter break! Luv you!

I would begin concocting murder plans for Madison over break. There would be no evidence of her demise.

Christos got out of his car and leaned against it, arms folded. "Need a ride?" He wore a leather motorcycle jacket, boots, and jeans. He was so damn sexy. Damn him. His hair was disheveled and he had the perfect amount of sexy stubble to make me swoon. I wasn't letting him get away with blatant manipulation.

"No, I can drive myself."

"You don't want to park at the airport. It costs a bundle."

I rolled my eyes.

"Let me drive you. I mean, we're still friends, right?"

I took a deep breath, released it. "Fine. But I'm only letting you drive me because were friends. How long did you and Madison plan this?"

"She called me last night. Jake gave her my number."

"That bitch, I knew she was a conniver."

He chuckled. He walked up the stairs and took my bags. "I'll carry those for you."

I followed him down the stairs and waited while he put them in the trunk.

He opened my door for me.

"Thank you, Christos."

"You're welcome." He closed my door for me, climbed into the driver's seat, and we drove off.

We barely talked on the twenty minute trip to the airport. There was zero traffic on the freeway at four-thirty.

When we got to the airport, he turned into the parking structure.

"Why are you parking? You could just drop me off." That's what my parents usually did.

"I always hate it when people do that. It's nice to have someone you know walk you to security and wave you off."

I couldn't disagree, not that I knew from experience. But it sounded good.

He found a space and we walked to the terminal. According to the monitors, my flight was on time.

"Which airport are you going to?" he asked as he scanned the monitor.

"Ronald Reagan."

"Which airline?"

"United."

"Looks like you're on time then."

I only had carry-on bags, so we walked to security.

"Well, thanks," I said. "I should get through security." The line was short, but I was uncomfortable. I braced for some sort of desperate, last minute plea.

"Okay. Have a safe trip." He smiled and walked away.

That was odd. Whatever. It was probably for the best.

Security took about five minutes to get through. I bought a muffin and a coffee on the other side. I sipped my brew and nibbled on my muffin until my flight boarded.

I had a seat near the back, next to the window. An old woman took the aisle seat. There was an empty seat between us.

"Good morning," she said. "What's your name?" She was way too peppy for the hour and her age.

"I'm Sam."

"Nice to meet you, Sam. I'm Gladys. I hate flying this early, but my son lives on the east coast. I'd rather arrive when it's still light out."

"I know what you mean."

"Are you going to see your parents for Christmas?"

"Yes."

"I bet they're looking forward to seeing you. They'll give you a big hug and smother you with kisses when you get there, won't they?"

She had no idea. How about a handshake and curbside pick up? I flashed her a fake smile. Gladys was going to make this a long flight.

"Is this seat taken?"

"Christos!" I almost hit my head on the overhead compartment when I jumped.

He flashed his grin at Gladys. "Do you mind if I squeeze in?"

"Not at all, young man." Gladys unbuckled and stood up, allowing Christos to squeeze between us.

He plopped into the seat. "Hi."

I looked around desperately for a flight attendant. But what was I going to do? Christos held a ticket in his hand.

"Passengers, please take your seats," a female flight attendant said over the loudspeaker. "We are now fully boarded and preparing for takeoff. Please fasten your safety belts and make sure your tray tables are in the upright and locked position. Please follow along while we walk you through our safety procedures."

Shit. I was stuck.

Christos buckled in and grinned at me.

"Did you just buy that ticket?" I asked.

"Yeah," he grinned.

"Geez, how much did it cost?"

"It was only four hundred bucks for a one-way. That's almost the normal price. I think they were trying to fill the flight. It's pretty empty."

"What about your car?"

"I'll leave it in parking."

"Aren't you in short term? How much is that going to cost?"

"I don't know. A few hundred bucks?"

"You can't do that! You shouldn't be here, Christos!"

"Why not?"

"Because…because, you can't fly home with me!"

"Who said anything about flying home? I told you my mom lived in New York. Maybe I'm going to visit her."

"But we're flying to D.C.!"

"So? I'll rent a car with a GPS and drive to Manhattan. It'll be an adventure."

"Jesus, Christos. You're crazy."

"Nope. Fearless."

"I think they're the same thing."

"Maybe they are." He smiled.

Christos and I spent the flight talking. It couldn't be avoided. It was better than having Gladys remind me of how much I wasn't looking forward to seeing my parents. They were the last people I wanted to bawl my eyes out to about everything that had happened. I was looking forward to two weeks of quiet, solitary misery. I knew how to do that just fine.

I'd have to wait until I parted ways with Christos in D.C. He managed to include Gladys in many of our conversations, and it turned out she was pretty funny. Despite my best effort, I always had fun with Christos around, no matter how hard I tried not to.

When the plane landed, Christos and I disembarked together. The cold air seeped into the airplane before we were on the jetway. I had already forgotten how cold D.C. was in the winter. While we waited for the passengers ahead of us to disembark, I put on my heavy coat and a wool cap.

I knew my parents would be waiting at the curb outside baggage claim, so I went that way. When we got to the rental car counters, Christos didn't stop.

"Aren't you going to rent a car?" I asked.

"Do you think I should?"

"What do you mean? I thought you were going to see your mom."

He lifted his eyebrows. "Ahh, yeah. About that."

"Were you not actually planning on going to New York?"

"Maybe not."

I was shocked. Had he flown across the country with me on a whim, totally unprepared, simply to be with me? He was a lunatic! "You're not even dressed for the east coast! It's freezing outside."

He examined my winter-wear outfit. "You look really cute with that cap on your head," he said.

"Christos! This is so not right. You can't come to my parents house!" Why was I saying that? I was just playing into his game. How did he get away with this behavior? It wasn't going to work on me. Nope, no way.

"I can get a hotel. Close to where you live."

"No!"

"Come on, *agápi mou*."

"Don't say that." But I wanted him to say it. I wanted him to tell me it over and over again, every day for the rest of my life. I wanted a 24/7 soundtrack of him saying that to me in his perfectly accented Greek.

"I love you, Samantha."

Crap, that wasn't fair.

"Sam?" It was my mom.

I turned around.

"Your father told me to come look for you. I thought maybe you'd forgotten about waiting for us at the curb. He told me you didn't forget things like that, so something must've been wrong."

"Hi," Christos waved at her sheepishly.

"Who's this," my mom asked, confused.

"This is Christos."

Christos offered his hand and my mom shook it warily. "I'm Linda Smith. Pleased to meet you." She was *so* totally confused.

"He's my friend."

"From school?"

"Yeah."

"Oh!" Relief washed over my mom. "You go to SDU?"

"Yeah."

"You look a little old for college."

"I'm in the graduate program."

"Oh. Do you live in D.C.?" Mom was still completely lost.

"No. My mom lives in New York. I thought I'd fly in with Samantha for fun. Drive to New York."

"The roads are terrible. Didn't Sam tell you?"

"Probably, but I thought it would be fun anyway," Christos smiled.

"Uh, all right, it was nice meeting you, Christos. Sam? Are you ready to go?"

This was my chance. I had a decision to make. Now or never. *What's it gonna be, Sam I am?* "Mom, since the roads are so bad, do you think Christos could stay with us for a couple days? Until they get better?"

Surprise lit up Christos' face.

My mom looked him up and down, taking in his bad boy motorcycle look. "I don't know, Sam. It's so last minute."

"We've got room. Is anybody visiting?" I knew the answer would be no.

"Well, no, but…"

"Then he can sleep in the guest bedroom. It'll only be a couple days till the weather clears, right?"

"I don't know, Sam, your father might—"

Without thinking, I grabbed my mom by the elbow, something I had never done before. I grabbed Christos too, and walked us all outside. "Dad won't mind, he'll totally understand." I wasn't entirely sure about it, but fuck it. I was going to try anyway.

My dad waited at the curb, standing beside the family Honda. I saw his face pinball uncertainly when he saw Christos.

"Hey, Dad!" I smiled brightly. "This is my friend Christos. He needs a place to stay for a couple days until the roads improve, then he's driving to New York to see his mom," I lied.

My dad was completely thrown off. "Uh?"

"I tried to tell her, Bill. We don't have room, do we, Bill?" Mom gave Dad a pointed look.

"Ahhh," my Dad stammered.

"Come on, you guys. It's no big deal."

My mom and dad exchanged a look like I had grown a second head.

Christos walked to my father and shook his hand. "I'm Christos Manos. A friend of your daughter's from SDU."

"Bill. Bill Smith."

"Pleased to meet you, Bill. I promise, as soon as the roads clear, I'll be outta your hair."

"Where's your car?"

"I'm going to rent one."

"Uh, okay?"

I gave my dad my best "begging daddy" pout. It never worked before, but I was desperate.

"If it's okay with your mother, it's okay with me."

My mom gave my dad a scolding look.

I looked at my mom. "Please, mom," I begged. "Christos will totally stay out of the way, won't you, Christos?"

"Your parents won't even know I'm there. I'll leave you guys alone to have family time together."

Family time? With *my* parents? I'm sure he meant that as some kind of joke, but hey, it sounded good, right?

Christos smiled at my mom flirtatiously. It didn't work on her.

"Well," my dad said, "our daughter's growing up. Learning to make her own choices. If her friend needs a place to stay for a couple days, we can't very well say no, can we, Linda?"

What sort of mind control parasite had taken over my dad's brain?

My mom spiraled her head in this angry corkscrew, like she was fighting off the urge to explode, but she didn't let her reluctance transform into words. Thankfully.

"Okay!" I cheered. "I guess that solves that! Let's go, everybody!"

My dad put my bags in the trunk. "Where are your bags, Christos?"

"I didn't bring any."

"What?" My dad looked like someone had just sunk his battleship.

"I travel light."

"I'll say," my mom miffed.

Christos and I rode in the back. My mom kept glancing at

Christos, like she was waiting for him to pull a gun or something and carjack the family Honda.

After we dropped off my bags at home, Christos insisted on taking us all out for dinner. He left the choice of restaurant up to my parents.

Dad suggested Chinese, meaning The Imperial Palace, the same place they always went to. We'd been going there since I was a kid. Most things with my parents never changed.

We all piled into my dad's car and drove to the restaurant.

It was so weird to have Christos sitting next to me in the booth opposite my parents. In the past, the seat next to me had always been empty. Not even Damian had the rare honor of going to the Imperial Palace with my parents. Christos' presence fulfilled my girlish fantasy to have the hottest guy in the world with me at a childhood haunt, like he was proof to both my parents and me that a world existed outside of the "same-old, same-old" that my parents continuously inhabited.

My dad ordered family style, picking out several dishes for everyone to share.

"I'm sure Sam has told you she's a business major?" my dad said to Christos, pausing with his chopsticks halfway to his mouth, a nugget of sweet and sour pork tweezed between them.

Christos sipped his green tea. "Yeah. I think it's great. You can get a job anywhere with a business degree."

"Business is the sensible choice," my mom said.

"I agree," my dad said, still chewing on sweet and sour pork. "Did Sam tell you she took that silly art class instead of Micro Economics?"

Christos played dumb. "She hadn't mentioned that, no."

Oh, gawd. My parents never quit with defining My Boring Life for me. I'm sure if they could surgically implant the Micro Economics class into my head, they would.

"Well," Christos said cheerily, "I look forward to hearing all about micro econ when Sam takes it. As it is, I'm always bugging Samantha to tell me what she's learning in her accounting class."

"Do tell," Dad said, chewing on more sweet and sour pork.

"As I'm sure you know, Mr. Smith, accounting is the language of business."

"It is."

"I figure, the best way for me to stay on top of my career is to understand the business side of things as well as everything else."

"Oh?" my mom said, her interest piqued. "Career? I thought Sam said you were in the graduate program."

"I am. But it's sort of a formality."

"How so?" my dad asked.

"Well, I'm already building my own business. In fact, I have significant cash flow already, and my profitability is through the roof." He winked at me on the sly.

I stifled a laugh by shoving a wad of moo shu pork in my mouth. Christos made it sound like his gallery show was some kind of factory making brake pads or computer chips.

"Really," my dad said, impressed. "What line of work is your business?"

"Painting."

"You mean like a painting contractor? How many employees do you have?"

"It's just me."

My dad frowned. "How much painting can one person do? Or do you sub-contract and manage a team of painters?"

"Nope. It's just me."

My dad chuckled. "Well, I hope you're painting mansions or executive board rooms, or whatever."

"Nope. I'm painting paintings."

"What?" my mom asked, confused.

"I'm a gallery painter. I paint pictures."

My dad reacted as if Christos had stood up and pulled his pants down and waggled his ding-dong over the table.

I rolled my eyes. "He's an artist, Dad." My parents were sometimes so one-track minded, I thought they might be no-track minded.

"Art?" My mom said like she wanted to hold the word "art" with a poop-scooper and rubber gloves.

"He's really good, Mom. He already had a sell-out gallery show. He sold every single painting in one night," I defended. My parents had no idea about the art world. Neither did I, but compared to them, I knew volumes.

My dad processed that thoughtfully. "Sell-out, huh? How much did you make?"

I knew enough to know that was rude as hell to ask. I can imagine how my dad would react if Christos asked him point blank how much he made. It wouldn't go over well, and that was an understatement.

"Mid six," Christos said casually, draping an arm over the bench seat behind me. It was like some kind of gentlemen's duel, and Christos had not only pulled out a Gatling gun, he had laid claim to the chieftain's daughter in the process. I was giddy with girlishness. *Go get 'em, Christos!*

"Six what?" Dad asked, still frowning, water glass to his mouth.

"Figures."

My dad coughed out his water into the glass. Mom reached over and patted his back. "Are you okay, Bill?"

"I'm fine," Dad choked. "Fine." He coughed some more. When he recovered, he said, "You made six figures? In one night?"

"Yup." A grin eased across Christos' face. "Not that I did all the work in one night. The paintings took months to finish. But that's not work. I love the painting part. It's the selling that's the job."

"In other words," I grinned, "Christos works one day a year."

My parents goggled, as if Christos had burst into flames.

"It's not quite that simple," Christos said thoughtfully. "I also have to schmooze a lot. Build rapport with my customer base over time. But that's about social visits, dinner parties, that kind of thing. Plus, my dad and grandfather have been doing the painting thing for decades. You could call it a family business."

If my parents weren't so uptight, their jaws would've dropped on the table. It was as if Christos had ridden in on a bejeweled elephant from distant lands and spun legendary stories about cities of gold and rivers of platinum that were real and true. My parents had never heard of such things. They couldn't wrap their heads around it.

My dad slowly recovered his composure. "Well, that's terrific, Christos. But our Samantha doesn't have access to that sort of thing. I mean, Linda and I aren't successful artists. We're business people. Always have been. And that's where Sam's talents lie, wouldn't you agree, Linda?"

"Of course," Mom said, taking my father's hand in hers, a show of solidarity.

I clenched my fists beneath the table, twisting my napkin into knots. I half-expected Christos to suddenly object and sing the praises of my art talents, thereby starting a fight with my parents that would lead to his ejection from their house. That was the last thing I wanted, now that he was here in D.C. with me.

"You have to do what's right for your daughter," Christos said ambiguously. "Whatever keeps her healthy and happy," he said pointedly.

"Exactly," my dad said, missing the point entirely. As always.

Christos picked up the check afterward, as promised. It was nearly freezing outside the restaurant, and all Christos wore was his leather jacket.

"Aren't you cold," I asked, hugging myself against the chill air. I wanted to lean into Christos, but not with my parents watching.

"I'll be fine," he smiled.

"Perhaps he can borrow one of Bill's coats while he's here?" my mom suggested.

"I don't know that they'll fit him, Linda. Christos is a bit taller than I am, and wider across the shoulders." My dad was a wee bit off the mark on that one. Christos towered over him.

"Thanks, Mr. and Mrs. Smith. I'll be fine."

We drove back to my parents house, Christos and I again in the back seat of my parents' Honda. The thought of holding Christos' hand crossed my mind. It was dark, but I somehow suspected my parents would intuitively know I was having a good time and put a stop to it immediately.

I kept my hands to myself. Besides, I didn't want to send mixed signals to Christos.

At the house, Mom automatically set about preparing the guest room for Christos. I'm sure my parents assumed I'd sleep in my bedroom, which appeared exactly how I'd left it in August.

I didn't argue the point of who slept where. I was just glad my parents let Christos stay without making a huge deal out of it.

Christos said good night and I laid in my bed alone. Knowing he was across the hall gave me a sense of peace I'd never felt in my parents' house. I had a protector, a guardian angel. He shielded me not only from the rest of the world, but from my parents' disconnected concern for my best interests.

I twisted in my bed, my thoughts rumbling chaotically.

How could I possibly get through life without Christos? I knew I wouldn't *die* without him, but I felt like my life would be significantly worse. It would be tolerable, but probably miserable. I mean, seriously, did I really want to be an accountant as badly as my parents wanted me to?

Not even close.

They didn't know the first thing about the art world. Art was an actual business. I had seen that from firsthand experience. What had I been thinking after Thanksgiving, pushing Christos away like I had?

Taylor.

Yeah. Taylor was always on my mind. Every single minute of every single day.

I rolled and tossed under my blankets. I wished Christos would come into my room and cuddle with me. But I suspected he wouldn't, out of respect for my parents. I could go into the guest room and crawl into his bed. But I had this nagging sense my parents would freak if they found me in there with him come morning.

Besides, I hadn't made my peace with Christos. He still didn't know about Taylor. He didn't know who I really was underneath the lies.

I faded in and out of sleep all night long. Every time I drifted off, the old nightmare assaulted me.

Taylor.

I saw the flash of color. I heard the horrible thump. I saw the blood.

I remembered the countless lies I had told every single day for almost three years. To everybody. To myself. To my parents. To my friends.

To the entire world.

To Christos.

I was a huge fucking lie.

I couldn't take it anymore. It was eating me alive. If I didn't put a stop to it once and for all, I would be slowly devoured by my own dishonesty.

I couldn't live that way any longer.

I wasn't going to give up on life or myself.

I was going to tell the truth tomorrow. For the first time.

Starting with Christos.

I was finally going to break my silence and talk about Taylor.

My mom cooked breakfast for everybody in the morning. French toast, bacon, OJ.

My dad and mom were already dressed for work when I walked into the kitchen. I was in sweats. Christos wore his clothes from yesterday, but left his leather jacket in the guest room.

"Aren't you cold in that t-shirt, Christos?" Mom asked.

"I'm fine," he smiled. He really did look fine.

"Maybe we can go to the mall today and get you some new clothes," I suggested.

"Sure," he smiled. "I could probably use a tooth brush, too."

I almost blurted he could borrow mine, but thought my parents would be weirded out by that.

"You can borrow my car after you have your breakfast," my mom said. "Your dad can take me to work."

My dad, who still read the newspaper, peeked over the business section, raising his eyebrows. "I can?"

"Yes, Bill. It's only a few minutes out of your way. Your daughter needs a car."

Dad submerged beneath the newspaper, grumbling.

"Eat while it's hot," Mom said. She served up plates full of steaming food for everybody.

Christos chewed on french toast. "Wow, Mrs. Smith. Great french toast. So fluffy."

My mom smiled. "It's the bread. I get it at a local bakery."

"Well, it's awesome. I love it."

"Thank you, Christos." She sipped her coffee.

When we finished eating, I cleared the table. "Thanks for breakfast, Mom."

"Thank you, Mrs. Smith," Christos said. "Everything was wonderful."

After my parents left for work, Christos and I took turns showering.

When Christos and I were dressed, I dug an old backpack out of the back of my closet, put it in the trunk of my mom's Honda, then we hopped inside.

My parents drove the identical model of Honda sedan. The only difference was that my dad's was silver, because he said it reflected heat better in the summer. My mom's was black because she thought it was more stylish. They were way too extreme for their own good. Not.

Inside the car, I cranked the heater up full-blast for Christos.

"Thanks," Christos said.

The roads were somewhat icy, but I was used to it. I drove us through neighborhood streets for awhile, knowing exactly where I was going. Eventually, we rolled to a stop on a residential street in nearby Maryland.

Christos looked around. "Aren't we going shopping for clothes?"

I turned off the car. "Christos, I need to tell you something."

"Okay."

I unbuckled my seatbelt. This was going to take awhile. "First of all, thank you for coming out with me."

"It was my pleasure. I couldn't think of a better way to spend winter break. Or a better person to spend it with." He reached over and cupped my chin. "I missed you so much, *agápi mou.*"

I reached up with both hands and pressed his hand against my cheek. I feared he wouldn't miss me ever again after I finished telling him about Taylor. I was pretty sure I'd be driving him to the airport, not to CVS for a new toothbrush.

"I'm not who you think I am, Christos."

"What do you mean?"

"I have a bit of a history."

"Oh? Are you a dude?" He grinned. "I mean, I should know better, based on what I've seen so far, but I hear those sex change operations have gotten really good."

"No, Christos." I frowned. "This is serious. I've been holding back on you big time. And I feel terrible."

"Samantha, whatever it is, I'm sure it's not as bad as you're making it sound."

I glanced out the front window of the Honda, to the simple two bedroom house across the street.

A mother and her daughter had walked outside and stood on the porch. The daughter was two years older than me. Her mother locked the front door, then the two of them made their way carefully down the short brick pathway.

The daughter limped noticeably. Her mother helped her down the two steps at the end of the path. Such a simple thing, walking down two steps. But the young woman couldn't do it confidently without help. They climbed into an older, rust-spotted minivan parked on the street.

"See that girl across the street?" I said.

"The one getting into the minivan?" Christos asked.

"Yeah. That's Taylor. Taylor Lamberth."

Recognition lit Christos' face. "*The* Taylor? The name you kept muttering in your sleep?"

"Yes. She didn't used to limp like that. Before I ruined her life."

I was pretty sure all the air in the car was sucked into Christos's lungs when he inhaled sharply.

Christos frowned. Then his frown turned to a doubtful smirk. "What do you mean, ruined?"

This was not going to be easy. At least the sun was up. For whatever reason, I didn't want to tell this story in the darkness. I didn't think I could do it. Because that's when it happened.

"Let me begin at the beginning. Remember I told you about Damian? The night we were supposed to have sex for the first time, but didn't?"

"Yeah?"

"I didn't tell you the whole story."

Chapter 24

THREE YEARS EARLIER...

Near Damian Wolfram's home.

The road leading away from Damian's parents' secluded mansion was long, windy and isolated. Except for the white headlights of Damian's BMW, it was pitch black. There were no street lights of any kind this far from the city. Dark woods and fields surrounded us.

Damian drove recklessly, taking the turns way too fast.

"Slow down, Damian! You're going to get us killed!" My voice was surprisingly calm, considering how angry and hurt and sad I was after Damian had destroyed what should've been an intimate evening.

"I just want to get you home, Sam," he seethed. "Like you asked, Sam. So if I'm driving too fast, Sam, I'm just giving you what the fuck you wanted, Sam. I'm taking you the fuck home. Sam."

He was in full-pout mode. I hated how he kept saying my name, but I wasn't going to ask him to stop, and risk triggering greater wrath.

A few minutes later, we rounded a tight turn and the car drifted into the oncoming lane. Luckily, there was no one else on the road this late. "Damian, you're scaring me. Please slow down."

"Calm down? Why the fuck do you think I'm so angry, Sam? Huh? Do you want to guess? Sam? I'll bet you know the answer."

I wasn't going to play into his tirade.

"Come on, Sam. Guess. I bet you'll get it in one try." He eyed me and his lips peeled back over his teeth. In the glow of the dashboard lights, he looked like a monster. "Not gonna play? Oh that's right. You don't play, do you? Because you're a fucking tease. Six months?" He scoffed. "Six fucking months. What were you waiting for? A fucking ring? Jesus Christ, Sam, how long does a guy have to wait until you give it up?"

I had done my best to stay calm, but he was prodding me so hard, I couldn't help myself. "I don't know, *Damian*. Maybe if you actually loved me, I would've gone through with it," I sneered.

"Love you? Fuck, fine. I love you, Sam. Now can we go fuck?"

"You don't know anything about love, Damian." I turned to stare out the window. There was no point in continuing the conversation any further. He was clueless.

"Well? I'm waiting for an answer. I love you, Sam. Let's fuck. I love you, Sam. Suck my dick. I love you, Sam. Let's have sex. COME ON, SAM! TAKE YOUR DRESS OFF! GIVE ME A BLOW JOB WHILE I'M DRIVING! ANYTHING, GOD DAMN IT!"

I seriously considered asking him to stop the car to let me out. But we were a long way from anywhere, and it was freezing outside. I wouldn't be able to get very far in my four-inch heels.

"HELLO! SAM! I'M TALKING TO YOU!! ANYBODY HOME?!"

Damian was looking at me, and not the road. He braked hard. "Shit," he growled through clenched teeth, fighting with the steering wheel as the car slid around another corner.

I looked up in time to see a flash of pink. Then I heard the thud.

"What the fuck was that!" Damian whipped his head around while he fought to control the car. I felt the rear end slide out. His arms flailed around the wheel and the car screeched to a stop.

We had narrowly missed slamming into the stout trees growing on the side of the road. If the car had spun into them, I would've been crushed.

My heart raced. My fingers dug into the armrest. I forced myself to let go. "I think you hit something."

"I didn't fucking hit anything."

"I'm going to check." I opened my door. Without thinking, I jumped out, leaving my jacket on the seat with my purse. I was so full of adrenaline, I didn't feel the cold as I walked up the road. My breath puffed out of my mouth in the frigid night air.

The driver's side window hummed downward. "Get back in the fucking car!" Damian yelled through the open window.

"No, Damian! We have to check."

"Check what?"

"You hit something!"

"It was probably a raccoon. Maybe a deer."

"A deer? I saw pink."

"Get in the car, goddammit."

"No!"

"I guess you want to walk your ass home? I'm not waiting around for you."

I ignored him and continued back the way we'd come. I could barely see anything in the red glow of the BMW's brake lights.

I heard Damian's door open. "Fine. What the fuck. I'm sure I killed Bambi or some stupid possum. So fucking what."

I walked around the tight curve quite a ways. We had been going pretty fast. At least forty. It had taken Damian several seconds to get the car under control and bring it to a stop.

Then I saw it.

A bare foot. Wet with dark blood. "Oh my god."

"What?" Damian asked, irritated.

"I think you hit someone." I crept closer. "Ohmygod, ohmygod. You hit someone!"

"I didn't hit anybody," he sneered. His rage was now tempered by doubt. He stood beside me.

The body of a young woman lay on the side of the road. She wore fall-weather running clothes. Long sleeve shirt, puffy pink down vest, thermal leggings, a pink beanie, mittens. Long hair fanned out from beneath the beanie. Her face was turned to the side. Her legs were bent in unnatural angles. Her gray leggings were splotchy with blood.

"Oh my god, Damian. I think you killed her."

"She's not dead."

She wore no shoes. One sock was still on, but the other was peeled off and lay next to her foot. Both socks were dotted with blood. I couldn't tell where all she bled from, or how badly. "She looks like she was out running. But where are her shoes?"

"How the fuck should I know? Who goes running without shoes?"

"You hit her, Damian!"

"No I didn't."

"I heard it! We need to call 911 right now." I'd stupidly left my purse in the car with my cell phone, otherwise I'd already be dialing. "Call 911!"

"Huh?"

"On your phone!"

"I'm not calling 911!" he growled.

I glared at him. "You hit her, Damian. You have to call the police. She needs help."

"We're going. Get in the car."

"What? Are you crazy?"

"Now. In the car." He narrowed his eyes and stalked toward me, clenching his fists. "Move it."

Damian had gone completely crazy, and I was in trouble. My purse was in the car with my phone and my jacket. I wore nothing but a thin dress, pantyhose and heels. Not nearly warm enough for the forty-degree chill. This road had almost zero traffic at this hour. If for some reason, Damian didn't wrestle me into the car against my will, I'd be stranded in a bad way. I wouldn't be able to help this girl. It would take forever for me to run into town wearing heels. If I didn't freeze first.

Damian stood in front of me. "Get in the car, or I will make you," he hissed.

"No, Damian. We have to help this girl."

"No we don't," he seethed. "I'm not warning you again."

"I'm not leaving until you call for help."

He shoved me in the chest with both his hands, hard. I stumbled backward and fell on my ass, skinning my palms on the asphalt.

"You're crazy, Damian! You're insane!" He didn't seem worried about what I thought of him. "You're a monster." I wept freely. Tears streamed down my face.

"So what? Get moving." He kicked me in the thigh. "In the car."

I stared at him from my position on the ground. "You're evil, Damian."

"In the car." When I didn't move, he circled around and hooked his arms under mine. He dragged me across the rough pavement. I stood up to avoid further abrasion on the gravelly road. I flailed at him, trying to claw and gouge with my nails, but he was behind me and there was nothing I could do. He was crushing my rib cage with his powerful arms.

I remembered how you're supposed to stomp on the attacker's toes if they're behind you, but I kept losing my footing as he pulled me backward. I was helpless.

Back at the BMW, I noticed one of my heels had broken off during the struggle. When Damian released one of his arms from my torso to open the passenger side door, I twisted out of his grasp.

"Get back here!"

I stumbled along the shoulder, trying to get away. He jogged up behind me and I dodged.

Because of my broken heel, my footing was off and I tripped and fell onto the shoulder. Damian dove for me. I rolled out of his reach. Right over the edge of a short, steep hill that led into a stand of dark trees.

The slope of the hill was severe. I tumbled down grass, dried leaves, and undergrowth. I narrowly missed bashing my head against several tree trunks at the bottom.

I was in so much shock, I couldn't tell whether or not I'd been hurt. Damian thundered down the hill toward me.

"Get the fuck back here, stupid bitch! I'm going to kill you! We have to get out of here, now!"

I wasn't going to wait and find out whether he was serious about killing me or not. I picked myself up and scrambled into the trees. Prickly bushes caught my pantyhose and tore them open.

I don't know how far I ran before stopping. When I looked behind me through the trees, I expected to see Damian barreling toward me. He was nowhere to be seen.

I held my breath and listened. A minute or two later, I heard a car door slam and an engine revving.

Damian's car drove away.

After a few minutes of silence, I crept back through the woods in the darkness. When I reached the road, I was a mess. My pantyhose were shredded. My dress was torn and falling off one shoulder. I'd completely lost my broken shoe in the brush. The remaining one still had its heel. Unsure what to do, I hobbled up the road to the injured girl. The rough pavement was murder on my bare foot.

I collapsed on the ground beside the girl and wept. I shivered and wrapped my arms around myself. I was going to freeze to death out here.

A moan escaped the girl.

Correction. *We* were going to freeze to death. "Are you okay?"

Another moan.

"Can you hear me? My name's Samantha. I'm right here. I'm going to help you. Everything's going to be all right." I had no idea what I was going to do, but I was going to do something.

If I had a jacket, I would've put it over her. I was afraid to touch her. I would probably make her injuries worse.

I stood up and looked at my surroundings. It was nothing but dark trees, fields, and road. I was screwed. There weren't even houses nearby to ask for help. My only option was to head for town. Then I'd knock on the first door I found.

After walking two hundred feet, I knew there was no way I could make it with one shoe, a four-inch heel at that. I plopped down in the middle of the road and removed my platform. Whoever said fashion didn't have to be functional was an idiot.

Who the hell invented high heels, anyway?

I tried to break the heel off but I wasn't strong enough. Shit. How was I going to make it two miles into town on one heel? I tried walking on the grass shoulder, but the grass was freezing. I'd have frostbite in no time. This wasn't going to work. That poor girl would die, and I would end up toeless, before I ever got to town.

If only I'd had my running shoes. I could jog. The running would keep me warm. But I didn't have my godforsaken running shoes.

Running shoes.

Wait a second.

That girl had been wearing running shoes. But they weren't on her feet. They had to be around somewhere!

I put my one heel back on and limped up the road and commenced searching for the girl's shoes. I heard her moan again, so I started talking to her. My teeth clacked while I spoke.

"Hey, I don't know what your name is, but I hope you have good taste in running shoes." I laughed. "Who am I kidding. I just hope your shoes fit my feet! You won't mind if I borrow them, will you? I know, I sound stupid."

My arms were pebbled with chill bumps. I hoped all my talking would help keep me warm, and give her something to hold onto. I heard her moan again. Good. She hadn't passed out completely. Or worse.

There was just enough moonlight for me to see. I kept talking to her as I walked back up the road, the way Damian and I had come. The first shoe was in the middle of the road. Thank god for small favors. I sat down on the pavement and put it on, tossing my useless heel aside. The ground froze my ass in two seconds. It was so freaking cold.

The girl's shoe was way too big, so I tightened the laces all the way. I stood and walked. My foot slid around quite a bit, but it was better than nothing. I continued searching for shoe number two.

I stood with hands on hips, scanning the area. Where the hell was that other shoe? I couldn't stand here all night. Could I make the run into town with one shoe? Probably not.

I turned my head, and a glint in the corner of my eye caught my attention. I whipped my head back. I frantically scanned the trees. Damn. I swore I'd seen a reflection.

Wait, there it was! I saw the shoe's tiny reflectors glinting in the moonlight. The shoe poked out from a fork in the trunk of a tree. I ran to it.

How'd it get way up in a tree? I'd never understood how people's shoes came off when they got hit, but they did. Just as sure as this one had.

I jumped up, trying to reach the shoe, but it was too high.

I'd climbed plenty of trees as a girl. I could do this, if I could find a low hanging branch. I circled the tree. No luck. But the trunk was narrow. I could wrap my legs around it and inch my way up.

If only I'd been wearing protective clothing like jeans, a long sleeved denim shirt, and sturdy hiking boots. Instead, I had only my sleeveless rayon dress, torn pantyhose, and one shoe. This was going to hurt.

I clenched my knees around the trunk. Fortunately, the bark was relatively smooth. I monkeyed my way up. My skin was instantly abraded. But I was getting that shoe.

The toe of the shoe poked out just beyond my reach, but I didn't need to grab it. I smacked the nose of the shoe with my finger tips. If I could knock it free and it fell to the ground, I was good to go.

It didn't work. I needed to climb higher to get a better reach. But my thighs were screaming. I'm pretty sure they were going to bleed soon, if they weren't already. I made one more swat at the shoe. Nope. It was lodged in good.

I took a deep breath, reached up with my arms, and inch-wormed up another foot. My thighs burned with white hot pain. I reached for the shoe and got a good grip. I wiggled it loose and tossed it to the ground.

I took a moment to decide if I should jump and risk twisting an ankle, or inch back down the tree. A broken ankle wasn't going to help that poor girl. I chose the abraded, bloody thighs. I worked down about a foot when my thigh jammed on a knot. Agony!

I let go and slid down to the ground.

I winced in pain. I touched my thighs to see if I felt any blood. I wasn't sure. Hopefully it was just sweat. My arms felt torn up too. But nothing I couldn't handle.

I put the running shoe on and laced it tight before climbing back up the slope. I trotted over to the girl.

"I'm going to run and get help. Next time, try to keep your shoes on," I joked. "It took me forever to find them."

She moaned. I hoped it was a moan of laughter.

I ran toward town. I went slowly at first, until my body warmed and my legs loosened. Then I sped up. I made good time because the road was slightly downhill the entire way. Thank you, gravity.

As long as some nut like Damian didn't run me over in the darkness, I'd find help in no time.

All my after-school jogging made this easy work. The skin on my torn up thighs started complaining immediately, but I ignored it.

The shoes were way too big for my tiny feet. I felt several hot spots forming on the balls of my feet already, but I kept reminding myself a few blisters were far better than what that poor girl had already suffered.

Eventually I saw a dark house. I hoped someone was home.

A car screeched to a stop in front of me. Damian's BMW. He jumped out and ran toward me. I sprinted in the opposite direction, but he caught up instantly. He grabbed me by the hair and jammed something in my back.

"Stop right now and get in my car or I'm going to shoot you."

I twisted and saw a silver pistol in his hand. My eyes popped wide. "Have you lost it, Damian?!"

"In the car." His grip on my neck tightened.

I didn't know what to do. I let him push me to his car.

"Open the door."

"No, this is crazy."

"Do it, or I will shoot you."

I studied his eyes. I had never seen them this cold. I opened the passenger side door and he forced me inside.

"Put the seatbelt on. Now."

I did.

"I'm going to get in the other side. If you try to run, I will hunt you down and kill you."

I was stunned by his viciousness.

He jogged around the car and climbed in. He squeezed the pistol between his legs while he made a U-turn and we drove away from the scene of the crime, and that poor girl.

I realized my jacket and purse were still in his car.

"Don't even think about going for your phone. I will shoot you if you try."

"Where are we going."

"I'm taking you home."

That wasn't what I'd been expecting. I was thinking more along the lines of some abandoned reservoir or coal mine. So he could dump my body after he did who knew what with me.

He was silent while we drove. We were definitely headed to my house.

"Damian, this isn't right. We have to call someone to help that girl."

"Do I need to drop you off at the asylum? I can't have this on my record. I'll never get into Columbia if I killed someone."

"She's not dead. I heard her moaning. If we get her help now, she'll survive. I know it."

"I can't take that chance."

"What? That she'll survive? Or you won't get into Columbia?"

"Either. No one's going to find out about this." At a stop sign, he cut me with his eyes. "If you tell anyone, I will kill you. If you call the cops, I will kill you. Look me in the eyes and tell me if you think I'm joking."

I examined his face. I barely recognized it. Had I thought this young man was attractive at some point? Desirable? My perfect fantasy? I was crazier than he was if I had. Wow, I had poor taste in men. And that was the understatement of the millennium.

"Say anything about this to *anybody*, and I will ruin you. Don't think I can't." He stroked the pistol between his legs. And I do mean the shining gun. Somehow, the way he did it was the foulest thing I had ever seen. It was grotesque, like he loved that gun more than he ever had me.

He pulled to a stop next to my parents' house, which was dark. They must've still been out with their friends.

Damian stared straight ahead, through the windshield. "Get out."

I opened the car door and stepped out. I leaned in to gather my jacket and my purse. He grabbed my wrist and squeezed it hard.

"Don't tell anyone. Or you're dead."

"I won't."

He yanked me back into the car.

My chin almost smashed into the stick shift. "Hey! Watch it!"

"I'm serious as a heart attack, you fucking cunt. If you tell, I will kill you before the cops get me. I can find you, no matter where you go." He clamped his fingers down harder, until the bones in my wrist ground together.

I felt like I was supposed to answer him, but I didn't know what to say. He glared at me.

A pair of headlights turned the corner onto my street. He released my arm.

"Close the fucking door."

I did. He drove off slowly.

I waited until he was gone before I dashed into my house. I bolted the front door behind me and leaned against it. When the tears started, I slid down until I sat on the floor. I bawled in the darkness and hugged my purse and jacket.

With Damian gone, I was free to let it out. All the fear that had raced through me for the last twenty minutes.

I had loved Damian. Until I realized he was such a monster. I would be lying if I said I never had any feelings for him. That's why it hurt so much. The love and sense of loss I'd felt wouldn't evaporate in a few seconds.

I shook with sobs for some time before I could begin to think clearly.

That's when I remembered the girl. She needed help. For all I knew, Damian was driving back up that road to push her off into a ditch so no one would find her. Was he capable of that? An accident was one thing. But finishing the job like that? Was Damian that cruel?

Maybe.

What the hell was I going to do?

I couldn't let that girl die all alone.

I put my hands on the tile floor and stood myself up. I tugged my coat on and rushed to my VW outside. I drove until I found a pay phone.

There was one beside the Italian restaurant a few blocks from my house. I always noticed the phone when I drove to school and wondered who actually used it. I parked on the street and ran up to it. I didn't have any change. I dialed 911 anyway.

The operator picked up.

"911. What's your emergency?"

"There's a girl on Deer Creek Road, she was hit by a car, she's bleeding, she needs an ambulance."

"Ma'am, please calm down."

"She's half way up Deer Creek Road! She's lying on the side of the road!"

"Ma'am? I'm going to ask you to take a deep breath and calm down."

"Send an ambulance! Deer Creek Road! Half way up! On the right side! Near a bunch of trees at the hairpin turn."

"Ma'am? Please calm down. Ma'am? What's your name, ma'am?"

I slammed the receiver into the cradle. I took a step back and folded my arms across my chest. I half-expected the phone to ring. I glanced from side to side. I wasn't going to wait to find out.

I jumped into my VW and drove toward Deer Creek Road. I needed to check on that girl. Screw crazy Damian.

I kept seeing his face in my mind, and hearing his words. *"Don't tell anyone. Or you're dead…If you tell, I will kill you before the cops get me."*

A half mile away from Deer Creek Road, an ambulance appeared in my rearview mirror with flashing lights and sirens. I pulled over and let it pass. Thank God. I was about to pull back onto the road when two police cars barreled past. I breathed a huge sigh of relief.

I drove toward Deer Creek, but a few blocks away, I contemplated making a U-turn and heading home.

No, I had to make sure the ambulance went to the right place.

I drove up Deer Creek. I imagined Damian waiting for me in his BMW, ready to chase my VW and run me into a tree. But he was nowhere to be found. When I could see the blue and red glow of emergency lights reflecting against the trees near the hair pin turn, I was confident they were in the right spot.

 I found a wide section of the road and turned my VW around. I drove home slowly. My hands shook so much, I had to squeeze the steering wheel as hard as I could to keep them steady.

Back at my house, I was ready to vomit. I ran inside and spilled Damian's home-cooked dinner into the toilet. That was the last of him I ever wanted to see. I flushed it down, rinsed my face, and brushed my teeth.

When I sat down to pee, the burning between my legs hit me full-force. I had blocked it completely out during my ordeal. My inner thighs were hamburger from climbing the tree. I used sterile pads and a bottle of antiseptic from under the sink to clean my wounds. They totally burned, but it wasn't as bad as I'd thought when I first looked at them in this light.

After I bandaged myself, I stuffed the wrappers in the bottom of my school backpack. I feared my parents might notice the wrappers and start asking questions if I put them in the bathroom wastebasket. I would throw them out at school the next day.

Finally, I crawled into bed.

When my parents came home, I pretended to be asleep. They didn't check up on me. They trusted me.

Dependable Samantha Smith. I never got in trouble.

The next morning, I watched the news before school while pretending to eat breakfast. I was sick to my stomach the whole time.

The local newscaster laid it all out.

"Taylor Lamberth, a local high school senior, is hospitalized this morning after a nearly fatal hit-and-run accident. According to Taylor's parents, Taylor went out for an evening jog last night, as usual. When Taylor didn't return home, her parents called local police.

"An anonymous 911 caller tipped off authorities to the location of Taylor. Emergency crews rushed to the scene. Taylor was taken to St. Mary's Hospital, where she is listed in critical condition. The extent of her injuries has not been determined. Police ask anyone who knows anything about this case to please come forward."

If I had actually eaten any of my cereal, I would've thrown it up into my bowl right at the table.

I spent the entire day at school nearly comatose.

All I could think about was poor Taylor Lamberth. I had contributed in some way to her injuries and worried she might die. I had no idea how bad a shape she was in.

Damian stalked me in the hallways that day, never talking to me. He shot me threatening looks at every opportunity.

He quickly spread word about our break up, claiming I was a huge slut, the campus pump, that he'd dropped me as soon as he'd found out.

I was labeled a bitch, a slut, a whore, and a tease. I never understood how you could be a slut and a tease at the same time, but I was now classified as both. It seemed like the entire high school shunned me. Everyone gave me dirty looks, stuffed nasty notes in my locker, the works.

I was so freaked out about the incident with Taylor, I stopped talking to my friends completely. I was afraid I would spill everything if I opened my mouth at all and that Damian would find out. The repercussions of my involvement scared me more than anything. I feared I was somehow an accomplice.

Over the coming weeks, my friends drifted away. They claimed they didn't know me anymore. I couldn't blame them because they were right. I used to tell them everything that went on in my life. Now I told them nothing.

To further distance myself, I started wearing black clothes, black makeup, and a black mood at all times. That's when I was labeled Emo, and Goth, and Witch.

Nobody really knew what was going on. But everyone saw how withdrawn I had become.

That's when they started calling me Suicide Watch. They all thought I was going to kill myself. Some days, I feared they were right. But mainly, I was too busy obsessing about Taylor Lamberth to think about myself. I desperately awaited good news in the local media.

I found out Taylor was eventually released from the hospital. She was supposed to go to University on a full-ride soccer scholarship in the fall, but due to the severity of her injuries sustained in the accident, her soccer days were over.

Both her knees were basically shattered and had to be bolted back together with titanium pins and rods. She would still be able to walk, doctors said, after tons of physical therapy. But she lost her scholarship, and her extensive medical bills were bankrupting her parents. The last I knew, Taylor was going to the local community college.

The day I got my acceptance letter from SDU, almost two years later, my parents celebrated. But I was miserable. I felt guilty because I was going off to have a great time while Taylor had to give up her childhood dreams.

And Damian got away with everything. He even went to Columbia, like he'd planned.

The cops never figured out who did it. I mean, how could they? There was no evidence. I imagine they found my high heels, but they had no way to connect them to me. I wasn't in any criminal databases.

I considered tipping off the police a thousand times, but I was too afraid of Damian.

He would know it was me.

Chapter 25

PRESENT DAY.

Tears had run freely down my face the whole time I told the story. My coat was wet with them. I sniffled and looked at Christos.

His blue eyes blazed. Was he angry? I felt cut off from him, like he wasn't even there. Maybe he wasn't anymore. Maybe his heart ran away the second he'd heard my story. I deserved it for what I'd done.

"It's not your fault, Samantha." He unbuckled his seat belt and reached over. His thumb brushed tears from my cheek. "You did everything you could. You called 911 as soon as you were able. So what if Damian got away with it? If he'd been caught, it wouldn't have helped the doctors fix Taylor's legs any better than they did."

"I still feel responsible," I sobbed.

"For what? If you hadn't called 911, who knows how long she would've been lying on the road? You said yourself she could've frozen to death."

"But if I'd just had sex with Damian, Taylor would be fine."

"Hold on a second." He pulled back and leveled a stern look at me. "Don't even go there. You can't tell yourself that. There's no way you could've known. Besides, you did the right thing by turning down sex with Damian. You weren't obligated to go through with it. He should've controlled his temper instead of flipping out and speeding on that road."

"Yeah, but would it really have been so bad? If I'd just had sex with stupid Damian? Taylor Lamberth would still have a soccer scholarship. Now her dreams are ruined. Because of me."

"Stop it, Samantha. That's insane. You did not need to have sex with Damian to save her."

I leaned back in my seat and sobbed.

Christos put an elbow on the center console and hugged me with his free arm. "Shh, shh, shh. Let it out. You did the best you could."

"I didn't though."

"Come on, *agápi mou*. It's not your fault."

"I should've realized long before that night that Damian was a total jerk. I should've seen what an asshole he was in advance."

"That's ridiculous."

"I should've known he was a terrible person beneath his looks and his money."

"That's crazy, Samantha. How old were you?"

"Sixteen."

"Nobody knows their way around relationships at that age. I mean, seriously, didn't he come on to you all romantic, with the flowers and the dinner and the fancy mansion?"

"Yeah."

"And I bet he was doing that shit all along, playing the part of perfect boyfriend until he got you into bed."

I sniffled. "Isn't that what you're doing?"

Christos froze. "What?" he asked in a low voice.

Oh no, I was ruining everything again. There was no way I could retract my words. There were out, and they had way too much power.

He frowned. "I'm sorry, but can you please repeat what you said? I want to make sure I heard you correctly before I say another word."

Fuck! What had I just done?

"Samantha? I need you to talk to me. Right now."

I quivered with fear, trying to burrow closer to him. He released me and sat back in his seat. I could tell he was done with me.

"Christos, please." I was crying again.

"I'm not him, Samantha. I'm nothing like Damian."

"But you *are!* You were arrested on the first day of school! That guy *shot* at you at Jake's party because you smashed him into the side of a car! I could've been killed! Those bikers at Xanadu chased us! You speed, you get into fights, you do crazy things all the time! When are *you* going to hit some girl jogging in the middle of the night and take away *her* dreams?!"

Dead silence.

"My parents were right! I need to give up all this craziness about art! I don't deserve for my dreams to come true! Taylor Lamberth doesn't get hers! Why should I get mine?!"

I was destroying everything I cared about.

Maybe it was for the best.

I opened the door of my parents' Honda and ran down the street. Tears poured from my eyes and I wailed as I ran. I needed to get away from everything and everyone.

But I couldn't escape *myself*.

I walked around Taylor Lamberth's neighborhood for over an hour. Even though the sun was out, I was chilled when I got back to the car. Christos sat on the hood, his boots resting on the front bumper.

He had to have been freezing in his leather jacket. I felt like a jerk.

I walked toward him tentatively, stopping a few feet away. My arms were folded across my chest, my chin tucked in my coat. I was afraid to look him in the eyes. "I have to fix what I've done," I said, shivering.

He stood up and walked to me. He placed his hands gently on my hips, and touched his forehead to mine.

"Whatever you decide, Samantha," he murmured, "I am here for you, *agápi mou*."

I leaned into him. "I love you, Christos."

Chapter 26

We climbed back into the Honda and I turned the engine on, running the heater full-blast.

At some point while I was gone on my impromptu walk, the Lamberth minivan had returned. I hoped both Taylor and her mother were inside.

"I have to apologize to Taylor," I told Christos. "I need to tell her what I know. Then I'm going to tell the police. If they end up arresting me for being an accessory or covering up, or whatever, and I go to jail? So be it."

"Are you sure?" Christos asked, looking distinctly pained.

"I love you, Christos. But I have to do this, no matter what happens."

"Do you want me to come with you?"

"I need to do this on my own. It's my responsibility."

"Okay, *agápi mou*. I'll be in the car, waiting for you."

I got out of my mom's Honda, took my old backpack out of the trunk, and walked up to the front door of the Lamberth house. Something I'd considered doing countless times, but never had the courage to until now.

I rang the doorbell. Taylor's mom answered.

"Yes?" She stood with the door open only a crack, keeping the heat in the house.

"Is Taylor home?"

"Yes. And you are?"

"A friend of hers," I lied.

The mom turned and hollered into the house. "Taylor, your friend is here to see you!" To me, "What's your name again?"

"Samantha Smith."

"It's Samantha Smith," she hollered into the house. "Hold on a second. I'll be right back."

She gently closed the door.

A minute later, Taylor opened the door. The mother stood behind her. Taylor looked confused. Of course she didn't know me.

"I owe you an apology," I said. "And I wanted to return these." I pulled her shoes out of my backpack.

Painful recognition widened Taylor's eyes. "My shoes," she gasped. "Those were my favorite running shoes! I was wearing them the night of the accident! Where did you get them?"

"From you." I didn't know how else to say it. "From the night you were hit by that car. My jerk ex-boyfriend was driving too fast. I used your shoes to run for help. I was wearing heels, but I found your shoes in the road."

Taylor's mother's brows knit with concern. She stepped protectively in front of her daughter. "Who are you? Is this some kind of a sick joke? What are you doing here?" She demanded angrily.

I panicked. "I need to tell your daughter what happened that night! I was the only person who knows and is willing to say anything. My boyfriend threatened to kill me if I ever told anybody," I pleaded.

Taylor's mom appeared both angry and confused. "We don't need you opening old wounds!" she spat, looming toward me.

"But wait! I—"

"I remember," Taylor said softly. "Your voice. You're her."

"Who?" Her mother halted, surprised. "Who is she, Taylor?"

"I know her voice, Mom." Taylor's eyes started to tear up. She locked eyes with me. "She was the one who talked to me, she told me she was going to help me. I always thought she was one of the EMTs."

I cried softly, nodding my head.

Taylor addressed me directly. "You told me to keep my shoes on next time." She laughed while weeping.

I nodded. "I thought it was a stupid joke."

"It was," Taylor smiled and laughed through tears. "I—I don't remember getting hit, but I remember pieces of what happened afterward, before the ambulance arrived. I remember lying on the side of the road in the darkness and being cold." She sniffled. "And I remember you."

I wanted to hug her, but I was afraid.

Taylor's mom was shocked, to say the least, but she seemed to understand what was happening between her daughter and me.

"What's your name?" Taylor asked.

"Samantha Smith."

"Would you like to come inside, Samantha?" the mom asked, opening the front door wide for me.

"Yes." I started sobbing when I crossed the threshold of the Lamberth's front doorstep.

"I never got to thank you," Taylor said. She threw her arms around me and hugged me fiercely. "You saved my life," she whispered into my ear.

I hugged her back.

I think she had just saved mine.

Epilogue

I told Taylor and her mother the entire story, from start to finish, over hot coffee and cookies. I began with my plan to lose my virginity to Damian, his ensuing tantrum, and his awful behavior and threats after the accident. I cried during most of it.

Afterward, we drove to the police station together. The Lamberths followed behind in their minivan while Christos sat beside me in my mom's car. He held my hand the entire way. At the station, I retold the entire story for the third time that day to a pair of detectives.

There's some old saying about the third time being the charm.

It turned out the police weren't going to arrest me for not reporting the crime. Because it was an accident, and I was not the person at fault, it wasn't a felony merely because I didn't come forward sooner.

The District Attorney eventually decided not to press charges against Damian. His BMW from that night had been sold a long time ago. Although the police tracked it down, they found it in a wrecking yard somewhere in New Mexico, battered and crushed beyond recognition. No surprise there. As a result, there wasn't enough evidence to press charges against Damian. All they really had was my testimony against his. The D.A. thought it wouldn't be a strong enough case to hold up in court.

Fortunately, the Lamberth family also immediately filed a civil suit against Damian. Just in time, too. If I had waited much longer, the statute of limitations would've passed, and Damian would've gotten completely off the hook. The reason was that Taylor's parents were the ones paying her medical bills. So even though Taylor was a minor at the time of the accident, the three year civil statute applied to her parents, not her.

Luckily, my testimony was enough to sway the civil jury against Damian. They awarded the Lamberth family enough money to cover all her medical expenses, the loss of her scholarship, and substantial pain and suffering.

And because the Wolfram family was so well-off financially, they actually paid. In installments, of course. They weren't paying out of the goodness of their hearts. Of that, I was sure.

Taylor's parents climbed out of debt, and Taylor finally went to a four-year college, like she'd always dreamed. She ended up majoring in Physical Therapy at the University of Delaware.

After telling everything to the police that day, Christos and I went back to my parents' neighborhood and bought Christos some new underwear, socks, a winter jacket, and a tooth brush.

For the fourth time in one day, I told my parents the whole story. I owed it to them. They were very supportive. I was sort of surprised.

At first, they had a hard time believing that Damian could be so heartless. But when I described how callous Damian had been, and that he'd threatened to shoot me and kill me, they actually believed me. I don't know why I thought they wouldn't, but they did.

I was extremely grateful for that.

Christos stayed at my parents' for the entire winter break. He didn't end up going to New York to see his mom, but that was okay. I was glad to have him with me for emotional support.

My parents didn't seem to mind his presence, and I think he grew on them by the end of the two weeks. He was so helpful, and did lots of dishes, and took me and my parents out for dinner several more times. I could tell my dad was getting irritated that Christos would never let him pay. Poor Dad.

The topic of my burgeoning art career never came up with my parents over the break, I think because everyone was so overwhelmed talking about the drama surrounding Taylor Lamberth and awful Damian Wolfram, especially after going to Taylor's attorney in Maryland to give my deposition. When my parents met Taylor and her parents face to face for the first time at the attorney's office, I think it made my story all the more real and shocking in Mom and Dad's minds. They had nothing but bad things to say about Damian after that.

All the distraction meant no lectures from my parents about focusing on a sensible business major. Somehow, I suspected it was only a temporary reprieve. Once the drama of Taylor Lamberth died down in our lives, I was sure discussions about my career path would come back with a vengeance.

Christos and I returned to San Diego at the end of December, giving us a few days to settle in before winter quarter started.

I still needed to figure out what was going on between me and Christos. I loved him, and I knew without a doubt that he loved me.

But could I be with him, considering all that I had been through?

Was I that Fearless?

Want to get an email when the sequel is released?

Sign up here: **http://eepurl.com/B7crf**

Find out how FEARLESS Samantha Smith is in:

the sequel to FEARLESS

coming October 2013

Personal thanks from Devon Hartford:

Thank you, dear reader, for taking the time to live with Samantha and Christos for awhile! If you enjoyed Fearless, please leave some positive feedback on Amazon, Goodreads, or any book blogs you frequent. Be sure to tell your friends about it!

If you want to drop me a line, you can find me at any of the links below. I love to hear what you have to say, and I love to talk books!

-Devon

Like me on Facebook: at Devon Hartford, NA & YA novelist

Friend me on Facebook at Devon Hartford

Follow me on Twitter @DevonHartford

Follow me on WordPress at devonhartford.com

ABOUT THE AUTHOR

Devon Hartford spent most of his life in Southern California, frequenting many of the locations in Fearless. Devon also paints. His background in the arts was the inspiration for this book.

ACKNOWLEDGMENTS

First and foremost I need to thank fellow New Adult author Elle Casey. She has gone above and beyond in her efforts to help me promote this book and get it into the hands of you, the reader. You should definitely check out her work!

Secondly, thanks to all my passionate and fantastic beta readers: Kimberlin Sanders, Sarah Welsh (a.k.a. Princess Frilly-Bottoms of the Land of Willow), Anne Berkeley, Emaleth Morrigan (mermaid), Whitney Marceleen Hutchinson, Mandy Jamerson, and Camie Laterza, for invaluable feedback and encouragement!

A special thanks to Jennifer Mignano, the official caretaker of the term "breasticles."

And thanks to everybody else who has helped make this book a reality!

www.ingramcontent.com/pod-product-compliance
Lightning Source LLC
Chambersburg PA
CBHW050920250626
47155CB00001B/307